A SELECTED EDITION OF W. D. HOWELLS

Volume 5

Their Wedding Journey

W. D. HOWELLS

Their Wedding Journey

Edited by John K. Reeves

EDWIN H. CADY, GENERAL EDITOR
RONALD GOTTESMAN, TEXTUAL EDITOR
SCOTT BENNETT AND DAVID J. NORDLOH,
ASSOCIATE TEXTUAL EDITORS

INDIANA UNIVERSITY PRESS

Bloomington and London

1968

ACKNOWLEDGMENTS

The Editorial Board is indebted to the Indiana University Foundation and the Research Committee of Indiana University for support which brought the Howells Center into being and continues to maintain it. For financial support essential to the operation of the Center and to the production of this volume, the Editorial Board gratefully acknowledges the assistance of the National Endowment for the Humanities, Barnaby C. Keeney, Chairman.

At every stage the hard work and advice of Thomas Wortham and Julene Dutton of the Howells Edition staff were instrumental. We are also indebted to:

John Alden, Boston Public Library
Paul Baender, University of Iowa
Ellen Ballou, Providence, Rhode Island
William H. Bond, Houghton Library, Harvard University
Matthew Bruccoli, Ohio State University
Cecil Byrd, Indiana University Library
William Cagle, Indiana University Library
Kenneth Carpenter, Belmont, Massachusetts
Flora D. Colton, Van Pelt Library, University of Pennsylvania
Mary Felix, New York State Library
Ray Heffner, Brown University
John Noyes Mead Howells, Kittery Point, Maine
William White Howells, Harvard University
Carolyn Jakeman, Houghton Library, Harvard University
Clara and Rudolf Kirk, University of Illinois, Chicago
Colin Kirkpatrick, T. & A. Constable, Ltd., London, England
Watt P. Marchman, Hayes Memorial Library
The late Frederic C. Marston, Jr., University of Vermont
Robert A. Miller, Indiana University Library
Ellen M. Oldham, Boston Public Library
David Randall, Lilly Library, Indiana University
The Staff of the Skidmore College Library
Emma Swift, Rochester (N.Y.) Public Library
Marcia Tuttle, Princeton University Library
Herman B Wells, Indiana University
Hilda M. Wick, Ohio Wesleyan University Library

Contents

INTRODUCTION   *xiii*

THEIR WEDDING JOURNEY

   I   The Outset   3
  II   A Midsummer-Day's Dream   24
 III The Night Boat   36
 IV A Day's Railroading   51
  V The Enchanted City, and Beyond   61
 VI Niagara   74
VII Down the St. Lawrence   107
VIII The Sentiment of Montreal   121
 IX Quebec   142
  X Homeward and Home   174
 XI Niagara Revisited, Twelve Years after Their
       Wedding Journey   180

     Notes to the Text   201

TEXTUAL APPARATUS

    Textual Commentary   205
    A Note on the Manuscript   215
    Commentary on Selected Leaves of the Manuscript   219
    Textual Notes   222
    Emendations   225
    Rejected Substantives   236
    Word-Division   238

Illustrations

Photograph by A. Sorgato of W. D. and Elinor Mead Howells
   taken in Venice soon after their marriage. Courtesy of
   The Rutherford B. Hayes Library

facing page xxxiv

Leaves of the Manuscript of *Their Wedding Journey*
   Chapter iii, page 111–112   *facing page 219*
   Chapter v, page 48   *facing page 220*

Introduction

A NEW PATH IN LITERATURE

On the 11th of December 1870, Howells wrote to his father:

> At last, I have fairly launched upon the story of our last summer's travels, which I'm giving the form of fiction so far as the characters are concerned. If I succeed in this—and I believe I shall—I see clear before me a path in literature which no one else has tried, and which I believe I can make most distinctly and entirely my own. I am going to take my people to Niagara, and then down the St. Lawrence, and so back to Boston.[1]

This story was *Their Wedding Journey*, serialized in the *Atlantic Monthly* from July through December 1871, and published in book form by James R. Osgood and Company on 19 December 1871.

Howells had scored his first important literary success with his sketches of Italian life and travel, collected as *Venetian Life* (1866) and *Italian Journeys* (1867), and for a time he continued to mine his Italian experience when his duties as assistant editor of the *Atlantic Monthly* permitted. He was also working intermittently on an Italian novel, about which he wrote to M. M. Hurd on 15 December 1867: "but it's slow business, and may turn out a failure" (*Life in Letters*, I, 125). It was the latter half of 1874 before it was finally finished and serialized in the *Atlantic* as *A Foregone Conclusion*.

Late in 1867 Howells began experimenting with American counterparts of his Italian sketches, which were later collected in *Suburban Sketches* (1870). At first he wrote about picturesque sights and people, as he had done in the Italian pieces, but later

---

1. Printed with slight variations in *Life in Letters of William Dean Howells*, ed. Mildred Howells (Garden City, N.Y., 1928), I, 162; hereafter cited as *Life in Letters*. The manuscripts of this and all other letters cited are at Harvard unless otherwise noted. For permission to quote see footnote 6.

in the book he satirized interest in the picturesque as being
sentimental and attempted to find sources of interest in the
average and ordinary. At the outset of his career as a novelist,
however, he found some difficulty in putting his belief into
practice. As he was nearing the end of the composition of *Their
Wedding Journey,* he wrote to his friend Ralph Keeler:

> I feel more and more persuaded that we have only to study
> American life with the naked eye in order to find it infinitely
> various and entertaining. The trouble has always been that we
> have looked at it through somebody else's confounded literary
> telescope. I find it hard work myself to trust my eyes, and I
> catch myself feeling for the telescope, but I hope to do without
> it, altogether, by and by.[2]

While Howells was experimenting with the American
sketches, he was also reviewing for the *Atlantic* current American
and European fiction, an activity which must have helped him
to clarify and formulate his views of what good fiction should
be. One of the American books which he reviewed during this
period of indecision may actually have suggested to him the
advantages of using his own experiences as a basis for fiction. In
an enthusiastic review of Thomas Bailey Aldrich's *The Story of a
Bad Boy* in January 1870, Howells wrote: "There must be a
great deal of fact mixed up with the feigning, but the author has
the art which imbues all with the same quality, and will not let
us tell one from the other."[3] Whatever the spur, it was at some
point not long after this review that Howells glimpsed his new
path in literature, a combination of the well-practiced travel and
character sketch with fiction, a form he had attempted un-
successfully ever since boyhood.

Although Howells' first literary ambition was to be a poet, he
also tried his hand at fiction in his teens and published several
pieces in his father's newspaper, the Ashtabula *Sentinel,* on which
the young Howells worked as typesetter and errand boy. The
longest of these pieces was a Dickensian novel entitled *The*

2. 23 September 1871. MS at the University of Southern California.
3. *Atlantic Monthly,* XXV (1870), 124.

Independent Candidate. Late in life he wrote that his hopes at this early stage were dealt an "all-but-mortal blow . . . in the failure of that story which I had begun printing in my father's news-paper before I had imagined an ending for it."[4] In spite of this blow, later in the 1850's he began work on a novel of village life entitled "Geoffrey Winter." From the point of view of plot it is a more fully developed novel than *Their Wedding Journey*; but although an early version of the first chapter was published by the *Knickerbocker Magazine* in August 1861, as "A Dream," the completed manuscript (now at Harvard) was rejected by a number of publishers in both the United States and England between 1861 and 1865.[5] These early failures in fiction and the subsequent success of the Italian travel sketches may well have been in Howells' mind as he searched for the literary path he was to follow at the end of the 1860's. The plan to combine the two types by fictionalizing his American travel experiences had the advantage of holding securely to a successful form with one hand while tentatively reaching with the other toward a form which had tempted him in the past.

Doubts at this stage about his ability to write successful fiction are reflected in Howells' careful limitation of the fictional element in *Their Wedding Journey*. At the beginning of the novel the first-person narrator says that he is not going to tell the honeymooners' "long love-story, which I do not think myself qualified to rehearse, distrusting my fitness for a sustained or involved narration." He adds that "in attempting to tell the reader of the wedding-journey of a newly married couple . . . I shall have nothing to do but to talk of some ordinary traits of American life as these appeared to them, to speak a little of well-known and easily accessible places, to present now a bit of land-scape and now a sketch of character" (page 3). In a passage canceled in the manuscript before publication the narrator says

---

4. *Years of My Youth* (New York, 1916), p. 209. The story appeared in the *Sentinel* between 23 November 1854 and 18 January 1855.

5. See *Years of My Youth*, p. 209, and Olov W. Fryckstedt, *In Quest of America: A Study of Howells' Early Development as a Novelist* (Upsala, 1958), pp. 67–68.

further: "It is with what they [the honeymooners] saw, and where they went, rather than what they are, that we have to do" (MS, page 3). At another point in the same passage the narrator characterizes the action of the story: "I will be so honest with the reader as to assure him that the coming adventures, if I may so call them, are trivial and unimpressive, ⟨any things that are not so, he will know by a certain clumsy air to be my fiction⟩ and that I have no idea of interesting him in anything like a plot" (MS, page 2). This tentative and tangential use of the fictional element indicates that Howells intended to keep a firm hold on the safe mooring of actual travel.

THE MATERIALS

In view of Howells' eventual distinction as a realistic novelist, it is particularly fortunate that materials have survived which enable us to trace the process by which he transformed his travel experience into his first successful piece of fiction. These materials are: (1) travel articles which as a young correspondent Howells had written for the *Ohio State Journal* and the Cincinnati *Gazette* in the summer of 1860, when on his famous pilgrimage to New England he covered some of the same ground over which he later sent his fictional honeymooners; (2) a diary of "last summer's travels" (i.e. 1870), which took him and Mrs. Howells over the entire route of the wedding journey; (3) a brief diary of a trip to Niagara Falls with his father probably in the early summer of 1871; and (4) the working manuscript of the novel.[6]

William M. Gibson has made a detailed study of Howells' use of the travel articles in the early novels.[7] He estimates that about a tenth of *Their Wedding Journey* was drawn, often ver-

---

6. The diaries are in a small pocket volume, in the Houghton Library at Harvard. The manuscript is in the possession of the present editor. Permission to quote unpublished passages from the diaries, the manuscript, and letters written by Howells has been granted by William White Howells for the heirs of the Howells Estate. Permission to quote from the diaries and unpublished letters owned by Harvard has been granted by William H. Bond, Librarian, for the Howells Committee of the Houghton Library. Republication of this material also requires these permissions.

7. "Materials and Form in Howells's First Novels," *American Literature*, XIX (1947), 158–166.

batim, from these newspaper pieces. Later, when the manuscript came to light, printed portions of these articles were in fact found pasted into the text.

Howells' use of the 1870 travel diary is more revealing of the way in which he transformed actual experience into fiction. The first entry, made in the Worcester Depot in Boston while he waited for a train to New York on 20 June 1870, suggests that he was consciously gathering material for his projected book. The diary of the entire trip occupies nineteen and a half pages of a small pocket volume, and Howells filled five and a half of these while he sat for two hours in the station. These notes supplied material for twelve pages of the novel. All nineteen of the people in the novel's depot scene had been noted in the diary, though several figures in the diary do not appear in the novel. Although sequences of people and incidents in the diary were frequently changed in the novel, incidents were not developed beyond the material provided by the diary except in the passages on the restaurant and the infirm old lady (pages 10–12).

After the first day's entry the diary became much less detailed, but most of the record was incorporated into the novel. Howells soon began to write fewer complete sentences in the diary, relying on single words and phrases to jog his memory. In fact, his memory, unaided by either diary or travel articles, became by far his richest source of material. His heavy reliance on a retentive memory may be illustrated by the fact that for the chapter which contains the much-quoted passage on an "ordinary carful of human beings" ("A Day's Railroading") Howells noted only two of them in his diary.

Perhaps because he had already written three detailed travel articles on Niagara in 1860, Howells made no entries in his diary on the scene which eventually became the subject of the longest chapter in the book. A year later, however, when the first installment of the novel was about to appear in the *Atlantic Monthly* (July 1871), Howells went back to Niagara to refresh his memory. A short diary of this trip with his father from Jefferson, Ohio, to Buffalo and Niagara follows the 1870 entries in the notebook.

Although the year of these new entries is not given, 1871 seems likely, for while little use was made of this diary in the novel, one note about elderly couples "evidently just married" became the subject of a paragraph inserted in the manuscript during a revision of the original version.

Brief as the diaries are in relation to the completed novel, they show that when Howells returned to Boston from his travels, he had a mine of written material on people, incidents, scenery, buildings, historical sites, and even weather on which to draw for his fictionalized account of his journey; and his memory was stocked with even more.[8]

COMPOSITION

Although Howells was well supplied with data for a travel book, the crucial problem involved his capacity to transform this material into fiction. His doubts about his ability and success during the composition of the book can be traced in his frequent letters to his father and his sister Annie in Jefferson and to a few other correspondents. The beginning of composition seems to have been delayed not only by his editorial duties on the *Atlantic* but also by his commitment to prepare and deliver a series of four lectures on "Italian Poets of Our Century" at the Lowell Institute during the fall of 1870. Although the Howellses had returned from their trip to their home in Cambridge early in August, the first reference to a book based on the trip appears in a letter to William Cooper Howells on 11 September 1870. Howells reported that he had received the "proofs of my new book, Suburban Sketches, up to the 110th page" and then added, "I'm next going to write out my summer's travel." There seems to have been further delay, however, for on 27 November he wrote to his father that he had two more of the lectures to give and would "be *so* glad when they are done. . . . The fact is, the

---

8. For historical material on Montreal and Quebec Howells drew extensively on Parkman's histories ("those precious books," Howells called them in the novel, p. 89). For a detailed discussion of Howells' use of Parkman see Fryckstedt, *In Quest of America*, pp. 115–120.

conviction has been growing upon me that I am a writer, and nothing else. . . . I am now going to push forward my American travel-sketches as fast as I can. Do you think I might make a tolerably accurate description of Jefferson, without giving offense?''

Two weeks later (11 December) he reported that he was "fairly launched" on his travel book and had decided to leave out Jefferson. By 1 January 1871 he was able to write that "Elinor approves of the opening of 'Their Wedding Journey'— under which title I'm writing out my sketches of our last summer's travel." This is the first reference to the nature of the story he was making of the travel material. On 12 March 1871 he wrote to his father: "I am getting on with 'Their Wedding Journey' at a pretty good rate. That is, I have the journeyers at Buffalo, now." He mentioned again his decision to omit Jefferson because it "would have involved a very difficult and delicate treatment of the subject, to which I'd rather recur some other time, if the present attempt succeeds at all."

His wife was not the only critic to whom he turned for an opinion at this stage. In this letter of 12 March he reported that he had read what he had written "to Harry James, and part of it to Lowell. They both praise it; but what the public, which isn't of my friendship may say, I don't know." As if to give a reason for his uncertainty he again spoke of the unusual nature of the book: "The thing is quite a new species of fiction: it isn't at all dependent on plot, but [merely?] has the interest of character, [seen?] and described, and some notable places. I feel as if I had got over the hardest part, but perhaps I haven't."

His reference to "the hardest part" may possibly be reflected in the manuscript of chapters iv and v, which deal with the train trip from Albany to Buffalo and a stopover in Rochester. Although it is difficult to determine just when any particular revision was made, the manuscript shows that the sections which are set on the train gave Howells a great deal of trouble. His chief problem was whether or not to include lengthy though interesting life stories of some of the passengers. In chapter iv some of the original sheets were canceled completely, some were cut up and re-arranged, eight new sheets were inserted, and then much of the new material was canceled either in the manuscript or later. The same pattern of addition of new material and eventual rejection through several stages also appears in chapter v.

Howells' continuing uncertainty about the book at this stage is seen in a letter to James R. Osgood on 1 April 1871 (MS at Yale). He enclosed sheets and described later scenes so that Osgood could consider illustrations and then added, "I should be glad to know what you think of the thing as literature. I vacillate between a pyramidal pride in it, and a colossal loathing of it." On the next day he wrote to his father that he was "making steady, but rather slow progress on my [latest?] novel, and expect to have it done in a month or two. If it succeeds at all in the magazine, it will be reprinted in book-form. I've just got some proofs of the beginning, and it reads decently enough, in print, which is of course the great test." By 6 April he reported to his father that the book was about half done, "and if I have luck, I can finish it in the next six weeks—that is, I can make a rough draft of it." On 23 April Howells sent his father "the proof of the first part of my story" (presumably chapter i, the first installment in the July *Atlantic*). He said, "Some changes will be in before publishing. I'd like to know what you and the girls think of it." His father apparently criticized the slow pace of the first chapter, for Howells wrote to him on 7 May: "I don't understand what you say about the chapter of Wedding Journey I sent you, not getting the people out of Boston. I carried them as far as to the Battery in New York."

During the first two or three weeks of June 1871, Howells left his desk and traveled through parts of Ohio and to Buffalo and Niagara Falls with his father. In the letter of 6 April to his father he wrote that it would be more convenient for him to make the trip in September but then concluded: "It won't make any *great* difference with me either way. For some reasons—such as looking over the ground of my story at Niagara, etc., I'd rather go out this spring." There is no further reference to Niagara in the extant letters about the trip, but the undated (as to year) diary of a trip with his father, mentioned above, seems pretty clearly the diary of this trip. Having made no notes on Niagara in the 1870 diary, Howells was apparently having trouble with the details of this chapter. In a letter of 17 March 1871, he had asked Annie to send him his guide to Niagara and down the St. Lawrence. "I've got my Wedding Journeyers to Niagara, and I've no means of showing them about."

Not long after his return from the trip with his father Howells asked (letter of 25 June) his family's opinion of "the second part of Their Wedding Journey" (presumably chapters ii and iii, the installment for the August *Atlantic*) and added, "I'm getting it forward as fast as I can, but I work slowly. My travellers have pretty nearly reached Montreal." Three weeks later, after the first installment had appeared, Howells wrote (16 July 1871) to his sister Annie that he had "got the people to Montreal and almost away again, so there isn't a great deal more to do about it. Sometimes it seems to me good, and again wretchedly flimsy."

On 30 July 1871 Howells wrote to his father: "I'm hurrying forward my serial, which I want to have sketched to the end before I leave for Canada." The Howellses spent most of their three-week holiday in Quebec, possibly in part for literary purposes. Back in Boston, Howells wrote to his father on 17 September that he was "deep" in the Quebec chapter. The manuscript of this chapter shows considerably less revision than the manuscript of earlier chapters, and Howells' letters as he neared the end of the story also suggest greater confidence in the work. On 23 September 1871, after five chapters had appeared in the *Atlantic*, he wrote to Ralph Keeler (MS at the University of Southern California): "I'm very glad you're pleased with Their W. J. Do you know, sometimes *I'm* pleased with it." On 15 October in a letter to his father he remarked that none of the Jefferson family had spoken about the Niagara chapter in the current *Atlantic*. "If you like it, don't be afraid of making me vain by saying so." Finally on 22 October he was able to write to

J. M. Comly (MS at the Ohio Historical Society Library) that he had finished *Their Wedding Journey* a few days before. Looking back on his experience he reflected: "I found a pleasure in writing the thing, though I groaned over it, too, which I miss now."

In spite of this growing confidence, Howells was still not completely certain about the book and continued to seek reassurance and cherish praise. On 3 December 1871 he replied to his father: "I'm glad that you're so well pleased with the close of my story. I had some qualms about the scene with the burlesqueress [burlesquerers?], thinking it might appear coarse; but it doesn't seem to have struck you unpleasantly. Did you really laugh? I couldn't tell, after it was done whether it was flat or funny. The other night I was at Mr. Longfellow's for supper, and he praised the passage about the nun giving the rose—'a beautiful poem,' he called it, saying that he had never read anything finer in its way."

The pleasure and the groaning during the process of composition had lasted a full year, and the result was beginning to be praised.

BECOMING HOWELLS

Since Howells' experiment did become both a popular and a critical success and since so many of the materials that went into it have survived, *Their Wedding Journey* offers a unique opportunity to see Howells the journalist, romantic poet, and travel essayist taking early steps towards becoming Howells the realistic novelist. His principal tool, besides his memory, was the travel diary, a tool which he had used in Italy to prepare the highly praised essays about what he had seen. But this time he had determined to interfuse the facts of travel with an element of fiction, and the first requisite was to create fictional characters to make the trip which he and his wife had just taken. In many respects Basil and Isabel March resemble the Howellses, and he found them so useful for creating fiction out of his actual experience that he used them in eight more stories at various times in his career. In their first incarnation, as a comparison of the diary and the fiction shows, the Marches' experiences and their reactions to them are for the most part the same as those of Howells and his wife.[9] However, the comparison also shows a significant difference between fact and fiction at several points. In these scenes we can catch a glimpse of Howells' imagination at work. One instance will serve as an illustration of his method. In the New York section of the diary most of the entry for 25 June is devoted to the sunstroke which Howells suffered on Broadway. Howells' use of this experience in the novel provides an early example of the way in which he achieved realistic objectivity by using the Marches as "witnesses of the events" rather than as "prominent actors."[10] The significant point is that in the novel it is not Basil March who suffers the stroke but an unnamed man in a drug store. The facts in the actual and fictional versions are very similar, but the attitude and tone are quite different. Howells described his personal experience in the diary as follows:

> Broadway was crowded and seemed black with heat. My heart labored terribly, and after getting my tickets [for the night boat] we took an omnibus to ride down to the first druggists. I did not find any till I reached the Astor House. By this time my arms and legs felt as if they had gone to sleep, and I was ready to faint. I ran in with Elinor, and told the apothecary I thought I was affected by the heat. He gave me instantly aromatic ammonia in plain soda to drink, and gave Elinor a handkerchief full of ice to rub over my head. I felt better directly, but was unable to leave for an hour and more, and was then very weak. Pushed out straight to Shepards.—Men who came in and looked at me. Succession of soda drinkers.

In the fictional transmutation of this experience Howells made Basil March one of the onlookers: "Basil drank his soda and paused to look upon this group [the stricken man and his wife], which he felt would commend itself to realistic sculpture as

---

9. For a detailed study of the relationship between the Marches and the Howellses see Clara M. Kirk, "Reality and Actuality in the March Family Narratives of W. D. Howells," *PMLA*, LXXIV (1959), 137–152.

10. See Howells' discussion of the Marches in this role in "Howells's Unpublished Prefaces," ed. George Arms, *New England Quarterly*, XVII (1944), 585–586.

eminently characteristic of the local life, and as 'The Sunstroke' would sell enormously in the hot season" (page 33). Isabel's feeling that the onlookers were inhumanly indifferent leads to their discussion of whether it would be better to suffer such a stroke in Broadway or in a village street, and Basil ends the discussion by saying, "But let us be selfishly thankful that it isn't you and I there in the apothecary's shop, as it might very well be" (page 35). In the manuscript Howells played with the identification and then canceled it. After Isabel's shock at the indifference of the people, Howells had her say, "Basil, that poor fellow looked enough like you to be your double," and Basil replied, "So he did! . . . and I'm obliged to his part of the duality for taking the sunstroke. I don't think I should carry it off so well"(MS, page 78). Although this is a minor episode, the diary and the manuscript allow us to see Howells creating fiction. Though the facts are drawn from his own experience, the point of view from which they are seen in the novel is the product of his imagination.[11]

At the outset Howells also envisaged another fictional character, the first-person narrator. Most of the first two and a half pages of the manuscript is devoted to a discussion of the relationship between the narrator and Basil and Isabel March. This remains uncanceled in the manuscript, but at some point before the appearance of the first installment Howells reduced the definition of the relationship to two sentences. Whether he recognized the awkwardness of having a third person go along on a honeymoon or whether he intuitively sensed the limitations of first-person narration, it is impossible to say; but the manuscript does not show that Howells attempted further development of the narrator as a character, and in the final version the narrator is omniscient and is, except at a few places, merely the voice which tells the story.

The diary of the 1870 trip makes it clear that the other char-

---

11. Col. and Mrs. Ellison, whom the Marches meet in Niagara and travel with as far as Quebec, may also be slightly drawn sketches of Howells and his wife; and Howells acknowledged that Kitty, Mrs. Ellison's cousin, had "some faint outlines" of his sister Annie (letters to his father, 9 April 1871 and 5 February 1873).

acters in the narrative are simply the keenly observed and amusingly described fellow travelers whom the Howellses encountered
along the way. They are not in the fictional sense created,
except in a few instances, like the man with the sunstroke, when
Howells transferred his own experiences and reactions to them.
The characters could be so simple and so successful in the roles
they play because there is no plot for them to motivate. The slight
narrative thread is based largely on fact and governed by the
simple principles of chronology and geography. The steps which
Howells took in *Their Wedding Journey* on the road to becoming a
novelist were few and elementary, but he had intended and attempted no more; and what is most important, he was successful.
Even as he wrote Comly (22 October 1871) that he had just
finished the book, he said, "I'm casting about for the frame-work
of some new serial. There's nothing like having railroads and
steamboats transact your plot for you, but I can't write two
W. J.s." The new path in literature was already beginning to
look like the highroad to the novel.

The question of whether Howells had left the romantic poet
behind on the road to becoming a realist is more complex because
it involves a conflict within him of which he was only partly
aware. Intellectually he had been dedicated, from at least the
time of "Geoffrey Winter," to the principle of telling the truth
about life, but his emotional nature often made him see this
"truth" in conventional romantic hues. His objection to contemporary sentimental fiction was chiefly against its falsity
rather than against its emotionalism. This head-heart conflict in
Howells was complicated by another element in his nature which
partakes of both intellect and feeling, his sense of humor. It
helped to chasten and control the emotional side of his nature
but never subdued it. The manuscript of *Their Wedding Journey*
shows revisions which suggest an attempt to cut down on romantic attitudes and responses, but at the same time there is his
unabashed pleasure in Longfellow's praise of the sentimental
passage about the pale rose which the nun gave to Isabel at the
convent in Quebec. Perhaps the key to Howells' attitude in 1870

is provided by the Marches' discussion of the ballad of Sam Patch, which describes in not very realistic terms his fatal leap over the Genesee Falls at Rochester. Isabel "refused to admit that tragical figure to the honor of her emotions" because his name was too homely "to be linked in our thoughts with this superb cataract." In Basil's objection we may well have Howells' attempt to define and defend a "realistic" kind of poetry: "We shall never have a poetry of our own till we get over this absurd reluctance from facts, till we make the ideal embrace and include the real, till we consent to face the music in our simple common names, and put Smith into a lyric and Jones into a tragedy. The Germans are braver than we, and in them you find facts and dreams continually blended and confronted" (pages 68–69). Clearly, the romantic poet was still very much alive in 1870, and the realistic novelist was only beginning to stir.

PUBLICATION

Setting a pattern which he followed until late in his career, Howells first published *Their Wedding Journey* as a magazine serial. On the retirement of James T. Fields, Howells took over as editor of the *Atlantic Monthly* on 1 July 1871; his story began to appear in the July issue and was concluded in December. Negotiations for book publication were opened by James R. Osgood in a letter to Howells on 11 August 1871, and the contract was signed on 1 November with Osgood agreeing to pay for the plates and to give Howells ten per cent royalty.

On 15 October 1871 Howells wrote to his father that Augustus Hoppin was going to illustrate the book, and commented, "I think he'll do it charmingly." Several times during the fall Hoppin wrote to Howells about the sketches, and on 19 November he reported that he had sent in the last plates. He returned with thanks some photographs of Quebec which Howells had loaned him and noted that for his sketch of the habit of the nun (pages 150–151) he had relied on the description and sketch supplied by Mrs. Howells.[12]

---

12. See Arthur A. Adrian, "Augustus Hoppin to William Dean Howells," *New England Quarterly*, XXIV (1951), 88.

On 3 December 1871 Howells wrote to his father that the book would be out on "Tuesday of next week" (12 December), but there was a delay of a week, and the book did not appear until 19 December. In his letter of 24 December Howells reported that by noon on Wednesday (20 December) "more than the whole 1500 were ordered from the publishers" and that he had "only secured 8 copies on Friday out of the last lot of the 1st edition." He continued: "Another 1000 will be out next Wednesday [27 December], but of course that will be too late for the holiday sales. 5000 could have been sold if the book had been printed a few weeks ago—Osgood says. Of course this is very harrowing as well as very flattering. I hope the sale will still continue. I send you one of the books to-day." The second printing was also delayed, for on 31 December Howells wrote to his father: "The second edition of my book is not yet out, and orders are lying unfilled. It's a great misfortune that it was so badly published, and I haven't the patience to think of it."[13]

As time went on, however, Howells had less and less cause for complaint. By the end of 1872 there had been six printings totaling 6,500 copies. In seven of the next eight years new impressions were issued with new dates on the title page, and in 1875 Osgood also brought out a pocket-sized edition. The publisher's royalty records show that by 1 May 1881, 9,671 copies of the original edition and 2,327 copies of the pocket edition had been sold. The figures for the next decade (1881–1891) are not complete, but the two editions sold approximately 2,700 and 1,000 copies respectively. In 1882 sheets made from the original plates were bound in paper for Houghton Mifflin's Riverside Paper Series and sold 2,842 copies in that year alone. Approximately 1,000 more were sold in the next three years before the Riverside Series was discontinued. On 3 November 1887 Howells wrote to the publishers: "I am sorry the Riverside series has failed, but I think you've done surprisingly well with my

---

13. William M. Gibson and George Arms, in *A Bibliography of William Dean Howells* (New York, 1948), p. 22, give the publication date as 27 December 1871. This is the copyright deposit date. Howells' letter of 24 December 1871, on which the revised publication date is based, is partly quoted in *Life in Letters*, I, 162–163, but the date of the letter is there incorrectly given as 14 December.

books in the other editions, and I am obliged to you for the interest you always show in them."[14]

In 1887 another chapter was added to *Their Wedding Journey*. It was called "Niagara Revisited, Twelve Years after Their Wedding Journey," and first appeared in the *Atlantic Monthly* in May 1883.[15] As early as 13 March 1883 Howells suggested to Osgood, his literary agent, that they let Houghton Mifflin add the sketch to the novel (MS at Columbia), but Osgood was reluctant to do so, "certainly not without consideration" (letter of 2 April 1883). Apparently Osgood's opinion prevailed at the time, but early in July 1887 Howells wrote to Houghton Mifflin suggesting that the chapter be added "if you think it would help *The Wedding Journey* to a fresh sale" (letter received 7 July 1887). The enlarged volume came out in time for the Christmas trade, and the sales figures for 1888 show a modest increase over those of the previous year.

Howells continued to show concern for the sale of his book. On 14 June 1890 he wrote to the publishers asking whether anything had been done about his earlier suggestion that they have "a lot of Wedding Journeys bound up in white cloth, and put in the trade, for wedding presents." However, when a new printing of the novel was issued in 1891, it was bound in what came to be the familiar red cloth with the title and Howells' signature stamped in gilt on the front cover (first used by Harper on *April Hopes* in 1888). Howells' suggestion of a bridal-white binding was eventually taken up in 1895 when Houghton Mifflin published a completely new edition from new plates and with new illustrations by Clifford Carleton, in both a limited,

---

14. Howells had signed an exclusive five-year contract with Harper in 1885. The data on printings and sales in this paragraph were drawn from the Houghton Mifflin papers in the Houghton Library, specifically "The Cost Books of Ticknor & Co. and Successors," vol. 6; "Copyrights, 1876–1881"; Houghton Mifflin sales records, 1880–1891, vol. IV; and "Journal, 1881–1885." Howells' letter is also in the Houghton Mifflin file. Permission to cite the records and quote from the letter has been granted by the Houghton Mifflin Company and by William H. Bond, Librarian of the Houghton Library.

15. For a full account of the vicissitudes of this sketch see Rudolf and Clara M. Kirk, "*Niagara Revisited* . . . The Story of Its Publication and Suppression," in *Essays in Literary History*, ed. Rudolf Kirk and C. F. Main (New Brunswick, N.J., 1960), pp. 177–195.

large-paper edition bound in vellum and a trade edition bound in white cloth. In the same year the publisher also issued a new printing from the original 1872 plates. Both editions were kept in print by new impressions at irregular intervals. The last of each bears the copyright date 1916, just four years before Howells' death.

Besides the foregoing editions published by Osgood and Houghton Mifflin there were four foreign editions of *Their Wedding Journey*. Belford Brothers and the Musson Book Co., Limited, both of Toronto, brought out pirated editions, and in 1882 David Douglas of Edinburgh incorporated the novel, with others by Howells, in his new "American Authors" series. Edmund Gosse in a letter to Howells attested to the popularity of the Douglas editions and playfully complained that "the question Have you read 'A Wedding Journey' is one of those tiresome things that make one loathe one's fellow-creatures."[16] The novel had thirteen known printings by Douglas between 1882 and 1911. In 1895 Douglas issued the new edition with the Carleton illustrations, using American sheets with a new title page bearing his imprint. The fourth foreign edition was brought out in 1883 by Bernhard Tauchnitz of Leipzig, who already had seven other Howells titles on his list.

As late as 1915 Houghton Mifflin had an offer from "parties in New York" who wanted to lease the plates of *Their Wedding Journey* and *A Chance Acquaintance* and bring out editions to sell for twenty-five cents. Apparently the offer was declined, but in 1960 Fawcett Publications added *Their Wedding Journey* to its paperback series of "Premier Classics of American Realism," with an admiring introduction by Van Wyck Brooks. The publishing history of the novel clearly attests to its vitality.

RECEPTION

Howells had little reason to be disappointed in the immediate reception of his experiment with fiction, though as late as 11

---

16. Letter of 12 October 1882 in *Transatlantic Dialogue: Selected American Correspondence of Edmund Gosse*, ed. Paul F. Mattheisen and Michael Millgate (Austin, Texas, 1965), pp. 99–100.

March 1872 he wrote with reservations about the book's success to Edward Eggleston (MS at Cornell). The serial installments had been given favorable notice in the New York *Daily Tribune* (20 June–13 November 1871) and in the *Nation* (13 July–30 November 1871). The *Independent* (27 July–30 November 1871) had mixed praise and censure but at the end noted the steady improvement in the installments. Also during the serialization several of Howells' literary friends—Bayard Taylor, Ralph Keeler, Whittier, Sarah Orne Jewett, and Clarence King—had written to express their pleasure in the work. Whittier wrote: "Nothing so graceful and pleasant has appeared for a long time."[17]

Less than a week after the book was published on 19 December 1871, John Hay wrote from New York to congratulate Howells on its success and to deplore the delay of the second printing, and early in January Oliver Wendell Holmes wrote to say how much he and Mrs. Holmes had enjoyed the story.[18] The weekly magazines were quick to notice the book. The *Literary World* (Boston) carried a brief but favorable review in the issue of 1 January 1872, and two weeks later *Appleton's Journal* (New York) warmly praised the book, which had "attracted so much deserved attention" during its serialization in the *Atlantic*.[19]

A sentence in the *Harper's* review of the book includes the principal qualities noted and praised by almost all of the reviewers: "the charm of Mr. Howells's style prevents his book from being in any sense commonplace, and we read it with wonder at the eyes which see so much to entertain and amuse where ordinary eyes see little or nothing."[20] Virtually every review noted the familiar and commonplace material, and most praised the keen observation which enabled Howells to find interest in

---

17. WDH to Taylor, 5 September 1871, MS at Cornell; WDH to Keeler, 23 September 1871, MS at UCLA; Whittier, 10 October 1871; Jewett, 17 October 1871; King, 17 December 1871.

18. Hay, 25 December 1871, printed in *Letters of John Hay*, ed. Clara S. Hay (Washington, 1908), II, 11; Holmes, 6 January 1872.

19. *Literary World*, II, 124; *Appleton's Journal*, VII (1872), 52.

20. *Harper's New Monthly Magazine*, XLIV (1872), 781.

such unpromising subject matter. The reviewer for the *Christian Union* wrote: "It is our American life exactly as we all see it. We are confident that we could write such a book ourselves, and we are equally confident on second thought that it would be barren of interest to the public at large."[21] The reviewer for the *Overland Monthly* said that if the reader wonders whether this is not a story founded on fact, his curiosity is "a tribute to the reality of the sketches." The *Overland* reviewer and three others cited the description of the hot summer day in New York as an excellent example of this realism. The reviewers for the *Galaxy* and the *Independent*, while admitting the reality of the descriptions, regretted the lack of character and story, but the *Independent* reviewer spoke for both when he added, "Even these omissions we might pardon were there more substance and thought beneath Mr. Howells's exquisite style." He revealed a romantic bias when he expressed his preference for the Italian travel books with their "rich colors" and "that glamour of marble palaces in which we of the West delight."[22]

Although the *Independent* reviewer caviled at an occasional Gallicism in Howells' style, liked best its literary allusiveness, and praised its delicacy and humor, his general praise of the style was duplicated in virtually every review. The qualities most frequently lauded were its charm, simple beauty, finish, ease, freshness, and delicacy. A writer for the Denver *Tribune* capped all by calling Howells the "most perfect master of the mysteries of the English speech that America has produced."[23]

Whether the humor was mentioned as an aspect of style or an element in itself, most of the reviewers praised it as a distinctive quality of the book. A few thought that the humor was too subtle and delicate for the average reader, and one or two saw its satirical note, which the *Appleton* reviewer called "subtle and

---

21. *Christian Union* (later *Outlook*), V (1872), 142.
22. *Overland Monthly*, VIII (1872), 482; *Galaxy*, XIII (1872), 426–427; *Independent*, XXIII (1871), 6.
23. Clipping enclosed in a letter to WDH from G. W. Curtis, 14 January 1872. MS at Hayes Memorial Library, Fremont, Ohio.

felicitous." Others described the humor as delightful, genial, quiet, and full of body. A perceptive comparison of Howells' humor with Mark Twain's appeared in the Boston *Globe* in a review of Osgood's new editions of the Italian travel books and *Suburban Sketches*, which were issued in May 1872. The reviewer, called by *Publishers' Weekly* "an accomplished critic," wrote:

> [Howells'] humor, however vivid in form, is subtle and elusive in its essence. He depends, perhaps, somewhat too much on the feeling of humor in his readers to appreciate his own. Everybody understands such a humorist as Mark Twain, because he storms down on our sense of the ludicrous in an overwhelming flood of eccentricity, oddity, and caricature. We roar with laughter as we read. Howells, on the contrary, has the true Addisonian touch; hits his mark in the white; and, instead of provoking uproarious laughter strives to evoke that satisfied smile which testifies to the quiet enjoyment of the reader. The humor is the humor of a poet.[24]

No less than three reviewers predicted a permanent place in literature for Howells' experimental hybrid of travel and fiction. Doubtless the opinion which Howells cherished most was that of Henry Adams, whose praise in the *North American Review* was something akin to nomination to New England's (and therefore America's) hall of fame. Adams wrote in part:

> An interesting question presents itself to the cautious critic who reads this little book, and who does not care to commit himself and his reputation for sound judgment irretrievably to the strength of such a gossamer-like web: it is whether the book will live. Why should it not live? If extreme and almost photographic truth to nature, and remarkable delicacy and lightness of touch, can give permanent life to a story, why should this one not be read with curiosity and enjoyment a hundred or two hundred years hence? Our descendants will find nowhere so faithful and so pleasing a picture of our American existence, and no writer is likely to rival Mr. Howells in this idealization

---

24. Reprinted in *Publishers' and Stationers' Weekly Trade Circular*, I (1872), 598.

of the commonplace. The vein which Mr. Howells has struck is hardly a deep one. His dexterity in following it, and in drawing out its slightest resources, seems at times almost marvellous, a perpetual succession of feats of sleight-of-hand, all the more remarkable because the critical reader alone will understand how difficult such feats are, and how much tact and wit is needed to escape a mortifying failure.[25]

Although as late as his letter to Eggleston in March 1872 Howells was still cautious about judging *Their Wedding Journey* a success, by February of the following year he had accepted the fact. He wrote to his father after the second installment of *A Chance Acquaintance* had appeared in the *Atlantic*, "The story seems to be gaining in popularity, each month, though it never will be as well liked as Their Wedding Journey" (16 February 1873). The accuracy of his prophecy is borne out by the publishing histories of the two books.

J.K.R.

---

25. *North American Review*, CXIV (1872), 444–445.

W.D. and Elinor Mead Howells

Their Wedding Journey

I

THE OUTSET

THEY FIRST MET in Boston, but the match was made in Europe, where they afterwards saw each other; whither, indeed, he followed her; and there the match was also broken off. Why it was broken off, and why it was renewed after a lapse of years, is part of quite a long love-story, which I do not think myself qualified to rehearse, distrusting my fitness for a sustained or involved narration; though I am persuaded that a skilful romancer could turn the courtship of Basil and Isabel March to excellent account. Fortunately for me, however, in attempting to tell the reader of the wedding-journey of a newly married couple, no longer very young, to be sure, but still fresh in the light of their love, I shall have nothing to do but to talk of some ordinary traits of American life as these appeared to them, to speak a little of well-known and easily accessible places, to present now a bit of landscape and now a sketch of character.

They had agreed to make their wedding-journey in the simplest and quietest way, and as it did not take place at once after their marriage, but some weeks later, it had all the desired charm of privacy from the outset.

"How much better," said Isabel, "to go now, when nobody cares whether you go or stay, than to have started off upon a wretched wedding-breakfast, all tears and trousseau, and had people wanting to see you aboard the cars. Now there will not be a suspicion of honeymoon-shine about us; we shall go just like anybody else—with a difference, dear, with a difference!" and

3

she took Basil's cheeks between her hands. In order to do this, she had to run round the table; for they were at dinner, and Isabel's aunt, with whom they had begun married life, sat substantial between them. It was rather a girlish thing for Isabel, and she added, with a conscious blush, "We are past our first youth, you know; and we shall not strike the public as bridal, shall we? My one horror in life is an evident bride."

Basil looked at her fondly, as if he did not think her at all too old to be taken for a bride; and for my part I do not object to a woman's being of Isabel's age, if she is of a good heart and temper. Life must have been very unkind to her if at that age she have not won more than she has lost. It seemed to Basil that his wife was quite as fair as when they met first, eight years before; but he could not help recurring with an inextinguishable regret to the long interval of their broken engagement, which but for that fatality they might have spent together, he imagined, in just such rapture as this. The regret always haunted him, more or less; it was part of his love; the loss accounted irreparable really enriched the final gain.

"I don't know," he said presently, with as much gravity as a man can whose cheeks are clasped between a lady's hands, "you don't begin very well for a bride who wishes to keep her secret. If you behave in this way, they will put us into the 'bridal chambers' at all the hotels. And the cars,—they're beginning to have them on the palace-cars."

Just then a shadow fell into the room.

"Wasn't that thunder, Isabel?" asked her aunt, who had been contentedly surveying the tender spectacle before her. "O dear! you'll never be able to go by the boat to-night, if it storms. It's actually raining now!"

In fact, it was the beginning of that terrible storm of June, 1870. All in a moment, out of the hot sunshine of the day it burst upon us before we quite knew that it threatened, even before we had fairly noticed the clouds, and it went on from passion to passion with an inexhaustible violence. In the square upon which our friends looked out of their dining-room windows the trees whitened in the gusts, and darkened in the driving floods of the rainfall, and in some paroxysms of the tempest bent themselves in desperate submission, and then with a great shudder rent away whole branches and flung them far off upon the ground. Hail mingled with the rain, and now the few umbrellas that had braved the storm vanished, and the hurtling ice crackled upon the pavement, where the lightning played like flames burning from the earth, while the thunder roared overhead without ceasing. There was something splendidly theatrical about it all; and when a street-car, laden to the last inch of its capacity, came by, with horses that pranced and leaped under the stinging blows of the hail-stones, our friends felt as if it were an effective and very naturalistic bit of pantomime contrived for their admiration. Yet as to themselves they were very sensible of a potent reality in the affair, and at intervals during the storm they debated about going at all that day, and decided to go and not to go, according to the changing complexion of the elements. Basil had said that as this was their first journey together in America, he wished to give it at the beginning as pungent a national character as possible, and that as he could imagine nothing more peculiarly American than a voyage to New York by a Fall River boat, they ought to take that route thither. So much upholstery, so much music, such variety of company, he understood, could not be got in any other way, and it might be that they would even catch a glimpse of the inventor of the combination, who represented the very excess and extremity of a certain kind of Americanism. Isabel had eagerly consented; but these aesthetic motives were paralyzed for her by the thought of passing Point Judith in a storm, and she descended from her high intents first to the Inside Boats, without the magnificence and the orchestra, and then to the idea of going by land in a sleeping-car. Having comfortably accomplished this feat, she treated Basil's consent as a matter of course, not because she did not regard him, but because as a woman she could not conceive of the steps to her conclusion as unknown to him, and always treated her own decisions as the product of their common reasoning. But her husband held out for the boat, and insisted that if the storm fell before seven o'clock, they could reach it at Newport by the last express; and it was this obstinacy that, in proof of Isabel's wisdom, obliged them to wait two hours in the station before going by the land route. The storm abated at five o'clock, and though the rain continued, it seemed well by a quarter of seven to set out for the Old Colony Depot, in sight of which a sudden and vivid flash of lightning caused Isabel to seize her husband's arm, and to implore him, "O *don't* go by the boat!" On this, Basil had the incredible weakness to yield; and bade the driver take them to the Worcester Depot. It was the first swerving from the ideal in their wedding journey, but it was by no means the last; though it must be confessed that it was early to begin.

They both felt more tranquil when they were irretrievably committed by the purchase of their tickets, and when they sat down in the waiting-room of the station, with all the time between seven and nine o'clock before them. Basil would have eked out the business of checking the trunks into an affair of some length, but the baggage-master did his duty with pitiless celerity; and so Basil, in the mere excess of his disoccupation, bought an accident-insurance ticket. This employed him half a minute, and then he gave up the unequal contest, and went and took his place beside Isabel, who sat prettily wrapt in her shawl, perfectly content.

"Isn't it charming," she said gayly, "having to wait so long? It puts me in mind of some of those other journeys we took together.—But I can't think of those times with any patience, when we might really have had each other, and didn't!—Do you remember how long we had to wait at Chambéry? and the numbers of military gentlemen that waited too, with their little waists, and their kisses when they met? and that poor married military gentleman, with the plain wife and the two children, and a tarnished uniform? He seemed to be somehow in misfortune, and his moustache hung down in such a spiritless way, while all the other military moustaches about curled and bristled with so much boldness. I think *salles d'attente* everywhere are delightful;

and there is such a community of interest in them all, that when I come here only to go out to Brookline, I feel myself a traveller once more—a blessed stranger in a strange land. O dear, Basil, those were happy times after all, when we might have had each other and didn't. And now we're the more precious for having been so long lost."

She drew closer and closer to him, and looked at him in a way that threatened betrayal of her bridal character.

"Isabel, you will be having your head on my shoulder, next," said he.

"Never!" she answered fiercely, recovering her distance with a start. "But, dearest, if you *do* see me going to—act absurdly, you know, do stop me."

"I'm very sorry, but I've got myself to stop. Besides, I didn't undertake to preserve the incognito of this bridal party."

If any accident of the sort dreaded had really happened, it would not have mattered so much, for as yet they were the sole occupants of the waiting-room. To be sure, the ticket-seller was there, and the lady who checked packages left in her charge; but these must have seen so many endearments pass between passengers, that a fleeting caress or two would scarcely have drawn their notice to our pair. Yet Isabel did not so much even as put her hand into her husband's; and as Basil afterwards said, it was very good practice.

Our temporary state, whatever it is, is often mirrored in all that come near us, and our friends were fated to meet frequent parodies of their happiness from first to last on this journey. The travesty began with the very first people who entered the waiting-room after themselves, and who were a very young couple starting like themselves upon a pleasure tour, which also was evidently one of the first tours of any kind that they had made. It was of modest extent, and comprised going to New York and back; but they talked of it with a fluttered and joyful expectation as if it were a voyage to Europe. Presently there appeared a burlesque of their happiness (but with a touch of tragedy) in that kind of young man who is called by the females of his class a fellow, and two young women of that kind known to him as girls. He took a place between these, and presently began a robust flirtation with one of them. He possessed himself, after a brief struggle, of her parasol, and twirled it about, as he uttered, with a sort of tender rudeness, inconceivable vapidities, such as you would expect from none but a man of the highest fashion. The girl thus courted became selfishly unconscious of everything but her own joy, and made no attempt to bring the other girl within its warmth, but left her to languish forgotten on the other side. The latter sometimes leaned forward, and tried to divert a little of the flirtation to herself, but the flirters snubbed her with short answers, and presently she gave up and sat still in the sad patience of uncourted women. In this attitude she became a burden to Isabel, who was glad when the three took themselves away, and were succeeded by a very stylish couple—from New York, she knew as well as if they had given her their address on West 999th Street. The lady was not pretty, and she was not, Isabel thought, dressed in the perfect taste of Boston; but she owned frankly to herself that the New-Yorkeress was stylish, undeniably effective. The gentleman bought a ticket for New York, and remained at the window of the office talking quite easily with the seller.

"You couldn't do that, my poor Basil," said Isabel, "you'd be afraid."

"O dear, yes; I'm only too glad to get off without browbeating; though I must say that this officer looks affable enough. Really," he added, as an acquaintance of the ticket-seller came in and nodded to him and said "Hot, to-day!" "this is very strange. I always felt as if these men had no private life, no friendships like the rest of us. On duty they seem so like sovereigns, set apart from mankind, and above us all, that it's quite incredible they should have the common personal relations."

At intervals of their talk and silence there came vivid flashes of lightning and quite heavy shocks of thunder, very consoling to our friends, who took them as so many compliments to their prudence in not going by the boat, and who had secret doubts of their wisdom whenever these acknowledgments were withheld. Isabel went so far as to say that she hoped nothing would happen to the boat, but I think she would cheerfully have learnt that the vessel had been obliged to put back to Newport, on account of the storm, or even that it had been driven ashore at a perfectly safe place.

People constantly came and went in the waiting-room, which was sometimes quite full, and again empty of all but themselves. In the course of their observations they formed many cordial friendships and bitter enmities upon the ground of personal appearance, or particulars of dress, with people whom they saw for half a minute upon an average; and they took such a keen interest in every one, that it would be hard to say whether they were more concerned in an old gentleman with vigorously upright iron-gray hair, who sat fronting them, and reading all the evening papers, or a young man who hurled himself through the door, bought a ticket with terrific precipitation, burst out again, and then ran down a departing train before it got out of the station: they loved the old gentleman for a certain stubborn benevolence of expression, and if they had been friends of the young man and his family for generations, and felt bound if any harm befell him to go and break the news gently to his parents, their nerves could not have been more intimately wrought upon by his hazardous behaviour. Still, as they had their tickets for New York, and he was going out on a merely local train—to Brookline, I believe— they could not, even in their anxiety, repress a feeling of contempt for his unambitious destination.

They were already as completely cut off from local associations and sympathies as if they were a thousand miles and many months away from Boston. They enjoyed the lonely flaring of the gas-jets as a gust of wind drew through the station; they shared the gloom and isolation of a man who took a seat in the darkest corner of the room, and sat there with folded arms, the genius of absence. In the patronizing spirit of travellers in a foreign country they noted and approved the vases of cut-flowers in the booth of the lady who checked packages, and the pots of ivy in her windows. "These poor Bostonians," they said, "have some love of the beautiful in their rugged natures."

But after all was said and thought, it was only eight o'clock, and they still had an hour to wait.

Basil grew restless, and Isabel said, with a subtle interpretation of his uneasiness, "*I* don't want anything to eat, Basil, but I think I know the weaknesses of men; and you had better go and pass the next half-hour over a plate of something indigestible."

This was said *con stizza,* the least little suggestion of it; but Basil rose with shameful alacrity. "Darling, if it's your wish—"

"It's my fate, Basil," said Isabel.

"—I'll go," he exclaimed, "because it isn't bridal, and will help us to pass for old married people."

"No, no, Basil, be honest; fibbing isn't your *forte:* I wonder you went into the insurance business; you ought to have been a lawyer. Go, because you like eating, and are hungry, perhaps, or think you may be so before we get to New York. I shall amuse myself well enough here."

I suppose it is always a little shocking and grievous to a wife when she recognizes a rival in butchers'-meat and the vegetables of the season. With her slender relishes for pastry and confectionery, and her dainty habits of lunching, she cannot reconcile with the ideal her husband's capacity for breakfasting, dining, supping, and hot meals at all hours of the day and night—as they write it on the sign-boards of barbaric eating-houses. But Isabel would have had only herself to blame if she had not perceived this trait of Basil's before marriage. She recurred now, as his figure disappeared down the station, to memorable instances of his appetite in their European travels during their first engagement. "Yes, he ate terribly at Susa, when I was too full of the notion of getting into Italy to care for *bouillon* and cold roast chicken. At Rome, I thought I must break with him on account of the wild-boar; and at Heidelberg, the sausage and the ham!— how could he, in my presence? But I took him with all his faults —and was glad to get him," she added, ending her meditation with a little burst of candor; and she did not even think of Basil's appetite when he reappeared.

With the thronging of many sorts of people, in parties and singly, into the waiting-room, they became once again mere observers of their kind, more or less critical in temper, until the crowd grew so that individual traits were merged in the character of multitude. Even then, they could catch glimpses of faces so sweet or fine that they made themselves felt like moments of repose in the tumult, and here and there was something so grotesque in dress or manner that it showed distinct from the rest. The ticket-seller's stamp clicked incessantly as he sold tickets to all points South and West: to New York, Philadelphia, Charleston, to New Orleans, Chicago, Omaha, to St. Paul, Duluth, St. Louis; and it would not have been hard to find in that anxious bustle, that unsmiling eagerness, an image of the whole busy affair of life. It was not a particularly sane spectacle, that impatience to be off to some place that lay not only in the distance, but also in the future—to which no line of road carries you with absolute certainty across an interval of time full of every imaginable chance and influence. It is easy enough to buy a ticket to Cincinnati, but it is somewhat harder to arrive there. Say that all goes well, is it exactly *you* who arrive?

In the midst of the disquiet there entered at last an old woman, so very infirm that she had to be upheld on either hand by her husband and the hackman who had brought them, while a young girl went before with shawls and pillows which she arranged upon the seat. There the invalid lay down, and turned towards the crowd a white, suffering face, which was yet so heavenly meek and peaceful that it comforted whoever looked at it. In spirit our happy friends bowed themselves before it and owned that there was something better than happiness in it.

"What is it like, Isabel?"

"O, I don't know, darling," she said; but she thought, "Perhaps it is like some blessed sorrow that takes us out of this prison of a world, and sets us free of our every-day hates and desires, our aims, our fears, ourselves. Maybe a long and mortal sickness might come to wear such a face in one of us two, and the other could see it, and not regret the poor mask of youth and pretty looks that had fallen away."

She rose and went over to the sick woman, on whose face beamed a tender smile, as Isabel spoke to her. A chord thrilled in two lives hitherto unknown to each other; but what was said Basil would not ask when the invalid had taken Isabel's hand between her own, as for adieu, and she came back to his side with swimming eyes. Perhaps his wife could have given no good reason for her emotion, if he had asked it. But it made her very sweet and dear to him; and I suppose that when a tolerably unselfish man is once secure of a woman's love, he is ordinarily more affected by her compassion and tenderness for other objects than by her feelings towards himself. He likes well enough to think, "She loves me," but still better, "How kind and good she is!"

They lost sight of the invalid in the hurry of getting places on the cars, and they never saw her again. The man at the wicket-gate leading to the train had thrown it up, and the people were pressing furiously through as if their lives hung upon the chance of instant passage. Basil had secured his ticket for the sleeping-car, and so he and Isabel stood aside and watched the tumult. When the rush was over they passed through, and as they walked up and down the platform beside the train, "I was thinking," said Isabel, "after I spoke to that poor old lady, of what Clara Williams says: that she wonders the happiest women in the world can look each other in the face without bursting into tears, their happiness is so unreasonable, and so built upon and hedged about with misery. She declares that there's nothing so sad to her as a bride, unless it's a young mother, or a little girl growing up in the innocent gayety of her heart. She wonders they can live through it."

"Clara is very much of a reformer, and would make an end of all of us men, I suppose,—except her father, who supports her in the leisure that enables her to do her deep thinking. She little knows what we poor fellows have to suffer, and how often we break down in business hours, and sob upon one another's necks. Did that old lady talk to you in the same strain?"

"O no! she spoke very calmly of her sickness, and said she had lived a blessed life. Perhaps it was that made me shed those few small tears. She seemed a very religious person."

"Yes," said Basil, "it is almost a pity that religion is going out. But then, you are to have the franchise."

"All aboard!"

This warning cry saved him from whatever heresy he might have been about to utter; and presently the train carried them out into the gas-sprinkled darkness, with an ever-growing speed that soon left the city lamps far behind. It is a phenomenon whose commonness alone prevents it from being most impressive, that departure of the night-express. The two hundred miles it is to travel stretch before it, traced by those slender clews, to lose which is ruin, and about which hang so many dangers. The draw-bridges that gape upon the way, the trains that stand smoking and steaming on the track, the rail that has borne the wear so long that it must soon snap under it, the deep-cut where the over-hanging mass of rock trembles to its fall, the obstruction that a pitiless malice may have placed in your path—you think of these after the journey is done, but they seldom haunt your fancy while it lasts. The knowledge of your helplessness in any circumstances is so perfect that it begets a sense of irresponsibility, almost of security; and as you drowse upon the pallet of the sleeping-car, and feel yourself hurled forward through the obscurity, you are almost thankful that you can do nothing, for it is upon this condition only that you can endure it; and some such condition as this, I suppose, accounts for many heroic facts in the world. To the fantastic mood which possesses you equally, sleeping or waking, the stoppages of the train have a weird character; and Worcester, Springfield, New Haven, and Stamford are rather points in dreamland than well-known towns of New England. As the train stops you drowse if you have been waking, and wake if you have been in a doze; but in any case you are aware of the locomotive hissing and coughing beyond the station, of flaring gas-jets, of clattering feet of passengers getting on and off; then of some one, conductor or station-master, walking the whole length of the train; and then you are aware of an insane satisfaction in renewed flight through the darkness. You think hazily of the folk in their beds in the town left behind, who stir uneasily at the sound of your train's departing whistle; and so all is a blank vigil or a blank slumber.

By daylight Basil and Isabel found themselves at opposite ends of the car, struggling severally with the problem of the morning's toilet. When the combat was ended, they were surprised at the decency of their appearance, and Isabel said, "I think I'm presentable to an early Broadway public, and I've a fancy for not going to a hotel. Lucy will be expecting us out there before noon; and we can pass the time pleasantly enough for a few hours just wandering about." She was a woman who loved any cheap defiance of custom, and she had an agreeable sense of adventure in what she proposed. Besides, she felt that nothing could be more in the unconventional spirit in which they meant to make their whole journey than a stroll about New York at half past six in the morning.

"Delightful!" answered Basil, who was always charmed with these small originalities. "You look well enough for an evening party; and besides, you won't meet one of your own critical class on Broadway at this hour. We will breakfast at one of those gilded metropolitan restaurants, and then go round to Leonard's, who will be able to give us just three unhurried seconds. After that we'll push on out to his place."

At that early hour there were not many people astir on the wide avenue down which our friends strolled when they left the station; but in the aspect of those they saw there was something that told of a greater heat than they had yet known in Boston, and they were sensible of having reached a more southern latitude. The air, though freshened by the over-night's storm, still wanted the briskness and sparkle and pungency of the Boston air, which is as delicious in summer as it is terrible in winter; and the faces that showed themselves were sodden from the yesterday's heat and perspiration. A corner-grocer, seated in a sort of fierce despondency upon a keg near his shop door, had lightly equipped himself for the struggle of the day in the battered armor of the day before, and in a pair of roomy pantaloons, and a baggy shirt of neutral tint—perhaps he had made a vow not to change it whilst the siege of the hot weather lasted—now confronted the advancing sunlight, before which the long shadows of the buildings were slowly retiring. A marketing mother of a family paused at a provision-store, and looking weakly in at the white-aproned butcher among his meats and flies, passed without an effort to purchase. Hurried and wearied shop-girls tripped by in the draperies that betrayed their sad necessity to be both fine and shabby; from a boarding-house door issued briskly one of those cool young New-Yorkers whom no circumstances can oppress: breezy-coated, white-linened, clean, with a good cigar in the mouth, a light cane caught upon the elbow of one of the arms holding up the paper from which the morning's news is snatched, whilst the person sways lightly with the walk; in the street-cars that slowly tinkled up and down were rows of people with baskets between their legs and papers before their faces; and all showed by some peculiarity of air or dress the excess of heat which they had already borne, and to which they seemed to look forward, and gave by the scantiness of their number a vivid impression of the uncounted thousands within doors prolonging, before the day's terror began, the oblivion of sleep.

As they turned into one of the numerical streets to cross to Broadway, and found themselves in a yet deeper seclusion, Basil began to utter in a musing tone:—

> "A city 'gainst the world's gray Prime,
> Lost in some desert, far from Time,
> Where noiseless Ages, gliding through,
> Have only sifted sands and dew—
> Yet still a marble hand of man
> Lying on all the haunted plan;
> The passions of the human heart
> Beating the marble breast of Art—

Were not more lone to one who first
Upon its giant silence burst,
Than this strange quiet, where the tide
Of life, upheaved on either side,
Hangs trembling, ready soon to beat
With human waves the Morning Street."

"How lovely!" said Isabel, swiftly catching at her skirt, and deftly escaping contact with one of a long row of ash-barrels posted sentinel-like on the edge of the pavement. "Whose is it, Basil?"

"Ah! a poet's," answered her husband, "a man of whom we shall one day any of us be glad to say that we liked him before he was famous. What a nebulous sweetness the first lines have, and what a clear, cool light of daybreak in the last!"

"You could have been as good a poet as that, Basil," said the ever-personal and concretely-speaking Isabel, who could not look at a mountain without thinking what Basil might have done in that way, if he had tried.

"O no, I couldn't, dear. It's very difficult being any poet at all, though it's easy to be like one. But I've done with it; I broke with the Muse the day you accepted me. She came into my office, looking *so* shabby—not unlike one of those poor shop-girls; and as I was very well dressed from having just been to see you, why, you know, I felt the difference. 'Well, my dear?' said I, not quite liking the look of reproach she was giving me. 'You are going to leave me,' she answered sadly. 'Well, yes; I suppose I must. You see the insurance business is very absorbing; and besides, it has a bad appearance, your coming about so in office hours, and in those clothes.' 'O,' she moaned out, 'you used to welcome me at all times, out in the country, and thought me prettily dressed.' 'Yes, yes; but this is Boston; and Boston makes a great difference in one's ideas; and I'm going to be married, too. Come, I don't want to seem ungrateful; we *have* had many pleasant times together, I own it; and I've no objections to your being present at Christmas and Thanksgiving and birthdays, but really I must draw the line there.' She gave me a look that made my heart ache, and went straight to my desk and took out of a pigeon-hole a lot of papers,—odes upon your cruelty, Isabel; songs to you; sonnets —the sonnet, a mighty poor one, I'd made the day before—and threw them all into the grate. Then she turned to me again, signed adieu with mute lips, and passed out. I could hear the bottom wire of the poor thing's hoop-skirt clicking against each step of the stairway, as she went slowly and heavily down to the street."

"O don't,—*don't*, Basil," said his wife, "it seems like something wrong. I think you ought to have been ashamed."

"Ashamed! I was heart-broken. But it had to come to that. As I got hopeful about you, the Muse became a sad bore; and more than once I found myself smiling at her when her back was turned. The Muse doesn't like being laughed at any more than another woman would, and she would have left me shortly. No, I couldn't be a poet like our Morning-Street friend. But see! the human wave is beginning to sprinkle the pavement with cooks and second-girls."

They were frowzy serving-maids and silent; each swept down her own doorsteps and the pavement in front of her own house, and then knocked her broom on the curbstone and vanished into the house, on which the hand of change had already fallen. It was no longer a street solely devoted to the domestic gods, but had been invaded at more than one point by the bustling deities of business: in such streets the irregular, inspired doctors and doctresses come first with inordinate door-plates; then a milliner filling the parlor window with new bonnets; here even a publisher had hung his sign beside a door, through which the feet of young ladies used to trip, and the feet of little children to patter. Here and there stood groups of dwellings unmolested as yet outwardly; but even these had a certain careworn and guilty air, as if they knew themselves to be cheapish boarding-houses or furnished lodgings for gentlemen, and were trying to hide it. To these belonged the frowzy serving-women; to these the rows of ash-barrels, in which the decrepit children and mothers of the streets were clawing for bits of coal.

By the time Basil and Isabel reached Broadway there were already some omnibuses beginning their long day's travel up and down the handsome, tiresome length of that avenue; but for the most part it was empty. There was, of course, a hurry of foot-passengers upon the sidewalks, but these were sparse and uncharacteristic, for New York proper was still fast asleep. The waiter at the restaurant into which our friends stepped was so well aware of this, and so perfectly assured they were not of the city, that he could not forbear a little patronage of them, which they did not resent. He brought Basil what he had ordered in barbaric abundance, and charged for it with barbaric splendor. It is all but impossible not to wish to stand well with your waiter: I have myself been often treated with conspicuous rudeness by the tribe, yet I have never been able to withhold the *douceur* that marked me for a gentleman in their eyes, and entitled me to their dishonorable esteem. Basil was not superior to this folly, and left the waiter with the conviction that, if he was not a New-Yorker, he was a high-bred man of the world at any rate.

Vexed by a sense of his own pitifulness, this man of the world continued his pilgrimage down Broadway, which even in that desert state was full of a certain interest. Troops of laborers straggled along the pavements, each with his dinner-pail in hand; and in many places the eternal building up and pulling down was already going on; carts were struggling up the slopes of vast cellars, with loads of distracting rubbish; here stood the half-demolished walls of a house, with a sad variety of wall-paper showing in the different rooms; there clinked the trowel upon the brick, yonder the hammer on the stone; overhead swung and threatened the marble block that the derrick was lifting to its place. As yet these forces of demolition and construction had the business of the street almost to themselves.

"Why, how shabby the street is!" said Isabel, at last. "When I landed, after being abroad, I remember that Broadway impressed me with its splendor."

"Ah! but you were merely coming from Europe then; and now you arrive from Boston, and are contrasting this poor Broadway with Washington Street. Don't be hard upon it, Isabel; every street can't be a Boston street, you know," said Basil. Isabel, herself a Bostonian of great intensity both by birth and conviction, believed her husband the only man able to have thoroughly baffled the malignity of the stars in causing him to be born out of Boston; yet he sometimes trifled with his hardly achieved triumph, and even showed an indifference to it, with an insincerity of which there can be no doubt whatever.

"O stuff!" she retorted, "as if I had any of that silly local pride! Though *you* know well enough that Boston *is* the best place in the world. But Basil! I suppose Broadway strikes us as so fine, on coming ashore from Europe, because we hardly expect anything of America then."

"Well, I don't know. Perhaps the street has some positive grandeur of its own, though it needs a multitude of people in it to bring out its best effects. I'll allow its disheartening shabbiness and meanness in many ways; but to stand in front of Grace Church, on a clear day—a day of late September, say—and look down the swarming length of Broadway, on the movement and the numbers, while the Niagara roar swelled and swelled from those human rapids, was always like strong new wine to me. I don't think the world affords such another sight; and for one moment, at such times, I'd have been willing to be an Irish councilman, that I might have some right to the pride I felt in the capital of the Irish Republic. What a fine thing it must be for each victim of six centuries of oppression to reflect that he owns at least a dozen Americans, and that, with his fellows, he rules a hundred helpless millionnaires!"

Like all daughters of a free country, Isabel knew nothing about politics, and she felt that she was getting into deep water; she answered buoyantly, but she was glad to make her weariness the occasion of hailing a stage, and changing the conversation. The farther down town they went the busier the street grew; and about the Astor House, where they alighted, there was already a bustle that nothing but a fire could have created at the same hour in Boston. A little further on the steeple of Trinity rose high into the scorching sunlight, while below, in the shadow that was darker than it was cool, slumbered the old graves among their flowers.

"How still they lie!" mused the happy wife, peering through the iron fence in passing.

"Yes, their wedding-journeys are ended, poor things!" said Basil; and through both their minds flashed the wonder if they should ever come to something like that; but it appeared so impossible that they both smiled at the absurdity.

"It's too early yet for Leonard," continued Basil; "what a pity the churchyard is locked up! We could spend the time so delightfully in it. But, never mind; let us go down to the Battery,—it's not a very pleasant place, but it's near, and it's historical, and it's open,—where these drowsy friends of ours used to take the air when they were in the fashion, and had some occasion for the element in its freshness. You can imagine—it's cheap—how they used to see Mr. Burr and Mr. Hamilton down there."

All places that fashion has once loved and abandoned are very melancholy; but of all such places, I think the Battery is the most forlorn. Are there some sickly locust-trees there that cast a tremulous and decrepit shade upon the mangy grass-plots? I believe so, but I do not make sure; I am certain only of the mangy grass-plots, or rather the spaces between the paths, thinly overgrown with some kind of refuse and opprobrious weed, a stunted and pauper vegetation proper solely to the New York Battery. At that hour of the summer morning when our friends, with the aimlessness of strangers who are waiting to do something else, saw the ancient promenade, a few scant and hungry-eyed little boys and girls were wandering over this weedy growth, not playing, but moving listlessly to and fro, fantastic in the wild inaptness of their costumes. One of these little creatures wore, with an odd involuntary jauntiness, the cast-off best dress of some happier child, a gay little garment cut low in the neck and short in the sleeves, which gave her the grotesque effect of having been at a party the night before. Presently came two jaded women, a mother and a grandmother, that appeared, when they had

crawled out of their beds, to have put on only so much clothing as
the law compelled. They abandoned themselves upon the green
stuff, whatever it was, and, with their lean hands clasped outside
their knees, sat and stared, silent and hopeless, at the eastern sky,
at the heart of the terrible furnace, into which in those days the
world seemed cast to be burnt up, while the child which the
younger woman had brought with her feebly wailed unheeded
at her side. On one side of these women were the shameless houses
out of which they might have crept, and which somehow suggested riotous maritime dissipation; on the other side were those
houses in which had once dwelt rich and famous folk, but which
were now dropping down the boarding-house scale through various unhomelike occupations to final dishonor and despair. Down
nearer the water, and not far from the castle that was once a
playhouse and is now the depot of emigration, stood certain
express-wagons, and about these lounged a few hard-looking
men. Beyond laughed and danced the fresh blue water of the
bay, dotted with sails and smoke-stacks.

"Well," said Basil, "I think if I could choose, I should like to
be a friendless German boy, setting foot for the first time on this
happy continent. Fancy his rapture on beholding this lovely spot,
and these charming American faces! What a smiling aspect life
in the New World must wear to his young eyes, and how his
heart must leap within him!"

"Yes, Basil; it's all very pleasing, and thank you for bringing
me. But if you don't think of any other New York delights to show
me, do let us go and sit in Leonard's office till he comes, and then
get out into the country as soon as possible."

Basil defended himself against the imputation that he had
been trying to show New York to his wife, or that he had any
thought but of whiling away the long morning hours, until it
should be time to go to Leonard. He protested that a knowledge
of Europe made New York the most uninteresting town in
America, and that it was the last place in the world where he
should think of amusing himself or any one else; and then they
both upbraided the city's bigness and dulness with an enjoyment

that none but Bostonians can know. They particularly derided the notion of New York's being loved by any one. It was immense, it was grand in some ways, parts of it were exceedingly handsome; but it was too vast, too coarse, too restless. They could imagine its being liked by a successful young man of business, or by a rich young girl, ignorant of life and with not too nice a taste in her pleasures; but that it should be dear to any poet or scholar, or any woman of wisdom and refinement, that they could not imagine. They could not think of any one's loving New York as Dante loved Florence, or as Madame de Staël loved Paris, or as Johnson loved black, homely, home-like London. And as they twittered their little dispraises, the giant Mother of Commerce was growing more and more conscious of herself, waking from her night's sleep and becoming aware of her fleets and trains, and the myriad hands and wheels that throughout the whole sea and land move for her, and do her will even while she sleeps. All about the wedding-journeyers swelled the deep tide of life back from its night-long ebb. Broadway had filled her length with people; not yet the most characteristic New York crowd, but the not less interesting multitude of strangers arrived by the early boats and trains, and that easily distinguishable class of lately New-Yorkized people from other places, about whom in the metropolis still hung the provincial traditions of early rising; and over all, from moment to moment, the eager, audacious, well-dressed, proper life of the mighty city was beginning to prevail, though this was not so notable where Basil and Isabel had paused at a certain window. It was the office of one of the English steamers, and he was saying, "It was by this line I sailed, you know—" and she was interrupting him with, "When who could have dreamed that you would ever be telling me of it here?" So the old marvel was wondered over anew, till it filled the world in which there was room for nothing but the strangeness that they should have loved each other so long and not made it known, that they should ever have uttered it, and that, being uttered, it should be so much more and better than ever could have been dreamed. The broken engagement was a fable of disaster that only made their present fortune more prosperous. The city ceased about them, and they walked on up the street, the first man and first woman in the garden of the new-made earth. As they were both very conscious people, they recognized in themselves some sense of this, and presently drolled it away, in the opulence of a time when every moment brought some beautiful dream, and the soul could be prodigal of its bliss.

"I think if I had the naming of the animals over again, this morning, I shouldn't call snakes *snakes;* should you, Eve?" laughed Basil in intricate acknowledgment of his happiness.

"O no, Adam; we'd look out all the most graceful euphemisms in the newspapers, and we wouldn't hurt the feelings of a spider."

A MIDSUMMER-DAY'S DREAM

THEY HAD WAITED to see Leonard, in order that they might learn better how to find his house in the country; and now, when they came in upon him at nine o'clock, he welcomed them with all his friendly heart. He rose from the pile of morning's letters to which he had but just sat down; he placed them the easiest chairs; he made a feint of its not being a busy hour with him, and would have had them look upon his office, which was still damp and odorous from the porter's broom, as a kind of down-town parlor; but after they had briefly accounted to his amazement for their appearance then and there, and Isabel had boasted of the original fashion in which they had that morning seen New York, they took pity on him, and bade him adieu till evening.

They crossed from Broadway to the noisome street by the ferry, and in a little while had taken their places in the train on the thither side of the water.

"Don't tell me, Basil," said Isabel, "that Leonard travels fifty miles every day by rail going to and from his work!"

"I must, dearest, if I would be truthful."

"Then, darling, there *are* worse things in this world than living up at the South End, aren't there?" And in agreement upon Boston as a place of the greatest natural advantages, as well as all acquirable merits, with after talk that need not be recorded, they arrived in the best humor at the little country station near which the Leonards dwelt.

I must inevitably follow Mrs. Isabel thither, though I do it at the cost of the reader, who suspects the excitements which a long description of the movement would delay. The ladies were very old friends, and they had not met since Isabel's return from Europe and renewal of her engagement. Upon the news of this, Mrs. Leonard had swallowed with surprising ease all that she had said in blame of Basil's conduct during the rupture, and exacted a promise from her friend that she should pay her the first visit after their marriage. And now that they had come together, their only talk was of husbands, whom they viewed in every light to which husbands could be turned, and still found an inexhaustible novelty in the theme. Mrs. Leonard beheld in her friend's joy the sweet reflection of her own honeymoon, and Isabel was pleased to look upon the prosperous marriage of the former as the image of her future. Thus, with immense profit and comfort, they reassured one another by every question and answer, and in their weak content lapsed far behind the representative women of our age, when husbands are at best a necessary evil, and the relation of wives to them is known to be one of pitiable subjection. When these two pretty fogies put their heads of false hair together, they were as silly and benighted as their great-grandmothers could have been in the same circumstances, and, as I say, shamefully encouraged each other in their absurdity. The absurdity appeared too good and blessed to be true. "Do you really suppose, Basil," Isabel would say to her oppressor, after having given him some elegant extract from the last conversation upon husbands, "that we shall get on as smoothly as the Leonards when we have been married ten years? Lucy says that things go more hitchily the first year than ever they do afterwards, and that people love each other better and better just because they've got used to it. Well, our bliss does seem a little crude and garish compared with their happiness; and yet,"— she put up both her palms against his, and gave a vehement little push—"there *is* something agreeable about it, even at this stage of the proceedings."

"Isabel," said her husband, with severity, "this is bridal!"

"No matter! I only want to seem an old married woman to the general public. But the application of it is that you must be careful not to contradict me, or cross me in anything, so that we can be like the Leonards very much sooner than they became so. The great object is not to have any hitchiness; and you know you *are* provoking—at times."

They both educated themselves for continued and tranquil happiness by the example and precept of their friends; and the time passed swiftly in the pleasant learning, and in the novelty of the life led by the Leonards. This indeed merits a closer study than can be given here, for it is the life led by vast numbers of prosperous New-Yorkers who love both the excitement of the city and the repose of the country, and who aspire to unite the enjoyment of both in their daily existence. The suburbs of the metropolis stretch landward fifty miles in every direction; and everywhere are handsome villas like Leonard's, inhabited by men like himself, whom strict study of the time-table enables to spend all their working hours in the city and all their smoking and sleeping hours in the country.

The home and the neighborhood of the Leonards put on their best looks for our bridal pair, and they were charmed. They all enjoyed the visit, said guests and hosts, they were all sorry to have it come to an end; yet they all resigned themselves to this conclusion. Practically, it had no other result than to detain the travellers into the very heart of the hot weather. In that weather it was easy to do anything that did not require an active effort, and resignation was so natural with the mercury at ninety, that I am not sure but there was something sinful in it.

They had given up their cherished purpose of going to Albany by the day boat, which was represented to them in every impossible phase. It would be dreadfully crowded, and whenever it stopped the heat would be insupportable. Besides, it would bring them to Albany at an hour when they must either spend the night there, or push on to Niagara by the night train. "You had better go by the evening boat. It will be light almost till you reach West Point, and you'll see all the best scenery. Then you can get a good night's rest, and start fresh in the morning." So they were counselled, and they assented, as they would have done if they had been advised: "You had better go by the morning boat. It's deliciously cool travelling; you see the whole of the river; you reach Albany for supper, and you push through to Niagara that night and are done with it."

They took leave of Leonard at breakfast and of his wife at noon, and fifteen minutes later they were rushing from the heat of the country into the heat of the city, where some affairs and pleasures were to employ them till the evening boat should start.

Their spirits were low, for the terrible spell of the great heat brooded upon them. All abroad burned the fierce white light of the sun, in which not only the earth seemed to parch and thirst, but the very air withered, and was faint and thin to the troubled respiration. Their train was full of people who had come long journeys from broiling cities of the West, and who were dusty and ashen and reeking in the slumbers at which some of them still vainly caught. On every one lay an awful languor. Here and there stirred a fan, like the broken wing of a dying bird; now and then a sweltering young mother shifted her hot baby from one arm to another; after every station the desperate conductor swung through the long aisle and punched the ticket, which each passenger seemed to yield him with a tacit malediction; a suffering child hung about the empty tank, which could only gasp out a cindery drop or two of ice-water. The wind buffeted faintly at the windows; when the door was opened, the clatter of the rails struck through and through the car like a demoniac yell.

Yet when they arrived at the station by the ferry-side, they seemed to have entered its stifling darkness from fresh and vigorous atmosphere, so close and dead and mixed with the carbonic breath of the locomotives was the air of the place. The thin old wooden walls that shut out the glare of the sun transmitted an intensified warmth; the roof seemed to hover lower and lower, and in its coal-smoked, raftery hollow to generate a heat deadlier than that poured upon it from the skies.

In a convenient place in the station hung a thermometer, before which every passenger, on going aboard the ferry-boat, paused as at a shrine, and mutely paid his devotions. At the altar of this fetish our friends also paused, and saw that the mercury was above ninety, and exulting with the pride that savages take in the cruel might of their idols, bowed their souls to the great god Heat.

On the boat they found a place where the breath of the sea struck cool across their faces, and made them forget the thermometer for the brief time of the transit. But presently they drew near that strange, irregular row of wooden buildings and jutting piers which skirts the river on the New York side, and before the boat's motion ceased the air grew thick and warm again, and tainted with the foulness of the street on which the buildings front. Upon this the boat's passengers issued, passing up through a gangway, on one side of which a throng of return-passengers was pent by a gate of iron bars, like a herd of wild animals. They were streaming with perspiration, and, according to their different temperaments, had faces of deep crimson or deadly pallor.

"Now the question is, my dear," said Basil when, free of the press, they lingered for a moment in the shade outside, "whether we had better walk up to Broadway, at an immediate sacrifice of fibre, and get a stage there, or take one of these cars here, and be landed a little nearer, with half the exertion. By this route we shall have sights and smells which the other can't offer us, but whichever we take we shall be sorry."

"Then I say take this," decided Isabel. "I want to be sorry upon the easiest possible terms, this weather."

They hailed the first car that passed, and got into it. Well for them both if she could have exercised this philosophy with regard to the whole day's business, or if she could have given up her plans for it with the same resignation she had practised in regard to the day boat! It seems to me a proof of the small advance our race has made in true wisdom, that we find it so hard to give up doing anything we have meant to do. It matters very little whether the affair is one of enjoyment or of business, we feel the same bitter need of pursuing it to the end. The mere fact of intention gives it a flavor of duty, and dutiolatry, as one may call the devotion, has passed so deeply into our life that we have scarcely a sense any more of the sweetness of even a neglected pleasure. We will not taste the fine, guilty rapture of a deliberate dereliction; the gentle sin of omission is all but blotted from the calendar of our crimes. If I had been Columbus, I should have thought twice before setting sail, when I was quite ready to do so; and as for Plymouth Rock, I should have sternly resisted the blandishments of those twin sirens, Starvation and Cold, who beckoned the Puritans shoreward, and as soon as ever I came in sight of their granite perch should have turned back to England. But it is now too late to repair these errors, and so, on one of the hottest days of last year, behold my obdurate bridal pair, in a Tenth or Twentieth Avenue horse-car, setting forth upon the fulfilment of a series of intentions, any of which had wiselier been left unaccomplished. Isabel had said they would call upon certain people in Fiftieth Street, and then shop slowly down, ice-cream-ing and staging and variously cooling and calming by the way, until they reached the ticket-office on Broadway, whence they could indefinitely betake themselves to the steamboat an hour or two before her departure. She felt that they had yielded suf-ficiently to circumstances and conditions already on this journey, and she was resolved that the present half-day in New York should be the half-day of her original design.

It was not the most advisable thing, as I have allowed, but it was inevitable, and it afforded them a spectacle which is by no means wanting in sublimity, and which is certainly unique,—the spectacle of that great city on a hot day, defiant of the elements, and prospering on with every form of labor, and at a terrible cost of life. The man carrying the hod to the top of the walls that rankly grow and grow as from his life's blood, will only lay down his load when he feels the mortal glare of the sun blaze in upon heart and brain; the plethoric millionnaire for whom he toils will plot and plan in his office till he swoons at the desk; the trembling beast must stagger forward while the flame-faced tor-mentor on the box has strength to lash him on; in all those vast palaces of commerce there are ceaseless sale and purchase, pack-ing and unpacking, lifting up and laying down, arriving and

departing loads; in thousands of shops is the unspared and unsparing weariness of selling; in the street, filled by the hurry and
suffering of tens of thousands, is the weariness of buying.

Their afternoon's experience was something that Basil and
Isabel could, when it was past, look upon only as a kind of vision,
magnificent at times, and at other times full of indignity and pain.
They seemed to have dreamed of a long horse-car pilgrimage
through that squalid street by the river-side, where presently
they came to a market, opening upon the view hideous vistas of
carnage, and then into a wide avenue, with processions of cars
like their own coming and going up and down the centre of a
foolish and useless breadth, which made even the tall buildings
(rising gauntly up among the older houses of one or two stories)
on either hand look low, and let in the sun to bake the dust that
the hot breaths of wind caught up and sent swirling into the
shabby shops. Here they dreamed of the eternal demolition and
construction of the city, and further on of vacant lots full of
granite boulders, clambered over by goats. In their dream they
had fellow-passengers, whose sufferings made them odious and
whom they were glad to leave behind when they alighted from
the car, and running out of the blaze of the avenue, quenched
themselves in the shade of the cross-street. A little strip of shadow
lay along the row of brown-stone fronts, but there were intervals
where the vacant lots cast no shadow. With great bestowal of
thought they studied hopelessly how to avoid these spaces as if
they had been difficult torrents or vast expanses of desert sand;
they crept slowly along till they came to such a place, and
dashed swiftly across it, and then, fainter than before, moved on.
They seemed now and then to stand at doors, and to be told that
people were out, and again that they were in; and they had a
sense of cool dark parlors, and the airy rustling of light-muslined
ladies, of chat and of fans and ice-water, and then they came
forth again; and evermore

"The day increased from heat to heat."

At last they were aware of an end of their visits, and of a

purpose to go down town again, and of seeking the nearest car by endless blocks of brown-stone fronts, which with their eternal brown-stone flights of steps, and their handsome, intolerable uniformity, oppressed them like a procession of houses trying to pass a given point and never getting by. Upon these streets there was seldom a soul to be seen, so that when their ringing at a door had evoked answer, it had startled them with a vague, sad surprise. In the distance on either hand they could see cars and carts and wagons toiling up and down the avenues, and on the next intersecting pavement sometimes a laborer with his jacket slung across his shoulder, or a dog that had plainly made up his mind to go mad. Up to the time of their getting into one of those phantasmal cars for the return downtownwards they had kept up a show of talk in their wretched dream; they had spoken of other hot days that they had known elsewhere; and they had wondered that the tragical character of heat had been so little recognized. They said that the daily New York murder might even at that moment be somewhere taking place; and that no murder of the whole homicidal year could have such proper circumstance; they morbidly wondered what that day's murder would be, and in what swarming tenement-house, or den of the assassin streets by the river-sides,—if indeed it did not befall in some such high, close-shuttered, handsome dwelling as those they passed, in whose twilight it would be so easy to strike down the master and leave him undiscovered and unmourned by the family ignorantly absent at the mountains or the seaside. They conjectured of the horror of midsummer battles, and pictured the anguish of shipwrecked men upon a tropical coast, and the grimy misery of stevedores unloading shiny cargoes of anthracite coal at city docks. But now at last, as they took seats opposite one another in the crowded car, they seemed to have drifted infinite distances and long epochs asunder. They looked hopelessly across the intervening gulf and mutely questioned when it was and from what far city they or some remote ancestors of theirs had set forth upon a wedding journey. They bade each other a tacit fare-well, and with patient, pathetic faces awaited the end of the world.

When they alighted, they took their way up through one of the streets of the great wholesale businesses to Broadway. On this street was a throng of trucks and wagons lading and unlading; bales and boxes rose and sank by pulleys overhead; the footway was a labyrinth of packages of every shape and size : there was no flagging of the pitiless energy that moved all forward, no sign of how heavy a weight lay on it, save in the reeking faces of its helpless instruments. But when the wedding-journeyers emerged upon Broadway, the other passages and incidents of their dream faded before the superior fantasticality of the spectacle. It was four o'clock, the deadliest hour of the deadly summer day. The spiritless air seemed to have a quality of blackness in it, as if filled with the gloom of low-hovering wings. One half the street lay in shadow, and one half in sun; but the sunshine itself was dim, as if a heat greater than its own had smitten it with languor. Little gusts of sick, warm wind blew across the great avenue at the corners of the intersecting streets. In the upward distance, at which the journeyers looked, the loftier roofs and steeples lifted themselves dim out of the livid atmosphere, and far up and down the length of the street swept a stream of tormented life. All sorts of wheeled things thronged it, conspicuous among which rolled and jarred the gaudily painted stages, with quivering horses driven each by a man who sat in the shade of a branching white umbrella, and suffered with a moody truculence of aspect, and as if he harbored the bitterness of death in his heart for the crowding passengers within, when one of them pulled the strap about his legs, and summoned him to halt. Most of the foot-passengers kept to the shady side, and to the unaccustomed eyes of the strangers they were not less in number than at any other time, though there were fewer women among them. Indomitably resolute of soul, they held their course with the swift pace of custom, and only here and there they showed the effect of the heat. One man, collarless, with waistcoat unbuttoned, and hat set far back from his forehead, waved a fan before his death-white flabby face, and set down one foot after the other with the heaviness of a somnambulist. Another, as they passed him, was saying huskily to the friend at his side, "I can't stand this much longer. My hands tingle as if they had gone to sleep; my heart—" But still the multitude hurried on, passing, repassing, encountering, evading, vanishing into shop doors and emerging from them, dispersing down the side streets, and swarming out of them. It was a scene that possessed the beholder with singular fascination, and in its effect of universal lunacy, it might well have seemed the last phase of a world presently to be destroyed. They who were in it but not of it, as they fancied,—though there was no reason for this,—looked on it amazed, and at last their own errands being accomplished, and themselves so far cured of the madness of purpose, they cried with one voice, that it was a hideous sight, and strove to take refuge from it in the nearest place where the soda-fountain sparkled. It was a vain desire. At the front door of the apothecary's hung a thermometer, and as they entered they heard the next comer cry out with a maniacal pride in the affliction laid upon mankind, "Ninety-seven degrees!" Behind them at the door there poured in a ceaseless stream of people, each pausing at the shrine of heat, before he tossed off the hissing draught that two pale, close-clipped boys served them from either side of the fountain. Then in the order of their coming they issued through another door upon the side street, each, as he disappeared, turning his face half round, and casting a casual glance upon a little group near another counter. The group was of a very patient, half-frightened, half-puzzled looking gentleman who sat perfectly still on a stool, and of a lady who stood beside him, rubbing all over his head a handkerchief full of pounded ice, and easing one hand with the other when the first became tired. Basil drank his soda and paused to look upon this group, which he felt would commend itself to realistic sculpture as eminently characteristic of the local life, and as "The Sunstroke" would sell enormously in the hot season. "Better take a little more of that," the apothecary said, looking up from his prescription, and, as the organized sympathy of the seemingly indifferent crowd, smiling very kindly at his patient, who thereupon tasted something in the glass he held. "Do you still feel like fainting?" asked the humane authority. "Slightly, now and then," answered the other, "but I'm hanging on hard to the bottom curve of that icicled S on your soda-fountain, and I feel that I'm all right as long as I can see that. The people get rather hazy, occasionally, and have no features to speak of. But I don't know that I look very impressive myself," he added in the jesting mood which seems the natural condition of Americans in the face of all embarrassments.

"O, you'll do!" the apothecary answered, with a laugh; but he said, in answer to an anxious question from the lady, "He mustn't be moved for an hour yet," and gayly pestled away at a prescription, while she resumed her office of grinding the pounded ice round and round upon her husband's skull. Isabel offered her the commiseration of friendly words, and of looks kinder yet, and then seeing that they could do nothing, she and Basil fell into the endless procession, and passed out of the side door. "What a shocking thing!" she whispered. "Did you see how all the people looked, one after another, so indifferently at that couple, and evidently forgot them the next instant? It was dreadful. I shouldn't like to have you sun-struck in New York."

"That's very considerate of you; but place for place, if any accident must happen to me among strangers, I think I should prefer to have it in New York. The biggest place is always the kindest as well as the cruellest place. Amongst the thousands of spectators the good Samaritan as well as the Levite would be sure to be. As for a sun-stroke, it requires peculiar gifts. But if you compel me to a choice in the matter, then I say, give me the busiest part of Broadway for a sun-stroke. There is such experience of calamity there that you could hardly fall the first victim to any misfortune. Probably the gentleman at the apothecary's was merely exhausted by the heat, and ran in there for revival. The apothecary has a case of the kind on his hands every blazing afternoon, and knows just what to do. The crowd may be a little *ennuyé* of sun-strokes, and to that degree indifferent, but they most likely know that they can only do harm by an expression of sympathy, and so they delegate their pity as they have delegated their helpfulness to the proper authority, and go about their business. If a man was overcome in the middle of a village street, the blundering country druggist wouldn't know what to do, and the tender-hearted people would crowd about so that no breath of air could reach the victim."

"May be so, dear," said the wife, pensively; "but if anything did happen to you in New York, I should like to have the spectators look as if they saw a human being in trouble. Perhaps I'm a little exacting."

"I think you are. Nothing is so hard as to understand that there are human beings in this world besides one's self and one's set. But let us be selfishly thankful that it isn't you and I there in the apothecary's shop, as it might very well be; and let us get to the boat as soon as we can, and end this horrible midsummer day's dream. We must have a carriage," he added with tardy wisdom, hailing an empty hack, "as we ought to have had all day; though I'm not sorry, now the worst's over, to have seen the worst."

THE NIGHT BOAT

THERE IS LITTLE proportion about either pain or pleasure: a headache darkens the universe while it lasts, a cup of tea really lightens the spirit bereft of all reasonable consolations. Therefore I do not think it trivial or untrue to say that there is for the moment nothing more satisfactory in life than to have bought your ticket on the night boat up the Hudson and secured your state-room key an hour or two before departure, and some time even before the pressure at the clerk's office has begun. In the transaction with this castellated baron, you have of course been treated with haughtiness, but not with ferocity, and your self-respect swells with a sense of having escaped positive insult; your key clicks cheerfully in your pocket against its gutta-percha number, and you walk up and down the gorgeously carpeted, single-columned, two-story cabin, amid a multitude of plush sofas and chairs, a glitter of glass, and a tinkle of prismatic chandeliers overhead, unawed even by the aristocratic gloom of the yellow waiters. Your own state-room as you enter it from time to time is an ever-new surprise of splendors, a magnificent effect of amplitude, of mahogany bedstead, of lace curtains, and of marble-topped washstand. In the mere wantonness of an unalloyed prosperity you say to the saffron nobleman nearest your door, "Bring me a pitcher of ice-water, quick, please!" and you do not find the half-hour that he is gone very long.

If the ordinary wayfarer experiences so much pleasure from these things, then imagine the infinite comfort of our wedding-journeyers, transported from Broadway on that pitiless afternoon to the shelter and the quiet of that absurdly palatial steamboat. It was not yet crowded, and by the riverside there was almost a freshness in the air. They disposed of their troubling bags and packages; they complimented the ridiculous princeliness of their state-room, and then they betook themselves to the sheltered space aft of the saloon, where they sat down for the tranquiller observance of the wharf and whatever should come to be seen by them. Like all people who have just escaped with their lives from some menacing calamity, they were very philosophical in spirit; and having got aboard of their own motion, and being neither of them apparently the worse for the ordeal they had passed through, were of a light, conversational temper.

"What an amusingly superb affair!" Basil cried as they glanced through an open window down the long vista of the saloon. "Good heavens! Isabel, does it take all this to get us plain republicans to Albany in comfort and safety, or are we really a nation of princes in disguise? Well, I shall never be satisfied with less hereafter," he added. "I am spoilt for ordinary paint and upholstery from this hour; I am a ruinous spendthrift, and a humble three-story swell-front up at the South End is no longer the place for me. Dearest,

'Let us swear an oath, and keep it with an equal mind,'

never to leave this Aladdin's-palace-like steamboat, but spend our lives in perpetual trips up and down the Hudson."

To which not very costly banter Isabel responded in kind, and rapidly sketched the life they could lead aboard. Since they could not help it, they mocked the public provision which, leaving no interval between disgraceful squalor and ludicrous splendor, accommodates our democratic *ménage* to the taste of the richest and most extravagant plebeian amongst us. He unhappily minds danger and oppression as little as he minds money, so long as he has a spectacle and a sensation; and it is this ruthless imbecile who will have lace curtains to the steamboat berth into which he gets with his pantaloons on, and out of which he may be blown by an exploding boiler at any moment; it is he who will have for supper that overgrown and shapeless dinner in the lower saloon, and will not let any one else buy tea or toast for a less sum than he pays for his surfeit; it is he who perpetuates the insolence of the clerk and the reluctance of the waiters; it is he, in fact, who now comes out of the saloon, with his womenkind, and takes chairs under the awning where Basil and Isabel sit. Personally, he is not so bad; he is good-looking, like all of us; he is better dressed than most of us; he behaves himself quietly, if not easily; and no lord so loathes a scene. Next year he is going to Europe, where he will not show to so much advantage as here; but for the present it would be hard to say in what way he is vulgar, and perhaps vulgarity is not so common a thing after all.

It was something besides the river that made the air so much more sufferable than it had been. Over the city, since our friends had come aboard the boat, a black cloud had gathered and now hung low upon it, while the wind from the face of the water took the dust in the neighboring streets, and frolicked it about the housetops, and in the faces of the arriving passengers, who, as the moment of departure drew near, appeared in constantly increasing numbers and in greater variety, with not only the trepidation of going upon them, but also with the electrical excitement people feel before a tempest. The breast of the black cloud was now zigzagged from moment to moment by lightning, and claps of deafening thunder broke from it. At last the long endurance of the day was spent, and out of its convulsion burst floods of rain, again and again sweeping the promenade-deck where the people sat, and driving them disconsolate into the saloon. The air was darkened as by night, and with many regrets for the vanishing prospect, mingled with a sense of relief from the heat, our friends felt the boat tremble away from her moorings and set forth upon her trip.

"Ah! if we had only taken the day boat!" moaned Isabel. "Now, we shall see nothing of the river landscape, and we shall never be able to put ourselves down, when we long for Europe, by declaring that the scenery of the Hudson is much finer than that of the Rhine."

Yet they resolved, this indomitably good-natured couple, that they would be just even to the elements, which had by no means been generous to them; and they owned that if so noble a storm had celebrated their departure upon some storied river from some more romantic port than New York, they would have thought it an admirable thing. Even whilst they contented themselves, the storm passed, and left a veiled and humid sky overhead, that gave a charming softness to the scene on which their eyes fell when they came out of the saloon again, and took their places with a largely increased companionship on the deck.

They had already reached that part of the river where the uplands begin, and their course was between stately walls of rocky steepness, or wooded slopes, or grassy hollows, the scene forever losing and taking grand and lovely shape. Wreaths of mist hung about the tops of the loftier headlands, and long shadows draped their sides. As the night grew, lights twinkled from a lonely house here and there in the valleys; a swarm of lamps showed a town where it lay upon the lap or at the foot of the hills. Behind them stretched the great gray river, haunted with many sails; now a group of canal-boats grappled together, and having an air of cosiness in their adventure upon this strange current out of their own sluggish waters, drifted out of sight; and now a smaller and slower steamer, making a laborious show of keeping up, was passed, and reluctantly fell behind; along the water's edge rattled and hooted the frequent trains. They could not tell at any time what part of the river they were on, and they could not, if they would, have made its beauty a matter of conscientious observation; but all the more, therefore, they deeply enjoyed it without reference to time or place. They felt some natural pain when they thought that they might unwittingly pass the scenes that Irving has made part of the common dreamland, and they would fain have seen the lighted windows of the house out of which a cheerful ray has penetrated to so many hearts; but being sure of nothing, as they were, they had the comfort of finding the Tappan Zee in every expanse of the river, and of discovering Sunny-Side on every pleasant slope. By virtue of this helplessness, the Hudson, without ceasing to be the Hudson, became from moment to moment all fair and stately streams upon which they had voyaged or read of voyaging, from the Nile to the Mississippi. There is no other travel like river travel; it is the perfection of movement, and one might well desire never to arrive at one's destination. The abundance of room, the free, pure air, the constant delight of the eyes in the changing landscape, the soft tremor of the boat, so steady upon her keel, the variety of the little world on board,—all form a charm which no good heart in a sound body can resist. So, whilst the twilight held, well content, in contiguous chairs, they purred in flattery of their kindly fate, imagining different pleasures, certainly, but none greater, and tasting to its subtlest flavor the happiness conscious of itself.

Their own satisfaction, indeed, was so interesting to them in this objective light, that they had little desire to turn from its contemplation to the people around them; and when at last they did so, it was still with lingering glances of self-recognition and enjoyment. They divined rightly that one of the main conditions of their present felicity was the fact that they had seen so much of time and of the world, that they had no longer any desire to take beholding eyes, or to make any sort of impressive figure, and they understood that their prosperous love accounted as much as years and travel for this result. If they had had a loftier opinion of themselves, their indifference to others might have made them offensive; but with their modest estimate of their own value in the world, they could have all the comfort of self-sufficiency, without its vulgarity.

"O, yes!" said Basil, in answer to some apostrophe to their bliss from Isabel, "it's the greatest imaginable satisfaction to have lived past certain things. I always knew that I was not a very handsome or otherwise captivating person, but I can remember years—now blessedly remote—when I never could see a young girl without hoping she would mistake me for something of that sort. I couldn't help desiring that some fascination of mine, which had escaped my own analysis, would have an effect

upon her. I dare say all young men are so. I used to live for the
possible interest I might inspire in your sex, Isabel. They controlled my movements, my attitudes; they forbade me repose;
and yet I believe I was no ass, but a tolerably sensible fellow.
Blessed be marriage, I am free at last! All the loveliness that
exists outside of you, dearest—and it's mighty little—is mere
pageant to me; and I thank heaven that I can meet the most
stylish girl now upon the broad level of our common humanity.
Besides, it seems to me that our experience of life has quieted us
in many other ways. What a luxury it is to sit here, and reflect
that we do not want any of these people to suppose us rich or
distinguished or beautiful or well dressed, and do not care to
show off in any sort of way before them!"

This content was heightened, no doubt, by a just sense of
their contrast to the group of people nearest them,—a young
man of the second or third quality and two young girls. The
eldest of these was carrying on a vivacious flirtation with the
young man, who was apparently an acquaintance of brief standing; the other was scarcely more than a child, and sat somewhat
abashed at the sparkle of the colloquy. They were conjecturally
sisters going home from some visit, and not skilled in the world,
but of a certain repute in their country neighborhood for beauty
and wit. The young man presently gave himself out as one who,
in pursuit of trade for the dry-goods house he represented, had
travelled many thousands of miles in all parts of the country. The
encounter was visibly that kind of adventure which both would
treasure up for future celebration to their different friends; and
it had a brilliancy and interest which they could not even now
consent to keep to themselves. They talked to each other and at
all the company within hearing, and exchanged curt speeches
which had for them all the sensation of repartee.

Young Man. They say that beauty unadorned is adorned the
most.

Young Woman (bridling, and twitching her head from side to
side, in the high excitement of the dialogue). Flattery is out of
place.

Young Man. Well, never mind. If you don't believe me, you ask your mother when you get home.

(Titter from the younger sister.)

Young Woman (scornfully). Umph! my mother has no control over me!

Young Man. Nobody else has, either, *I* should say. (Admiringly.)

Young Woman. Yes, you've told the truth for once, for a wonder. I'm able to take care of myself—perfectly. (Almost hoarse with a sense of sarcastic performance.)

Young Man. "Whole team and big dog under the wagon," as they say out West.

Young Woman. Better a big dog than a puppy, *any* day.

(Giggles and horror from the younger sister, sensation in the young man, and so much rapture in the young woman that she drops the key of her state-room from her hand. They both stoop, and a jocose scuffle for it ensues, after which the talk takes an autobiographical turn on the part of the young man, and drops into an unintelligible murmur. Ah! poor Real Life, which I love, can I make others share the delight I find in thy foolish and insipid face?)

Not far from this group sat two Hebrews, one young and the other old, talking of some business out of which the latter had retired. The younger had been asked his opinion upon some point, and he was expanding with a flattered consciousness of the elder's perception of his importance, and toadying to him with the pleasure which all young men feel in winning the favor of seniors in their vocation. "Well, as I was a-say'n', Isaac don't seem to haf no natcheral pent for the glothing business. Man gomes in and wands a goat,"—he seemed to be speaking of a garment and not a domestic animal,—"Isaac'll zell him the goat he wands him to puy, and he'll make him believe it's the goat he was a-lookin' for. Well, now, that's well enough as far as it goes; but *you* know and *I* know, Mr. Rosenthal, that that's no way to do business. A man gan't zugzeed that goes upon that brincible. Id's wrong. Id's easy enough to make a man puy the goat you want him to, if he wands a goat, but the thing is to *make him puy the goat that you wand to zell when he don't wand no goat at all*. You've asked me what I thought and I've dold you. Isaac'll never zugzeed in the redail glothing business in the world!"

"Well," sighed the elder, who filled his arm-chair quite full, and quivered with a comfortable jelly-like tremor in it, at every pulsation of the engine, "I was afraid of something of the gind. As you say, Benjamin, he don't seem to have no pent for it. And yet I proughd him up to the business; I drained him to it, my-self."

Besides these talkers, there were scattered singly, or grouped about in twos and threes and fours, the various people one encounters on a Hudson River boat, who are on the whole different from the passengers on other rivers, though they all have features in common. There was that man of the sudden gains, who has already been typified; and there was also the smoother rich man of inherited wealth, from whom you can somehow know the former so readily. They were each attended by their several retinues of womankind, the daughters all much alike, but the mothers somewhat different. They were going to Saratoga, where perhaps the exigencies of fashion would bring them acquainted, and where the blue blood of a quarter of a century would be kind to the yesterday's fluid of warmer hue. There was something pleasanter in the face of the hereditary aristocrat, but not so strong nor, altogether, so admirable; particularly if you reflected that he really represented nothing in the world, no great culture, no political influence, no civic aspiration, not even a pecuniary force, nothing but a social set, an alien club-life, a tradition of dining. We live in a true fairy-land after all, where the hoarded treasure turns to a heap of dry leaves. The almighty dollar defeats itself and finally buys nothing that a man cares to have. The very highest pleasure that such an American's money can purchase is exile, and to this rich man doubtless Europe is a twice-told tale. Let us clap our empty pockets, dearest reader, and be glad.

We can be as glad, apparently, and with the same reason as the poorly dressed young man standing near beside the guard, whose face Basil and Isabel chose to fancy that of a poet, and concerning whom they romanced that he was going home, wherever his home was, with the manuscript of a rejected book in his pocket. They imagined him no great things of a poet, to be sure, but his pensive face claimed delicate feeling for him, and a graceful, sombre fancy, and they conjectured unconsciously caught flavors of Tennyson and Browning in his verse, with a moderner tint from Morris; for was it not a story out of mythology, with gods and heroes of the nineteenth century, that he was now carrying back from New York with him? Basil sketched from the colors of his own long-accepted disappointments a moving little picture of this poor imagined poet's adventures; with what kindness and unkindness he had been put to shame by publishers, and how, descending from his high hopes of a book, he had tried to sell to the magazines some of the shorter pieces out of the "And other Poems" which were to have filled up the volume. "He's going back rather stunned and bewildered; but it's something to have tasted the city, and its bitter may turn to sweet on his palate, at last, till he finds himself longing for the tumult that he abhors now. Poor fellow! one compassionate cutthroat of a publisher even asked him to lunch, being struck, as we are, with something fine in his face. I hope he's got somebody who believes in him, at home. Otherwise he'd be more comfortable, for the present, if he went over the railing there."

So the play of which they were both actors and spectators went on about them. Like all passages of life, it seemed now a grotesque mystery, with a bluntly enforced moral, now a farce of the broadest, now a latent tragedy folded in the disguises of comedy. All the elements, indeed, of either were at work there, and this was but one brief scene of the immense complex drama which was to proceed so variously in such different times and places, and to have its *dénouement* only in eternity. The contrasts were sharp; each group had its travesty in some other; the talk of one seemed the rude burlesque, the bitter satire of the next; but of all these parodies none was so terribly effective as the two women, who sat in the midst of the company, yet were somehow distinct from the rest. One wore the deepest black of widowhood, the other was dressed in bridal white, and they were both alike awful in their mockery of guiltless sorrow and guiltless joy. They were not old, but the soul of youth was dead in their pretty, lamentable faces, and ruin ancient as sin looked from their eyes; their talk and laughter seemed the echo of an innumerable multitude of the lost haunting the world in every land and time, each solitary forever, yet all bound together in the unity of an imperishable slavery and shame.

What a stale effect! What hackneyed characters! Let us be glad the night drops her curtain upon the cheap spectacle, and shuts these with the other actors from our view.

Within the cabin through which Basil and Isabel now slowly moved there were numbers of people lounging about on the sofas, in various attitudes of talk or vacancy; and at the tables there were others reading "Lothair," a new book in the remote epoch of which I write, and a very fashionable book indeed. There was in the air that odor of paint and carpet which prevails on steamboats; the glass drops of the chandeliers ticked softly against each other, as the vessel shook with her respiration, like a comfortable sleeper, and imparted a delicious feeling of cosiness and security to our travellers.

A few hours later they struggled awake at the sharp sound of the pilot's bell signalling the engineer to slow the boat. There was a moment of perfect silence; then all the drops of the chandeliers in the saloon clashed musically together; then fell another silence; and at last came wild cries for help, strongly qualified with blasphemies and curses. "Send out a boat!" "There was a woman aboard that steamboat!" "Lower your boats!" "Run a craft right down, with your big boat!" "Send out a boat and pick up the crew!" The cries rose and sank, and finally ceased; through the lattice of the state-room window some lights shone faintly on the water at a distance.

"Wait here, Isabel!" said her husband. "We've run down a boat. We don't seem hurt; but I'll go see. I'll be back in a minute."

Isabel had emerged into a world of dishabille, a world wildly unbuttoned and unlaced, where it was the fashion for ladies to wear their hair down their backs, and to walk about in their stockings, and to speak to each other without introduction. The place with which she had felt so familiar a little while before was now utterly estranged. There was no motion of the boat, and in the momentary suspense a quiet prevailed, in which those grotesque shapes of disarray crept noiselessly round whispering panic-stricken conjectures. There was no rushing to and fro, nor tumult of any kind, and there was not a man to be seen, for apparently they had all gone like Basil to learn the extent of the calamity. A mist of sleep involved the whole, and it was such a topsy-turvy world that it would have seemed only another dreamland, but that it was marked for reality by one signal fact. With the rest appeared the woman in bridal white and the woman in widow's black, and there, amidst the fright that made all others friends, and for aught that most knew, in the presence of death itself, these two moved together shunned and friendless.

Somehow, even before Basil returned, it had become known to Isabel and the rest that their own steamer had suffered no harm, but that she had struck and sunk another convoying a flotilla of canal-boats, from which those alarming cries and curses had come. The steamer was now lying by for the small boats she had sent out to pick up the crew of the sunken vessel.

"Why, I only heard a little tinkling of the chandeliers," said one of the ladies. "Is it such a very slight matter to run down another boat and sink it?"

She appealed indirectly to Basil, who answered lightly, "I don't think you ladies ought to have been disturbed at all. In running over a common tow-boat on a perfectly clear night like this there should have been no noise and no perceptible jar. They manage better on the Mississippi, and both boats often go down without waking the lightest sleeper on board."

The ladies, perhaps from a deficient sense of humor, listened with undisguised displeasure to this speech. It dispersed them, in fact; some turned away to bivouac for the rest of the night upon the arm-chairs and sofas, while others returned to their rooms. With the latter went Isabel. "Lock me in, Basil," she said, with a bold meekness, "and if anything more happens don't wake me till the last moment." It was hard to part from him, but she felt that his vigil would somehow be useful to the boat, and she confidingly fell into a sleep that lasted till daylight.

Meantime, her husband, on whom she had tacitly devolved so great a responsibility, went forward to the promenade in front of the saloon, in hopes of learning something more of the catastrophe from the people whom he had already found gathered there.

A large part of the passengers were still there, seated or standing about in earnest colloquy. They were in that mood which follows great excitement, and in which the feeblest-minded are sure to lead the talk. At such times one feels that a sensible frame of mind is unsympathetic, and if expressed, unpopular, or perhaps not quite safe; and Basil, warned by his fate with the ladies, listened gravely to the voice of the common imbecility and incoherence.

The principal speaker was a tall person, wearing a silk travelling-cap. He had a face of stupid benignity and a self-satisfied smirk; and he was formally trying to put at his ease, and hopelessly confusing the loutish youth before him. "You say you saw the whole accident, and you're probably the only passenger that did see it. You'll be the most important witness at the trial," he added, as if there would ever be any trial about it. "Now, how did the tow-boat hit us?"

"Well, she came bows on."

"Ah! bows on," repeated the other, with great satisfaction; and a little murmur of "Bows on!" ran round the listening circle.

"That is," added the witness, "it seemed as if we struck her amidships, and cut her in two, and sunk her."

"Just so," continued the examiner, accepting the explanation, "bows on. Now I want to ask if you saw our captain or any of the crew about?"

"Not a soul," said the witness, with the solemnity of a man already on oath.

"That'll do," exclaimed the other. "This gentleman's experience coincides exactly with my own. I didn't see the collision, but I did see the cloud of steam from the sinking boat, and I saw her go down. There wasn't an officer to be found anywhere on board our boat. I looked about for the captain and the mate myself, and couldn't find either of them high or low."

"The officers ought all to have been sitting here on the promenade deck," suggested one ironical spirit in the crowd, but no one noticed him.

The gentleman in the silk travelling-cap now took a chair, and a number of sympathetic listeners drew their chairs about him, and then began an interchange of experience, in which each related to the last particular all that he felt, thought, and said, and, if married, what his wife felt, thought, and said, at the moment of the calamity. They turned the disaster over and over in their talk, and rolled it under their tongues. Then they reverted to former accidents in which they had been concerned; and the silk-capped gentleman told, to the common admiration, of a fearful escape of his on the Erie Road, from being thrown down a steep embankment fifty feet high by a piece of rock that had fallen on the track. "Now just see, gentlemen, what a little thing, humanly speaking, life depends upon. If that old woman had been able to sleep, and hadn't sent that boy down to warn the train, we should have run into the rock and been dashed to pieces. The passengers made up a purse for the boy, and I wrote a full account of it to the papers."

"Well," said one of the group, a man in a hard hat, "I never lie down on a steamboat or a railroad train. I want to be ready for whatever happens."

The others looked at this speaker with interest, as one who had invented a safe method of travel.

"I happened to be up to-night, but I almost always undress

and go to bed, just as if I were in my own house," said the gentleman of the silk cap. "I don't say your way isn't the best, but that's
my way."

The champions of the rival systems debated their merits with
suavity and mutual respect, but they met with scornful silence a
compromising spirit who held that it was better to throw off your
coat and boots, but keep your pantaloons on. Meanwhile, the
steamer was hanging idle upon the current, against which it
now and then stirred a careless wheel, still waiting for the return
of the small boats. Thin gray clouds, through rifts of which a star
sparkled keenly here and there, veiled the heavens; shadowy
bluffs loomed up on either hand; in a hollow on the left twinkled
a drowsy little town; a beautiful stillness lay on all.

After an hour's interval a shout was heard from far down the
river; then later the plash of oars; then a cry hailing the ap-
roaching boats, and the answer, "All safe!" Presently the boats
had come alongside, and the passengers crowded down to the
guard to learn the details of the search. Basil heard a hollow,
moaning, gurgling sound, regular as that of the machinery, for
some note of which he mistook it. "Clear the gangway there!"
shouted a gruff voice; "man scalded, here!" And a burden was
carried by from which fluttered, with its terrible regularity, that
utterance of mortal anguish.

Basil went again to the forward promenade, and sat down to
see the morning come.

The boat swiftly ascended the current, and presently the
steeper shores were left behind and the banks fell away in long
upward sloping fields, with farm-houses and with stacks of har-
vest dimly visible in the generous expanses. By and by they passed
a fisherman drawing his nets, and bending from his boat, there
near Albany, N. Y., in the picturesque immortal attitudes of
Raphael's Galilean fisherman; and now a flush mounted the
pale face of the east, and through the dewy coolness of the dawn
there came, more to the sight than any other sense, a vague
menace of heat. But as yet the air was deliciously fresh and sweet,
and Basil bathed his weariness in it, thinking with a certain

luxurious compassion of the scalded man, and how he was to fare that day. This poor wretch seemed of another order of beings, as the calamitous always seem to the happy, and Basil's pity was quite an abstraction; which, again, amused and shocked him, and he asked his heart of bliss to consider of sorrow a little more earnestly as the lot of all men, and not merely of an alien creature here and there. He dutifully tried to imagine another issue to the disaster of the night, and to realize himself suddenly bereft of her who so filled his life. He bade his soul remember that, in the security of sleep, Death had passed them both so close that his presence might well have chilled their dreams, as the iceberg that grazes the ship in the night freezes all the air about it. But it was quite idle: where love was, life only was; and sense and spirit alike put aside the burden that he would have laid upon them; his revery reflected with delicious caprice the looks, the tones, the movements that he loved, and bore him far away from the sad images that he had invited to mirror themselves in it.

IV

A DAY'S RAILROADING

HAPPINESS has commonly a good appetite; and the thought of the fortunately ended adventures of the night, the fresh morning air, and the content of their own hearts, gifted our friends, by the time the boat reached Albany, with a wholesome hunger, so that they debated with spirit the question of breakfast and the best place of breakfasting in a city which neither of them knew, save in the most fugitive and sketchy way.

They decided, at last, in view of the early departure of the train, and the probability that they would be more hurried at a hotel, to breakfast at the station, and thither they went and took places at one of the many tables within, where they seemed to have been expected only by the flies. The waitress plainly had not looked for them, and for a time found their presence so incredible that she would not acknowledge the rattling that Basil was obliged to make on his glass. Then it appeared that the cook would not believe in them, and he did not send them till they were quite faint the peppery and muddy draught which impudently affected to be coffee, the oily slices of fugacious potatoes slipping about in their shallow dish and skilfully evading pursuit, the pieces of beef that simulated steak, the hot, greasy biscuit, steaming evilly up into the face when opened, and then soddening into masses of condensed dyspepsia.

The wedding-journeyers looked at each other with eyes of sad amaze. They bowed themselves for a moment to the viands, and then by an equal impulse refrained. They were sufficiently young, they were happy, they were hungry: nature is great and strong, but art is greater, and before these triumphs of the cook at the Albany depot appetite succumbed. By a terrible *tour de force* they swallowed the fierce and turbid liquor in their cups, and then speculated fantastically upon the character and history of the materials of that breakfast.

Presently Isabel paused, played a little with her knife, and, after a moment, looked up at her husband with an arch regard and said: "I was just thinking of a small station somewhere in the South of France where our train once stopped for breakfast. I remember the freshness and brightness of everything on the little tables,—the plates, the napkins, the gleaming half-bottles of wine. They seemed to have been preparing that breakfast for us from the beginning of time, and we were hardly seated before they served us with great cups of *café-au-lait*, and the sweetest rolls and butter; then a delicate cutlet, with an unspeakable gravy, and potatoes—such potatoes! Dear me, how little I ate of it! I wish, for once, I'd had your appetite, Basil; I do indeed."

She ended with a heartless laugh, in which, despite the tragical contrast her words had suggested, Basil finally joined. So much amusement had probably never been got before out of the misery inflicted in that place; but their lightness did not at all commend them. The waitress had not liked it from the first, and had served them with reluctance; and the proprietor did not like it, and kept his eye upon them as if he believed them about to escape without payment. Here, then, they had enforced a great fact of travelling,—that people who serve the public are kindly and pleasant in proportion as they serve it well. The unjust and the inefficient have always that consciousness of evil which will not let a man forgive his victim, or like him to be cheerful.

Our friends, however, did not heat themselves over the fact. There was already such heat from without, even at eight o'clock in the morning, that they chose to be as cool as possible in mind, and they placidly took their places in the train, which had been made up for departure. They had deliberately rejected the notion of a drawing-room car as affording a less varied prospect of humanity, and as being less in the spirit of ordinary American travel. Now, in reward, they found themselves quite comfortable in the common passenger-car, and disposed to view the scenery, into which they struck an hour after leaving the city, with much complacency. There was sufficient draught through the open window to make the heat tolerable, and the great brooding warmth gave to the landscape the charm which it alone can impart. It is a landscape that I greatly love for its mild beauty and tranquil picturesqueness, and it is in honor of our friends that I say they enjoyed it. There are nowhere any considerable hills, but everywhere generous slopes and pleasant hollows and the wide meadows of a grazing country, with the pretty brown Mohawk River rippling down through all, and at frequent intervals the life of the canal, now near, now far away, with the lazy boats that seem not to stir, and the horses that the train passes with a whirl, and leaves slowly stepping forward and swiftly slipping backward. There are farms that had once, or still have, the romance to them of being Dutch farms,—if there is any romance in that,—and one conjectures a Dutch thrift in their waving grass and grain. Spaces of woodland here and there dapple the slopes, and the cosey red farm-houses repose by the side of their capacious red barns. Truly, there is no ground on which to defend the idleness, and yet as the train strives furiously onward amid these scenes of fertility and abundance, I like in fancy to loiter behind it, and to saunter at will up and down the landscape. I stop at the farm-yard gates, and sit upon the porches or thresholds, and am served with cups of buttermilk by old Dutch ladies who have done their morning's work and have leisure to be knitting or sewing; or if there are no old ladies, with decent caps upon their gray hair, then I do not complain if the drink is brought me by some red-cheeked, comely young girl, out of Washington Irving's pages, with no cap on her golden braids, who mirrors my diffidence, and takes an attitude of pretty awkwardness while she waits till I have done drinking. In the same easily contented spirit as I lounge through the barn-yard, if I find the old hens gone about their family affairs, I do not mind a meadow-lark's singing in the top of the elm-tree beside the pump. In these excursions the watch-dogs know me for a harmless person, and will not open their eyes as they lie coiled up in the sun before the gate. At all the places, I have the people keep bees, and, in the garden full of worthy potherbs, such idlers in the vegetable world as hollyhocks and larkspurs and four-o'clocks, near a great bed in which the asparagus has gone to sleep for the season with a dream of delicate spray hanging over it. I walk unmolested through the farmer's tall grass, and ride with him upon the perilous seat of his voluble mowing-machine, and learn to my heart's content that his name begins with Van, and that his family has owned that farm ever since the days of the Patroon; which I dare say is not true. Then I fall asleep in a corner of the hay-field, and wake up on the tow-path of the canal beside that wonderfully lean horse, whose bones you cannot count only because they are so many. He never wakes up, but with a faltering under lip and half-shut eyes hobbles stiffly on, unconscious of his anatomical interest. The captain hospitably asks me on board, with a twist of the rudder swinging the stern of the boat up to the path, so that I can step on. She is laden with flour from the valley of the Genesee, and may have started on her voyage shortly after the canal was made. She is succinctly manned by the captain, the driver, and the cook, a fiery-haired lady of imperfect temper; and the cabin, which I explore, is plainly furnished with a cook-stove and a flask of whiskey. Nothing but profane language is allowed on board; and so, in a life of wicked jollity and ease, we glide imperceptibly down the canal, unvexed by the far-off future of arrival.

Such, I say, are my own unambitious mental pastimes, but I am aware that less superficial spirits could not be satisfied with them, and I do not pretend that my wedding-journeyers were so. They cast an absurd poetry over the landscape; they invited themselves to be reminded of passages of European travel by it; and they placed villas and castles and palaces upon all the eligible building-sites. Ashamed of these devices, presently, Basil patriotically tried to reconstruct the Dutch and Indian past of the Mohawk Valley, but here he was foiled by the immense ignorance of his wife, who, as a true American woman, knew nothing of the history of her own country, and less than nothing of the barbarous regions beyond the borders of her native province. She proved a bewildering labyrinth of error concerning the events which Basil mentioned; and she had never even heard of the massacres by the French and Indians at Schenectady, which he in his boyhood had known so vividly that he was scalped every night in his dreams, and woke up in the morning expecting to see marks of the tomahawk on the headboard. So, failing at last to extract any sentiment from the scenes without, they turned their faces from the window, and looked about them for amusement within the car.

It was in all respects an ordinary carful of human beings, and it was perhaps the more worthy to be studied on that account. As in literature the true artist will shun the use even of real events if they are of an improbable character, so the sincere observer of man will not desire to look upon his heroic or occasional phases, but will seek him in his habitual moods of vacancy and tiresomeness. To me, at any rate, he is at such times very precious; and I never perceive him to be so much a man and a brother as when I feel the pressure of his vast, natural, unaffected dulness. Then I am able to enter confidently into his life and inhabit there, to think his shallow and feeble thoughts, to be moved by his dumb, stupid desires, to be dimly illumined by his stinted inspirations, to share his foolish prejudices, to practise his obtuse selfishness. Yes, it is a very amusing world, if you do not refuse to be amused; and our friends were very willing to be entertained. They delighted in the precise, thick-fingered old ladies who bought sweet apples of the boys come aboard with baskets, and who were so long in finding the right change, that our travellers, leaping in thought with the boys from the moving train, felt that they did so at the peril of their lives. Then they were interested in people who went out and found their friends waiting for them, or else did not find them, and wandered disconsolately up and down before the country stations, carpet-bag in hand; in women who came aboard, and were awkwardly shaken hands with or sheepishly kissed by those who hastily got seats for them, and placed their

bags or their babies in their laps, and turned for a nod at the door;
in young ladies who were seen to places by young men (the latter
seemed not to care if the train did go off with them), and then
threw up their windows and talked with girl-friends on the platform without, till the train began to move, and at last turned with
gleaming eyes and moist red lips, and panted hard in the excitement of thinking about it, and could not calm themselves to the
dull level of the travel around them; in the conductor, coldly
and inaccessibly vigilant, as he went his rounds, reaching blindly
for the tickets with one hand while he bent his head from time
to time, and listened with a faint, sarcastic smile to the questions
of passengers who supposed they were going to get some information out of him; in the train-boy, who passed through on his
many errands with prize-candies, gum-drops, pop-corn, papers
and magazines, and distributed books and the police journals
with a blind impartiality, or a prodigious ignorance, or a supernatural perception of character in those who received them.

A through train from East to West presents some peculiar features as well as the traits common to all railway travel; and our
friends decided that this was not a very well-dressed company,
and would contrast with the people on an express-train between
Boston and New York to no better advantage than these would
show beside the average passengers between London and Paris.
And it seems true that on a westering line, the blacking fades
gradually from the boots, the hat softens and sinks, the coat loses
its rigor of cut, and the whole person lounges into increasing in-
formality of costume. I speak of the undressful sex alone:
woman, wherever she is, appears in the last attainable effects of
fashion, which are now all but telegraphic and universal. But
most of the passengers here were men, and they were plainly of
the free-and-easy West rather than the dapper East. They wore
faces thoughtful with the problem of buying cheap and selling
dear, and they could be known by their silence from the loqua-
cious acquaintance-making way-travellers. In these, the mere
coming aboard seemed to beget an aggressively confidential
mood. Perhaps they clutched recklessly at any means of relieving

their *ennui;* or they felt that they might here indulge safely in the pleasures of autobiography, so dear to all of us; or else, in view of the many possible catastrophes, they desired to leave some little memory of themselves behind. At any rate, whenever the train stopped, the wedding-journeyers caught fragments of the personal histories of their fellow-passengers which had been re-hearsing to those that sat next the narrators. It was no more than fair that these should somewhat magnify themselves, and put the best complexion on their actions and the worst upon their suffer-ings; that they should all appear the luckiest or the unluckiest, the healthiest or the sickest, people that ever were, and should all have made or lost the most money. There was a prevailing desire among them to make out that they came from or were going to some very large place; and our friends fancied an actual mortification in the face of a modest gentleman who got out at Penelope (or some other insignificant classical station, in the ancient Greek and Roman part of New York State), after having listened to the life of a somewhat rustic-looking person who had described himself as belonging *near* New York City.

Basil also found diversion in the tender couples, who publicly comported themselves as if in a sylvan solitude, and, as it had been on the bank of some umbrageous stream, far from the ken of envious or unsympathetic eyes, reclined upon each other's shoulders and slept; but Isabel declared that this behaviour was perfectly indecent. She granted, of course, that they were foolish, innocent people, who meant no offence, and did not feel guilty of an impropriety, but she said that this sort of thing was a national reproach. If it were merely rustic lovers, she should not care so much, but you saw people who ought to know better, well-dressed, stylish people, flaunting their devotion in the face of the world, and going to sleep on each other's shoulders on every rail-road train. It was outrageous, it was scandalous, it was really in-famous. Before she would allow herself to do such a thing she would —well, she hardly knew what she would not do; she would have a divorce, at any rate. She wondered that Basil could laugh at it; and he would make her hate him if he kept on.

From the seat behind their own they were now made listeners to the history of a ten weeks' typhoid fever, from the moment when the narrator noticed that he had not felt very well for a day or two back, and all at once a kind of shiver took him, till he lay fourteen days perfectly insensible, and could eat nothing but a little pounded ice; and his wife—a small woman, too—used to lift him back and forth between the bed and sofa like a feather, and the neighbors did not know half the time whether he was dead or alive. This history, from which not the smallest particular or the least significant symptom of the case was omitted, occupied an hour in recital, and was told as it seemed for the entertainment of one who had been five minutes before it began a stranger to the historian.

At last the train came to a stand, and Isabel wailed forth in accents of desperation the words, "O, disgusting!" The monotony of the narrative in the seat behind, fatally combining with the heat of the day, had lulled her into slumbers from which she awoke at the stopping of the train, to find her head resting tenderly upon her husband's shoulder.

She confronted his merriment with eyes of mournful rebuke; but as she could not find him, by the harshest construction, in the least to blame, she was silent.

"Never mind, dear, never mind," he coaxed, "you were really not responsible. It was fatigue, destiny, the spite of fortune—whatever you like. In the case of the others, whom you despise so justly, I dare say it is sheer, disgraceful affection. But see that ravishing placard, swinging from the roof: 'This train stops twenty minutes for dinner at Utica.' In a few minutes more we shall be at Utica. If they have anything edible there, it shall never contract *my* powers. I could dine at the Albany station, even."

In a little while they found themselves in an airy, comfortable dining-room, eating a dinner, which it seemed to them France in the flush of her prosperity need not have blushed to serve; for if it wanted a little in the last graces of art, it redeemed itself in abundance, variety, and wholesomeness. At the elbow of every famishing passenger stood a beneficent, coal-black glossy fairy in a white linen apron and jacket, serving him with that alacrity and kindliness and grace which make the negro waiter the master, not the slave of his calling, which disenthral it of servility, and constitute him your eager host, not your menial, for the moment. From table to table passed a calming influence in the person of the proprietor, who, as he took his richly earned money, checked the rising fears of the guests by repeated proclamations that there was plenty of time, and that he would give them due warning before the train started. Those who had flocked out of the cars, to prey with beak and claw, as the vulture-like fashion is, upon everything in reach, remained to eat like Christians; and even a poor, scantily-Englished Frenchman, who wasted half his time in trying to ask how long the cars stopped and in looking at his watch, made a good dinner in spite of himself.

"O Basil, Basil!" cried Isabel, when the train was again in motion, "have we really dined once more? It seems too good to be true. Cleanliness, plenty, wholesomeness, civility! Yes, as you say, they cannot be civil where they are not just; honesty and courtesy go together; and wherever they give you outrageous things to eat, they add indigestible insults. Basil, dear, don't be jealous; I shall never meet him again; but I'm in love with that black waiter at our table. I never saw such perfect manners, such a winning and affectionate politeness. He made me feel that every mouthful I ate was a personal favor to him. What a complete gentleman! There ought never to be a white waiter. None but negroes are able to render their service a pleasure and distinction to you."

So they prattled on, doing, in their eagerness to be satisfied, a homage perhaps beyond its desert to the good dinner and the decent service of it. But here they erred in the right direction, and I find nothing more admirable in their behaviour throughout a wedding journey which certainly had its trials, than their willingness to make the very best of whatever would suffer itself to be made anything at all of. They celebrated its pleasures with magnanimous excess, they passed over its griefs with a wise forbearance. That which they found the most difficult of management was the want of incident for the most part of the time; and I who write their history might also sink under it, but that I am supported by the fact that it is so typical in this respect. I even imagine that ideal reader for whom one writes as yawning over these barren details with the life-like weariness of an actual travelling companion of theirs. Their own silence often sufficed my wedded lovers, or then, when there was absolutely nothing to engage them, they fell back upon the story of their love, which they were never tired of hearing as they severally knew it. Let it not be a reproach to human nature or to me if I say that there was something in the comfort of having well dined which now touched the springs of sentiment with magical effect, and that they had never so rejoiced in these tender reminiscences.

They had planned to stop over at Rochester till the morrow, that they might arrive at Niagara by daylight, and at Utica they had suddenly resolved to make the rest of the day's journey in a drawing-room car. The change gave them an added reason for content; and they realized how much they had previously sacrificed to the idea of travelling in the most American manner, without achieving it after all, for this seemed a touch of Americanism beyond the old-fashioned car. They reclined in luxury upon the easy-cushioned, revolving chairs; they surveyed with infinite satisfaction the elegance of the flying-parlor in which they sat, or turned their contented regard through the broad plate-glass windows upon the landscape without. They said that none but Americans or enchanted princes in the Arabian Nights ever travelled in such state; and when the stewards of the car came round successively with tropical fruits, ice-creams, and claret-punches—they felt a heightened assurance that they were either enchanted princes—or Americans. There were more ladies and more fashion than in the other cars; and prettily dressed children played about on the carpet; but the general appearance of the passengers hardly suggested greater wealth than elsewhere; and they were plainly in that car because they were of the American race, which finds nothing too good for it that its money can buy.

V

————

THE ENCHANTED CITY, AND BEYOND

THEY KNEW none of the hotels in Rochester, and they had chosen a certain one in reliance upon their handbook. When they named it, there stepped forth a porter of an incredibly cordial and pleasant countenance, who took their travelling-bags, and led them to the omnibus. As they were his only passengers, the porter got inside with them, and seeing their interest in the streets through which they rode, he descanted in a strain of cheerful pride upon the city's prosperity and character, and gave the names of the people who lived in the finer houses, just as if it had been an Old-World town, and he some eager historian expecting reward for his comment upon it. He cast quite a glamour over Rochester, so that in passing a body of water, bordered by houses, and overlooked by odd balconies and galleries, and crossed in the distance by a bridge upon which other houses were built, they boldly declared, being at their wit's end for a comparison, and taken with the unhoped-for picturesqueness, that it put them in mind of Verona. Thus they reached their hotel in almost a spirit of foreign travel, and very willing to verify the pleasant porter's assurance that they would like it, for everybody liked it; and it was with a sudden sinking of the heart that Basil beheld presiding over the register the conventional American hotel clerk. He was young, he had a neat moustache and well-brushed hair; jewelled studs sparkled in his shirt-front, and rings on his white hands; a gentle disdain of the travelling public breathed from his person in the mystical odors of Ihlang-ihlang. He did not lift his haughty head to look at the wayfarer who meekly wrote his name in the register; he did not answer him when he begged for a cool room; he turned to the board on which the keys hung, and, plucking one from it, slid it towards Basil on the marble counter, touched a bell for a call-boy, whistled a bar of Offenbach, and as he wrote the number of the room against Basil's name, said to a friend lounging near him, as if resuming a conversation, "Well, she's a mighty pooty gul, any way, Chawley!"

When I reflect that this was a type of the hotel clerk through-out the United States, that behind unnumbered registers at this moment he is snubbing travellers into the dust, and that they are suffering and perpetuating him, I am lost in wonder at the na-tional meekness. Not that I am one to refuse the humble pie his jewelled fingers offer me. Abjectly I take my key, and creep off up stairs after the call-boy, and try to give myself the genteel air of one who has not been stepped upon. But I think homicidal things, all the same, and I rejoice that in the safety of print I can cry out against the despot, whom I have not the presence to defy. "You vulgar and cruel little soul," I say, and I imagine myself breathing the words to his teeth, "why do you treat a weary stranger with this ignominy? I am to pay well for what I get, and I shall not complain of that. But look at me, and own my humanity; confess by some civil action, by some decent phrase, that I have rights and that they shall be respected. Answer my proper questions; respond to my fair demands. Do not slide my key at me; do not deny me the poor politeness of a nod as you give it in my hand. I am not your equal; few men are; but I shall not presume upon your clemency. Come, I also am human!"

Basil found that, for his sin in asking for a cool room, the clerk had given them a chamber into which the sun had been shining the whole afternoon; but when his luggage had been put in it seemed useless to protest, and like a true American, like you, like me, he shrank from asserting himself. When the sun went down it would be cool enough; and they turned their thoughts to supper, not venturing to hope that, as it proved, the handsome clerk was the sole blemish of the house.

Isabel viewed with innocent surprise the evidences of luxury afforded by all the appointments of a hotel so far west of Boston, and they both began to feel that natural ease and superiority which an inn always inspires in its guests, and which our great hotels, far from impairing, enhance in flattering degree; in fact, the clerk once forgotten, I protest, for my own part, I am never more conscious of my merits and riches in any other place. One has there the romance of being a stranger and a mystery to every one else, and lives in the alluring possibility of not being found out a most ordinary person.

They were so late in coming to the supper-room, that they found themselves alone in it. At the door they had a bow from the head-waiter, who ran before them and drew out chairs for them at a table, and signalled waiters to serve them, first laying before them with a gracious flourish the bill of fare. A force of servants flocked about them, as if to contest the honor of ordering their supper; one set upon the table a heaping vase of strawberries, another flanked it with flagons of cream, a third accompanied it with cates of varied flavor and device; a fourth obsequiously smoothed the table-cloth; a fifth, the youngest of the five, with folded arms stood by and admired the satisfaction the rest were giving. When these had been despatched for steak, for broiled white-fish of the lakes—noblest and delicatest of the fish that swim—for broiled chicken, for fried potatoes, for muffins, for whatever the lawless fancy and ravening appetites of the wayfarers could suggest, this fifth waiter remained to tempt them to further excess and vainly proposed some kind of eggs,—fried eggs, poached eggs, scrambled eggs, boiled eggs, or omelette.

"O, you're sure, dearest, that this isn't a vision of fairy-land, which will vanish presently, and leave us empty and forlorn?" plaintively murmured Isabel, as the menial train re-appeared, bearing the supper they had ordered, and set it smoking down.

Suddenly a look of apprehension dawned upon her face, and she let fall her knife and fork. "You *don't* think, Basil," she faltered, "that they *could* have found out we're a bridal party, and that they're serving us so magnificently because—because—O, I shall be miserable every moment we're here!" she concluded, desperately.

She looked, indeed, extremely wretched for a woman with so much broiled white-fish on her plate, and such a banquet array about her; and her husband made haste to reassure her. "You're still demoralized, Isabel, by our sufferings at the Albany depot, and you exaggerate the blessings we enjoy, though I should be sorry to undervalue them. I suspect it's the custom to use people well at this hotel; or if we are singled out for uncommon favor, I think I can explain the cause. It has been discovered by the register that we are from Boston, and we are merely meeting the reverence, affection, and homage which the name everywhere commands. It's our fortune to represent for the time being the intellectual and moral virtue of Boston. This supper is not a tribute to you as a bride, but as a Bostonian."

It was a cheap kind of raillery, to be sure, but it served. It kindled the local pride of Isabel to self-defence, and in the distraction of the effort she forgot her fears; she returned with renewed appetite to the supper, and in its excellence they both let fall their dispute,—which ended, of course, in Basil's abject confession that Boston was the best place in the world, and nothing but banishment could make him live elsewhere,—and gave themselves up, as usual, to the delight of being just what and where they were. At last, the natural course brought them to the strawberries, and when the fifth waiter approached from the corner of the table at which he stood, to place the vase near them, he did not retire at once, but presently asked if they were from the West.

Isabel smiled, and Basil answered that they were from the East.

He faltered at this, as if doubtful of the result if he went further, but took heart, then, and asked, "Don't you think this is a pretty nice hotel"—hastily adding as a concession of the probable existence of much finer things at the East—"for a *small* hotel?"

They imagined this waiter as new to his station in life, as perhaps just risen to it from some country tavern, and unable to repress his exultation in what seemed their sympathetic presence. They were charmed to have invited his guileless confidence, to have evoked possibly all the simple poetry of his soul; it was what might have happened in Italy, only there so much *naïveté* would have meant money; they looked at each other with rapture, and Basil answered warmly while the waiter flushed as at a personal compliment: "Yes, it's a nice hotel; one of the best I ever saw, East or West, in Europe or America."

They rose and left the room, and were bowed out by the head-waiter.

"How perfectly idyllic!" cried Isabel. "Is this Rochester, New York, or is it some vale of Arcady? Let's go out and see."

They walked out into the moonlit city, up and down streets that seemed very stately and fine, amidst a glitter of shop-window lights; and then, less of their own motion than of mere error, they quitted the business quarter, and found themselves in a quiet avenue of handsome residences,—the Beacon Street of Rochester, whatever it was called. They said it was a night and a place for lovers, for none but lovers, for lovers newly plighted, and they made believe to bemoan themselves that, hold each other dear as they would, the exaltation, the thrill, the glory of their younger love was gone. Some of the houses had gardened spaces about them, from which stole, like breaths of sweetest and saddest regret, the perfume of midsummer flowers—the despair of the rose for the bud. As they passed a certain house, a song fluttered out of the open window and ceased, the piano warbled at the final rush of fingers over its chords, and they saw *her* with her fingers resting lightly on the keys, and her graceful head lifted to look into his; they saw *him* with his arm yet stretched across to the leaves of music he had been turning, and his face lowered to meet her gaze.

"Ah, Basil, I wish it was we, there!"

"And if they knew that we, on our wedding journey, stood outside, would not they wish it was they, here?"

"I suppose so, dearest, and yet, once-upon-a-time was sweet. Pass on; and let us see what charm we shall find next in this enchanted city."

"Yes, it is an enchanted city to us," mused Basil, aloud, as they wandered on, "and all strange cities are enchanted. What is Rochester to the Rochesterese? A place of a hundred thousand people, as we read in our guide, an immense flour interest, a great railroad *entrepôt*, an unrivalled nursery trade, a university, two commercial colleges, three collegiate institutes, eight or ten newspapers, and a free library. I dare say any respectable resident would laugh at us sentimentalizing over his city. But Rochester is for us, who don't know it at all, a city of any time or country, moonlit, filled with lovers hovering over piano-fortes, of a palatial hotel with pastoral waiters and porters,—a city of handsome streets wrapt in beautiful quiet and dreaming of the golden age. The only definite association with it in our minds is the tragically romantic thought that here Sam Patch met his fate."

"And who in the world was Sam Patch?"

"Isabel, your ignorance of all that an American woman should be proud of distresses me. Have you really, then, never heard of the man who invented the saying, 'Some things can be done as well as others,' and proved it by jumping over Niagara Falls twice? Spurred on by this belief, he attempted the leap of the Genesee Falls. The leap was easy enough, but the coming up again was another matter. He failed in that. It was the one thing that could not be done as well as others."

"Dreadful!" said Isabel, with the cheerfullest satisfaction. "But what has all that to do with Rochester?"

"Now, my dear! You don't mean to say you didn't know that the Genesee Falls were at Rochester? Upon my word, I'm ashamed. Why, we're within ten minutes' walk of them now."

"Then walk to them at once!" cried Isabel, wholly unabashed, and in fact unable to see what he had to be ashamed of. "Actually, I believe you would have allowed me to leave Rochester without telling me the falls were here, if you hadn't happened to think of Sam Patch."

Saying this, she persuaded herself that a chief object of their journey had been to visit the scene of Sam Patch's fatal exploit, and she drew Basil with a nervous swiftness in the direction of the railroad station, beyond which he said were the falls. Presently, after threading their way among a multitude of locomotives, with and without trains attached, that backed and advanced, or stood still, hissing impatiently on every side, they passed through the station to a broad planking above the river on the other side, and thence, after encounter of more locomotives, they found, by dint of much asking, a street winding up the hillside to the left, and leading to the German Bierhaus that gives access to the best view of the cataract.

The Americans have characteristically bordered the river with manufactures, making every drop work its passage to the brink; while the Germans have as characteristically made use of the beauty left over, and have built a Bierhaus where they may regale both soul and sense in the presence of the cataract. Our travellers might, in another mood and place, have thought it droll to arrive at that sublime spectacle through a Bierhaus, but in this enchanted city it seemed to have a peculiar fitness.

A narrow corridor gave into a wide festival space occupied by many tables, each of which was surrounded by a group of clamorous Germans of either sex and every age, with tall beakers of beaded lager before them, and slim flasks of Rhenish; overhead flamed the gas in globes of varicolored glass; the walls were painted like those of such haunts in the fatherland; and the wedding-journeyers were fain to linger on their way, to dwell upon that scene of honest enjoyment, to inhale the mingling odors of beer and of pipes, and of the pungent cheeses in which the children of the fatherland delight. Amidst the inspiriting clash of plates and glasses, the rattle of knives and forks, and the hoarse rush of gutturals, they could catch the words Franzosen, Kaiser, König, and Schlacht, and they knew that festive company to be exulting in the first German triumphs of the war, which were then the day's news; they saw fists shaken at noses in fierce exchange of joy, arms tossed abroad in wild congratulation, and health-pouring goblets of beer lifted in air. Then they stepped into the moonlight again, and heard only the solemn organ stops of the cataract. Through garden-ground they were led by the little maid, their guide, to a small pavilion that stood on the edge of the precipitous shore, and commanded a perfect view of the falls. As they entered this pavilion, a youth and maiden, clearly lovers, passed out, and they were left alone with that sublime presence. Something of definiteness was to be desired in the spectacle, but there was ample compensation in the mystery with which the broad effulgence and the dense unluminous shadows of the moonshine invested it. The light touched all the tops of the rapids, that seemed to writhe away from the brink of the cataract, and then desperately breaking and perishing to fall, the white disembodied ghosts of rapids, down to the bottom of the vast and deep ravine through which the river rushed away. Now the waters seemed to mass themselves a hundred feet high in a wall of snowy compactness, now to disperse into their multitudinous particles and hang like some vaporous cloud from the cliff. Every moment renewed the vision of beauty in some rare and fantastic shape; and its loveliness isolated it, in spite of the great town on the other shore, the station with its bridge and its trains, the mills that supplied their feeble little needs from the cataract's strength.

At last Basil pointed out the table-rock in the middle of the fall, from which Sam Patch had made his fatal leap; but Isabel refused to admit that tragical figure to the honors of her emotions. "I don't care for him!" she said fiercely. "Patch! What a name to be linked in our thoughts with this superb cataract."

"Well, Isabel, I think you are very unjust. It's as good a name as Leander, to my thinking, and it was immortalized in support of a great idea—the feasibility of all things; while Leander's has come down to us as that of the weak victim of a passion. We shall never have a poetry of our own till we get over this absurd reluctance from facts, till we make the ideal embrace and include the real, till we consent to face the music in our simple common names, and put Smith into a lyric and Jones into a tragedy. The Germans are braver than we, and in them you find facts and dreams continually blended and confronted. Here is a fortunate illustration. The people we met coming out of this pavilion were lovers, and they had been here sentimentalizing on this superb cataract, as you call it, with which my heroic Patch is not worthy to be named. No doubt they had been quoting Uhland or some other of their romantic poets, perhaps singing some of their tender German love-songs, the tenderest, unearthliest love-songs in the world. At the same time they did not disdain the matter-of-fact corporeity in which their sentiment was enshrined; they fed it heartily and abundantly with the banquet whose relics we see here."

On a table before them stood a pair of beer-glasses, in the bottoms of which lurked scarce the foam of the generous liquor lately brimming them; some shreds of sausage, some rinds of Swiss cheese, bits of cold ham, crusts of bread, and the ashes of a pipe.

Isabel shuddered at the spectacle, but made no comment, and Basil went on: "Do you suppose *they* scorned the idea of Sam Patch as they gazed upon the falls? On the contrary, I've no doubt that he recalled to her the ballad which a poet of their language made about him. It used to go the rounds of the German newspapers, and I translated it, a long while ago, when I thought that I too was in Arkadien geboren.

> " 'In the Bierhausgarten I linger
>   By the Falls of the Genesee:
> From the Table-Rock in the middle
>   Leaps a figure bold and free.
>
> 'Aloof in the air it rises
>   O'er the rush, the plunge, the death;
> On the thronging banks of the river
>   There is neither pulse nor breath.
>
> 'Forever it hovers and poises
>   Aloof in the moonlit air;

As light as mist from the rapids,
　As heavy as nightmare.

'In anguish I cry to the people,
　The long-since vanished hosts;
I see them stretch forth in answer,
　The helpless hands of ghosts.'

I once met the poet who wrote this. He drank too much beer."

"I don't see that he got in the name of Sam Patch, after all," said Isabel.

"O yes, he did; but I had to yield to our taste, and where he said, 'Springt der Sam Patsch kühn und frei,' I made it 'Leaps a figure bold and free.'"

As they passed through the house on their way out, they saw the youth and maiden they had met at the pavilion door. They were seated at a table; two glasses of beer towered before them; on their plates were odorous crumbs of Limburger cheese. They both wore a pensive air.

The next morning the illusion that had wrapt the whole earth was gone with the moonlight. By nine o'clock, when the wedding-journeyers resumed their way toward Niagara, the heat had already set in with the effect of ordinary midsummer's heat at high noon. The car into which they got had come the past night from Albany, and had an air of almost conscious shabbiness, griminess, and over-use. The seats were covered with cinders, which also crackled under foot. Dust was on everything, especially the persons of the crumpled and weary passengers of overnight. Those who came aboard at Rochester failed to lighten the spiritual gloom, and presently they sank into the common bodily wretchedness. The train was somewhat belated, and as it drew nearer Buffalo they knew the conductor to have abandoned himself to that blackest of the arts, making time. The long irregular jolt of the ordinary progress was reduced to an incessant shudder and a quick lateral motion. The air within the cars was deadly; if a window was raised, a storm of dust and cinders blew in and quick gusts caught away the breath. So they sat with closed windows, sweltering and stifling, and all the faces on which a lively horror was not painted were dull and damp with apathetic misery.

The incidents were in harmony with the abject physical tone of the company. There was a quarrel between a thin, shrill-voiced, highly dressed, much-bedizened Jewess, on the one side, and a fat, greedy old woman, half asleep, and a boy with large pink transparent ears that stood out from his head like the handles of a jar, on the other side, about a seat which the Hebrew wanted, and which the others had kept filled with packages on the pretence that it was engaged. It was a loud and fierce quarrel enough, but it won no sort of favor; and when the Jewess had given a final opinion that the greedy old woman was no lady, and the boy, who disputed in an ironical temper, replied, "High-ly complimentary, I *must* say," there was no sign of relief or other acknowledgment in any of the spectators, that there had been a quarrel.

There was a little more interest taken in the misfortune of an old purblind German and his son, who were found by the conductor to be a few hundred miles out of the direct course to their destination, and were with some trouble and the aid of an Americanized fellow-countryman made aware of the fact. The old man then fell back in the prevailing apathy, and the child naturally cared nothing. By and by came the unsparing train-boy on his rounds, bestrewing the passengers successively with papers, magazines, fine-cut tobacco, and packages of candy. He gave the old man a package of candy, and passed on. The German took it as the bounty of the American people, oddly manifested in a situation where he could otherwise have had little proof of their care. He opened it and was sharing it with his son when the train-boy came back, and metallically, like a part of the machinery, demanded, "Ten cents!" The German stared helplessly, and the boy repeated, "Ten cents! ten cents!" with tiresome patience, while the other passengers smiled. When it had passed through the alien's head that he was to pay for this national gift and he took with his tremulous fingers from the recesses of his pocket-book a ten-cent note and handed it to his tormentor, some of the people laughed. Among the rest, Basil and Isabel laughed, and then looked at each other with eyes of mutual reproach.

"Well, upon my word, my dear," he said, "I think we've fallen pretty low. I've never felt such a poor, shabby ruffian before. Good heavens! To think of our immortal souls being moved to mirth by such a thing as this—so stupid, so barren of all reason of laughter. And then the cruelty of it! What ferocious imbeciles we are! Whom have I married? A woman with neither heart nor brain!"

"O Basil, dear, pay him back the money—do."

"I can't. That's the worst of it. He's money enough, and might justly take offence. What breaks my heart is that we could have the depravity to smile at the mistake of a friendless stranger, who supposed he had at last met with an act of pure kindness. It's a thing to weep over. Look at these grinning wretches! What a fiendish effect their smiles have, through their cinders and sweat! O, it's the terrible weather; the despotism of the dust and heat; the wickedness of the infernal air. What a squalid and loathsome company!"

At Buffalo, where they arrived late, they found themselves with several hours' time on their hands before the train started for Niagara, and in the first moments of tedium, Isabel forgot herself into saying, "Don't you think we'd have done better to go directly from Rochester to the Falls, instead of coming this way?"

"Why certainly. I didn't propose coming this way."

"I know it, dear. I was only asking," said Isabel, meekly. "But I should think you'd have generosity enough to take a little of the blame, when I wanted to come out of a romantic feeling for you."

This romantic feeling referred to the fact that, many years before, when Basil made his first visit to Niagara, he had approached from the west by way of Buffalo; and Isabel, who tenderly begrudged his having existed before she knew him, and longed to ally herself retrospectively with his past, was resolved to draw near the great cataract by no other route.

She fetched a little sigh which might mean the weather or his hard-heartedness. The sigh touched him, and he suggested a carriage-ride through the city; she assented with eagerness, for it was what she had been thinking of. She had never seen a lake-side city before, and she was taken by surprise. "If ever we leave Boston," she said, "we will not live at Rochester, as I thought last night; we'll come to Buffalo." She found that the place had all the picturesqueness of a seaport, without the ugliness that attends the rising and falling tides. A delicious freshness breathed from the lake, which lying so smooth, faded into the sky at last, with no line between sharper than that which divides drowsing from dreaming. But the color was the most charming thing, that delicate blue of the lake, without the depth of the sea-blue, but infinitely softer and lovelier. The nearer expanses rippled with dainty waves, silver and lucent; the further levels made, with the sun-dimmed summer sky, a vague horizon of turquoise and amethyst, lit by the white sails of ships, and stained by the smoke of steamers.

"Take me away now," said Isabel, when her eyes had feasted upon all this, "and don't let me see another thing till I get to Niagara. Nothing less sublime is worthy the eyes that have beheld such beauty."

However, on the way to Niagara she consented to glimpses of the river which carries the waters of the lake for their mighty plunge, and which shows itself very nobly from time to time as you draw toward the cataract, with wooded or cultivated islands, and rich farms along its low shores, and at last flashes upon the eye the shining white of the rapids,—a hint, no more, of the splendor and awfulness to be revealed.

VI

NIAGARA

As the train stopped, Isabel's heart beat with a childlike exultation, as I believe every one's heart must who is worthy to arrive at Niagara. She had been trying to fancy, from time to time, that she heard the roar of the cataract, and now, when she alighted from the car, she was sure she should have heard it but for the vulgar little noises that attend the arrival of trains at Niagara as well as everywhere else. "Never mind, dearest; you shall be stunned with it before you leave," promised her husband; and, not wholly disconsolate, she rode through the quaint streets of the village, where it remains a question whether the lowliness of the shops and private houses makes the hotels look so vast, or the bigness of the hotels dwarfs all the other buildings. The immense caravansaries swelling up from among the little bazaars (where they sell feather fans, and miniature bark canoes, and jars and vases and bracelets and brooches carved out of the local rocks), made our friends with their trunks very conscious of their disproportion to the accommodations of the smallest. They were the sole occupants of the omnibus, and they were embarrassed to be received at their hotel with a burst of minstrelsy from a whole band of music. Isabel felt that a single stringed instrument of some timid note would have been enough; and Basil was going to express his own modest preference for a jew's-harp, when the music ceased with a sudden clash of the cymbals. But the next moment it burst out with fresh sweetness, and in alighting they perceived that another omnibus had turned the corner and was drawing up to the pillared portico of the hotel. A small family

74

dismounted, and the feet of the last had hardly touched the pavement when the music again ended as abruptly as those flourishes of trumpets that usher player-kings upon the stage. Isabel could not help laughing at this melodious parsimony. "I hope they don't let on the cataract and shut it off in this frugal style; do they, Basil?" she asked, and passed jesting through a pomp of unoccupied porters and call-boys. Apparently there were not many people stopping at this hotel, or else they were all out looking at the Falls or confined to their rooms. However, our travellers took in the almost weird emptiness of the place with their usual gratitude to fortune for all queerness in life, and followed to the pleasant quarters assigned them. There was time before supper for a glance at the cataract, and after a brief toilet they sallied out again upon the holiday street, with its parade of gay little shops, and thence passed into the grove beside the Falls, enjoying at every instant their feeling of arrival at a sublime destination.

In this sense Niagara deserves almost to rank with Rome, the metropolis of history and religion; with Venice, the chief city of sentiment and fantasy. In either you are at once made at home by a perception of its greatness, in which there is no quality of aggression, as there always seems to be in minor places as well as in minor men, and you gratefully accept its sublimity as a fact in no way contrasting with your own insignificance.

Our friends were beset of course by many carriage-drivers, whom they repelled with the kindly firmness of experienced travel. Isabel even felt a compassion for these poor fellows who had seen Niagara so much as to have forgotten that the first time one must see it alone or only with the next of friendship. She was voluble in her pity of Basil that it was not as new to him as to her, till between the trees they saw a white cloud of spray, shot through and through with sunset, rising, rising, and she felt her voice softly and steadily beaten down by the diapason of the cataract.

I am not sure but the first emotion on viewing Niagara is that of familiarity. Ever after, its strangeness increases; but in that earliest moment, when you stand by the side of the American fall, and take in so much of the whole as your glance can compass, an impression of having seen it often before is certainly very vivid. This may be an effect of that grandeur which puts you at your ease in its presence; but it also undoubtedly results in part from lifelong acquaintance with every variety of futile picture of the scene. You have its outward form clearly in your memory; the shores, the rapids, the islands, the curve of the Falls, and the stout rainbow with one end resting on their top and the other lost in the mists that rise from the gulf beneath. On the whole I do not account this sort of familiarity a misfortune. The surprise is none the less a surprise because it is kept till the last, and the marvel, making itself finally felt in every nerve, and not at once through a single sense, all the more fully possesses you. It is as if Niagara reserved her magnificence, and preferred to win your heart with her beauty; and so Isabel, who was instinctively prepared for the reverse, suffered a vague disappointment, for a little instant, as she looked along the verge from the water that caressed the shore at her feet before it flung itself down, to the wooded point that divides the American from the Canadian fall, beyond which showed dimly through its veil of golden and silver mists the emerald wall of the great Horse-Shoe. "How still it is!" she said, amidst the roar that shook the ground under their feet and made the leaves tremble overhead, and "How lonesome!" amidst the people lounging and sauntering about in every direction among the trees. In fact that prodigious presence does make a solitude and silence round every spirit worthy to perceive it, and it gives a kind of dignity to all its belongings, so that the rocks and pebbles in the water's edge, and the weeds and grasses that nod above it, have a value far beyond that of such common things elsewhere. In all the aspects of Niagara there seems a grave simplicity, which is perhaps a reflection of the spectator's soul for once utterly dismantled of affectation and convention. In the vulgar reaction from this, you are of course as trivial, if you like, at Niagara, as anywhere.

Slowly Isabel became aware that the sacred grove beside the

fall was profaned by some very common presences indeed, that tossed bits of stone and sticks into the consecrated waters, and struggled for handkerchiefs and fans, and here and there put their arms about each other's waists, and made a show of laughing and joking. They were a picnic party of rude, silly folks of the neighborhood, and she stood pondering them in sad wonder if anything could be worse, when she heard a voice saying to Basil, "Take you next, sir? Plenty of light yet, and the wind's down the river, so the spray won't interfere. Make a capital picture of you; falls in the background." It was the local photographer urging them to succeed the young couple he had just posed at the brink: the gentleman was sitting down, with his legs crossed and his hands elegantly disposed; the lady was standing at his side, with one arm thrown lightly across his shoulder, while with the other hand she thrust his cane into the ground; you could see it was going to be a splendid photograph.

Basil thanked the artist, and Isabel said, trusting as usual to his sympathy for perception of her train of thought, "Well, I'll never try to be high-strung again. But shouldn't you have thought, dearest, that I might expect to be high-strung with success at Niagara if anywhere?" She passively followed him into the long, queer, downward-sloping edifice on the border of the grove, unflinchingly mounted the car that stood ready, and descended the incline. Emerging into the light again, she found herself at the foot of the fall by whose top she had just stood.

At first she was glad there were other people down there, as if she and Basil were not enough to bear it alone, and she could almost have spoken to the two hopelessly pretty brides, with parasols and impertinent little boots, whom their attendant husbands were helping over the sharp and slippery rocks, so bare beyond the spray, so green and mossy within the fall of mist. But in another breath she forgot them, as she looked on that dizzied sea, hurling itself from the high summit in huge white knots, and breaks and masses, and plunging into the gulf beside her, while it sent continually up a strong voice of lamentation, and crawled away in vast eddies, with somehow a look of human terror, bewilderment, and pain. It was bathed in snowy vapor to its crest, but now and then heavy currents of air drew this aside, and they saw the outline of the Falls almost as far as the Canada side. They remembered afterwards how they were able to make use of but one sense at a time, and how when they strove to take in the forms of the descending flood, they ceased to hear it; but as soon as they released their eyes from this service, every fibre in them vibrated to the sound, and the spectacle dissolved away in it. They were aware, too, of a strange capriciousness in their senses, and of a tendency of each to palter with the things perceived. The eye could no longer take truthful note of quality, and now beheld the tumbling deluge as a Gothic wall of carven marble, white, motionless; and now as a fall of lightest snow, with movement in all its atoms, and scarce so much cohesion as would hold them together; and again they could not discern if this course were from above or from beneath, whether the water rose from the abyss or dropped from the height. The ear could give the brain no assurance of the sound that filled it, and whether it were great or little: the prevailing softness of the cataract's tone seemed so much opposed to ideas of prodigious force or of prodigious volume. It was only when the sight, so idle in its own behalf, came to the aid of the other sense, and showed them the mute movement of each other's lips, that they dimly appreciated the depth of sound that involved them.

"I think you might have been high-strung there, for a second or two," said Basil, when, ascending the incline, he could make himself heard. "We will try the bridge next."

Over the river, so still with its oily eddies and delicate wreaths of foam, just below the Falls they have in late years woven a web of wire high in air, and hung a bridge from precipice to precipice. Of all the bridges made with hands it seems the lightest, most ethereal; it is ideally graceful, and droops from its slight towers like a garland. It is worthy to command, as it does, the whole grandeur of Niagara, and to show the traveller the vast spectacle, from the beginning of the American fall to the furthest limit of the Horse-Shoe, with all the awful pomp of the rapids, the solemn darkness of the wooded islands, the mystery of the vaporous gulf, the indomitable wildness of the shores, as far as the eye can reach up or down the fatal stream.

To this bridge our friends now repaired, by a path that led through another of those groves which keep the village back from the shores of the river on the American side, and greatly help the sight-seer's pleasure in the place. The exquisite structure, which sways so tremulously from its towers, and seems to lay so slight a hold on earth where its cables sink into the ground, is to other bridges what the blood horse is to the common breed of roadsters; and now they felt its sensitive nerves quiver under them and sympathetically through them as they advanced further and further towards the centre. Perhaps their sympathy with the bridge's trepidation was too great for unalloyed delight, and yet the thrill was a glorious one, to be known only there; and afterwards, at least, they would not have had their airy path seem more secure.

The last hues of sunset lingered in the mists that sprung from the base of the Falls with a mournful, tremulous grace, and a movement weird as the play of the northern lights. They were touched with the most delicate purples and crimsons, that darkened to deep red, and then faded from them at a second look, and they flew upward, swiftly upward, like troops of pale, transparent ghosts; while a perfectly clear radiance, better than any other for local color, dwelt upon the scene. Far under the bridge the river smoothly swam, the undercurrents forever unfolding themselves upon the surface with a vast rose-like evolution, edged all round with faint lines of white, where the air that filled the water freed itself in foam. What had been clear green on the face of the cataract was here more like rich verd-antique, and had a look of firmness almost like that of the stone itself. So it showed beneath the bridge, and down the river till the curving shores hid it. These, springing abruptly from the water's brink, and shagged with pine and cedar, displayed the tender verdure of grass and bushes intermingled with the dark evergreens that climb from ledge to ledge, till they point their speary tops above the crest of bluffs. In front, where tumbled rocks and expanses of naked clay varied the gloomier and gayer green, sprung those spectral mists; and through them loomed out, in its manifold majesty, Niagara, with the seemingly immovable white Gothic screen of the American fall, and the green massive curve of the Horse-Shoe, solid and simple and calm as an Egyptian wall; while behind this, with their white and black expanses broken by dark foliaged little isles, the steep Canadian rapids billowed down between their heavily wooded shores.

The wedding-journeyers hung, they knew not how long, in rapture on the sight; and then, looking back from the shore to the spot where they had stood, they felt relieved that unreality should possess itself of all, and that the bridge should swing there in mid-air like a filmy web, scarce more passable than the rainbow that flings its arch above the mists.

On the portico of the hotel they found half a score of gentlemen smoking, and creating together that collective silence which passes for sociality on our continent. Some carriages stood before the door, and within, around the base of a pillar, sat a circle of idle call-boys. There were a few trunks heaped together in one place, with a porter standing guard over them; a solitary guest was buying a cigar at the newspaper stand in one corner; another friendless creature was writing a letter in the reading-room; the clerk, in a seersucker coat and a lavish shirt-bosom, tried to give the whole an effect of watering-place gayety and bustle, as he provided a newly arrived guest with a room.

Our pair took in these traits of solitude and repose with indifference. If the hotel had been thronged with brilliant company, they would have been no more and no less pleased; and when, after supper, they came into the grand parlor, and found nothing there but a marble-topped centre-table, with a silver-plated ice-pitcher and a small company of goblets, they sat down perfectly content in a secluded window-seat. They were not seen by the three people who entered soon after, and halted in the centre of the room.

"Why, Kitty!" said one of the two ladies, who must be in any travelling-party of three, "this is more inappropriate to your gorgeous array than the supper-room, even."

She who was called Kitty was armed, as for social conquest, in some kind of airy evening-dress, and was looking round with bewilderment upon that forlorn waste of carpeting and up-holstery. She owned, with a smile, that she had not seen so much of the world yet as she had been promised; but she liked Niagara very much, and perhaps they should find the world at breakfast.

"No," said the other lady, who was as unquiet as Kitty was calm, and who seemed resolved to make the most of the worst, "it isn't probable that the hotel will fill up overnight; and I feel personally responsible for this state of things. Who would ever have supposed that Niagara would be so empty? I thought the place was thronged the whole summer long. How do you account for it, Richard?"

The gentleman looked fatigued, as from a long-continued discussion elsewhere of the matter in hand, and he said that he had not been trying to account for it.

"Then you don't care for Kitty's pleasure at all, and you don't want her to enjoy herself. Why don't you take some interest in the matter?"

"Why, if I accounted for the emptiness of Niagara in the most satisfactory way, it wouldn't add a soul to the floating population. Under the circumstances I prefer to leave it unexplained."

"Do you think it's because it's such a hot summer? Do you suppose it's not exactly the season? Didn't you expect there'd be more people? Perhaps Niagara isn't as fashionable as it used to be."

"It looks something like that."

"Well, what under the sun do you think *is* the reason?"

"I don't know."

"Perhaps," interposed Kitty, placidly, "most of the visitors go to the other hotel, now."

"It's altogether likely," said the other lady, eagerly. "There are just such caprices."

"Well," said Richard, "I wanted you to go there."

"But you said that you always heard this was the most fashionable."

"I know it. I didn't want to come here for that reason. But fortune favors the brave."

"Well, it's too bad! Here we've asked Kitty to come to Niagara with us, just to give her a little peep into the world, and you've brought us to a hotel where we're—"

"Monarchs of all we survey," suggested Kitty.

"Yes, and start at the sound of our own," added the other lady, helplessly.

"Come now, Fanny," said the gentleman, who was but too clearly the husband of the last speaker. "You know you insisted, against all I could say or do, upon coming to this house; I implored you to go to the other, and now you blame me for bringing you here."

"So I do. If you'd let me have my own way without opposition about coming here, I dare say I should have gone to the other place. But never mind. Kitty knows whom to blame, I hope. She's *your* cousin."

Kitty was sitting with her hands quiescently folded in her lap. She now rose and said that she did not know anything about the other hotel, and perhaps it was just as empty as this.

"It can't be. There can't be *two* hotels so empty," said Fanny. "It don't stand to reason."

"If you wish Kitty to see the world so much," said the gentleman, "why don't you take her on to Quebec, with us?"

Kitty had left her seat beside Fanny, and was moving with a listless content about the parlor.

"I wonder you ask, Richard, when you know she's only come for the night, and has nothing with her but a few cuffs and collars! I certainly never heard of anything so absurd before!"

The absurdity of the idea then seemed to cast its charm upon her, for, after a silence, "I could lend her some things," she said musingly. "But don't speak of it to-night, please. It's *too* ridiculous. Kitty!" she called out, and, as the young lady drew near, she continued, "How would you like to go to Quebec, with us?"

"O Fanny!" cried Kitty, with rapture; and then, with dismay, "How *can* I?"

"Why, very well, I think. You've got this dress, and your travelling-suit; and I can lend you whatever you want. Come!" she added joyously, "let's go up to your room, and talk it over!"

The two ladies vanished upon this impulse, and the gentleman followed. To their own relief the guiltless eavesdroppers, who found no moment favorable for revealing themselves after the comedy began, issued from their retiracy.

"What a remarkable little lady!" said Basil, eagerly turning to Isabel for sympathy in his enjoyment of her inconsequence.

"Yes, poor thing!" returned his wife; "it's no light matter to invite a young lady to take a journey with you, and promise her all sorts of gayety, and perhaps beaux and flirtations, and then find her on your hands in a desolation like this. It's dreadful, I think."

Basil stared. "O, certainly," he said. "But what an amusingly illogical little body!"

"I don't understand what you mean, Basil. It was the only thing that she could do, to invite the young lady to go on with them. I wonder her husband had the sense to think of it first. Of *course* she'll have to lend her things."

"And you didn't observe anything peculiar in her way of reaching her conclusions?"

"Peculiar? What *do* you mean?"

"Why, her blaming her husband for letting her have her own way about the hotel; and her telling him not to mention his proposal to Kitty, and then doing it herself, just after she'd pronounced it absurd and impossible." He spoke with heat at being forced to make what he thought a needless explanation.

"O!" said Isabel, after a moment's reflection. "*That!* Did you think it so very odd?"

Her husband looked at her with the gravity a man must feel when he begins to perceive that he has married the whole mystifying world of womankind in the woman of his choice, and made no answer. But to his own soul he said: "I supposed I had the pleasure of my wife's acquaintance. It seems I have been flattering myself."

The next morning they went out, as they had planned, for an exploration of Goat Island, after an early breakfast. As they sauntered through the village's contrasts of pygmy and colossal in architecture, they praisefully took in the unalloyed holiday character of the place, enjoying equally the lounging tourists at the hotel doors, the drivers and their carriages to let, and the little shops, with nothing but mementos of Niagara, and Indian bead-work, and other trumpery, to sell. Shops so useless, they agreed, could not be found outside the Palais Royale, or the Square of St. Mark, or anywhere else in the world but here. They felt themselves once more a part of the tide of mere sight-seeing pleasure-travel, on which they had drifted in other days, and in an eddy of which their love itself had opened its white blossom, and lily-like dreamed upon the wave.

They were now also part of the great circle of newly wedded bliss, which, involving the whole land during the season of bridal-tours, may be said to show richest and fairest at Niagara, like the costly jewel of a precious ring. The place is, in fact, almost abandoned to bridal couples, and any one out of his honeymoon is in some degree an alien there, and must discern a certain im-modesty in his intrusion. Is it for his profane eyes to look upon all that blushing and trembling joy? A man of any sensibility must desire to veil his face, and, bowing his excuses to the col-lective rapture, take the first train for the wicked outside world to which he belongs. Everywhere, he sees brides and brides. Three or four, with the benediction still on them, come down in the same car with him; he hands her travelling-shawl after one as she springs from the omnibus into her husband's arms; there are two or three walking back and forth with their new lords upon the porch of the hotel; at supper they are on every side of him, and he feels himself suffused, as it were, by a roseate atmos-phere of youth and love and hope. At breakfast it is the same, and then, in his wanderings about the place, he constantly meets them. They are of all manners of beauty, fair and dark, slender and plump, tall and short; but they are all beautiful with the radiance of loving and being loved. Now, if ever in their lives, they are charmingly dressed, and ravishing toilets take the willing eye from the objects of interest. How high the heels of the pretty boots, how small the tender-tinted gloves, how electrical the flutter of the snowy skirts! What is Niagara to these things?

Isabel was not willing to own her bridal sisterhood to these blessed souls; but she secretly rejoiced in it, even while she joined Basil in noting their number and smiling at their innocent abandon. She dropped his arm at encounter of the first couple, and walked carelessly at his side; she made a solemn vow never to take hold of his watch-chain in speaking to him; she trusted that she might be preserved from putting her face very close to his at dinner in studying the bill of fare; getting out of carriages, she forbade him ever to take her by the waist. All ascetic resolutions are modified by experiment; but if Isabel did not rigorously keep these, she is not the less to be praised for having formed them.

Just before they reached the bridge to Goat Island, they passed a little group of the Indians still lingering about Niagara, who make the barbaric wares in which the shops abound, and, like the woods and the wild faces of the cliffs and precipices, help to keep the cataract remote, and to invest it with the charm of primeval loneliness. This group were women, and they sat motionless on the ground, smiling sphinx-like over their laps full of bead-work, and turning their dark liquid eyes of invitation upon the passers. They wore bright kirtles, and red shawls fell from their heads over their plump brown cheeks and down their comfortable persons. A little girl with them was attired in like gayety of color. "What is her name?" asked Isabel, paying for a bead pin-cushion. "Daisy Smith," said her mother, in distressingly good English. "But her Indian name?" "She has none," answered the woman, who told Basil that her village numbered five hundred people, and that they were Protestants. While they talked they were joined by an Indian, whom the women saluted musically in their native tongue. This was somewhat consoling; but he wore trousers and a waistcoat, and it could have been wished that he had not a silk hat on.

"Still," said Isabel, as they turned away, "I'm glad he hasn't Lisle-thread gloves, like that chieftain we saw putting his forest queen on board the train at Oneida. But, how shocking that they should be Christians, and Protestants! It would have been bad enough to have them Catholics. And that woman said that they were increasing. They ought to be fading away."

On the bridge, they paused and looked up and down the rapids rushing down the slope in all their wild variety with the white crests of breaking surf, the dark massiveness of heavy-climbing waves, the fleet, smooth sweep of currents over broad shelves of sunken rock, the dizzy swirl and suck of whirlpools.

Spellbound, the journeyers pored upon the deathful course beneath their feet, gave a shudder to the horror of being cast upon it, and then hurried over the bridge to the island, in the shadow of whose wildness they sought refuge from the sight and sound.

There had been rain in the night; the air was full of forest fragrance, and the low, sweet voice of twittering birds. Presently they came to a bench set in a corner of the path, and commanding a pleasant vista of sunlit foliage, with a mere gleam of the foaming river beyond. As they sat down here loverwise, Basil, as in the early days of their courtship, began to recite a poem. It was one which had been haunting him since his first sight of the rapids, one of many that he used to learn by heart in his youth; the rhyme of some poor newspaper poet, whom the third or fourth editor copying his verses consigned to oblivion by carelessly clipping his name from the bottom. It had always lingered in Basil's memory, rather from the interest of the awful fact it recorded, than from any merit of its own; and now he recalled it with a distinctness that surprised him.

AVERY.

I.

All night long they heard in the houses beside the shore,
Heard, or seemed to hear, through the multitudinous roar,
Out of the hell of the rapids as 'twere a lost soul's cries:

Heard and could not believe; and the morning mocked their eyes,
Showing where wildest and fiercest the waters leaped up and ran
Raving round him and past, the visage of a man
Clinging, or seeming to cling, to the trunk of a tree that, caught
Fast in the rocks below, scarce out of the surges raught.
Was it a life, could it be, to yon slender hope that clung?
Shrill, above all the tumult the answering terror rung.

II.

Under the weltering rapids a boat from the bridge is drowned,
Over the rocks the lines of another are tangled and wound,
And the long, fateful hours of the morning have wasted soon,
As it had been in some blessed trance, and now it is noon.
Hurry, now with the raft! But O, build it strong and stanch,
And to the lines and the treacherous rocks look well as you launch!
Over the foamy tops of the waves, and their foam-sprent sides,
Over the hidden reefs, and through the embattled tides,
Onward rushes the raft, with many a lurch and leap,—
Lord! if it strike him loose from the hold he scarce can keep!
No! through all peril unharmed, it reaches him harmless at last,
And to its proven strength he lashes his weakness fast.
Now, for the shore! But steady, steady, my men, and slow;
Taut, now, the quivering lines; now slack; and so, let her go!
Thronging the shores around stands the pitying multitude;
Wan as his own are their looks, and a nightmare seems to brood
Heavy upon them, and heavy the silence hangs on all,
Save for the rapids' plunge, and the thunder of the fall.
But on a sudden thrills from the people still and pale,
Chorussing his unheard despair, a desperate wail:
Caught on a lurking point of rock it sways and swings,
Sport of the pitiless waters, the raft to which he clings.

III.

All the long afternoon it idly swings and sways;
And on the shore the crowd lifts up its hands and prays:
Lifts to heaven and wrings the hands so helpless to save,
Prays for the mercy of God on him whom the rock and the wave
Battle for, fettered betwixt them, and who amidst their strife
Struggles to help his helpers, and fights so hard for his life,—
Tugging at rope and at reef, while men weep and women swoon.

Priceless second by second, so wastes the afternoon.
And it is sunset now; and another boat and the last
Down to him from the bridge through the rapids has safely passed.

IV.

Wild through the crowd comes flying a man that nothing can stay,
Maddening against the gate that is locked athwart his way.
"No! we keep the bridge for them that can help him. You,
Tell us, who are you?" "His brother!" "God help you both! Pass
    through."
Wild, with wide arms of imploring he calls aloud to him,
Unto the face of his brother, scarce seen in the distance dim:
But in the roar of the rapids his fluttering words are lost
As in a wind of autumn the leaves of autumn are tossed.
And from the bridge he sees his brother sever the rope
Holding him to the raft, and rise secure in his hope;
Sees all as in a dream the terrible pageantry,—
Populous shores, the woods, the sky, the birds flying free;
Sees, then, the form—that, spent with effort and fasting and fear,
Flings itself feebly and fails of the boat that is lying so near,—
Caught in the long-baffled clutch of the rapids, and rolled and hurled
Headlong on to the cataract's brink, and out of the world.

"O Basil!" said Isabel, with a long sigh breaking the hush that best praised the unknown poet's skill, "it *isn't* true, is it?"

"Every word, almost, even to the brother's coming at the last moment. It's a very well-known incident," he added, and I am sure the reader whose memory runs back twenty years cannot have forgotten it.

Niagara, indeed, is an awful homicide; nearly every point of interest about the place has killed its man, and there might well be a deeper stain of crimson than it ever wears in that pretty bow overarching the falls. Its beauty is relieved against an historical background as gloomy as the lightest-hearted tourist could desire. The abominable savages, revering the cataract as a kind of august devil, and leading a life of demoniacal misery and wickedness, whom the first Jesuits found here two hundred years ago; the ferocious Iroquois bloodily driving out these squalid devil-worshippers; the French planting the fort that yet guards the mouth of the river, and therewith the seeds of war that fruited afterwards in murderous strifes throughout the whole Niagara country; the struggle for the military posts on the river, during the wars of France and England; the awful scene in the conspiracy of Pontiac, where a detachment of English troops was driven by the Indians over the precipice near the great Whirlpool; the sorrow and havoc visited upon the American settlements in the Revolution by the savages who prepared their attacks in the shadow of Fort Niagara; the battles of Chippewa and of Lundy's Lane, that mixed the roar of their cannon with that of the fall; the savage forays with tomahawk and scalping-knife, and the blazing villages on either shore in the War of 1812: these are the memories of the place, the links in a chain of tragical interest scarcely broken before our time since the white man first beheld the mist-veiled face of Niagara. The facts lost nothing of their due effect as Basil, in the ramble across Goat Island, touched them with the reflected light of Mr. Parkman's histories—those precious books that make our meagre past wear something of the rich romance of old European days, and illumine its savage solitudes with the splendor of medieval chivalry, and the glory of medieval martyrdom—and then, lacking this light, turned upon them the feeble glimmer of the guide-books. He and Isabel enjoyed the lurid picture with all the zest of sentimentalists dwelling upon the troubles of other times from the shelter of the safe and peaceful present. They were both poets in their quality of bridal couple, and so long as their own nerves were unshaken they could transmute all facts to entertaining fables. They pleasantly exercised their sympathies upon those who every year perish at Niagara in the tradition of its awful power; only they refused their cheap and selfish compassion to the Hermit of Goat Island, who dwelt so many years in its conspicuous seclusion, and was finally carried over the cataract. This public character they suspected of design in his death as in his life, and they would not be moved by his memory; though they gave a sigh to that dream, half pathetic, half ludicrous, yet not ignoble, of Mordecai

Noah, who thought to assemble all the Jews of the world, and all the Indians, as remnants of the lost tribes, upon Grand Island, there to rebuild Jerusalem, and who actually laid the corner-stone of the new temple there.

Goat Island is marvellously wild for a place visited by so many thousands every year. The shrubbery and undergrowth remain unravaged, and form a deceitful privacy, in which, even at that early hour of the day, they met many other pairs. It seemed incredible that the village and the hotels should be so full, and that the wilderness should also abound in them; yet on every embowered seat, and going to and from all points of interest and danger, were these new-wedded lovers with their interlacing arms and their fond attitudes, in which each seemed to support and lean upon the other. Such a pair stood prominent before them when Basil and Isabel emerged at last from the cover of the woods at the head of the island, and glanced up the broad swift stream to the point where it ran smooth before breaking into the rapids; and as a soft pastoral feature in the foreground of that magnificent landscape, they found them far from unpleasing. Some such pair is in the foreground of every famous American landscape; and when I think of the amount of public love-making in the season of pleasure-travel, from Mount Desert to the Yosemite, and from the parks of Colorado to the Keys of Florida, I feel that our continent is but a larger Arcady, that the middle of the nineteenth century is the golden age, and that we want very little of being a nation of shepherds and shepherdesses.

Our friends returned by the shore of the Canadian rapids, having traversed the island by a path through the heart of the woods, and now drew slowly near the falls again. All parts of the prodigious pageant have an eternal novelty, and they beheld the ever-varying effect of that constant sublimity with the sense of discoverers, or rather of people whose great fortune it is to see the marvel in its beginning, and new from the creating hand. The morning hour lent its sunny charm to this illusion, while in the cavernous precipices of the shores, dark with evergreens, a mystery as of primeval night seemed to linger. There was a wild fluttering of their nerves, a rapture with an under-consciousness of pain, the exaltation of peril and escape, when they came to the three little isles that extend from Goat Island, one beyond another, far out into the furious channel. Three pretty suspension-bridges connect them now with the larger island, and under each of these flounders a huge rapid, and hurls itself away to mingle with the ruin of the fall. The Three Sisters are mere fragments of wilderness, clumps of vine-tangled woods, planted upon masses of rock; but they are part of the fascination of Niagara which no one resists; nor could Isabel have been persuaded from exploring them. It wants no courage to do this, but merely submission to the local sorcery, and the adventurer has no other reward than the consciousness of having been where but a few years before no human being had perhaps set foot. She crossed from bridge to bridge with a quaking heart, and at last stood upon the outermost isle, whence, through the screen of vines and boughs, she gave fearful glances at the heaving and tossing flood beyond, from every wave of which at every instant she rescued herself with a desperate struggle. The exertion told heavily upon her strength unawares, and she suddenly made Basil another revelation of character. Without the slightest warning she sank down at the root of a tree, and said, with serious composure, that she could never go back on those bridges; they were not safe. He stared at her cowering form in blank amaze, and put his hands in his pockets. Then it occurred to his dull masculine sense that it must be a joke; and he said, "Well, I'll have you taken off in a boat."

"O *do*, Basil, *do* have me taken off in a boat!" implored Isabel. "You see yourself the bridges are not safe. *Do* get a boat."

"Or a balloon," he suggested, humoring the pleasantry.

Isabel burst into tears; and now he went on his knees at her side, and took her hands in his. "Isabel! Isabel! Are you crazy?" he cried, as if he meant to go mad himself. She moaned and shuddered in reply; he said, to mend matters, that it was a jest, about the boat; and he was driven to despair when Isabel repeated, "I never can go back by the bridges, never."

"But what do you propose to do?"

"I don't know. I don't know!"

He would try sarcasm. "Do you intend to set up a hermitage here, and have your meals sent out from the hotel? It's a charming spot, and visited pretty constantly; but it's small, even for a hermitage."

Isabel moaned again with her hands still on her eyes, and wondered that he was not ashamed to make fun of her.

He would try kindness. "Perhaps, darling, you'll let me carry you ashore."

"No, that will bring double the weight on the bridge at once."

"Couldn't you shut your eyes, and let me lead you?"

"Why, it isn't the *sight* of the rapids," she said, looking up fiercely. "*The bridges are not safe.* I'm not a *child*, Basil. O, *what shall we do?*"

"I don't know," said Basil, gloomily. "It's an exigency for which I wasn't prepared." Then he silently gave himself to the Evil One, for having probably overwrought Isabel's nerves by repeating that poem about Avery, and by the ensuing talk about Niagara, which she had seemed to enjoy so much. He asked her if that was it; and she answered, "O no, it's nothing but the bridges." He proved to her that the bridges, upon all known principles, were perfectly safe, and that they could not give way. She shook her head, but made no answer, and he lost his patience.

"Isabel," he cried, "I'm ashamed of you!"

"Don't say anything you'll be sorry for afterwards, Basil," she replied, with the forbearance of those who have reason and justice on their side.

The rapids beat and shouted round their little prison-isle, each billow leaping as if possessed by a separate demon. The absurd horror of the situation overwhelmed him. He dared not attempt to carry her ashore, for she might spring from his grasp into the flood. He could not leave her to call for help; and what if nobody came till she lost her mind from terror? Or, what if somebody should come and find them in that ridiculous affliction?

Somebody *was* coming!

"Isabel!" he shouted in her ear, "here come those people we saw in the parlor last night."

Isabel dashed her veil over her face, clutched Basil's with her icy hand, rose, drew her arm convulsively through his, and walked ashore without a word.

In a sheltered nook they sat down, and she quickly "repaired her drooping head and tricked her beams" again. He could see her tearfully smiling through her veil. "My dear," he said, "I don't ask an explanation of your fright, for I don't suppose you could give it. But should you mind telling me why those people were so sovereign against it?"

"Why, dearest! Don't you understand? That Mrs. Richard— whoever she is—is so much like *me*."

She looked at him as if she had made the most satisfying statement, and he thought he had better not ask further then, but wait in hope that the meaning would come to him. They walked on in silence till they came to the Biddle Stairs, at the head of which is a notice that persons have been killed by pieces of rock from the precipice overhanging the shore below, and warning people that they descend at their peril. Isabel declined to visit the Cave of the Winds, to which these stairs lead, but was willing to risk the ascent of Terrapin Tower. "Thanks; no," said her husband. "You might find it unsafe to come back the way you went up. We can't count certainly upon the appearance of the lady who is so much like you; and I've no fancy for spending my life on Terrapin Tower." So he found her a seat, and went alone to the top of the audacious little structure standing on the verge of the cataract, between the smooth curve of the Horse-Shoe and the sculptured front of the Central Fall, with the stormy sea of the Rapids behind, and the river, dim seen through the mists, crawling away between its lofty bluffs before. He knew again the awful delight with which so long ago he had watched the changes in the beauty of the Canadian Fall as it hung a mass of translucent green from the brink, and a pearly white seemed to crawl up from the abyss, and penetrate all its substance to the very crest, and then suddenly vanished from it, and perpetually renewed the same effect. The mystery of the rising vapors veiled the gulf into which the cataract swooped; the sun shone, and a rainbow dreamed upon them.

Near the foot of the tower, some loose rocks extend quite to the verge, and here Basil saw an elderly gentleman skipping from one slippery stone to another, and looking down from time to time into the abyss, who, when he had amused himself long enough in this way, clambered up on the plank bridge. Basil, who had descended by this time, made bold to say that he thought the diversion an odd one and rather dangerous. The gentleman took this in good part, and owned it might seem so, but added that a distinguished phrenologist had examined his head, and told him he had equilibrium so large that he could go anywhere.

"On your bridal tour, I presume," he continued, as they approached the bench where Basil had left Isabel. She had now the company of a plain, middle-aged woman, whose attire hesitatingly expressed some inward festivity, and had a certain reluctant fashionableness. "Well, this is my third bridal tour to Niagara, and wife's been here once before on the same business. We see a good many changes. I used to stand on Table Rock with the others. Now that's *all* gone. Well, old lady, shall we move on?" he asked; and this bridal pair passed up the path, attended, haply, by the guardian spirits of those who gave the place so many sad yet pleasing associations.

At dinner, Mr. Richard's party sat at the table next Basil's, and they were all now talking cheerfully over the emptiness of the spacious dining-hall.

"Well, Kitty," the married lady was saying, "you can tell the girls what you please about the gayeties of Niagara, when you get home. They'll believe anything sooner than the truth."

"O, yes, indeed," said Kitty, "I've got a good deal of it made up already. I'll describe a grand hop at the hotel, with fashionable people from all parts of the country, and the gentlemen I danced with the most. I'm going to have had quite a flirtation with the gentleman of the long blond moustache, whom we met on the bridge this morning, and he's got to do duty in accounting for my missing glove. It'll never do to tell the girls I dropped it from the top of Terrapin Tower. Then, you know, Fanny, I really *can* say something about dining with aristocratic Southerners, waited upon by their black servants."

This referred to the sad-faced patrician whom Basil and Isabel had noted in the cars from Buffalo as a Southerner probably coming North for the first time since the war. He had an air at once fierce and sad, and a half-barbaric, homicidal gentility of manner fascinating enough in its way. He sat with his wife at a table further down the room, and their child was served in part by a little tan-colored nurse-maid. The fact did not quite answer to the young lady's description of it, and yet it certainly afforded her a ground-work. Basil fancied a sort of bewilderment in the Southerner, and explained it upon the theory that he used to come every year to Niagara before the war, and was now puzzled to find it so changed.

"Yes," he said, "I can't account for him except as the ghost of Southern travel, and I can't help feeling a little sorry for him. I suppose that almost any evil commends itself by its ruin; the wrecks of slavery are fast growing a fungus crop of sentiment, and they may yet outflourish the remains of the feudal system in the kind of poetry they produce. The impoverished slaveholder *is* a pathetic figure, in spite of all justice and reason; the beaten rebel *does* move us to compassion, and it is of no use to think of Andersonville in his presence. This gentleman, and others like him, used to be the lords of our summer resorts. They spent the money they did not earn like princes; they held their heads high; they trampled upon the Abolitionist in his lair; they received the homage of the doughface in his home. They came up here from their rice-swamps and cotton-fields, and bullied the whole busy civilization of the North. Everybody who had merchandise or principles to sell truckled to them, and travel amongst us was a triumphal progress. Now they're moneyless and subjugated (as they call it), there's none so poor to do them reverence, and it's left for me, an Abolitionist from the cradle, to sigh over their fate. After all, they had noble traits, and it was no great wonder they got to despise us, seeing what most of us were. It seems to me I should like to know our friend. I can't help feeling towards him as towards a fallen prince, heaven help my craven spirit! I wonder how our colored waiter feels towards him. I dare say he admires him immensely."

There were not above a dozen other people in the room, and Basil contrasted the scene with that which the same place formerly presented. "In the old time," he said, "every table was full, and we dined to the music of a brass band. I can't say I liked the band, but I miss it. I wonder if our Southern friend misses it? They gave us a very small allowance of brass band when we arrived, Isabel. Upon my word, I wonder what's come over the place," he said, as the Southern party, rising from the table, walked out of the dining-room, attended by many treacherous echoes in spite of an ostentatious clatter of dishes that the waiters made.

After dinner they drove on the Canada shore up past the Clifton House, towards the Burning Spring, which is not the least wonder of Niagara. As each bubble breaks upon the troubled surface, and yields its flash of infernal flame and its whiff of sulphurous stench, it seems hardly strange that the Neutral Nation should have revered the cataract as a demon; and another subtle spell (not to be broken even by the business-like composure of the man who shows off the hell-broth) is added to those successive sorceries by which Niagara gradually changes from a thing of beauty to a thing of terror. By all odds, too, the most tremendous view of the Falls is afforded by the point on this drive whence you look down upon the Horse-Shoe, and behold its three massive walls of sea rounding and sweeping into the gulf together, the color gone, and the smooth brink showing black and ridgy.

Would they not go to the battle-field of Lundy's Lane? asked the driver at a certain point on their return; but Isabel did not care for battle-fields, and Basil preferred to keep intact the reminiscence of his former visit. "They have a sort of tower of observation built on the battle-ground," he said, as they drove on down by the river, "and it was in charge of an old Canadian militia-man, who had helped his countrymen to be beaten in the fight. This hero gave me a simple and unintelligible account of the battle, asking me first if I had ever heard of General Scott, and adding without flinching that here he got his earliest laurels. He seemed to go just so long to every listener, and nothing could stop him short, so I fell into a revery until he came to an end. It was hard to remember, that sweet summer morning, when the sun shone, and the birds sang, and the music of a piano and a girl's voice rose from a bowery cottage near, that all the pure air had once been tainted with battle-smoke, that the peaceful fields had been planted with cannon, instead of potatoes and corn, and that where the cows came down the farmer's lane, with tinkling bells, the shock of armed men had befallen. The blue and tranquil Ontario gleamed far away, and far away rolled the beautiful land, with farm-houses, fields, and woods, and at the foot of the tower lay the pretty village. The battle of the past seemed only a vagary of mine; yet how could I doubt the warrior at my elbow?—grieved though I was to find that a habit of strong drink had the better of his utterance that morning. My driver explained afterwards, that persons visiting the field were commonly so much pleased with the captain's eloquence, that they kept the noble old soldier in a brandy-and-water rapture throughout the season, thereby greatly refreshing his memory, and making the battle bloodier and bloodier as the season advanced and the number of visitors increased. There, my dear," he suddenly broke off, as they came in sight of a slender stream of water that escaped from the brow of a cliff on the American side below the Falls, and spun itself into a gauze of silvery mist, "that's the Bridal Veil; and I suppose you think the stream, which is making such a fine display, yonder, is some idle brooklet, ending a long course of error and worthlessness by that spectacular plunge. It's nothing of the kind; it's an honest hydraulic canal, of the most straightforward character, a poor but respectable mill-race which has devoted itself strictly to business, and has turned mill-wheels instead of fooling round water-lilies. It can afford that ultimate finery. What you behold in the Bridal Veil, my love, is the apotheosis of industry."

"What I can't help thinking of," said Isabel, who had not paid the smallest attention to the Bridal Veil, or anything about it, "is the awfulness of stepping off these places in the night-time." She referred to the road which, next the precipice, is unguarded by any sort of parapet. In Europe a strong wall would secure it, but we manage things differently on our continent, and carriages go ruining over the brink from time to time.

"If your thoughts have that direction," answered her husband, "we had better go back to the hotel, and leave the Whirlpool for to-morrow morning. It's late for it to-day, at any rate." He had treated Isabel since the adventure on the Three Sisters with a superiority which he felt himself to be very odious, but which he could not disuse.

"I'm not afraid," she sighed, "but in the words of the retreating soldier, 'I'm awfully demoralized';" and added, "You know we must reserve some of the vital forces for shopping this evening."

Part of their business also was to buy the tickets for their return to Boston by way of Montreal and Quebec, and it was part of their pleasure to get these of the heartiest imaginable ticket-agent. He was a colonel or at least a major, and he made a polite feint of calling Basil by some military title. He commended the trip they were about to make as the most magnificent and beautiful on the whole continent, and he commended them for intending to make it. He said that was Mrs. General Bowder of Philadelphia who just went out; did they know her? Somehow, the titles affected Basil as of older date than the late war, and as belonging to the militia period; and he imagined for the agent the romance of a life spent at a watering-place, in contact with rich money-spending, pleasure-taking people, who formed his whole jovial world. The Colonel, who included them in this world and thereby brevetted them rich and fashionable, could not secure a state-room for them on the boat,—a perfectly splendid Lake steamer, which would take them down the rapids of the

St. Lawrence, and on to Montreal without change,—but he would give them a letter to the captain, who was a very *particular* friend of his, and would be happy to show them as his *friends* every attention; and so he wrote a note ascribing peculiar merits to Basil, and in spite of all reason making him feel for the moment that he was privileged by a document which was no doubt part of every such transaction. He spoke in a loud cheerful voice; he laughed jollily at no apparent joke; he bowed very low and said, "*Good* evening!" at parting, and they went away as if he had blessed them.

The rest of the evening they spent in wandering through the village, charmed with its bizarre mixture of quaintness and commonplaceness; in hanging about the shop-windows with their monotonous variety of feather fans—each with a violently red or yellow bird painfully sacrificed in its centre—moccasons, bead-wrought work-bags, tobacco-pouches, bows and arrows, and whatever else the savage art of the neighboring squaws can invent; in sauntering through these gay booths, pricing many things and in hanging long and undecidedly over cases full of feldspar crosses, quartz bracelets and necklaces, and every manner of vase, inoperative pitcher, and other vessel that can be fashioned out of the geological formations at Niagara, tormented meantime by the heat of the gas-lights and the persistence of the mosquitoes. There were very few people besides themselves in the shops, and Isabel's purchases were not lavish. Her husband had made up his mind to get her some little keepsake; and when he had taken her to the hotel he ran back to one of the shops, and hastily bought her a feather fan,—a magnificent thing of deep magenta dye shading into blue, with a whole yellow-bird trans-fixed in the centre. When he triumphantly displayed it in their room, "Who's *that* for, Basil?" demanded his wife; "the cook?" But seeing his ghastly look at this, she fell upon his neck, crying, "O you poor old tasteless darling! You've got it for *me!*" and seemed about to die of laughter.

"Didn't you start and throw up your hands," he stammered, "when you came to that case of fans?"

"*Yes*—in horror! Did you think I *liked* the cruel things, with their dead birds and their hideous colors? O Basil, dearest! You *are* incorrigible. *Can't* you learn that magenta is the vilest of all the hues that the perverseness of man has invented in defiance of nature? Now, my love, just promise me one thing," she said pathetically. "We're going to do a little shopping in Montreal, you know; and perhaps you'll be wanting to surprise me with something there. Don't do it. Or if you must, do tell me all about it beforehand, and what the color of it's to be; and I can say whether to get it or not, and then there'll be some taste about it, and I shall be *truly* surprised and pleased."

She turned to put the fan into her trunk, and he murmured something about exchanging it. "No," she said, "we'll keep it as a—a—monument." And she deposed him, with another peal of laughter, from the proud height to which he had climbed in pity of her nervous fears of the day. So completely were their places changed, that he doubted if it were not he who had made that scene on the Third Sister; and when Isabel said, "O, why *won't* men use their reasoning faculties?" he could not for himself have claimed any, and he could not urge the truth: that he had bought the fan more for its barbaric brightness than for its beauty. She would not let him get angry, and he could say nothing against the half-ironical petting with which she soothed his mortification.

But all troubles passed with the night, and the next morning they spent a charming hour about Prospect Point, and in sauntering over Goat Island, somewhat daintily tasting the flavors of the place on whose wonders they had so hungrily and indiscriminately feasted at first. They had already the feeling of veteran visitors, and they loftily marvelled at the greed with which newer comers plunged at the sensations. They could not conceive why people should want to descend the inclined railway to the foot of the American Fall; they smiled at the idea of going up Terrapin Tower; they derided the vulgar daring of those who went out upon the Three Weird Sisters; for some whom they saw about to go down the Biddle Stairs to the Cave of the Winds, they had no words to express their contempt.

Then they made their excursion to the Whirlpool, mistakenly going down on the American side, for it is much better seen from the other, though seen from any point it is the most impressive feature of the whole prodigious spectacle of Niagara.

Here within the compass of a mile, those inland seas of the North, Superior, Huron, Michigan, Erie, and the multitude of smaller lakes, all pour their floods, where they swirl in dreadful vortices, with resistless under-currents boiling beneath the surface of that mighty eddy. Abruptly from this scene of secret power, so different from the thunderous splendors of the cataract itself, rise lofty cliffs on every side, to a height of two hundred feet, clothed from the water's edge almost to their crests with dark cedars. Noiselessly, so far as your senses perceive, the lakes steal out of the whirlpool, then, drunk and wild, with brawling rapids roar away to Ontario through the narrow channel of the river. Awful as the scene is, you stand so far above it that you do not know the half of its terribleness; for those waters that look so smooth are great ridges and rings, forced, by the impulse of the currents, twelve feet higher in the centre than at the margin. Nothing can live there, and with what is caught in its hold, the maelstrom plays for days, and whirls and tosses round and round in its toils, with a sad, maniacal patience. The guides tell ghastly stories, which even their telling does not wholly rob of ghastliness, about the bodies of drowned men carried into the whirlpool and made to enact upon its dizzy surges a travesty of life, apparently floating there at their pleasure, diving and frolicking amid the waves, or frantically struggling to escape from the death that has long since befallen them.

On the American side, not far below the railway suspension bridge, is an elevator more than a hundred and eighty feet high, which is meant to let people down to the shore below, and to give a view of the rapids on their own level. From the cliff opposite, it looks a terribly frail structure of pine sticks, but is doubtless stronger than it looks; and at any rate, as it has never yet fallen to pieces, it may be pronounced perfectly safe.

In the waiting-room at the top, Basil and Isabel found Mr.

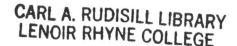

Richard and his ladies again, who got into the movable chamber with them, and they all silently descended together. It was not a time for talk of any kind, either when they were slowly and not quite smoothly dropping through the lugubrious upper part of the structure, where it was darkened by a rough weather-boarding, or lower down where the unobstructed light showed the grim tearful face of the cliff, bedrabbled with oozy springs, and the audacious slightness of the elevator. An abiding distrust of the machinery overhead mingled in Isabel's heart with a doubt of the value of the scene below, and she could not look forward to escape from her present perils by the conveyance which had brought her into them, with any satisfaction. She wanly smiled, and shrank closer to Basil; while the other matron made nothing of seizing her husband violently by the arm and imploring him to stop it whenever they experienced a rougher jolt than usual.

At the bottom of the cliff they were helped out of their prison by a humid young Englishman, with much clay on him, whose face was red and bathed in perspiration, for it was very hot down there in his little enclosure of baking pine boards, and it was not much cooler out on the rocks upon which the party issued, descending and descending by repeated and desultory flights of steps, till at last they stood upon a huge fragment of stone right abreast of the rapids. Yet it was a magnificent sight, and for a moment none of them were sorry to have come. The surges did not look like the gigantic ripples on a river's course as they were, but like a procession of ocean billows; they arose far aloft in vast bulks of clear green, and broke heavily into foam at the crest. Great blocks and shapeless fragments of rock strewed the margin of the awful torrent; gloomy walls of dark stone rose naked from these, bearded here and there with cedar, and everywhere frowning with shaggy brows of evergreen. The place is inexpressibly lonely and dreadful, and one feels like an alien presence there, or as if he had intruded upon some mood or haunt of Nature in which she had a right to be forever alone. The slight, impudent structure of the elevator rises through the solitude, like a thing that merits ruin, yet it is better than something more elaborate, for it looks temporary, and since there must be an elevator, it is well to have it of the most transitory aspect. Some such quality of rude impermanence consoles you for the presence of most improvements by which you enjoy Niagara; the suspension bridges for their part being saved from offensiveness by their beauty and unreality.

Ascending, none of the party spoke; Isabel and the other matron blanched in each other's faces; their husbands maintained a stolid resignation. When they stepped out of their trap into the waiting-room at the top, "What I like about these little adventures," said Mr. Richard to Basil, abruptly, "is getting safely out of them. Good morning, sir." He bowed slightly to Isabel, who returned his politeness, and exchanged faint nods, or glances, with the ladies. They got into their separate carriages, and at that safe distance made each other more decided obeisances.

"Well," observed Basil, "I suppose we're introduced now. We shall be meeting them from time to time throughout our journey. You know how the same faces and the same trunks used to keep turning up in our travels on the other side. Once meet people in travelling, and you can't get rid of them."

"Yes," said Isabel, as if continuing his train of thought, "I'm glad we're going to-day."

"O dearest!"

"Truly. When we first arrived I felt only the loveliness of the place. It seemed more familiar, too, then; but ever since, it's been growing stranger and dreadfuller. Somehow it's begun to pervade me and possess me in a very uncomfortable way: I'm tossed upon rapids, and flung from cataract brinks, and dizzied in whirlpools; I'm no longer yours, Basil; I'm most unhappily married to Niagara. Fly with me, save me from my awful lord!"

She lightly burlesqued the woes of a *prima donna*, with clasped hands and uplifted eyes.

"That'll do very well," Basil commented, "and it implies a reality that can't be quite definitely spoken. We come to Niagara in the patronizing spirit in which we approach everything nowadays, and for a few hours we have it our own way, and pay our little tributes of admiration with as much complacency as we feel in acknowledging the existence of the Supreme Being. But after a while we are aware of some potent influence undermining our self-satisfaction; we begin to conjecture that the great cataract does not exist by virtue of our approval, and to feel that it will not cease when we go away. The second day makes us its abject slaves, and on the third we want to fly from it in terror. I believe some people stay for weeks, however, and hordes of them have written odes to Niagara."

"I can't understand it, at all," said Isabel. "I don't wonder now that the town should be so empty this season, but that it should ever be full. I wish we'd gone after our first look at the Falls from the suspension bridge. How beautiful that was! I rejoice in everything that I haven't done. I'm so glad I haven't been in the Cave of the Winds; I'm so happy that Table Rock fell twenty years ago! Basil, I couldn't stand another rainbow today. I'm sorry we went out on the Three Weird Sisters. O, I shall dream about it! and the rush, and the whirl, and the dampness in one's face, and the everlasting chir-r-r-r of everything!"

She dipped suddenly upon his shoulder for a moment's oblivion, and then rose radiant with a question: "Why in the world, if Niagara is really what it seems to us, now, do so many bridal parties come here?"

"Perhaps they're the only people who've the strength to bear up against it, and are not easily dispersed and subjected by it."

"But *we*'re dispersed and subjected."

"Ah, my dear, we married a little late. Who knows how it would be if you were nineteen instead of twenty-seven, and I twenty-five and not turned of thirty?"

"Basil, you're very cruel."

"No, no. But don't you see how it is? We've known too much of life to desire any gloomy background for our happiness. We're quite contented to have things gay and bright about us. Once we couldn't have made the circle dark enough. Well, my dear, that's the effect of age. We're superannuated."

"I used to think *I* was before we were married," answered Isabel simply; "but now," she added triumphantly, "I'm rescued from all that. I shall never be old again, dearest; never, as long as you—love me!"

They were about to enter the village, and he could not make any open acknowledgment of her tenderness; but her silken mantle (or whatever) slipped from her shoulder, and he embracingly replaced it, flattering himself that he had delicately seized this chance of an unavowed caress and not knowing (O such is the blindness of our sex!) that the opportunity had been yet more subtly afforded him, with the art which women never disuse in this world, and which I hope they will not forget in the next.

They had an early dinner, and looked their last upon the nuptial gayety of the otherwise forlorn hotel. Three brides sat down with them in travelling-dress; two occupied the parlor as they passed out; half a dozen happy pairs arrived (to the music of the band) in the omnibus that was to carry our friends back to the station; they caught sight of several about the shop-windows, as they drove through the streets. Thus the place perpetually renews itself in the glow of love as long as the summer lasts. The moon which is elsewhere so often of wormwood, or of the ordinary green cheese at the best, is of lucent honey there from the first of June to the last of October; and this is a great charm in Niagara. I think with tenderness of all the lives that have opened so fairly there; the hopes that have reigned in the glad young hearts; the measureless tide of joy that ebbs and flows with the arriving and departing trains. Elsewhere there are carking cares of business and of fashion, there are age, and sorrow, and heartbreak: but here only youth, faith, rapture. I kiss my hand to Niagara for that reason, and would I were a poet for a quarter of an hour.

Isabel departed in almost a forgiving mood towards the weak sisterhood of evident brides, and both our friends felt a lurking fondness for Niagara at the last moment. I do not know how much of their content was due to the fact that they had suffered no sort of wrong there, from those who are apt to prey upon travellers. In the hotel a placard warned them to have nothing to do with the miscreant hackmen on the streets, but always to order their carriage at the office; on the street the hackmen whispered to them not to trust the exorbitant drivers in league with the landlords; yet their actual experience was great reasonableness and facile contentment with the sum agreed upon. This may have been because the hackmen so far outnumbered the visitors, that the latter could dictate terms; but they chose to believe it a triumph of civilization; and I will never be the cynic to sneer at their faith. Only at the station was the virtue of the Niagarans put in doubt, by the hotel porter who professed to find Basil's trunk enfeebled by travel, and advised a strap for it, which a friend of his would sell for a dollar and a half. Yet even he may have been a benevolent nature unjustly suspected.

VII

DOWN THE ST. LAWRENCE

THEY WERE TO TAKE the Canadian steamer at Charlotte, the port of Rochester, and they rattled uneventfully down from Niagara by rail. At the broad, low-banked river-mouth the steamer lay beside the railroad station; and while Isabel disposed of herself on board, Basil looked to the transfer of the baggage, novelly comforted in the business by the respectfulness of the young Canadian who took charge of the trunks for the boat. He was slow, and his sytem was not good; he did not give checks for the pieces, but marked them with the name of their destination, and there was that indefinable something in his manner which hinted his hope that you would remember the porter; but he was so civil that he did not snub the meekest and most vexatious of the passengers, and Basil mutely blessed his servile soul. Few white Americans, he said to himself, would behave so decently in his place; and he could not conceive of the American steamboat clerk who would use the politeness towards a waiting crowd that the Canadian purser showed when they all wedged themselves in about his window to receive their state-room keys. He was somewhat awkward, like the porter, but he was patient, and he did not lose his temper even when some of the crowd, finding he would not bully them, made bold to bully him. He was three times as long in serving them as an American would have been, but their time was of no value there, and he served them well. Basil made a point of speaking him fair, when his turn came, and the purser did not trample on him for a base truckler, as an American jack-in-office would have done.

Our tourists felt at home directly on this steamer, which was very comfortable, and in every way sufficient for its purpose, with a visible captain, who answered two or three questions very pleasantly, and bore himself towards his passengers in some sort like a host.

In the saloon Isabel had found among the passengers her semi-acquaintances of the hotel parlor and the Rapids-elevator, and had glanced tentatively towards them. Whereupon the matron of the party had made advances that ended in their all sitting down together, and wondering when the boat would start, and what time they would get to Montreal next evening, with other matters that strangers going upon the same journey may properly marvel over in company. The introduction having thus accomplished itself, they exchanged addresses, and it appeared that Richard was Colonel Ellison, of Milwaukee, and that Fanny was his wife. Miss Kitty Ellison was of western New York, not far from Erie. There was a diversion presently towards the different state-rooms; but the new acquaintances sat *vis-à-vis* at the table, and after supper the ladies drew their chairs together on the promenade deck, and enjoyed the fresh evening breeze. The sun set magnificent upon the low western shore which they had now left an hour away, and a broad stripe of color stretched behind the steamer. A few thin, luminous clouds darkened momently along the horizon, and then mixed with the land. The stars came out in a clear sky, and a light wind softly buffeted the cheeks, and breathed life into nerves that the day's heat had wasted. It scarcely wrinkled the tranquil expanse of the lake, on which loomed, far or near, a full-sailed schooner, and presently melted into the twilight, and left the steamer solitary upon the waters. The company was small, and not remarkable enough in any way to take the thoughts of any one off his own comfort. A deep sense of the coseyness of the situation possessed them all, which was if possible intensified by the spectacle of the captain, seated on the upper deck, and smoking a cigar that flashed and fainted like a stationary firefly in the gathering dusk.

How very distant, in this mood, were the most recent events! Niagara seemed a fable of antiquity; the ride from Rochester a myth of the Middle Ages. In this cool, happy world of quiet lake, of starry skies, of air that the soul itself seemed to breathe, there was such consciousness of repose as if one were steeped in rest and soaked through and through with calm.

The points of likeness between Isabel and Mrs. Ellison shortly made them mutually uninteresting, and, leaving her husband to the others, Isabel frankly sought the companionship of Miss Kitty, in whom she found a charm of manner which puzzled at first, but which she presently fancied must be perfect trust of others mingling with a peculiar self-reliance.

"Can't you see, Basil, what a very flattering way it is?" she asked of her husband, when, after parting with their friends for the night, she tried to explain the character to him. "Of course no art could equal such a natural gift; for that kind of belief in your good-nature and sympathy makes you feel worthy of it, don't you know; and so you can't help being good-natured and sympathetic. This Miss Ellison, why, I can tell you, I shouldn't be ashamed of her anywhere." By anywhere Isabel meant Boston, and she went on to praise the young lady's intelligence and refinement, with those expressions of surprise at the existence of civilization in a westerner which westerners find it so hard to receive graciously. Happily, Miss Ellison had not to hear them. "The reason she happened to come with only two dresses is, she lives so near Niagara that she could come for one day, and go back the next. The colonel's her cousin, and he and his wife go East every year, and they asked her this time to see Niagara with them. She told me all over again what we eavesdropped so shamefully in the hotel parlor; and I don't know whether she was better pleased with the prospect of what's before her, or with the notion of making the journey in this original way. She didn't force her confidence upon me, any more than she tried to withhold it. We got to talking in the most natural manner; and she seemed to tell these things about herself because they amused her and she liked me. I had been saying how my trunk got left behind once on the French side of Mont Cenis, and I had to wear aunt's things at Turin till it could be sent for.''

"Well, I don't see but Miss Ellison could describe you to her friends very much as you've described her to me," said Basil. "How did these mutual confidences begin? Whose trustfulness first flattered the other's? What else did you tell about yourself?"

"I said we were on our wedding journey," guiltily admitted Isabel.

"O, you did!"

"Why, dearest! I wanted to know, for once, you see, whether we seemed honeymoon-struck."

"And do we?"

"No," came the answer, somewhat ruefully. "Perhaps, Basil," she added, "we've been a little *too* successful in disguising our bridal character. Do you know," she continued, looking him anxiously in the face, "this Miss Ellison took me at first for— your sister!"

Basil broke forth in outrageous laughter. "One more such victory," he said, "and we are undone"; and he laughed again immoderately. "How sad is the fruition of human wishes! There's nothing, after all, like a good thorough failure for making people happy."

Isabel did not listen to him. Safe in a dim corner of the deserted saloon, she seized him in a vindictive embrace; then, as if it had been he who suggested the idea of such a loathsome relation, hissed out the hated words, "*Your sister!*" and released him with a disdainful repulse.

A little after daybreak the steamer stopped at the Canadian city of Kingston, a handsome place, substantial to the water's edge, and giving a sense of English solidity by the stone of which it is largely built. There was an accession of many passengers here, and they and the people on the wharf were as little like Americans as possible. They were English or Irish or Scotch, with the healthful bloom of the Old World still upon their faces, or if Canadians they looked not less hearty; so that one must wonder if the line between the Dominion and the United States did not also sharply separate good digestion and dyspepsia. These provincials had not our regularity of features, nor the best of them our careworn sensibility of expression; but neither had they our complexions of *adobe;* and even Isabel was forced to allow that the men were, on the whole, better dressed than the same number of average Americans would have been in a city of that size and remoteness. The stevedores who were putting the freight aboard were men of leisure; they joked in a kindly way with the orange-women and the old women picking up chips on the pier; and our land of hurry seemed beyond the ocean rather than beyond the lake.

Kingston has romantic memories of being Fort Frontenac two hundred years ago; of Count Frontenac's splendid advent among the Indians; of the brave La Salle, who turned its wooden walls to stone; of wars with the savages and then with the New York colonists, whom the French and their allies harried from this point; of the destruction of La Salle's fort in the old French War; and of final surrender a few years later to the English. It is as picturesque as it is historical. All about the city the shores are beautifully wooded, and there are many lovely islands,—the first indeed of those Thousand Islands with which the head of the St. Lawrence is filled, and among which the steamer was presently threading her way. They are still as charming and still almost as wild as when, in 1673, Frontenac's flotilla of canoes passed through their labyrinth and issued upon the lake. Save for a lighthouse upon one of them, there is almost nothing to show that the foot of man has ever pressed the thin grass clinging to their rocky surfaces, and keeping its green in the eternal shadow of their pines and cedars. In the warm morning light they gathered or dispersed before the advancing vessel, which some of them almost touched with the plumage of their evergreens; and where none of them were large, some were so small that it would not have been too bold to figure them as a vaster race of water-birds assembling and separating in her course. It is curiously affecting to find them so unclaimed yet from the solitude of the vanished wilderness, and scarcely touched even by tradition. But for the interest left them by the French, these tiny islands have scarcely any associations, and must be enjoyed for their beauty alone. There is indeed about them a faint light of legend concerning the Canadian rebellion of 1837, for several patriots are said to have taken refuge amidst their lovely multitude; but this episode of modern history is difficult for the imagination to manage, and somehow one does not take sentimentally even to that daughter of a lurking patriot, who long baffled her father's pursuers by rowing him from one island to another, and supplying him with food by night.

Either the reluctance is from the natural desire that so recent a heroine should be founded on fact, or it is mere perverseness. Perhaps I ought to say, in justice to her, that it was one of her own sex who refused to be interested in her, and forbade Basil to care for her. When he had read of her exploit from the guide-book, Isabel asked him if he had noticed that handsome girl in the blue and white striped Garibaldi and Swiss hat, who had come aboard at Kingston. She pointed her out, and courageously made him admire her beauty, which was of the most bewitching Canadian type. The young girl was redeemed by her New World birth from the English heaviness; a more delicate bloom lighted her cheeks; a softer grace dwelt in her movement; yet she was round and full, and she was in the perfect flower of youth. She was not so ethereal in her loveliness as an American girl, but she was not so nervous and had none of the painful fragility of the latter. Her expression was just a little vacant, it must be owned; but so far as she went she was faultless. She looked like the most tractable of daughters, and as if she would be the most obedient of wives. She had a blameless taste in dress, Isabel declared, her costume of blue and white striped Garibaldi and Swiss hat (set upon heavy masses of dark brown hair) being completed by a black silk skirt. "And you can see," she added, "that it's an old skirt made over, and that she's dressed as cheaply as she is prettily." This surprised Basil, who had imputed the young lady's personal sumptuousness to her dress, and had thought it enormously rich.

When she got off with her *chaperone* at one of the poorest-looking country landings, she left them in hopeless conjecture about her. Was she visiting there, or was the interior of Canada full of such stylish and exquisite creatures? Where did she get her taste, her fashions, her manners? As she passed from sight towards the shadow of the woods, they felt the poorer for her going; yet they were glad to have seen her, and on second thoughts they felt that they could not justly ask more of her than to have merely existed for a few hours in their presence. They perceived that beauty was not only its own excuse for being, but that it flattered and favored and profited the world by consenting to be.

At Prescott, the boat on which they had come from Charlotte, and on which they had been promised a passage without change to Montreal, stopped, and they were transferred to a smaller steamer with the uncomfortable name of Banshee. She was very old, and very infirm and dirty, and in every way bore out the character of a squalid Irish goblin. Besides, she was already heavily laden with passengers, and, with the addition of the other steamer's people, had now double her complement; and our friends doubted if they were not to pass the Rapids in as much danger as discomfort. Their fellow-passengers were in great variety, however, and thus partly atoned for their numbers. Among them of course there was a full force of brides from Niagara and elsewhere, and some curious forms of the prevailing infatuation appeared. It is well enough, if she likes, and it may even be very noble for a passably good-looking young lady to marry a gentleman of venerable age; but to intensify the idea of self-devotion by furtively caressing his wrinkled front seems too reproachful of the general public; while, on the other hand, if the bride is very young and pretty, it enlists in behalf of the white-haired husband the unwilling sympathies of the spectator to see her the centre of a group of young people, and him only acknowledged from time to time by a Parthian snub. Nothing, however, could have been more satisfactory than the sisterly surrounding of this latter bride. They were of a better class of Irish people; and if it had been any sacrifice for her to marry so old a man, they were doing their best to give the affair at least the liveliness of a wake. There were five or six of those great handsome girls, with their generous curves and wholesome colors, and they were every one attended by a good-looking colonial lover, with whom they joked in slightly brogued voices, and laughed with careless Celtic laughter. One of the young fellows presently lost his hat overboard, and had to wear the handkerchief of his lady about his head; and this appeared to be really one of the best things in the world, and led to endless banter. They were well dressed, and it could be imagined that the ancient bridegroom had come in for the support of the whole good-looking, healthy, light-hearted family. In some degree he looked it, and wore but a rueful countenance for a bridegroom; so that a very young newly married couple, who sat next the jolly sister-and-loverhood could not keep their pitying eyes off his downcast face. "What if he, too, were young at heart!" the kind little wife's regard seemed to say.

For the sake of the slight air that was stirring, and to have the best view of the Rapids, the Banshee's whole company was gathered upon the forward promenade, and the throng was almost as dense as in a six-o'clock horse-car out from Boston. The standing and sitting groups were closely packed together, and the expanded parasols and umbrellas formed a nearly unbroken roof. Under this Isabel chatted at intervals with the Ellisons, who sat near; but it was not an atmosphere that provoked social feeling, and she was secretly glad when after a while they shifted their position.

It was deadly hot, and most of the people saddened and silenced in the heat. From time to time the clouds idling about overhead met and sprinkled down a cruel little shower of rain that seemed to make the air less breathable than before. The lonely shores were yellow with drought; the islands grew wilder and barrener; the course of the river was for miles at a stretch through country which gave no signs of human life. The St. Lawrence has none of the bold picturesqueness of the Hudson, and is far more like its far-off cousin the Mississippi. Its banks are low like the Mississippi's, its current swift, its way through solitary lands. The same sentiment of early adventure hangs about each: both are haunted by visions of the Jesuit in his priestly robe, and the soldier in his medieval steel; the same gay, devout, and dauntless race has touched them both with immortal romance. If the water were of a dusky golden color, instead of translucent green, and the shores and islands were covered with cottonwoods and willows instead of dark cedars, one could with no great effort believe one's self on the Mississippi between Cairo and St. Louis, so much do the great rivers strike one as kindred in the chief features of their landscape. Only, in tracing this resemblance you do not know just what to do with the purple mountains of Vermont seen vague against the horizon from the St. Lawrence, or with the quaint little French villages that begin to show themselves as you penetrate further down into Lower Canada. These look so peaceful, with their dormer-windowed cottages clustering about their church-spires, that it seems impossible they could once have been the homes of the savages and the cruel peasants, who with firebrand and scalping-knife and tomahawk harassed the borders of New England for a hundred years. But just after you descend the Long Sault you pass the hamlet of St. Regis, in which was kindled the torch that wrapt Deerfield in flames, waking her people from their sleep to meet instant death or taste the bitterness of a captivity. The bell which was sent out from France for the Indian converts of the Jesuits, and was captured by an English ship and carried into Salem, and thence sold to Deerfield, where it called the Puritans to prayer, till at last it also summoned the priest-led Indians and *habitans* across hundreds of miles of winter and of wilderness to reclaim it from that desecration,—this fateful bell still hangs in the church-tower of St. Regis, and has invited to matins and vespers for nearly two centuries the children of those who fought so pitilessly and dared and endured so much for it. Our friends would fain have heard it as they passed, hoping for some mournful note of history in its sound; but it hung silent over the silent hamlet, which, as it lay in the hot afternoon sun by the river's side, seemed as lifeless as the Deerfield burnt long ago.

They turned from it to look at a gentleman who had just appeared in a mustard-colored linen duster, and Basil asked, "Shouldn't you like to know the origin, personal history, and secret feelings of a gentleman who goes about in a duster of that particular tint? Or, that gentleman yonder with his eye tied up in a wet handkerchief, do you suppose he's travelling for pleassure? Look at those young people from Omaha: they haven't ceased flirting or cackling since we left Kingston. Do you think everybody has such spirits out at Omaha? But behold a yet more surprising figure than any we have yet seen among this boat-load of nondescripts!"

This was a tall, handsome young man, with a face of somewhat foreign cast, and well dressed, with a certain impressive difference from the rest in the cut of his clothes. But what most drew the eye to him was a large cross, set with brilliants, and surmounted by a heavy double-headed eagle in gold. This ornament dazzled from a conspicuous place on the left lappel of his coat; on his hand shone a magnificent diamond ring, and he bore a stately opera-glass, with which, from time to time, he imperiously, as one may say, surveyed the landscape. As the imposing apparition grew upon Isabel, "O here," she thought, "is something truly distinguished. Of course, dear," she added aloud to Basil, "he's some foreign nobleman travelling here"; and she ran over in her mind the newspaper announcements of patrician visitors from abroad, and tried to identify him with some one of them. The cross must be the decoration of a foreign order, and Basil suggested that he was perhaps a member of some legation at Washington, who had run up there for his summer vacation. The cross puzzled him, but the double-headed eagle, he said, meant either Austria or Russia; probably Austria, for the wearer looked a trifle too civilized for a Russian.

"Yes, indeed! What an air he *has*. Never tell *me*, Basil, that there's nothing in *blood!*" cried Isabel, who was a bitter aristocrat at heart, like all her sex, though in principle she was democratic enough. As she spoke, the object of her regard looked about him on the different groups, not with pride, not with hauteur, but with a glance of unconscious, unmistakable superiority. "O, that stare!" she added; "nothing but high birth and long descent can give it! Dearest, he's becoming a great affliction to me. I want to know who he is. Couldn't you invent some pretext for speaking to him?"

"No, I couldn't do it decently; and no doubt he'd snub me as I deserved if I intruded upon him. Let's wait for fortune to reveal him."

"Well, I suppose I must, but it's dreadful; it's really dreadful. You can easily see *that's* distinction," she continued, as her hero moved about the promenade and gently but loftily made a way for himself among the other passengers and favored the scenery through his opera-glass from one point and another. He spoke to no one, and she reasonably supposed that he did not know English.

In the mean time it was drawing near the hour of dinner, but no dinner appeared. Twelve, one, two came and went, and then at last came the dinner, which had been delayed, it seemed, till the cook could recruit his energies sufficiently to meet the wants of double the number he had expected to provide for. It was observable of the officers and crew of the Banshee, that while they did not hold themselves aloof from the passengers in the disdainful American manner, they were of feeble mind, and not only did everything very slowly (in the usual Canadian fashion), but with an inefficiency that among us would have justified them in being insolent. The people sat down at several successive tables to the worst dinner that ever was cooked; the ladies first, and the gentlemen afterwards, as they made conquest of places. At the second table, to Basil's great satisfaction, he found a seat, and on his right hand the distinguished foreigner.

"Naturally, I was somewhat abashed," he said in the account he was presently called to give Isabel of the interview, "but I remembered that I was an American citizen, and tried to maintain a decent composure. For several minutes we sat silent behind a dish of flabby cucumbers, expecting the dinner, and I was wondering whether I should address him in French or German,

—for I knew you'd never forgive me if I let slip such a chance,— when he turned and spoke himself."

"O *what* did he say, dearest?"

"He said, 'Pretty tejious waitin', ain't it?' in the best New York State accent."

"You don't mean it!" gasped Isabel.

"But I do. After that I took courage to ask what his cross and double-headed eagle meant. He showed the condescension of a true nobleman. 'O,' says he, 'I'm glad you like it, and it's not the least offence to ask,' and he told me. Can you imagine what it is? It's the emblem of the fifty-fourth degree in the secret society he belongs to!"

"I don't believe it!"

"Well, ask him yourself, then," returned Basil; "he's a very good fellow. 'O, that stare! nothing but high birth and long descent could give it!' " he repeated, abominably implying that he had himself had no share in their common error.

What retort Isabel might have made cannot now be known, for she was arrested at this moment by a rumor amongst the passengers that they were coming to the Long Sault Rapids. Looking forward she saw the tossing and flashing of surges that, to the eye, are certainly as threatening as the rapids above Niagara. The steamer had already passed the Deplau and the Galopes, and they had thus had a foretaste of whatever pleasure or terror there is in the descent of these nine miles of stormy sea. It is purely a matter of taste, about shooting the rapids of the St. Lawrence. The passengers like it better than the captain and the pilot, to guess by their looks, and the women and children like it better than the men. It is no doubt very thrilling and picturesque and wildly beautiful: the children crow and laugh, the women shout forth their delight, as the boat enters the seething current; great foaming waves strike her bows, and brawl away to the stern, while she dips, and rolls, and shoots onward, light as a bird blown by the wind; the wild shores and islands whirl out of sight; you feel in every fibre the career of the vessel. But the captain sits in front of the pilot-house smoking with a grave face, the pilots tug hard at the wheel; the hoarse roar of the waters fills the air; beneath the smoother sweeps of the current you can see the brown rocks; as you sink from ledge to ledge in the writhing and twisting steamer, you have a vague sense that all this is perhaps an achievement rather than an enjoyment. When, descending the Long Sault, you look back up hill, and behold those billows leaping down the steep slope after you, "No doubt," you confide to your soul, "it is magnificent; but it is not pleasure." You greet with silent satisfaction the level river, stretching between the Long Sault and the Coteau, and you admire the delightful tranquillity of that beautiful Lake St. Francis into which it expands. Then the boat shudders into the Coteau Rapids, and down through the Cedars and Cascades. On the rocks of the last lies the skeleton of a steamer wrecked upon them, and gnawed at still by the white-tusked wolfish rapids. No one, they say, was lost from her. "But how," Basil thought, "would it fare with all these people packed here upon her bow, if the Banshee should swing round upon a ledge?" As to Isabel, she looked upon the wrecked steamer with indifference, as did all the women; but then they could not swim, and would not have to save themselves. "The La Chine's to come yet," they exulted, "and that's the awfullest of all!"

They passed the Lake St. Louis; the La Chine Rapids flashed into sight. The captain rose up from his seat, took his pipe from his mouth, and waved a silence with it. "Ladies and gentlemen," said he, "it's very important in passing these rapids to keep the boat perfectly trim. Please to remain just as you are."

It was twilight, for the boat was late. From the Indian village on the shore they signalled to know if he wanted the local pilot; the captain refused; and then the steamer plunged into the leaping waves. From rock to rock she swerved and sank; on the last ledge she scraped with a deadly touch that went to the heart.

Then the danger was passed, and the noble city of Montreal was in full sight, lying at the foot of her dark green mountain, and lifting her many spires into the rosy twilight air: massive and grand showed the sister towers of the French cathedral.

Basil had hoped to approach this famous city with just associations. He had meant to conjure up for Isabel's sake some reflex, however faint, of that beautiful picture Mr. Parkman has painted of Maisonneuve founding and consecrating Montreal. He flushed with the recollection of the historian's phrase; but in that moment there came forth from the cabin a pretty young person who gave every token of being a pretty young actress, even to the duenna-like, elderly female companion, to be detected in the remote background of every young actress. She had flirted audaciously during the day with some young Englishmen and Canadians of her acquaintance, and after passing the La Chine Rapids she had taken the hearts of all the men by springing suddenly to her feet, apostrophizing the tumult with a charming attitude, and warbling a delicious bit of song. Now as they drew near the city the Victoria Bridge stretched its long tube athwart the river, and looked so low because of its great length that it seemed to bar the steamer's passage.

"I wonder," said one of the actress's adorers,—a Canadian, whose face was exactly that of the beaver on the escutcheon of his native province, and whose heavy gallantries she had constantly received with a gay, impertinent nonchalance,—"I wonder if we can be going right under that bridge?"

"No, sir!" answered the pretty young actress with shocking promptness, "we're going right over it:

> "Three groans and a guggle,
> And an awful struggle,
> And over we go!"

At this witless, sweet impudence the Canadian looked very sheepish—for a beaver; and all the other people laughed; but the noble historical shades of Basil's thought vanished in wounded dignity beyond recall, and left him feeling rather ashamed,—for he had laughed too.

VIII

THE SENTIMENT OF MONTREAL

THE FEELING of foreign travel for which our tourists had striven throughout their journey, and which they had known in some degree at Kingston and all the way down the river, was intensified from the first moment in Montreal; and it was so welcome that they were almost glad to lose money on their greenbacks, which the conductor of the omnibus would take only at a discount of twenty cents. At breakfast next morning they could hardly tell on what country they had fallen. The waiters had but a thin varnish of English speech upon their native French, and they spoke their own tongue with each other; but most of the meats were cooked to the English taste, and the whole was a poor imitation of an American hotel. During their stay the same commingling of usages and races bewildered them; the shops were English and the clerks were commonly French; the carriage-drivers were often Irish, and up and down the streets with their pious old-fashioned names, tinkled American horse-cars. Everywhere were churches and convents that recalled the ecclesiastical and feudal origin of the city; the great tubular bridge, the superb water-front with its long array of docks only surpassed by those of Liverpool, the solid blocks of business houses, and the substantial mansions on the quieter streets, proclaimed the succession of Protestant thrift and energy.

Our friends cared far less for the modern splendor of Montreal than for the remnants of its past, and for the features that identified it with another faith and another people than their own. Isabel would almost have confessed to any one of the black-robed

priests upon the street; Basil could easily have gone down upon
his knees to the white-hooded, pale-faced nuns gliding among
the crowd. It was rapture to take a carriage, and drive, not to the
cemetery, not to the public library, not to the rooms of the Young
Men's Christian Association, or the grain elevators, or the new
park just tricked out with rockwork and sprigs of evergreen,—
not to any of the charming resorts of our own cities, but as in
Europe to the churches, the churches of a pitiless superstition, the
churches with their atrocious pictures and statues, their lingering smell of the morning's incense, their confessionals, their fee-
taking sacristans, their worshippers dropped here and there upon
their knees about the aisles, and saying their prayers with shut
or wandering eyes according as they were old women or young!
I do not defend the feeble sentimentality,—call it wickedness if
you like,—but I understand it, and I forgive it from my soul.

They went first, of course, to the French cathedral, pausing
on their way to alight and walk through the Bonsecours Market,
where the *habitans* have all come in their carts, with their various
stores of poultry, fruit, and vegetables, and where every cart is a
study. Here is a simple-faced young peasant-couple with butter
and eggs and chickens ravishingly displayed; here is a smooth-
cheeked, black-eyed, black-haired young girl, looking as if an
infusion of Indian blood had darkened the red of her cheeks,
presiding over a stock of onions, potatoes, beets, and turnips;
there an old woman with a face carven like a walnut behind a
flattering array of cherries and pears; yonder a whole family
trafficking in loaves of brown-bread and maple-sugar in many
shapes of pious and grotesque device. There are gay shows of
bright scarfs and kerchiefs and vari-colored yarns, and sad shows
of old clothes and second-hand merchandise of other sorts; but
above all prevails the abundance of orchard and garden, while
within the fine edifice are the stalls of the butchers, and in the
basement below a world of household utensils, glass-ware, hard-
ware, and wooden-ware. As in other Latin countries, each
peasant has given a personal interest to his wares, but the bar-
gains are not clamored over as in Latin lands abroad. Whatever

protest and concession and invocation of the saints attend the transaction of business at Bonsecours Market are in a subdued tone. The fat huckster-women drowsing beside their wares, scarce send their voices beyond the borders of their broad-brimmed straw hats, as they softly haggle with purchasers, or tranquilly gossip together.

At the cathedral there are, perhaps, the worst paintings in the world, and the massive pine-board pillars are unscrupulously smoked to look like marble; but our tourists enjoyed it as if it had been St. Peter's; in fact it has something of the barn-like immensity and impressiveness of St. Peter's. They did not ask it to be beautiful or grand; they desired it only to recall the beloved ugliness, the fondly cherished hideousness and incongruity of the average Catholic churches of their remembrance, and it did this and more: it added an effect of its own; it offered the spectacle of a swarthy old Indian kneeling before the high altar, telling his beads, and saying with many sighs and tears the prayers which it cost so much martyrdom and heroism to teach his race. "O, it is only a savage man," said the little French boy who was showing them the place, impatient of their interest in a thing so unworthy as this groaning barbarian. He ran swiftly about from object to object, rapidly lecturing their inattention. "It is now time to go up into the tower," said he, and they gladly made that toilsome ascent, though it is doubtful if the ascent of towers is not too much like the ascent of mountains ever to be compensatory. From the top of Notre Dame is certainly to be had a prospect upon which, but for his fluttered nerves and trembling muscles and troubled respiration, the traveller might well look with delight, and as it is must behold with wonder. So far as the eye reaches it dwells only upon what is magnificent. All the features of that landscape are grand. Below you spreads the city, which has less that is merely mean in it than any other city of our continent, and which is everywhere ennobled by stately civic edifices, adorned by tasteful churches, and skirted by full-foliaged avenues of mansions and villas. Behind it rises the beautiful mountain, green with woods and gardens to its crest, and flanked on the east by an endless fertile plain, and on the west by another expanse, through which the Ottawa rushes, turbid and dark, to its confluence with the St. Lawrence. Then these two mighty streams commingled flow past the city, lighting up the vast champagne country to the south, while upon the utmost southern verge, as on the northern, rise the cloudy summits of far-off mountains.

As our travellers gazed upon all this grandeur, their hearts were humbled to the tacit admission that the colonial metropolis was not only worthy of its seat, but had traits of a solid prosperity not excelled by any of the abounding and boastful cities of the Republic. Long before they quitted Montreal they had rallied from this weakness, but they delighted still to honor her superb beauty.

The tower is naturally bescribbled to its top with the names of those who have climbed it, and most of these are Americans, who flock in great numbers to Canada in summer. They modify its hotel life, and the objects of interest thrive upon their bounty. Our friends met them at every turn, and knew them at a glance from the native populations, who are also easily distinguishable from each other. The French Canadians are nearly always of a peasant-like commonness, or where they rise above this, have a bourgeois commonness of face and manner; and the English Canadians are to be known from the many English sojourners by the effort to look much more English than the latter. The social heart of the colony clings fast to the mother-country, that is plain, whatever the political tendency may be; and the public monuments and inscriptions celebrate this affectionate union.

At the English cathedral the effect is deepened by the epitaphs of those whose lives were passed in the joint service of England and her loyal child; and our travellers, whatever their want of sympathy with the sentiment, had to own to a certain beauty in that attitude of proud reverence. Here, at least, was a people not cut off from its past, but holding, unbroken in life and death, the ties which exist for us only in history. It gave a glamour of olden

time to the new land; it touched the prosaic democratic present
with the waning poetic light of the aristocratic and monarchical
tradition. There was here and there a title on the tablets, and
there was everywhere the formal language of loyalty and of
veneration for things we have tumbled into the dust. It is a beautiful church, of admirable English Gothic; if you are so happy,
you are rather curtly told you may enter by a burly English figure
in some kind of sombre ecclesiastical drapery, and within its
quiet precincts you may feel yourself in England if you like,—
which, for my part, I do not. Neither did our friends enjoy it so
much as the Church of the Jesuits, with its more than tolerable
painting, its coldly frescoed ceiling, its architectural taste of subdued Renaissance, and its black-eyed peasant-girl telling her
beads before a side altar, just as in the enviably deplorable countries we all love; nor so much even as the Irish cathedral which
they next visited. That is a very gorgeous cathedral indeed,
painted and gilded *à merveille*, and everywhere stuck about with
big and little saints and crucifixes, and pictures incredibly bad—
but for those in the French cathedral. There is, of course, a series
representing Christ's progress to Calvary; and there was a very
tattered old man,—an old man whose voice had been long ago
drowned in whiskey, and who now spoke in a ghostly whisper,—
who, when he saw Basil's eye fall upon the series, made him go
the round of them, and tediously explained them.

"Why did you let that old wretch bore you, and then pay him
for it?" Isabel asked.

"O, it reminded me so sweetly of the swindles of other lands
and days, that I couldn't help it," he answered; and straightway
in the eyes of both that poor, whiskeyfied, Irish tatterdemalion
stood transfigured to the glorious likeness of an Italian beggar.

They were always doing something of this kind, those absurdly sentimental people, whom yet I cannot find it in my heart to
blame for their folly, though I could name ever so many reasons
for rebuking it. Why, in fact, should we wish to find America like
Europe? Are the ruins and impostures and miseries and superstitions which beset the traveller abroad so precious, that he

should desire to imagine them at every step in his own hemisphere? Or have we then of our own no effective shapes of ignorance and want and incredibility, that we must forever seek an alien contrast to our native intelligence and comfort? Some such questions this guilty couple put to each other, and then drove off to visit the convent of the Gray Nuns with a joyful expectation which I suppose the prospect of the finest public-school exhibition in Boston could never have inspired. But, indeed, since there must be Gray Nuns, is it not well that there are sentimentalists to take a mournful pleasure in their sad, pallid existence?

The convent is at a good distance from the Irish cathedral, and in going to it the tourists made their driver carry them through one of the few old French streets which still remain in Montreal. Fires and improvements had made havoc among the quaint houses since Basil's first visit; but at last they came upon a narrow, ancient Rue Saint Antoine,—or whatever other saint it was called after,—in which there was no English face or house to be seen. The doors of the little one-story dwellings opened from the pavement, and within you saw fat madame the mother moving about her domestic affairs, and spare monsieur the elderly husband smoking beside the open window; French babies crawled about the tidy floors; French martyrs (let us believe Lalement or Brébeuf, who gave up their heroic lives for the conversion of Canada) lifted their eyes in high-colored lithographs on the wall; among the flower-pots in the dormer-window looking from every tin roof sat and sewed a smooth-haired young girl, I hope,—the romance of each little mansion. The antique and foreign character of the place was accented by the inscription upon a wall of "Sirop adoucissant de Madame Winslow."

Ever since 1692 the Gray Nuns have made a refuge within the ample borders of their convent for infirm old people and for foundling children, and it is now in the regular course of sight-seeing for the traveller to visit their hospital at noonday, when he beholds the Sisters at their devotions in the chapel. It is a bare, white-walled, cold-looking chapel, with the usual paraphernalia of pictures and crucifixes. Seated upon low benches on either side of the aisle were the curious or the devout; the former in greater number and chiefly Americans, who were now and then whispered silent by an old pauper zealous for the sanctity of the place. At the stroke of twelve the Sisters entered two by two, followed by the lady-superior with a prayer-book in her hand. She clapped the leaves of this together in signal for them to kneel, to rise, to kneel again and rise, while they repeated in rather harsh voices their prayers, and then clattered out of the chapel as they had clattered in, with resounding shoes. The two young girls at the head were very pretty, and all the pale faces had a corpse-like peace. As Basil looked at their pensive sameness, it seemed to him that those prettiest girls might very well be the twain that he had seen there so many years ago, stricken forever young in their joyless beauty. The ungraceful gowns of coarse gray, the blue checked aprons, the black crape caps, were the same; they came and went with the same quick tread, touching their brows with holy water and kneeling and rising now as then with the same constrained and ordered movements. Would it be too cruel if they were really the same persons? or would it be yet more cruel if every year two girls so young and fair were self-doomed to renew the likeness of that youthful death?

The visitors went about the hospital, and saw the old men and the little children to whom these good pure lives were given, and they could only blame the system, not the instruments or their work. Perhaps they did not judge wisely of the amount of self-sacrifice involved, for they judged from hearts to which love was the whole of earth and heaven; but nevertheless they pitied the Gray Nuns amidst the unhomelike comfort of their convent, the unnatural care of those alien little ones. Poor Sœurs Grises! in their narrow cells; at the bedside of sickness and age and sorrow; kneeling with clasped hands and yearning eyes before the bloody spectacle of the cross!—the power of your Church is shown far more subtly and mightily in such as you, than in her grandest fanes or the sight of her most august ceremonies, with praying priests, swinging censers, tapers and pictures and images, under a gloomy heaven of cathedral arches. There, indeed, the faithful have given their substance; but here the nun has given up the most precious part of her woman's nature, and all the tenderness that clings about the thought of wife and mother.

"There are some things that always greatly afflict me in the idea of a new country," said Basil, as they loitered slowly through the grounds of the convent towards the gate. "Of course, it's absurd to think of men as other than men, as having changed their natures with their skies; but a new land always does seem at first thoughts like a new chance afforded the race for goodness and happiness, for health and life. So I grieve for the earliest dead at Plymouth more than for the multitude that the plague swept away in London; I shudder over the crime of the first guilty man, the sin of the first wicked woman in a new country; the trouble of the first youth or maiden crossed in love there is intolerable. All should be hope and freedom and prosperous life upon that virgin soil. It never was so since Eden; but none the less I feel it ought to be; and I am oppressed by the thought that among the earliest walls which rose upon this broad meadow of Montreal were those built to immure the innocence of such young girls as these, and shut them from the life we find so fair. Wouldn't you like to know who was the first that took the veil in this wild new country? Who was she, poor soul, and what was her deep sorrow or lofty rapture? You can fancy her some Indian maiden lured to the renunciation by the splendor of symbols and promises seen vaguely through the lingering mists of her native superstitions; or some weary soul, sick from the vanities and vices, the bloodshed and the tears of the Old World, and eager for a silence profounder than that of the wilderness into which she had fled. Well, the Church knows and God. She was dust long ago."

From time to time there had fallen little fitful showers during the morning. Now as the wedding-journeyers passed out of the convent gate the rain dropped soft and thin, and the gray clouds that floated through the sky so swiftly were as far-seen Gray Sisters in flight for heaven.

"We shall have time for the drive round the mountain before dinner," said Basil, as they got into their carriage again; and he was giving the order to the driver, when Isabel asked how far it was.

"Nine miles."

"O, then we can't think of going with one horse. You know," she added, "that we always intended to have two horses for going round the mountain."

"No," said Basil, not yet used to having his decisions reached without his knowledge. "And I don't see why we should. Everybody goes with one. You don't suppose we're too heavy, do you?"

"I had a party from the States, ma'am, yesterday," interposed the driver; "two ladies, real heavy ones, two gentlemen, weighin' two hundred apiece, and a stout young man on the box with me. You'd 'a' thought the horse was drawin' an empty carriage, the way she darted along."

"Then his horse must be perfectly worn out to-day," said Isabel, refusing to admit the poor fellow directly even to the honors of a defeat. He had proved too much, and was put out of court with no hope of repairing his error.

"Why, it seems a pity," whispered Basil, dispassionately, "to turn this man adrift, when he had a reasonable hope of being with us all day, and has been so civil and obliging."

"O yes, Basil, sentimentalize him, do! Why don't you sentimentalize his helpless, overworked horse?—all in a reek of perspiration."

"Perspiration! Why, my dear, it's the rain!"

"Well, rain or shine, darling, I don't want to go round the mountain with one horse; and it's very unkind of you to insist now, when you've tacitly promised me all along to take two."

"Now, this is a little too much, Isabel. You know we never mentioned the matter till this moment."

"It's the same as a promise, your not saying you wouldn't. But I don't *ask* you to keep your word. *I* don't want to go round the mountain. I'd *much* rather go to the hotel. I'm tired."

"Very well, then, Isabel, I'll leave you at the hotel."

In a moment it had come, the first serious dispute of their wedded life. It had come as all such calamities come, from nothing, and it was on them in full disaster ere they knew. Such a very little while ago, there in the convent garden, their lives had been drawn closer in sympathy than ever before; and now that blessed time seemed ages since, and they were further asunder than those who have never been friends. "I thought," bitterly mused Isabel, "that he would have done anything for me." "Who could have dreamed that a woman of her sense would be so unreasonable," he wondered. Both had tempers, as I know my dearest reader has (if a lady), and neither would yield; and so, presently, they could hardly tell how, for they were aghast at it all, Isabel was alone in her room amidst the ruins of her life, and Basil alone in the one-horse carriage, trying to drive away from the wreck of his happiness. All was over; the dream was past; the charm was broken. The sweetness of their love was turned to gall; whatever had pleased them in their loving moods was loathsome now, and the things they had praised a moment before were hateful. In that baleful light, which seemed to dwell upon all they ever said or did in mutual enjoyment, how poor and stupid and empty looked their wedding-journey! Basil spent five minutes in arraigning his wife and convicting her of every folly and fault. His soul was in a whirl,—

> "For to be wroth with one we love
> Doth work like madness in the brain."

In the midst of his bitter and furious upbraidings he found himself suddenly become her ardent advocate, and ready to denounce her judge as a heartless monster. "On our wedding journey, too! Good heavens, what an incredible brute I am!" Then he said, "What an ass I am!" And the pathos of the case having yielded to its absurdity, he was helpless. In five minutes more he was at Isabel's side, the one-horse carriage driver dismissed with a handsome *pour-boire,* and a pair of lusty bays with a glittering barouche waiting at the door below. He swiftly accounted for his presence, which she seemed to find the most natural thing that could be, and she met his surrender with the openness of a heart that forgives but does not forget, if indeed the most gracious art is the only one unknown to the sex.

She rose with a smile from the ruins of her life, amidst which she had heart-brokenly sat down with all her things on. "I knew you'd come back," she said.

"So did I," he answered. "I am much too good and noble to sacrifice my preference to my duty."

"I didn't care particularly for the two horses, Basil," she said, as they descended to the barouche. "It was your refusing them that hurt me."

"And I didn't want the one-horse carriage. It was your insisting so that provoked me."

"Do you think people *ever* quarrelled before on a wedding journey?" asked Isabel as they drove gayly out of the city.

"Never! I can't conceive of it. I suppose if this were written down, nobody would believe it."

"No, nobody could," said Isabel, musingly; and she added after a pause, "I wish you would tell me just what you thought of me, dearest. Did you feel as you did when our little affair was broken off, long ago? Did you hate me?"

"I did, most cordially; but not half so much as I despised myself the next moment. As to its being like a lover's quarrel, it wasn't. It was more bitter: so much more love than lovers ever give had to be taken back. Besides, it had no dignity, and a lover's quarrel always has. A lover's quarrel always springs from a more serious cause, and has an air of romantic tragedy. This had no grace of the kind. It was a poor shabby little squabble."

"O, don't call it so, Basil! I should like you to respect even a quarrel of ours more than that. It was tragical enough with me, for I didn't see how it could ever be made up. I knew *I* couldn't make the advances. I don't think it is quite feminine to be the first to forgive, is it?"

"I'm sure I can't say. Perhaps it *would* be rather unladylike."

"Well, you see, dearest, what I am trying to get at is this:

whether we shall love each other the more or the less for it. *I* think
we shall get on all the better for a while, on account of it. But I
should have said it was totally out of character. It's something
you might have expected of a very young bridal couple; but after
what we've been through, it seems too improbable."

"Very well," said Basil, who, having made all the concessions,
could not enjoy the quarrel as she did, simply because it was
theirs; "let's behave as if it had never been."

"O no, we can't. To me, it's as if we had just won each other."

In fact it gave a wonderful zest and freshness to that ride
round the mountain, and shed a beneficent glow upon the rest of
their journey. The sun came out through the thin clouds, and
lighted up the vast plain that swept away north and east, with
the purple heights against the eastern sky. The royal mountain
lifted its graceful mass beside them, and hid the city wholly from
sight. Peasant-villages, in the shade of beautiful elms, dotted the
plain in every direction, and at intervals crept up to the side of the
road along which they drove. But these had been corrupted by a
more ambitious architecture since Basil saw them last, and were
no longer purely French in appearance. Then, nearly every
house was a tannery in a modest way, and poetically published
the fact by the display of a sheep's tail over the front door, like a
bush at a wine-shop. Now, if the tanneries still existed, the poetry
of the sheep's tails had vanished from the portals. But our friends
were consoled by meeting numbers of the peasants jolting home
from market in the painted carts, which are doubtless of the
pattern of the carts first built there two hundred years ago. They
were grateful for the immortal old women, crooked and brown
with the labor of the fields, who abounded in these vehicles;
when a huge girl jumped from the tail of her cart, and showed the
thick, clumsy ankles of a true peasant-maid, they could only sigh
out their unspeakable satisfaction.

Gardens embowered and perfumed the low cottages, through
the open doors of which they could see the exquisite neatness of
the life within. One of the doors opened into a school-house,
where they beheld with rapture the schoolmistress, book in hand,

and with a quaint cap on her gray head, and encircled by her flock of little boys and girls.

By and by it began to rain again; and now while their driver stopped to put up the top of the barouche, they entered a country church which had taken their fancy, and walked up the aisle with the steps that blend with silence rather than break it, while they heard only the soft whisper of the shower without. There was no one there but themselves. The urn of holy water seemed not to have been troubled that day, and no penitent knelt at the shrine, before which twinkled so faintly one lighted lamp. The white roof swelled into dim arches over their heads; the pale day like a visible hush stole through the painted windows; they heard themselves breathe as they crept from picture to picture.

A narrow door opened at the side of the high altar, and a slender young priest appeared in a long black robe, and with shaven head. He, too, as he moved with noiseless feet, seemed a part of the silence; and when he approached with dreamy black eyes fixed upon them, and bowed courteously, it seemed impossible he should speak. But he spoke, the pale young priest, the dark-robed tradition, the tonsured vision of an age and a church that are passing.

"Do you understand French, monsieur?"

"A very little, monsieur."

"A very little is more than my English," he said, yet he politely went the round of the pictures with them, and gave them the names of the painters between his crossings at the different altars. At the high altar there was a very fair Crucifixion; before this the priest bent one knee. "Fine picture, fine altar, fine church," he said in English. At last they stopped near the poor-box. As their coins clinked against those within, he smiled serenely upon the good heretics. Then he bowed, and, as if he had relapsed into the past, he vanished through the narrow door by which he had entered.

Basil and Isabel stood speechless a moment on the church steps. Then she cried,—

"O, why *did*n't something happen?"

"Ah, my dear! what could have been half so good as the noth-ing that did happen? Suppose we knew him to have taken orders because of a disappointment in love: how common it would have made him; everybody has been crossed in love once or twice." He bade the driver take them back to the hotel. "This is the very *bouquet* of adventure: why should we care for the grosser body? I dare say if we knew all about yonder pale young priest, we should not think him half so interesting as we do now."

At dinner they spent the intervals of the courses in guessing the nationality of the different persons, and in wondering if the Canadians did not make it a matter of conscientious loyalty to out-English the English even in the matter of pale-ale and sherry, and in rotundity of person and freshness of face, just as they emu-lated them in the cut of their clothes and whiskers. Must they found even their health upon the health of the mother-country?

Our friends began to detect something servile in it all, and but that they were such amiable persons, the loyally perfect di-gestion of Montreal would have gone far to impair their own.

The loyalty, which had already appeared to them in the cathedral, suggested itself in many ways upon the street, when they went out after dinner to do that little shopping which Isabel had planned to do in Montreal. The booksellers' windows were full of Canadian editions of our authors, and English copies of English works, instead of our pirated editions; the dry-goods stores were gay with fabrics in the London taste and garments of the London shape; here was the sign of a photographer to the Queen, there of a hatter to H. R. H., the Prince of Wales; a barber was "under the patronage of H. R. H., the Prince of Wales, H. E., the Duke of Cambridge, and the gentry of Mon-treal." *Ich dien* was the motto of a restaurateur; a hosier had gal-lantly labelled his stock in trade with *Honi soit qui mal y pense.* Again they noted the English solidity of the civic edifices, and already they had observed in the foreign population a difference from that at home. They saw no German faces on the streets, and the Irish faces had not that truculence which they wear some-times with us. They had not lost their native simpleness and kindliness; the Irishmen who drove the public carriages were as civil as our own Boston hackmen, and behaved as respectfully under the shadow of England here, as they would have done under it in Ireland. The problem which vexes us seems to have been solved pleasantly enough in Canada. Is it because the Celt cannot brook equality; and where he has not an established and recognized caste above him, longs to trample on those about him; and if he cannot be lowest, will at least be highest?

However, our friends did not suffer this or any other advantage of the colonial relation to divert them from the opinion to which their observation was gradually bringing them, that its overweening loyalty placed a great country like Canada in a very silly attitude, the attitude of an overgrown, unmanly boy, clinging to the maternal skirts, and though spoilt and wilful, without any character of his own. The constant reference of local hopes to that remote centre beyond seas, the test of success by the criterions of a necessarily different civilization, the social and intellectual dependence implied by traits that meet the most hurried glance in the Dominion, give an effect of meanness to the whole fabric. Doubtless it is a life of comfort, of peace, of irresponsibility they live there, but it lacks the grandeur which no sum of material prosperity can give; it is ignoble, like all voluntarily subordinate things. Somehow, one feels that it has no basis in the New World, and that till it is shaken loose from England it cannot have.

It would be a pity, however, if it should be parted from the parent country merely to be joined to an unsympathetic halfbrother like ourselves; and nothing, fortunately, seems to be further from the Canadian mind. There are some experiments no longer possible to us which could still be tried there to the advantage of civilization, and we were better two great nations side by side than a union of discordant traditions and ideas. But none the less does the American traveller, swelling with forgetfulness of the shabby despots who govern New York, and the swindling railroad kings whose word is law to the whole land, feel like saying to the hulking young giant beyond St. Lawrence and the Lakes,

"Sever the apron-strings of allegiance, and try to be yourself, whatever you are."

Something of this sort Basil said, though of course not in apostrophic phrase, nor with Isabel's entire concurrence, when he explained to her that it was to the colonial dependence of Canada she owed the ability to buy things so cheaply there.

The fact is that the ladies' parlor at the hotel had been after dinner no better than a den of smugglers, in which the fair contra-bandists had debated the best means of evading the laws of their country. At heart every man is a smuggler, and how much more every woman! She would have no scruple in ruining the silk and woollen interest throughout the United States. She is a free-trader by intuitive perception of right, and is limited in practice by nothing but fear of the statute. What could be taken into the States without detection, was the subject before that wicked con-clave; and next, what it would pay to buy in Canada. It seemed that silk umbrellas were most eligible wares; and in the display of such purchases the parlor was given the appearance of a vio-lent thunder-storm. Gloves it was not advisable to get; they were better at home, as were many kinds of fine woollen goods. But laces, which you could carry about you, were excellent; and so was any kind of silk. Could it be carried if simply cut, and not made up? There was a difference about this: the friend of one lady had taken home half a trunkful of cut silks; the friend of another had "run up the breadths" of one lone little silk skirt, and then lost it by the rapacity of the customs officers. It was pretty much luck, and whether the officers happened to be in good-humor or not. You must not try to take in anything out of season, however. One had heard of a Boston lady going home in July, who "had the furs taken off her back," in that inclement month. Best get everything seasonable, and put it on at once. "And then, you know, if they ask you, you can say it's been worn." To this black wisdom came the combined knowledge of those miscreants. Basil could not repress a shudder at the innate depravity of the female heart. Here were virgins nurtured in the most spotless purity of life, here were virtuous mothers of families, here were venerable matrons, patterns in society and the church, —smugglers to a woman, and eager for any guilty subterfuge! He glanced at Isabel to see what effect the evil conversation had upon her. Her eyes sparkled; her cheeks glowed; all the woman was on fire for smuggling. He sighed heavily and went out with her to do the little shopping.

Shall I follow them upon their excursion? Shopping in Montreal is very much what it is in Boston or New York, I imagine, except that the clerks have a more honeyed sweetness of manners towards the ladies of our nation, and are surprisingly generous constructionists of our revenue laws. Isabel had profited by every word that she had heard in the ladies' parlor, and she would not venture upon unsafe ground; but her tender eyes looked her unutterable longing to believe in the charming possibilities that the clerks suggested. She bemoaned herself before the corded silks, which there was no time to have made up; the piece-velvets and the linens smote her to the heart. But they also stimulated her invention, and she bought and bought of the made-up wares in real or fancied needs, till Basil represented that neither their purses nor their trunks could stand any more. "O, don't be troubled about the trunks, dearest," she cried, with that gayety which nothing but shopping can kindle in a woman's heart; while he faltered on from counter to counter, wondering at which he should finally swoon from fatigue. At last, after she had declared repeatedly, "There, now, I *am* done," she briskly led the way back to the hotel to pack up her purchases.

Basil parted with her at the door. He was a man of high principle himself, and that scene in the smugglers' den, and his wife's preparation for transgression, were revelations for which nothing could have consoled him but a paragon umbrella for five dollars and an excellent business suit of Scotch goods for twenty.

When some hours later he sat with Isabel on the forward promenade of the steamboat for Quebec, and summed up the profits of their shopping, they were both in the kindliest mood towards the poor Canadians, who had built the admirable city before them.

For miles the water front of Montreal is superbly faced with quays and locks of solid stone masonry, and thus she is clean and beautiful to the very feet. Stately piles of architecture, instead of the foul old tumble-down warehouses that dishonor the water-side in most cities, rise from the broad wharves; behind these spring the twin towers of Notre Dame, and the steeples of the other churches above the city roofs.

"It's noble, yes, it's noble, after the best that Europe can show," said Isabel, with enthusiasm; "and what a pleasant day we've had here! Doesn't even our quarrel show *couleur de rose* in this light?"

"One side of it," answered Basil, dreamily, "but all the rest is black."

"What do you mean, my dear?"

"Why, the Nelson Monument, with the sunset on it, at the head of the street there."

The effect was so fine that Isabel could not be angry with him for failing to heed what she had said, and she mused a moment with him.

"It seems rather far-fetched," she said presently, "to erect a monument to Nelson in Montreal, doesn't it? But then, it's a very absurd monument when you're near it," she added, thoughtfully.

Basil did not answer at once, for gazing on this Nelson column in Jacques Cartier Square, his thoughts wandered away, not to the hero of the Nile, but to the doughty old Breton navigator, the first white man who ever set foot upon that shore, and who more than three hundred years ago explored the St. Lawrence as far as Montreal, and in the splendid autumn weather climbed to the top of her green height and named it. The scene that Jacques Cartier then beheld, like a mirage of the past projected upon the present, floated before him, and he saw at the mountain's foot the Indian city of Hochelaga, with its vast and populous lodges of bark, its encircling palisades, and its wide outlying fields of yellow maize. He heard with Jacques Cartier's sense the blare of his followers' trumpets down in the open square of the barbarous city, where the soldiers of many an Old-World fight, "with moustached lip and bearded chin, with arquebuse and glittering halberd, helmet, and cuirass," moved among the plumed and painted savages; then he lifted Jacques Cartier's eyes, and looked out upon the magnificent landscape. "East, west, and south, the mantling forest was over all, and the broad blue ribbon of the great river glistened amid a realm of verdure. Beyond, to the bounds of Mexico, stretched a leafy desert, and the vast hive of industry, the mighty battle-ground of later centuries, lay sunk in savage torpor, wrapped in illimitable woods."

A vaguer picture of Champlain, who, seeking a westward route to China and the East, some three quarters of a century later, had fixed the first trading-post at Montreal, and camped upon the spot where the convent of the Gray Nuns now stands, appeared before him, and vanished with all its fleets of fur-traders' boats and hunters' birch canoes, and the watch-fires of both; and then in the sweet light of the spring morning, he saw Maisonneuve leaping ashore upon the green meadows, that spread all gay with early flowers where Hochelaga once stood, and with the black-robed Jesuits, the high-born, delicately nurtured, and devoted nuns, and the steel-clad soldiers of his train, kneeling about the altar raised there in the wilderness, and silent amidst the silence of nature at the lifted Host.

He painted a semblance of all this for Isabel, using the colors of the historian who has made these scenes the beautiful in-heritance of all dreamers, and sketched the battles, the miracles, the sufferings, and the penances through which the pious colony was preserved and prospered, till they both grew impatient of modern Montreal, and would fain have had the ancient Ville-marie back in its place.

"Think of Maisonneuve, dearest, climbing in mid-winter to the top of the mountain there, under a heavy cross set with the bones of saints, and planting it on the summit, in fulfilment of a vow to do so if Villemarie were saved from the freshet; and then of Madame de la Peltrie romantically receiving the sacrament there, while all Villemarie fell down adoring! Ah, that was a picturesque people! When did ever a Boston governor climb to the top of Beacon Hill in fulfilment of a vow? To be sure, we may yet see a New York governor doing something of the kind—if he can find a hill. But this ridiculous column to Nelson, who never had anything to do with Montreal," he continued; "it really seems to me the perfect expression of snobbish colonial dependence and sentimentality, seeking always to identify itself with the mother-country, and ignoring the local past and its heroic figures. A column to Nelson in Jacques Cartier Square, on the ground that was trodden by Champlain, and won for its present masters by the death of Wolfe!"

The boat departed on her trip to Quebec. During supper they were served by French waiters, who, without apparent English of their own, miraculously understood that of the passengers, except in the case of the furious gentleman who wanted English breakfast tea; to so much English as that their inspiration did not reach, and they forced him to compromise on coffee. It was a French boat, owned by a French company, and seemed to be officered by Frenchmen throughout; certainly, as our tourists in the joy of their good appetites affirmed, the cook was of that culinarily delightful nation.

The boat was almost as large as those of the Hudson, but it was not so lavishly splendid, though it had everything that could minister to the comfort and self-respect of the passengers. These were of all nations, but chiefly Americans, with some French Canadians. The former gathered on the forward promenade, enjoying what little of the landscape the growing night left visible, and the latter made society after their manner in the saloon. They were plain-looking men and women, mostly, and provincial, it was evident, to their inmost hearts; provincial in origin, provincial by inheritance, by all their circumstances, social and political. Their relation with France was not a proud one, but it was not like submersion by the slip-slop of English colonial loyalty; yet they seem to be troubled by no memories of their hundred years' dominion of the land that they rescued from the wilderness, and that was wrested from them by war.

It is a strange fate for any people thus to have been cut off from the parent-country, and abandoned to whatever destiny their conquerors chose to reserve for them; and if each of the race wore the sadness and strangeness of that fate in his countenance it would not be wonderful. Perhaps it is wonderful that none of them shows anything of the kind. In their desertion they have multiplied and prospered; they may have a national grief, but they hide it well; and probably they have none.

Later, one of them appeared to Isabel in the person of the pale, slender young ecclesiastic who had shown her and Basil the pictures in the country church. She was confessing to the priest, and she was not at all surprised to find that he was Basil in a suit of medieval armor. He had an immense cross on his shoulder.

"To get this cross to the top of the mountain," thought Isabel, "we must have two horses. Basil," she added, aloud, "we must have two horses!"

"Ten, if you like, my dear," answered his voice, cheerfully, "though I think we'd better ride up in the omnibus."

She opened her eyes, and saw him smiling. "We're in sight of Quebec," he said. "Come out as soon as you can,—come out into the seventeenth century."

IX

_____

QUEBEC

ISABEL hurried out upon the forward promenade, where all the other passengers seemed to be assembled, and beheld a vast bulk of gray and purple rock, swelling two hundred feet up from the mists of the river, and taking the early morning light warm upon its face and crown. Black-hulked, red-chimneyed Liverpool steamers, gay river-craft and ships of every sail and flag, filled the stream athwart which the ferries sped their swift traffic-laden shuttles; a lower town clung to the foot of the rock, and crept, populous and picturesque, up its sides; from the massive citadel on its crest flew the red banner of Saint George, and along its brow swept the gray wall of the famous, heroic, beautiful city, overtopped by many a gleaming spire and antique roof.

Slowly out of our work-day, business-suited, modern world the vessel steamed up to this city of an olden time and another ideal—to her who was a lady from the first, devout and proud and strong, and who still, after two hundred and fifty years, keeps perfect the image and memory of the feudal past from which she sprang. Upon her height she sits unique; and when you say Quebec, having once beheld her, you invoke a sense of medieval strangeness and of beauty which the name of no other city could intensify.

As they drew near the steamboat wharf they saw, swarming over a broad square, a market beside which the Bonsecours Market would have shown as common as the Quincy, and up the odd wooden-sidewalked street stretched an aisle of carriages and those high-swung calashes, which are to Quebec what the gondolas are to Venice. But the hand of destiny was upon our tourists, and they rode up town in an omnibus. They were going to the dear old Hotel Musty in —— Street, wanting which Quebec is not to be thought of without a pang. It is now closed, and Prescott Gate, through which they drove into the Upper Town, has been demolished since the summer of last year. Swiftly whirled along the steep winding road, by those Quebec horses which expect to gallop up hill, whatever they do going down, they turned a corner of the towering weed-grown rock, and shot in under the low arch of the gate, pierced with smaller doorways for the foot-passengers. The gloomy masonry dripped with damp, the doors were thickly studded with heavy iron spikes; old cannon, thrust endwise into the ground at the sides of the gate, protected it against passing wheels. Why did not some semiforbidding commissary of police, struggling hard to overcome his native politeness, appear and demand their passports? The illusion was otherwise perfect, and it needed but this touch. How often in the adored Old World, which we so love and disapprove, had they driven in through such gates at that morning hour! On what perverse pretext, then, was it not some ancient town of Normandy?

"Put a few enterprising Americans in here, and they'd soon rattle this old wall down, and let in a little fresh air!" said a patriotic voice at Isabel's elbow, and continued to find fault with the narrow, irregular streets, the huddling gables, the quaint roofs, through which and under which they drove on to the hotel.

As they dashed into a broad open square, "Here is the French Cathedral; there is the Upper Town Market; yonder are the Jesuit Barracks!" cried Basil; and they had a passing glimpse of gray stone towers at one side of the square, and a low, massive yellow building at the other, and, between the two, long ranks of carts, and fruit and vegetable stands, protected by canvas awnings and broad umbrellas. Then they dashed round the corner of a street, and drew up before the hotel door. The low ceilings, the thick walls, the clumsy wood-work, the wandering corridors, gave the hotel all the desired character of age, and its slovenly state bestowed an additional charm. In another place they might have demanded neatness, but in Quebec they would almost have resented it. By a chance they had the best room in the house, but they held it only till certain people who had engaged it by telegraph should arrive in the hourly expected steamer from Liverpool; and, moreover, the best room at Hotel Musty was consolingly bad. The house was very full, and the Ellisons (who had come on with them from Montreal) were bestowed in less state only on like conditions.

The travellers all met at breakfast, which was admirably cooked, and well served, with the attendance of those swarms of flies which infest Quebec, and especially infested the old Musty House in summer. It had, of course, the attraction of broiled salmon, upon which the traveller breakfasts every day as long as he remains in Lower Canada; and it represented the abundance of wild berries in the Quebec market; and it was otherwise a breakfast worthy of the appetites that honored it.

There were not many other Americans besides themselves at this hotel, which seemed, indeed, to be kept open to oblige such travellers as had been there before, and could not persuade themselves to try the new Hotel St. Louis, whither the vastly greater number resorted. Most of the faces our tourists saw were English or English-Canadian, and the young people from Omaha, who had got here by some chance, were scarcely in harmony with the place. They appeared to be a bridal party, but which of the two sisters, in buff linen clad from head to foot, was the bride, never became known. Both were equally free with the husband, and he was impartially fond of both: it was quite a family affair.

For a moment Isabel harbored the desire to see the city in company with Miss Ellison; but it was only a passing weakness. She remembered directly the coolness between friends which she had seen caused by objects of interest in Europe, and she wisely deferred a more intimate acquaintance till it could have a purely social basis. After all, nothing is so tiresome as continual exchange of sympathy, or so apt to end in mutual dislike,—except gratitude. So the ladies parted friends till dinner, and drove off in separate carriages.

As in other show cities, there is a routine at Quebec for travellers who come on Saturday and go on Monday, and few depart from it. Our friends necessarily, therefore, drove first to the citadel. It was raining one of those cold rains by which the scarce-banished winter reminds the Canadian fields of his nearness even in midsummer, though between the bitter showers the air was sultry and close; and it was just the light in which to see the grim strength of the fortress next strongest to Gibraltar in the world. They passed a heavy iron gateway, and up through a winding lane of masonry to the gate of the citadel, where they were delivered into the care of Private Joseph Drakes, who was to show them such parts of the place as are open to curiosity. But, a citadel which has never stood a siege, or been threatened by any danger more serious than Fenianism, soon becomes, however strong, but a dull piece of masonry to the civilian; and our tourists more rejoiced in the crumbling fragment of the old French wall which the English destroyed than in all they had built; and they valued the latter work chiefly for the glorious prospects of the St. Lawrence and its mighty valleys which it commanded. Advanced into the centre of an amphitheatre inconceivably vast, that enormous beak of rock overlooks the narrow angle of the river and then, in every direction, immeasurable stretches of gardened vale, and wooded upland, till all melts into the purple of the encircling mountains. Far and near are lovely white villages nestling under elms, in the heart of fields and meadows; and everywhere the long, narrow, accurately divided farms stretch downward to the river-shores. The best roads on the continent make this beauty and richness accessible; each little village boasts some natural wonder in stream, or lake, or cataract; and this landscape, magnificent beyond any in Eastern America, is historical and interesting beyond all others. Hither came Jacques Cartier three hundred and fifty years ago, and wintered on the low point there by the St. Charles; here, nearly a century after, but still fourteen years before the landing at

Plymouth, Champlain founded the missionary city of Quebec; round this rocky beak came sailing the half-piratical armament of the Calvinist Kirks in 1629, and seized Quebec in the interest of the English, holding it three years; in the Lower Town, yonder, first landed the coldly welcomed Jesuits, who came with the returning French and made Quebec forever eloquent of their zeal, their guile, their heroism; at the foot of this rock lay the fleet of Sir William Phipps, governor of Massachusetts, and vainly assailed it in 1698; in 1759 came Wolfe and embattled all the region, on river and land, till at last the bravely defended city fell into his dying hand on the Plains of Abraham; here Montgomery laid down his life at the head of the boldest and most hopeless effort of our War of Independence.

Private Joseph Drakes, with the generosity of an enemy expecting drink-money, pointed out the sign-board on the face of the crag commemorating Montgomery's death; and then showed them the officers' quarters and those of the common soldiers, not far from which was a line of hang-dog fellows drawn up to receive sentence for divers small misdemeanors, from an officer whose blond whiskers drooped Dundrearily from his fresh English cheeks. There was that immense difference between him and the men in physical grandeur and beauty, which is so notable in the aristocratically ordered military services of Europe, and which makes the rank seem of another race from the file. Private Drakes saluted his superior, and visibly deteriorated in his presence, though his breast was covered with medals, and he had fought England's battles in every part of the world. It was a gross injustice, the triumph of a thousand years of wrong; and it was touching to have Private Drakes say that he expected in three months to begin life for himself, after twenty years' service of the Queen; and did they think he could get anything to do in the States? He scarcely knew what he was fit for, but he thought—to so little in him came the victories he had helped to win in the Crimea, in China, and in India—that he could take care of a gentleman's horse and work about his place. He looked inquiringly at Basil, as if he might be a gentleman with a horse to be taken care of and a place to be worked about, and made him regret that he was not a man of substance enough to provide for Private Drakes and Mrs. Drakes and the brood of Ducklings, who had been shown to him stowed away in one of those cavernous rooms in the earthworks where the married soldiers have their quarters. His regret enriched the reward of Private Drakes's service,—which perhaps answered one of Private Drakes's purposes, if not his chief aim. He promised to come to the States upon the pressing advice of Isabel, who, speaking from her own large experience, declared that everybody got on there; and he bade our friends an affectionate farewell as they drove away to the Plains of Abraham.

The fashionable surburban cottages and places of Quebec are on the St. Louis Road leading northward to the old battleground and beyond it; but these face chiefly towards the rivers St. Lawrence and St. Charles, and lofty hedges and shrubbery hide them in an English seclusion from the highway; so that the visitor may uninterruptedly meditate whatever emotion he will for the scene of Wolfe's death as he rides along. His loftiest emotion will want the noble height of that heroic soul, who must always stand forth in history a figure of beautiful and singular distinction, admirable alike for the sensibility and daring, the poetic pensiveness, and the martial ardor that mingled in him and taxed his feeble frame with tasks greater than it could bear. The whole story of the capture of Quebec is full of romantic splendor and pathos. Her fall was a triumph for all the English-speaking race, and to us Americans, long scourged by the cruel Indian wars plotted within her walls or sustained by her strength, such a blessing as was hailed with ringing bells and blazing bonfires throughout the Colonies; yet now we cannot think without pity of the hopes extinguished and the labors brought to naught in her overthrow. That strange colony of priests and soldiers, of martyrs and heroes, of which she was the capital, willing to perish for an allegiance to which the mother-country was indifferent, and fighting against the armies with which England was prepared to outnumber the whole Canadian population, is a magnificent spectacle; and Montcalm laying down his life to lose Quebec is not less affecting than Wolfe dying to win her. The heart opens towards the soldier who recited, on the eve of his costly victory, the Elegy in a Country Churchyard, which he would "rather have written than beat the French to-morrow"; but it aches for the defeated general, who, hurt to death, answered, when told how brief his time was, "So much the better; then I shall not live to see the surrender of Quebec."

In the city for which they perished their fame has never been divided. The English have shown themselves very generous victors; perhaps nothing could be alleged against them, but that they were victors. A shaft common to Wolfe and Montcalm celebrates them both in the Governor's Garden; and in the Chapel of the Ursuline Convent a tablet is placed, where Montcalm died, by the same conquerors who raised to Wolfe's memory the column on the battle-field.

A dismal prison covers the ground where the hero fell, and the monument stands on the spot where Wolfe breathed his last, on ground lower than the rest of the field; the friendly hollow that sheltered him from the fire of the French dwarfs his monument; yet it is sufficient, and the simple inscription, "Here died Wolfe victorious," gives it a dignity which many cubits of added stature could not bestow. Another of those bitter showers, which had interspersed the morning's sunshine, drove suddenly across the open plain, and our tourists comfortably sentimentalized the scene behind the close-drawn curtains of their carriage. Here a whole empire had been lost and won, Basil reminded Isabel; and she said, "Only think of it!" and looked to a wandering fold of her skirt, upon which the rain beat through a rent of the curtain.

Do I pitch the pipe too low? We poor honest men are at a sad disadvantage; and now and then I am minded to give a loose to fancy, and attribute something really grand and fine to my people, in order to make them worthier the reader's respected acquaintance. But again, I forbid myself in a higher interest; and I am afraid that even if I were less virtuous, I could not exalt their mood upon a battle-field; for of all things of the past a battle is the least conceivable. I have heard men who fought in many battles say that the recollection was like a dream to them; and what can the merely civilian imagination do on the Plains of Abraham, with the fact that there, more than a century ago, certain thousands of Frenchmen marched out, on a bright September morning, to kill and maim as many Englishmen? This ground so green and soft with grass beneath the feet, was it once torn with shot and soaked with the blood of men? Did they lie here in ranks and heaps, the miserable slain, for whom tender hearts away yonder over the sea were to ache and break? Did the wretches that fell wounded stretch themselves here, and writhe beneath the feet of friend and foe, or crawl away for shelter into little hollows, and behind bushes and fallen trees? Did he, whose soul was so full of noble and sublime impulses, die here, shot through like some ravening beast? The loathsome carnage, the shrieks, the hellish din of arms, the cries of victory, —I vainly strive to conjure up some image of it all now; and God be thanked, horrible spectre! that, fill the world with sorrow as thou wilt, thou still remainest incredible in its moments of sanity and peace. Least credible art thou on the old battle-fields, where the mother of the race denies thee with breeze and sun and leaf and bird and every blade of grass! The red stain in Basil's thought yielded to the rain sweeping across the pasture-land from which it had long since faded, and the words on the monument, "Here died Wolfe victorious," did not proclaim his bloody triumph over the French, but his self-conquest, his victory over fear and pain and love of life. Alas! when shall the poor, blind, stupid world honor those who renounce self in the joy of their kind, equally with those who devote themselves through the anguish and loss of thousands? So old a world, and groping still!

The tourists were better fitted for the next occasion of sentiment, which was at the Hôtel Dieu, whither they went after returning from the battle-field. It took all the mal-address of which travellers are masters to secure admittance, and it was not till they had rung various wrong bells, and misunderstood many soft nun-voices speaking French through grated doors, and set divers sympathetic spectators doing ineffectual services, that they at last found the proper entrance, and were answered in English that the porter would ask if they might see the chapel. They hoped to find there the skull of Brébeuf, one of those Jesuit martyrs who perished long ago for the conversion of a race that has perished, and whose relics they had come, fresh from their reading of Parkman, with some vague and patronizing intention to revere. An elderly sister with a pale, kind face led them through a ward of the hospital into the chapel, which they found in the expected taste, and exquisitely neat and cool, but lacking the martyr's skull. They asked if it were not to be seen. "Ah, yes, poor Père Brébeuf!" sighed the gentle sister, with the tone and manner of having lost him yesterday; "we had it down only last week, showing it to some Jesuit fathers; but it's in the convent now, and isn't to be seen." And there mingled apparently in her regret for Père Brébeuf a confusing sense of his actual state as a portable piece of furniture. She would not let them praise the chapel. It was very clean, yes, but there was nothing to see in it. She deprecated their compliments with many shrugs, but she was pleased; for when we renounce the pomps and vanities of this world, we are pretty sure to find them in some other,—if we are women. She, good and pure soul, whose whole life was given to self-denying toil, had yet something angelically coquettish in her manner, a spiritual-worldliness which was the clarified likeness of this-worldliness. O, had they seen the Hôtel Dieu at Montreal? Then (with a vivacious wave of the hands) they would not care to look at this, which by comparison was nothing. Yet she invited them to go through the wards if they would, and was clearly proud to have them see the wonderful cleanness and comfort of the place. There were not many patients, but here and there a wan or fevered face looked at them from its pillow, or a weak form drooped beside a bed, or a group of convalescents softly talked together. They came presently to the last hall, at the end of which sat another nun, beside a window that gave a view of the busy port, and beyond it the landscape of village-lit plain and forest-darkened height. On a table at her elbow stood a rose-tree on which hung only two pale tea-roses, so fair, so perfect, that Isabel cried out in wonder and praise. Ere she could prevent it, the nun, to whom there had been some sort of presentation, gathered one of the roses, and with a shy grace offered it to Isabel, who shrank back a little as from too costly a gift. "Take it," said the first nun, with her pretty French accent; while the other, who spoke no English at all, beamed a placid smile; and Isabel took it. The flower, lying light in her palm, exhaled a delicate odor, and a thrill of exquisite compassion for it trembled through her heart, as if it had been the white, cloistered life of the silent nun: with its pallid loveliness, it was as a flower that had taken the veil. It could never have uttered the burning passion of a lover for his mistress; the nightingale could have found no thorn on it to press his aching poet's heart against; but sick and weary eyes had dwelt gratefully upon it; at most it might have expressed, like a prayer, the nun's stainless love of some favorite saint in paradise. Cold, and pale, and sweet,—was it indeed only a flower, this cloistered rose of the Hôtel Dieu?

"Breathe it," said the gentle Gray Sister; "sometimes the air of the hospital offends. Not us, no; we are used; but you come from the outside." And she gave her rose for this humble use as lovingly as she devoted herself to her lowly cares.

"It is very little to see," she said at the end; "but if you are pleased, I am very glad. Good by, good by!" She stood with her arms folded, and watched them out of sight with her kind, coquettish little smile, and then the mute, blank life of the nun resumed her.

From Hôtel Dieu to Hotel Musty it was but a step; both were in the same street; but our friends fancied themselves to have come an immense distance when they sat down at an early dinner, amidst the clash of crockery and cutlery, and looked round upon all the profane travelling world assembled. Their regard presently fixed upon one company which monopolized a whole table, and were defined from the other diners by peculiarities as marked as those of the Sœurs Grises themselves. There were only two men among some eight or ten women; one of the former had a bad amiable face, with eyes full of a merry deviltry; the other, clean shaven and dark, was demure and silent as a priest. The ladies were of various types, but of one effect, with large rolling eyes, and faces that somehow regarded the beholder as from a distance, and with an impartial feeling for him as for an element of publicity. One of them, who caressed a lapdog with one hand while she served herself with the other, was, as she seemed to believe, a blonde; she had pale blue eyes, and her hair was cut in front so as to cover her forehead with a straggling sandy-colored fringe. She had an English look, and three or four others, with dark complexion and black, unsteady eyes, and various abandon of back-hair, looked like Cockney houris of Jewish blood; while two of the lovely company were clearly of our own nation, as was the young man with the reckless laughing face. The ladies were dressed and jewelled with a kind of broad effectiveness, which was to the ordinary style of society what scene-painting is to painting, and might have borne close inspection no better. They seemed the best-humored people in the world, and on the kindliest terms with each other. The waiters shared their pleasant mood, and served them affectionately, and were now and then invited to join in the gay talk which babbled on over dislocated aspirates, and filled the air with a sentiment of vaga-bond enjoyment, of the romantic freedom of violated convention, of something Gil Blas-like, almost picaresque.

If they had needed explanation it would have been given by the announcement in the office of the hotel that a troupe of British blondes was then appearing in Quebec for one week only.

After dinner they took possession of the parlor, and while one strummed fitfully upon the ailing hotel piano, the rest talked, and talked shop, of course, as all of us do when several of a trade are got together.

"W'at," said the eldest of the dark-faced, black-haired British blondes of Jewish race,—"w'at are we going to give at Mon-trehal?"

"We're going to give 'Pygmalion,' at Montrehal," answered

the British blonde of American birth, good-humoredly bur-
lesquing the erring *h* of her sister.

"But we cahn't, you know," said the lady with the fringed
forehead; "Hagnes is gone on to New York, and there's nobody
to do Wenus."

"Yes, you know," demanded the first speaker, "'oo's to do
Wenus?"

"Bella's to do Wenus," said a third.

There was an outcry at this, and "'Ow ever would she get herself up for Wenus?" and "W'at a guy she'll look!" and "Nonsense! Bella's too 'eavy for Wenus!" came from different lively
critics; and the debate threatened to become too intimate for the
public ear, when one of their gentlemen came in and said,
"Charley don't seem so well this afternoon." On this the chorus
changed its note, and at the proposal, "Poor Charley, let's go
and cheer 'im hup a bit," the whole good-tempered company
trooped out of the parlor together.

Our tourists meant to give the rest of the afternoon to that sort
of aimless wandering to and fro about the streets which seizes a
foreign city unawares, and best develops its charm of strangeness.
So they went out and took their fill of Quebec with appetites keen
through long fasting from the quaint and old, and only sharpened
by Montreal, and impartially rejoiced in the crooked up-and-
down hill streets; the thoroughly French domestic architecture
of a place that thus denied having been English for a hundred
years; the *porte-cochères* beside every house; the French names
upon the doors, and the oddity of the bell-pulls; the rough-paved,
rattling streets; the shining roofs of tin, and the universal dormer-
windows; the littleness of the private houses, and the greatness
of the high-walled and garden-girdled convents; the breadths of
weather-stained city wall, and the shaggy cliff beneath; the bat-
teries, with their guns peacefully staring through loopholes of
masonry, and the red-coated sergeants flirting with nursery-
maids upon the carriages, while the children tumbled about over
the pyramids of shot and shell; the sloping market-place before

the cathedral, where yet some remnant of the morning's traffic lingered under canvas canopies, and where Isabel bought a bouquet of marigolds and asters of an old woman peasant enough to have sold it in any market-place of Europe; the small, dark shops beyond the quarter invaded by English retail trade; the movement of all the strange figures of cleric and lay and military life; the sound of a foreign speech prevailing over the English; the encounter of other tourists, the passage back and forth through the different city gates; the public wooden stairways, dropping flight after flight from the Upper to the Lower Town; the bustle of the port, with its commerce and shipping and seafaring life huddled close in under the hill; the many desolate streets of the Lower Town, as black and ruinous as the last great fire left them; and the marshy meadows beyond, memorable of Recollets and Jesuits, of Cartier and Montcalm.

They went to the chapel of the Seminary at Laval University, and admired the Le Brun, and the other paintings of less merit, but equal interest through their suggestion of a whole dim religious world of paintings; and then they spent half an hour in the cathedral, not so much in looking at the Crucifixion by Vandyck which is there, as in revelling amid the familiar *rococo* splendors of the temple. Every swaggering statue of a saint, every ropedancing angel, every cherub of those that on the carven and gilded clouds above the high altar float

"Like little wanton boys that swim on bladders,"

was precious to them; the sacristan dusting the sacred properties with a feather brush, and giving each shrine a business-like nod as he passed, was as a long-lost brother; they had hearts of aggressive tenderness for the young girls and old women who stepped in for a half-hour's devotion, and for the men with bourgeois or peasant faces, who stole a moment from affairs and crops, and gave it to the saints. There was nothing in the place that need remind them of America, and its taste was exactly that of a thousand other churches of the eighteenth century. They could easily have believed themselves in the furthest Catholic

South, but for the two great porcelain stoves that stood on either side of the nave near the entrance, and that too vividly reminded them of the possibility of cold.

In fact, Quebec is a little painful in this and other confusions of the South and North, and one never quite reconciles himself to them. The Frenchmen, who expected to find there the climate of their native land, and ripen her wines in as kindly a sun, have perpetuated the image of home in so many things, that it goes to the heart with a painful emotion to find the sad, oblique light of the North upon them. As you ponder some characteristic aspect of Quebec,—a bit of street with heavy stone houses, opening upon a stretch of the city wall, with a Lombardy poplar rising slim against it,—you say to your satisfied soul, "Yes, it is the real thing!" and then all at once a sense of that northern sky strikes in upon you, and makes the reality a mere picture. The sky is blue, the sun is often fiercely hot; you could not perhaps prove that the pathetic radiance is not an efflux of your own consciousness that summer is but hanging over the land, briefly poising on wings which flit at the first dash of rain, and will soon vanish in long retreat before the snow. But somehow, from without or from within, that light of the North is there.

It lay saddest, our travellers thought, upon the little circular garden near Durham Terrace, where every brightness of fall flowers abounded,—marigold, coxcomb, snap-dragon, dahlia, hollyhock, and sunflower. It was a substantial and hardy efflorescence, and they fancied that fainter-hearted plants would have pined away in that garden, where the little fountain, leaping up into the joyless light, fell back again with a musical shiver. The consciousness of this latent cold, of winter only held in abeyance by the bright sun, was not deeper even in the once magnificent, now neglected Governor's Garden, where there was actually a rawness in the late afternoon air, and whither they were strolling for the view from its height, and to pay their duty to the obelisk raised there to the common fame of Wolfe and Montcalm. The sounding Latin inscription celebrates the royal governor-general who erected it almost as much as the heroes to whom it was raised; but these spectators did not begrudge the space given to his praise, for so fine a thought merited praise. It enforced again the idea of a kind of posthumous friendship between Wolfe and Montcalm, which gives their memory its rare distinction, and unites them, who fell in fight against each other, as closely as if they had both died for the same cause.

Some lasting dignity seems to linger about the city that has once been a capital; and this odor of fallen nobility belongs to Quebec, which was a capital in the European sense, with all the advantages of a small vice-regal court, and its social and political intrigues, in the French times. Under the English, for a hundred years it was the centre of Colonial civilization and refinement, with a governor-general's residence and a brilliant, easy, and delightful society, to which the large garrison of former days gave gayety and romance. The honors of a capital, first shared with Montreal and Toronto, now rest with half-savage Ottawa; and the garrison has dwindled to a regiment of rifles, whose presence would hardly be known, but for the natty serjeants lounging, stick in hand, about the streets and courting the nurse-maids. But in the days of old there were scenes of carnival pleas-ure in the Governor's Garden, and there the garrison band still plays once a week, when it is filled by the fashion and beauty of Quebec, and some semblance of the past is recalled. It is other-wise a lonesome, indifferently tended place, and on this after-noon there was no one there but a few loafing young fellows of low degree, French and English, and children that played screaming from seat to seat and path to path and over the too-heavily shaded grass. In spite of a conspicuous warning that any dog entering the garden would be destroyed, the place was thronged with dogs unmolested and apparently in no danger of the threatened doom. The seal of a disagreeable desolation was given in the legend rudely carved upon one of the benches, "Success to the Irish Republic!"

The morning of the next day our tourists gave to hearing mass at the French cathedral, which was not different, to their heretical senses, from any other mass, except that the ceremony was performed with a very full clerical force, and was attended by an uncommonly devout congregation. With Europe constantly in their minds, they were bewildered to find the worshippers not chiefly old and young women, but men also of all ages and of every degree, from the neat peasant in his Sabbath-day best to the modish young Quebecker, who spread his handkerchief on the floor to save his pantaloons during supplication. There was fashion and education in large degree among the men, and there was in all a pious attention to the function in poetical keeping with the origin and history of a city which the zeal of the Church had founded.

A magnificent beadle, clothed in a gold-laced coat and bearing a silver staff, bowed to them when they entered, and, leading them to a pew, punched up a kneeling peasant, who mutely resumed his prayers in the aisle outside, while they took his place. It appeared to Isabel very unjust that their curiosity should displace his religion; but she consoled herself by making Basil give a shilling to the man who, preceded by the shining beadle, came round to take up a collection. The peasant could have given nothing but copper, and she felt that this restored the lost balance of righteousness in their favor. There was a sermon, very sweetly and gracefully delivered by a young priest of singular beauty, even among clergy whose good looks are so notable as those of Quebec; and then they followed the orderly crowd of worshippers out, and left the cathedral to the sacristan and the odor of incense.

They thought the type of French-Canadian better here than at Montreal, and they particularly noticed the greater number of pretty young girls. All classes were well dressed; for though the best dressed could not be called stylish according to the American standard, as Isabel decided, and had only a provincial gentility, the poorest wore garments that were clean and whole. Everybody, too, was going to have a hot Sunday dinner, if there was any truth in the odors that steamed out of every door and window; and this dinner was to be abundantly garnished with onions, for the dullest nose could not err concerning that savor.

Numbers of tourists, of a nationality that showed itself superior

to every distinction of race, were strolling vaguely, and not always quite happily about; but they made no impression on the
proper local character, and the air throughout the morning was
full of the sentiment of Sunday in a Catholic city. There was the
apparently meaningless jangling of bells, with profound hushes
between, and then more jubilant jangling, and then deeper
silence; there was the devout trooping of the crowds to the
churches; and there was the beginning of the long afternoon's
lounging and amusement with which the people of that faith
reward their morning's devotion. Little stands for the sale of
knotty apples and choke-cherries and cakes and cider sprang
magically into existence after service, and people were already
eating and drinking at them. The carriage-drivers resumed their
chase of the tourists, and the unvoiceful stir of the new week had
begun again. Quebec, in fact, is but a pantomimic reproduction
of France; it is as if two centuries in a new land, amidst the
primeval silences of nature and the long hush of the Northern
winters, had stilled the tongues of the lively folk and made them
taciturn as we of a graver race. They have kept the ancestral
vivacity of manner; the elegance of the shrug is intact; the talking hands take part in dialogue; the agitated person will have its
share of expression. But the loud and eager tone is wanting, and
their dumb show mystifies the beholder almost as much as the
Southern architecture under the slanting Northern sun. It is not
America; if it is not France, what is it?

Of the many beautiful things to see in the neighborhood of
Quebec, our wedding-journeyers were in doubt on which to
bestow their one precious afternoon. Should it be Lorette, with
its cataract and its remnant of bleached and fading Hurons, or
the Isle of Orleans with its fertile farms and its primitive peasant
life, or Montmorenci, with the unrivalled fall and the long drive
through the beautiful village of Beauport? Isabel chose the
last, because Basil had been there before, and it had to it the
poetry of the wasted years in which she did not know him. She
had possessed herself of the journal of his early travels, among the
other portions and parcels recoverable from the dreadful past,

and from time to time on this journey she had read him passages out of it, with mingled sentiment and irony, and, whether she was mocking or admiring, equally to his confusion. Now, as they smoothly bowled away from the city, she made him listen to what he had written of the same excursion long ago.

It was, to be sure, a sad farrago of sentiment about the village and the rural sights, and especially a girl tossing hay in the field. Yet it had touches of nature and reality, and Basil could not utterly despise himself for having written it. "Yes," he said, "life was then a thing to be put into pretty periods; now it's something that has risks and averages, and may be insured."

There was regret, fancied or expressed, in his tone, that made her sigh, "Ah! if I'd only had a *little* more money, you might have devoted yourself to literature"; for she was a true Bostonian in her honor of our poor craft.

"O, you're not greatly to blame," answered her husband, "and I forgive you the little wrong you've done me. I was quits with the Muse, at any rate, you know, before we were married; and I'm very well satisfied to be going back to my applications and policies to-morrow."

To-morrow? The word struck cold upon her. Then their wedding journey would begin to end to-morrow! So it would, she owned with another sigh; and yet it seemed impossible.

"There, ma'am," said the driver, rising from his seat and facing round, while he pointed with his whip towards Quebec, "that's what we call the Silver City."

They looked back with him at the city, whose thousands of tinned roofs, rising one above the other from the water's edge to the citadel, were all a splendor of argent light in the afternoon sun. It was indeed as if some magic had clothed that huge rock, base and steepy flank and crest, with a silver city. They gazed upon the marvel with cries of joy that satisfied the driver's utmost pride in it, and Isabel said, "To live there, there in that Silver City, in perpetual sojourn! To be always going to go on a morrow that never came! To be forever within one day of the end of a wedding journey that never ended!"

From far down the river by which they rode came the sound of a cannon, breaking the Sabbath repose of the air. "That's the gun of the Liverpool steamer, just coming in," said the driver.

"O," cried Isabel, "I'm thankful we're only to stay one night more, for now we shall be turned out of our nice room by those people who telegraphed for it!"

There is a continuous village along the St. Lawrence from Quebec, almost to Montmorenci; and they met crowds of villagers coming from the church as they passed through Beauport. But Basil was dismayed at the change that had befallen them. They had their Sunday's best on, and the women, instead of wearing the peasant costume in which he had first seen them, were now dressed as if out of "Harper's Bazar" of the year before. He anxiously asked the driver if the broad straw hats and the bright sacks and kirtles were no more. "O, you'd see them on weekdays, sir," was the answer, "but they're not so plenty any time as they used to be." He opened his store of facts about the *habitans,* whom he praised for every virtue,—for thrift, for sobriety, for neatness, for amiability; and his words ought to have had the greater weight, because he was of the Irish race, between which and the Canadians there is no kindness lost. But the looks of the passers-by corroborated him, and as for the little houses, open-doored beside the way, with the pleasant faces at window and portal, they were miracles of picturesqueness and cleanliness. From each the owner's slim domain, narrowing at every successive division among the abundant generations, runs back to hill or river in well-defined lines, and beside the cottage is a garden of pot-herbs, bordered with a flame of bright autumn flowers; somewhere in decent seclusion grunts the fattening pig, which is to enrich all those peas and onions for the winter's broth; there is a cheerfulness of poultry about the barns; I dare be sworn there is always a small girl driving a flock of decorous ducks down the middle of the street; and of the priest with a book under his arm, passing a wayside shrine, what possible doubt? The houses, which are of one model, are built by the peasants themselves with the stone which their land yields more abundantly than any other crop, and are furnished with galleries and balconies to catch every ray of the fleeting summer, and perhaps to remember the long-lost ancestral summers of Normandy. At every moment, in passing through this ideally neat and pretty village, our tourists must think of the lovely poem of which all French Canada seems but a reminiscence and illustration. It was Grand Pré, not Beauport; and they paid an eager homage to the beautiful genius which has touched those simple village aspects with an undying charm, and which, whatever the land's political allegiance, is there perpetual Seigneur.

The village, stretching along the broad intervale of the St. Lawrence, grows sparser as you draw near the Falls of Montmorenci, and presently you drive past the grove shutting from the road the country-house in which the Duke of Kent spent some merry days of his jovial youth, and come in sight of two lofty towers of stone,—monuments and witnesses of the tragedy of Montmorenci.

Once a suspension-bridge, built sorely against the will of the neighboring *habitans*, hung from these towers high over the long plunge of the cataract. But one morning of the fatal spring after the first winter's frost had tried the hold of the cable on the rocks, an old peasant and his wife with their little grandson set out in their cart to pass the bridge. As they drew near the middle the anchoring wires suddenly lost their grip upon the shore, and whirled into the air; the bridge crashed under the hapless passengers and they were launched from its height upon the verge of the fall and thence plunged, two hundred and fifty feet, into the ruin of the abyss.

The *habitans* rebuilt their bridge of wood upon low stone piers, so far up the river from the cataract that whoever fell from it would yet have many a chance for life; and it would have been perilous to offer to replace the fallen structure, which, in the belief of faithful Christians, clearly belonged to the numerous bridges built by the Devil, in times when the Devil did not call himself a civil engineer.

The driver, with just unction, recounted the sad tale as he

halted his horses on the bridge; and as his passengers looked down the rock-fretted brown torrent towards the fall, Isabel seized the occasion to shudder that ever she had set foot on that suspension-bridge below Niagara, and to prove to Basil's confusion that her doubt of the bridges between the Three Sisters was not a case of nerves, but an instinctive wisdom concerning the unsafety of all bridges of that design.

From the gate opening into the grounds about the fall two or three little French boys, whom they had not the heart to forbid, ran noisily before them with cries in their sole English, "This way, sir!" and led towards a weather-beaten summer-house that tottered upon a projecting rock above the verge of the cataract. But our tourists shook their heads, and turned away for a more distant and less dizzy enjoyment of the spectacle, though any commanding point was sufficiently chasmal and precipitous. The lofty bluff was scooped inward from the St. Lawrence in a vast irregular semicircle, with cavernous hollows, one within another, sinking far into its sides, and naked from foot to crest or meagrely wooded here and there with evergreen. From the central brink of these gloomy purple chasms the foamy cataract launched itself, and like a cloud

"Along the cliff to fall and pause and fall did seem."

I say a cloud, because I find it already said to my hand, as it were, in a pretty verse, and because I must needs liken Montmorenci to something that is soft and light. Yet a cloud does not represent the glinting of the water in its downward swoop; it is like some broad slope of sun-smitten snow; but snow is coldly white and opaque, and this has a creamy warmth in its luminous mass; and so, there hangs the cataract unsaid as before. It is a mystery that anything so grand should be so lovely, that anything so tenderly fair in whatever aspect should yet be so large that one glance fails to comprehend it all. The rugged wildness of the cliffs and hollows about it is softened by its gracious beauty, which half redeems the vulgarity of the timber-merchant's uses in setting the river at work in his saw-mills and choking its outlet into the St.

Lawrence with rafts of lumber and rubbish of slabs and shingles. Nay, rather, it is alone amidst these things, and the eye takes note of them by a separate effort.

Our tourists sank down upon the turf that crept with its white clover to the edge of the precipice, and gazed dreamily upon the fall, filling their vision with its exquisite color and form. Being wiser than I, they did not try to utter its loveliness; they were content to feel it, and the perfection of the afternoon, whose low sun slanting over the landscape gave, under that pale, greenish-blue sky, a pensive sentiment of autumn to the world. The crickets cried amongst the grass; the hesitating chirp of birds came from the tree overhead; a shaggy colt left off grazing in the field and stalked up to stare at them; their little guides having found that these people had no pleasure in the sight of small boys scuffling on the verge of a precipice, threw themselves also down upon the grass and crooned a long, long ballad in a mournful minor key about some maiden whose name was La Belle Adeline. It was a moment of unmixed enjoyment for every sense, and through all their being they were glad; which considering, they ceased to be so, with a deep sigh, as one reasoning that he dreams must presently awake. They never could have an emotion without desiring to analyze it; but perhaps their rapture would have ceased as swiftly, even if they had not tried to make it a fact of consciousness.

"If there were not dinner after such experiences as these," said Isabel, as they sat at table that evening, "I don't know what would become of one. But dinner unites the idea of pleasure and duty, and brings you gently back to earth. You *must* eat, don't you see, and there's nothing disgraceful about what you're obliged to do; and so—it's all right."

"Isabel, Isabel," cried her husband, "you have a wonderful mind, and its workings always amaze me. But be careful, my dear; be careful. Don't work it too hard. The human brain, you know; delicate organ."

"Well, you understand what I mean; and I think it's one of the great charms of a husband, that you're not forced to express yourself to him. A husband," continued Isabel, sententiously, poising a bit of meringue between her thumb and finger,—for they had reached that point in the repast,—"a husband is almost as good as another woman!"

In the parlor they found the Ellisons, and exchanged the history of the day with them.

"Certainly," said Mrs. Ellison, at the end, "it's been a pleasant day enough, but what of the night? You've been turned out, too, by those people who came on the steamer, and who might as well have stayed on board to-night; have you got another room?"

"Not precisely," said Isabel, "we have a coop in the fifth story, right under the roof."

Mrs. Ellison turned energetically upon her husband and cried in tones of reproach, "Richard, Mrs. March has a room!"

"A coop, she *said*," retorted that amiable Colonel, "and we're too good for that. The clerk is keeping us in suspense about a room, because he means to surprise us with something palatial at the end. It's his joking way."

"Nonsense!" said Mrs. Ellison. "Have you seen him since dinner?"

"I have made life a burden to him for the last half-hour," returned the Colonel, with the kindliest smile.

"O Richard," cried his wife, in despair of his amendment, "you wouldn't make life a burden to a mouse!" And having nothing else for it, she laughed, half in sorrow, half in fondness.

"Well, Fanny," the Colonel irrelevantly answered, "put on your hat and things, and let's all go up to Durham Terrace for a promenade. I know our friends want to go. It's something worth seeing; and by the time we get back, the clerk will have us a perfectly sumptuous apartment."

Nothing, I think, more enforces the illusion of Southern Europe in Quebec than the Sunday-night promenading on Durham Terrace. This is the ample space on the brow of the cliff to the left of the citadel, the noblest and most commanding position in the whole city, which was formerly occupied by the old castle of Saint Louis, where dwelt the brave Count Frontenac and his splendid successors of the French *régime*. The castle went the way of Quebec by fire some forty years ago, and Lord Durham levelled the site and made it a public promenade. A stately arcade of solid masonry supports it on the brink of the rock, and an iron parapet encloses it; there are a few seats to lounge upon, and some idle old guns for the children to clamber over and play with. A soft twilight had followed the day, and there was just enough obscurity to hide from a willing eye the Northern and New World facts of the scene, and to bring into more romantic relief the citadel dark against the mellow evening, and the people gossiping from window to window across the narrow streets of the Lower Town. The Terrace itself was densely thronged, and there was a constant coming and going of the promenaders, who each formally paced back and forth upon the planking for a certain time, and then went quietly home, giving place to the new arrivals. They were nearly all French, and they were not generally, it seemed, of the first fashion, but rather of middling condition in life; the English being represented only by a few young fellows and now and then a red-faced old gentleman with an Indian scarf trailing from his hat. There were some fair American costumes and faces in the crowd, but it was essentially Quebecian. The young girls walking in pairs, or with their lovers, had the true touch of provincial unstylishness, the young men the ineffectual excess of the second-rate Latin dandy; their elders the rich inelegance of a *bourgeoisie* in their best. A few better-figured *avocats* or *notaires* (their profession was as unmistakable as if they had carried their well-polished brass doorplates upon their breasts) walked and gravely talked with each other. The non-American character of the scene was not less vividly marked in the fact that each person dressed according to his own taste and frankly indulged private preferences in shapes and colors. One of the promenaders was in white, even to his canvas shoes; another, with yet bolder individuality, appeared in perfect purple. It had a strange, almost portentous effect when these two startling figures met as friends and joined each other in the promenade with linked arms; but the evening was already be-

ginning to darken round them, and presently the purple com-
rade was merely a sombre shadow beside the glimmering white.

The valleys and the heights now vanished; but the river defined itself by the varicolored lights of the ships and steamers that
lay, dark, motionless bulks, upon its broad breast; the lights of
Point Levis swarmed upon the other shore; the Lower Town,
two hundred feet below them, stretched an alluring mystery of
clustering roofs and lamplit windows and dark and shining
streets around the mighty rock, mural-crowned. Suddenly a
spectacle peculiarly Northern and characteristic of Quebec revealed itself; a long arch brightened over the northern horizon;
the tremulous flames of the aurora, pallid violet or faintly tinged
with crimson, shot upward from it, and played with a weird apparition and evanescence to the zenith. While the strangers
looked, a gun boomed from the citadel, and the wild sweet notes
of the bugle sprang out upon the silence.

Then they all said, "How perfectly in keeping everything has
been!" and sauntered back to the hotel.

The Colonel went into the office to give the clerk another turn
on the rack, and make him confess to a hidden apartment somewhere, while Isabel left her husband to Mrs. Ellison in the parlor,
and invited Miss Kitty to look at her coop in the fifth story. As
they approached, light and music and laughter stole out of an
open door next hers, and Isabel, distinguishing the voices of the
theatrical party, divined that this was the sick-chamber, and
that they were again cheering up the afflicted member of the
troupe. Some one was heard to say, "Well, 'ow do you feel now,
Charley?" and a sound of subdued swearing responded, followed
by more laughter, and the twanging of a guitar, and a snatch of
song, and a stir of feet and dresses as for departure.

The two listeners shrank together; as women they could not
enjoy these proofs of the jolly *camaraderie* existing among the
people of the troupe. They trembled as before the merriment of
as many light-hearted, careless, good-natured young men: it
was no harm, but it was dismaying; and, "Dear!" cried Isabel,
"what shall we do?"

"Go back," said Miss Ellison, boldly, and back they ran to the parlor, where they found Basil and the Colonel and his wife in earnest conclave. The Colonel, like a shrewd strategist, was making show of a desperation more violent than his wife's, who was thus naturally forced into the attitude of moderating his fury.

"Well, Fanny, that's all he can do for us; and I do think it's the most outrageous thing in the world! It's real mean!"

Fanny perceived a bold parody of her own denunciatory manner, but just then she was obliged to answer Isabel's eager inquiry whether they had got a room yet. "Yes, *a* room," she said, "with two beds. But what are we to do with one room? That clerk—I don't know what to call him"—("Call him a hotel-clerk, my dear; you can't say anything worse," interrupted her husband) —"seems to think the matter perfectly settled."

"You see, Mrs. March," added the Colonel, "he's able to bully us in this way because he has the architecture on his side. There isn't another room in the house."

"Let me think a moment," said Isabel not thinking an instant. She had taken a fancy to at least two of these people from the first, and in the last hour they had all become very well acquainted; now she said, "I'll tell you: there are two beds in our room also; we ladies will take one room, and you gentlemen the other!"

"Mrs. March, I bow to the superiority of the Boston mind," said the Colonel, while his females civilly protested and consented; "and I might almost hail you as our preserver. If ever you come to Milwaukee,—which is the centre of the world, as Boston is,—we—I—shall be happy to have you call at my place of business.—I didn't commit myself, did I, Fanny?—I am sometimes hospitable to excess, Mrs. March," he said, to explain his aside. "And now, let us reconnoitre. Lead on, madam, and the gratitude of the houseless stranger will follow you."

The whole party explored both rooms, and the ladies decided to keep Isabel's. The Colonel was despatched to see that the wraps and traps of his party were sent to this number, and Basil went with him. The things came long before the gentlemen returned, but the ladies happily employed the interval in talking over the excitements of the day, and in saying from time to time, "So very kind of you, Mrs. March," and "I don't know what we should have done," and "Don't speak of it, please," and "I'm sure it's a great pleasure to me."

In the room adjoining theirs, where the invalid actor lay, and where lately there had been minstrelsy and apparently dancing for his solace, there was now comparative silence. Two women's voices talked together, and now and then a guitar was touched by a wandering hand. Isabel had just put up her handkerchief to conceal her first yawn, when the gentlemen, odorous of cigars, returned to say good night.

"It's the second door from this, isn't it, Isabel?" asked her husband.

"Yes, the second door. Good night."

"Good night."

The two men walked off together; but in a minute afterwards they had returned and were knocking tremulously at the closed door.

"O, what has happened?" chorussed the ladies in woful tune, seeing a certain wildness in the faces that confronted them.

"We don't know!" answered the others in as fearful a key, and related how they had found the door of their room ajar, and a bright light streaming into the corridor. They did not stop to ponder this fact, but, with the heedlessness of their sex, pushed the door wide open, when they saw seated before the mirror a bewildering figure, with dishevelled locks wandering down the back, and in dishabille expressive of being quite at home there, which turned upon them a pair of pale blue eyes, under a forehead remarkable for the straggling fringe of hair that covered it. They professed to have remained transfixed at the sight and to have noted a like dismay on the visage before the glass, ere they summoned strength to fly. These facts Colonel Ellison gave at the command of his wife, with many protests and insincere delays amidst which the curiosity of his hearers alone prevented them from rending him in pieces.

"And what do you suppose it was?" demanded his wife, with forced calmness, when he had at last made an end of the story and his abominable hypocrisies.

"Well, *I* think it was a mermaid."

"A mermaid!" said his wife, scornfully. "How do you know?"

"It had a comb in its hand, for one thing; and besides, my dear, I hope I know a mermaid when I see it."

"Well," said Mrs. Ellison, "it was no mermaid, it was a mistake; and I'm going to see about it. Will you go with me, Richard?"

"No money could induce me! If it's a mistake, it isn't proper for me to go; if it's a mermaid, it's dangerous."

"O you coward!" said the intrepid little woman to a hero of all the fights on Sherman's march to the sea; and presently they heard her attack the mysterious enemy with a lady-like courage, claiming the invaded chamber. The foe replied with like civility, saying the clerk had given her that room with the understanding that another lady was to be put there with her, and she had left the door unlocked to admit her. The watchers with the sick man next door appeared and confirmed this speech; a feeble voice from the bedclothes swore to it.

"Of course," added the invader, "if I'd known 'ow it really was, I never would 'ave listened to such a thing, never. And there isn't another 'ole in the 'ouse to lay me 'ead," she concluded.

"Then it's the clerk's fault," said Mrs. Ellison, glad to retreat unharmed; and she made her husband ring for the guilty wretch, a pale, quiet young Frenchman, whom the united party, sallying into the corridor, began to upbraid in one breath, the lady in dishabille vanishing as often as she remembered it, and reappearing whenever some strong point of argument or denunciation occurred to her.

The clerk, who was the Benjamin of his wicked tribe, threw himself upon their mercy and confessed everything: the house was so crowded, and he had been so crazed by the demands upon him, that he had understood Colonel Ellison's application to be for a bed for the young lady in his party, and he had done the very best he could. If the lady there—she vanished again—would give up the room to the two gentlemen, he would find her a place with the housekeeper. To this the lady consented without difficulty, and the rest dispersing, she kissed one of the sick man's watchers with "Isn't it a shame, Bella?" and flitted down the darkness of the corridor. The rooms upon it seemed all, save the two assigned our travellers, to be occupied by ladies of the troupe; their doors successively opened, and she was heard explaining to each as she passed. The momentary displeasure which she had shown at her banishment was over. She detailed the facts with perfect good-nature, and though the others appeared no more than herself to find any humorous cast in the affair, they received her narration with the same amiability. They uttered their sympathy seriously, and each parted from her with some friendly word. Then all was still.

"Richard," said Mrs. Ellison, when in Isabel's room the travellers had briefly celebrated these events, "I should think you'd hate to leave us alone up here."

"I do; but you can't think how I hate to go off alone. I wish you'd come part of the way with us, ladies; I do, indeed. Leave your door unlocked, at any rate."

This prayer, uttered at parting outside the room, was answered from within by a sound of turning keys and sliding bolts, and a low thunder as of bureaus and washstands rolled against the door. "The ladies are fortifying their position," said the Colonel to Basil, and the two returned to their own chamber. "I don't wish any intrusions," he said, instantly shutting himself in, "my nerves are too much shaken now. What an awfully mysterious old place this Quebec is, Mr. March! I'll tell you what: it's my opinion that this is an enchanted castle, and if my ribs are not walked over by a muleteer in the course of the night, it's all I ask."

In this and other discourse recalling the famous adventure of Don Quixote, the Colonel beguiled the labor of disrobing, and had got as far as his boots, when there came a startling knock at the door. With one boot in his hand and the other on his foot, the

Colonel limped forward. "I suppose it's that clerk has sent to say he's made some other mistake," and he flung wide the door, and then stood motionless before it, dumbly staring at a figure on the threshold,—a figure with the fringed forehead and pale blue eyes of her whom they had so lately turned out of that room.

Shrinking behind the side of the doorway, "Excuse me, gentlemen," she said, with a dignity that recalled their scattered senses, "but will you 'ave the goodness to look if my beads are on your table? O thanks, thanks, thanks!" she continued, showing her face and one hand, as Basil blushingly advanced with a string of heavy black beads, piously adorned with a large cross. "I'm sure, I'm greatly obliged to you, gentlemen, and I hask a thousand pardons for troublin' you," she concluded in a somewhat severe tone, that left them abashed and culpable; and vanished as mysteriously as she had appeared.

"Now, see here," said the Colonel, with a huge sigh as he closed the door again, and this time locked it, "I should like to know how long this sort of thing is to be kept up? Because, if it's to be regularly repeated during the night, I'm going to dress again." Nevertheless, he finished undressing and got into bed, where he remained for some time silent. Basil put out the light. "O, I'm sorry you did that, my dear fellow," said the Colonel; "but never mind, it was an idle curiosity, no doubt. It's my belief that in the landlord's extremity of bed-linen, I've been put to sleep between a pair of tablecloths; and I thought I'd like to look. It seems to me that I make out a checkered pattern on top and a flowered or arabesque pattern underneath. I wish they had given me mates. It's pretty hard having to sleep between *odd* tablecloths. I shall complain to the landlord of this in the morning. I've never had to sleep between *odd* tablecloths at *any* hotel before."

The Colonel's voice seemed scarcely to have died away upon Basil's drowsy ear, when suddenly the sounds of music and laughter from the invalid's room startled him wide awake. The sick man's watchers were coquetting with some one who stood in the little court-yard five stories below. A certain breadth of repartee was naturally allowable at that distance; the lover avowed his passion in ardent terms, and the ladies mocked him with the same freedom, now and then totally neglecting him while they sang a snatch of song to the twanging of the guitar, or talked professional gossip, and then returning to him with some tormenting expression of tenderness.

All this, abstractly speaking, was nothing to Basil; yet he could recollect few things intended for his pleasure that had given him more satisfaction. He thought, as he glanced out into the moonlight on the high-gabled silvery roofs around and on the gardens of the convents and the towers of the quaint city, that the scene wanted nothing of the proper charm of Spanish humor and romance, and he was as grateful to those poor souls as if they had meant him a favor. To us of the hither side of the foot-lights, there is always something fascinating in the life of the strange beings who dwell beyond them, and who are never so unreal as in their own characters. In their shabby bestowal in those mean upper rooms, their tawdry poverty, their merry submission to the errors and caprices of destiny, their mutual kindliness and careless friendship, these unprofitable devotees of the twinkling-footed burlesque seemed to be playing rather than living the life of strolling players; and their love-making was the last touch of a comedy that Basil could hardly accept as reality, it was so much more like something seen upon the stage. He would not have detracted anything from the commonness and cheapness of the *mise en scène*, for that, he reflected drowsily and confusedly, helped to give it an air of fact and make it like an episode of fiction. But above all, he was pleased with the natural eventlessness of the whole adventure, which was in perfect agreement with his taste; and just as his reveries began to lose shape in dreams, he was aware of an absurd pride in the fact that all this could have happened to him in our commonplace time and hemisphere. "Why," he thought, "if I were a student in Alcalá, what better could I have asked?" And as at last his soul swung out from its moorings and lapsed down the broad slowly circling tides out in the sea of sleep, he was conscious of one subtle touch of compassion for those poor strollers,—a pity so delicate and fine and tender that it hardly seemed his own but rather a sense of the compassion that pities the whole world.

X

HOMEWARD AND HOME

THE TRAVELLERS all met at breakfast and duly discussed the adventures of the night; and for the rest, the forenoon passed rapidly and slowly with Basil and Isabel, as regret to leave Quebec, or the natural impatience of travellers to be off, overcame them. Isabel spent part of it in shopping, for she had found some small sums of money and certain odd corners in her trunks still unappropriated, and the handsome stores on the Rue Fabrique were very tempting. She said she would just go in and look; and the wise reader imagines the result. As she knelt over her boxes, trying so to distribute her purchases as to make them look as if they were old, old things of hers, which she had brought all the way round from Boston with her, a fleeting touch of conscience stayed her hand.

"Basil," she said, "perhaps we'd better declare *some* of these things. What's the duty on those?" she asked, pointing to certain articles.

"I don't know. About a hundred per cent *ad valorem.*"

"*C'est à dire— ?*"

"As much as they cost."

"O *then*, dearest," responded Isabel, indignantly, "it *can't* be wrong to smuggle! I won't declare a thread!"

"That's very well for you, whom they won't ask. But what if they ask *me* whether there's anything to declare?"

Isabel looked at her husband and hesitated. Then she replied in terms that I am proud to record in honor of American womanhood: "You mustn't fib about it, Basil" (heroically), "I couldn't respect you if you did" (tenderly); "but" (with decision) *"you must slip out of it some way!"*

The ladies of the Ellison party, to whom she put the case in the parlor, agreed with her perfectly. They also had done a little shopping in Quebec, and they meant to do more at Montreal before they returned to the States. Mrs. Ellison was disposed to look upon Isabel's compunctions as a kind of treason to the sex, to be forgiven only because so quickly repented.

The Ellisons were going up the Saguenay before coming on to Boston, and urged our friends hard to go with them. "No, that must be for another time," said Isabel. "Mr. March has to be home by a certain day; and we shall just get back in season." Then she made them promise to spend a day with her in Boston, and the Colonel coming to say that he had a carriage at the door for their excursion to Lorette, the two parties bade good by with affection and many explicit hopes of meeting soon again.

"What do you think of them, dearest?" demanded Isabel, as she sallied out with Basil for a final look at Quebec.

"The young lady is the nicest; and the other is well enough, too. She is a good deal like you, but with the sense of humor left out. You've only enough to save you."

"Well, her husband is jolly enough for both of them. He's funnier than you, Basil, and he hasn't any of your little languid airs and affectations. I don't know but I'm a bit disappointed in my choice, darling; but I dare say I shall work out of it. In fact, I don't know but the Colonel is a little *too* jolly. This drolling everything is rather fatiguing." And having begun, they did not stop till they had taken their friends to pieces. Dismayed then, they hastily reconstructed them, and said that they were among the pleasantest people they ever knew, and they were really very sorry to part with them, and they should do everything to make them have a good time in Boston.

They were sauntering towards Durham Terrace, where they leaned long upon the iron parapet and blest themselves with the beauty of the prospect. A tender haze hung upon the landscape and subdued it till the scene was as a dream before them. As in a dream the river lay, and dream-like the shipping moved or rested on its deep, broad bosom. Far off stretched the happy fields with their dim white villages; further still the mellow heights melted into the low hovering heaven. The tinned roofs of the Lower Town twinkled in the morning sun; around them on every hand, on that Monday forenoon when the States were stirring from ocean to ocean in feverish industry, drowsed the gray city within her walls; from the flag-staff of the citadel hung the red banner of Saint George in sleep.

Their hearts were strangely and deeply moved. It seemed to them that they looked upon the last stronghold of the Past, and that afar off to the southward they could hear the marching hosts of the invading Present; and as no young and loving soul can relinquish old things without a pang, they sighed a long, mute farewell to Quebec.

Next summer they would come again, yes; but, ah me! every one knows what next summer is!

Part of the burlesque troupe rode down in the omnibus to the Grand Trunk Ferry with them, and were good-natured to the last, having shaken hands all round with the waiters, chambermaids, and porters of the hotel. The young fellow with the bad amiable face came in a calash, and refused to overpay the driver with a gay decision that made him Basil's envy till he saw his tribulation in getting the troupe's luggage checked. There were forty pieces, and it always remained a mystery, considering the small amount of clothing necessary to those people on the stage, what could have filled their trunks. The young man and the two English blondes of American birth found places in the same car with our tourists, and enlivened the journey with their frolics. When the young man pretended to fall asleep, they wrapt his golden curly head in a shawl, and vexed him with many thumps and thrusts, till he bought a brief truce with a handful of almonds; and the ladies having no other way to eat them, one of them saucily snatched off her shoe, and cracked them hammerwise with the heel. It was all so pleasant that it ought to have been all right; and in their merry world of outlawry perhaps things are not so bad as we like to think them.

The country into which the train plunges as soon as Quebec is out of sight is very stupidly savage, and our friends had little else to do but to watch the gambols of the players, till they came to the river St. Francis, whose wandering loveliness the road follows through an infinite series of soft and beautiful landscapes, and finds everywhere glassing in its smooth current the elms and willows of its gentle shores. At one place, where its calm broke into foamy rapids, there was a huge saw-mill, covering the stream with logs and refuse, and the banks with whole cities of lumber; which also they accepted as no mean elements of the picturesque. They clung the most tenderly to traces of the peasant life they were leaving. When some French boys came aboard with wild raspberries to sell in little birch-bark canoes, they thrilled with pleasure, and bought them, but sighed then, and said, "What thing characteristic of the local life will they sell us in Maine when we get there? A section of pie poetically wrapt in a broad leaf of the squash-vine, or pop-corn in its native tissue-paper, and advertising the new Dollar Store in Portland?" They saw the quaintness vanish from the farm-houses; first the dormer-windows, then the curve of the steep roof, then the steep roof itself. By and by they came to a store with a Grecian portico and four square pine pillars. They shuddered and looked no more.

The guiltily dreaded examination of baggage at Island Pond took place at nine o'clock, without costing them a cent of duty or a pang of conscience. At that charming station the trunks are piled higgledy-piggledy into a room beside the track, where a few inspectors with stifling lamps of smoky kerosene await the passengers. There are no porters to arrange the baggage, and each lady and gentleman digs out his box, and opens it before the lordly inspector, who stirs up its contents with an unpleasant hand and passes it. He makes you feel that you are once more in the land of official insolence, and that, whatever you are collectively, you are nothing personally. Isabel, who had sent her husband upon this business with quaking meekness of heart, experienced the bold indignation of virtue at his account of the way people were made their own baggage-smashers, and would not be amused when he painted the vile terrors of each husband as he tremblingly unlocked his wife's store of contraband.

The morning light showed them the broad elmy meadows of western-looking Maine; and the Grand Trunk brought them, of course, an hour behind time into Portland. All breakfastless they hurried aboard the Boston train on the Eastern Road, and all along that line (which is built to show how uninteresting the earth can be when she is *ennuyée* of both sea and land), Basil's life became a struggle to construct a meal from the fragmentary opportunities of twenty different stations where they stopped five minutes for refreshments. At one place he achieved two cups of shameless chickory, at another three sardines, at a third a dessert of elderly bananas.

"Home again, home again, from a foreign shore,"

they softly sang as the successive courses of this feast were disposed of.

The drouth and heat, which they had briefly escaped during their sojourn in Canada, brooded sovereign upon the tiresome landscape. The red granite rocks were as if red-hot; the banks of the deep cuts were like ash-heaps; over the fields danced the sultry atmosphere; they fancied that they almost heard the grasshoppers sing above the rattle of the train. When they reached Boston at last, they were dustier than most of us would like to be a hundred years hence. The whole city was equally dusty; and they found the trees in the square before their own door gray with dust. The bit of Virginia-creeper planted under the window hung shrivelled upon its trellis.

But Isabel's aunt met them with a refreshing shower of tears and kisses in the hall, throwing a solid arm about each of them. "O you dears!" the good soul cried, "you don't know how anxious I've been about you; so many accidents happening all the time. I've never read the 'Evening Transcript' till the next morning, for fear I should find your names among the killed and wounded."

"O aunty, you're too good, always!" whimpered Isabel; and neither of the women took note of Basil, who said, "Yes, it's probably the only thing that preserved our lives."

The little tinge of discontent, which had colored their sentiment of return faded now in the kindly light of home. Their holiday was over, to be sure, but their bliss had but begun; they had entered upon that long life of holidays which is happy marriage. By the time dinner was ended they were both enthusiastic at having got back, and taking their aunt between them walked up and down the parlor with their arms round her massive waist, and talked out the gladness of their souls.

Then Basil said he really must run down to the office that afternoon, and he issued all aglow upon the street. He was so full of having been long away and of having just returned, that he unconsciously tried to impart his mood to Boston, and the dusty composure of the street and houses, as he strode along, bewildered him. He longed for some familiar face to welcome him, and in the horse-car into which he stepped he was charmed to see an acquaintance. This was a man for whom ordinarily he cared nothing, and whom he would perhaps rather have gone out upon the platform to avoid than have spoken to; but now he plunged at him with effusion, and wrung his hand, smiling from ear to ear.

The other remained coldly unaffected, after a first start of surprise at his cordiality, and then reviled the dust and heat. "But I'm going to take a little run down to Newport, to-morrow, for a week," he said. "By the way, you look as if *you* needed a little change. Aren't you going anywhere this summer?"

"So you see, my dear," observed Basil, when he had recounted the fact to Isabel at tea, "our travels are incommunicably our own. We had best say nothing about our little jaunt to other people, and they won't know we've been gone. Even if we tried, we couldn't make our wedding-journey theirs."

She gave him a great kiss of recompense and consolation. "Who wants it," she demanded, "to be Their Wedding Journey?"

XI

NIAGARA REVISITED, TWELVE YEARS AFTER THEIR WEDDING JOURNEY

LIFE HAD NOT used them ill in this time, and the fairish treatment they had received was not wholly unmerited. The twelve years past had made them older, as the years must in passing. Basil was now forty-two, and his moustache was well sprinkled with gray. Isabel was thirty-nine, and the parting of her hair had thinned and retreated; but she managed to give it an effect of youthful abundance by combing it low down upon her forehead, and roughing it there with a wet brush. By gaslight she was still very pretty; she believed that she looked more interesting, and she thought Basil's gray moustache distinguished. He had grown stouter; he filled his double-breasted frock coat compactly, and from time to time he had the buttons set forward; his hands were rounded up on the backs, and he no longer wore his old number of gloves by two sizes; no amount of powder or manipulation from the young lady in the shop would induce them to go on. But this did not matter much now, for he seldom wore gloves at all. He was glad that the fashion suffered him to spare in that direction, for he was obliged to look somewhat carefully after the outgoes. The insurance business was not what it had been, and though Basil had comfortably established himself in it, he had not made money. He sometimes thought that he might have done quite as well if he had gone into literature; but it was now too late. They had not a very large family: they had a boy of eleven, who "took after" his father, and a girl of nine, who took after the boy; but with the American feeling that their children must have the best of everything, they made it an expensive family, and they spent nearly all Basil earned.

The narrowness of their means, as well as their household cares, had kept them from taking many long journeys. They passed their winters in Boston, and their summers on the South Shore,— cheaper than the North Shore, and near enough for Basil to go up and down every day for business; but they promised themselves that some day they would revisit certain points on their wedding journey, and perhaps somewhere find their lost second-youth on the track. It was not that they cared to be young, but they wished the children to see them as they used to be when they thought themselves very old; and one lovely afternoon in June they started for Niagara.

It had been very hot for several days, but that morning the east wind came in, and crisped the air till it seemed to rustle like tinsel, and the sky was as sincerely and solidly blue as if it had been chromoed. They felt that they were really looking up into the roof of the world, when they glanced at it; but when an old gentleman hastily kissed a young woman, and commended her to the conductor as being one who was going all the way to San Francisco alone, and then risked his life by stepping off the moving train, the vastness of the great American fact began to affect Isabel disagreeably. "Isn't it *too* big, Basil?" she pleaded, peering timidly out of the little municipal consciousness in which she had been so long housed. In that seclusion she had suffered certain original tendencies to increase upon her: her nerves were more sensitive and electrical; her apprehensions had multiplied quite beyond the ratio of the dangers that beset her; and Basil had counted upon a tonic effect of the change the journey would make in their daily lives. She looked ruefully out of the window at the familiar suburbs whisking out of sight, and the continental immensity that advanced devouringly upon her. But they had the best section in the very centre of the sleeping-car,—she drew what consolation she could from the fact,—and the children's premature demand for lunch helped her to forget her anxieties; they began to be hungry as soon as the train started. She found that she had not put up sandwiches enough; and when she told Basil that he would have to get out somewhere and buy some cold chicken, he asked her what in the world had become of that whole ham she had had boiled. It seemed to him, he said, that there was enough of it to subsist them to Niagara and back; and he went on as some men do, while Somerville vanished, and even Tufts College, which assails the Bostonian vision from every point of the compass, was shut out by the curve at the foot of the Belmont hills.

They had chosen the Hoosac Tunnel route to Niagara, because, as Basil said, their experience of travel had never yet included a very long tunnel, and it would be a signal fact by which the children would always remember the journey, if nothing else remarkable happened to impress it upon them. Indeed, they were so much concerned in it that they began to ask when they should come to this tunnel, even before they began to ask for lunch; and the long time before they reached it was not perceptibly shortened by Tom's quarter-hourly consultations of his father's watch.

It scarcely seemed to Basil and Isabel that their fellow-passengers were so interesting as their fellow-passengers used to be in their former days of travel. They were soberly dressed, and were all of a middle-aged sobriety of deportment, from which nothing salient offered itself for conjecture or speculation; and there was little within the car to take their minds from the brilliant young world that flashed and sang by them outside. The belated spring had ripened, with its frequent rains, into the perfection of early summer; the grass was thicker and the foliage denser than they had ever seen it before; and when they had run out into the hills beyond Fitchburg, they saw the laurel in bloom. It was everywhere in the woods, lurking like drifts among the underbrush, and overflowing the tops, and stealing down the hollows, of the railroad embankments; a snow of blossom flushed with a mist of pink. Its shy, wild beauty ceased whenever the train stopped, but the orioles made up for its absence with their singing in the village trees about the stations; and though Fitchburg and Ayer's Junction and Athol are not names that invoke historical or romantic associations, the hearts of Basil and Isabel began to stir with the joy of travel before they had passed these points. At the first Basil got out to buy the cold chicken which had been commanded, and he recognized in the keeper of the railroad restaurant their former conductor, who had been warned by the spirits never to travel without a flower of some sort carried between his lips, and who had preserved his own life and the lives of his passengers for many years by this simple device. His presence lent the sponge cake and rhubarb pie and baked beans a supernatural interest, and reconciled Basil to the toughness of the athletic bird which the mystical ex-partner of fate had sold him; he justly reflected that if he had heard the story of the restaurateur's superstition in a foreign land, or another time, he would have found in it a certain poetry. It was this willingness to find poetry in things around them that kept his life and Isabel's fresh, and they taught their children the secret of their elixir. To be sure, it was only a *genre* poetry, but it was such as has always inspired English art and song; and now the whole family enjoyed, as if it had been a passage from Goldsmith or Wordsworth, the flying sentiment of the railroad side. There was a simple interior at one place,— a small shanty, showing through the open door a cook stove surmounted by the evening coffee-pot, with a lazy cat outstretched upon the floor in the middle distance, and an old woman standing just outside the threshold to see the train go by,—which had an unrivaled value till they came to a superannuated car on a siding in the woods, in which the railroad workmen boarded: some were lounging on the platform and at the open windows, while others were "washing up" for supper, and the whole scene was full of holiday ease and sylvan comradery that went to the hearts of the sympathetic spectators. Basil had lately been reading aloud the delightful history of Rudder Grange, and the children, who had made their secret vows never to live in anything but an old canal-boat when they grew up, owned that there were fascinating possibilities in a worn-out railroad car.

The lovely Deerfield Valley began to open on either hand,

with smooth stretches of the quiet river, and breadths of grassy intervale and table-land; the elms grouped themselves like the trees of a park; here and there the nearer hills broke away, and revealed long, deep, chasmed hollows, full of golden light and delicious shadow. There were people rowing on the water; and every pretty town had some touch of picturesqueness or pastoral charm to offer: at Greenfield, there were children playing in the new-mown hay along the railroad embankment; at Shelburne Falls, there was a game of cricket going on (among the English operatives of the cutlery works, as Basil boldly asserted). They looked down from their car-window on a young lady swinging in a hammock, in her door-yard, and on an old gentleman hoeing his potatoes; a group of girls waved their handkerchiefs to the passing train, and a boy paused in weeding a garden bed,—and probably denied that he had paused, later. In the mean time the golden haze along the mountain side changed to a clear, pearly lustre, and the quiet evening possessed the quiet land-scape. They confessed to each other that it was all as sweet and beautiful as it used to be; and in fact they had seen palaces, in other days, which did not give them the pleasure they found in a woodcutter's shanty, losing itself among the shadows in a solitude of the hills. The tunnel, after this, was a gross and material sensa-tion; but they joined the children in trying to hold and keep it, and Basil let the boy time it by his watch. "Now," said Tom, when five minutes were gone, "we are under the very centre of the mountain." But the tunnel was like all accomplished facts, all hopes fulfilled, valueless to the soul, and scarcely appreciable to the sense; and the children emerged at North Adams with but a mean opinion of that great feat of engineering. Basil drew a pretty moral from their experience. "If you rode upon a comet you would be disappointed. Take my advice, and never ride upon a comet. I shouldn't object to your riding on a little meteor, —you wouldn't expect much of that; but I warn you against comets; they are as bad as tunnels."

The children thought this moral was a joke at their expense, and as they were a little sleepy they permitted themselves the

luxury of feeling trifled with. But they woke, refreshed and encouraged, from slumbers that had evidently been unbroken,
though they both protested that they had not slept a wink the
whole night, and gave themselves up to wonder at the intermina-
ble levels of Western New York over which the train was running. The longing to come to an edge, somewhere, that the New
England traveller experiences on this plain was inarticulate
with the children; but it breathed in the sigh with which Isabel
welcomed even the architectural inequalities of a city into which
they drew in the early morning. This city showed to their weary
eyes a noble stretch of river, from the waters of which lofty
piles of buildings rose abruptly; and Isabel, being left to guess
where they were, could think of no other place so picturesque
as Rochester.

"Yes," said her husband; "it is our own Enchanted City. I
wonder if that unstinted hospitality is still dispensed by the good
head waiter at the hotel where we stopped, to bridal parties who
have passed the ordeal of the haughty hotel clerk. I wonder what
has become of that hotel clerk. Has he fallen, through pride, to
some lower level, or has he bowed his arrogant spirit to the demands of advancing civilization, and realized that he is the serv-
ant, and not the master, of the public? I think I've noticed, since
his time, a growing kindness in hotel clerks; or perhaps I have
become of a more impressive presence; they certainly unbend to
me a little more. I should like to go up to our hotel, and try myself on our old enemy, if he is still there. I can fancy how his shirt
front has expanded in these twelve years past; he has grown a
little bald, after the fashion of middle-aged hotel clerks, but he
parts his hair very much on one side, and brushes it squarely
across his forehead to hide his loss; the forefinger that he touches
that little snap-bell with, when he doesn't look at you, must be
very pudgy now. Come, let us get out and breakfast at Rochester;
they will give us broiled white-fish; and we can show the children
where Sam Patch jumped over Genesee Falls, and"—

"No, no, Basil," cried his wife. "It would be sacrilege! All
that is sacred to those dear young days of ours; and I wouldn't

think of trying to repeat it. Our own ghosts would rise up in that dining-room to reproach us for our intrusion! O, perhaps we have done a wicked thing in coming this journey! We ought to have left the past alone; we shall only mar our memories of all these beautiful places. Do you suppose Buffalo *can* be as poetical as it was then? Buffalo! The name doesn't invite the Muse very much. Perhaps it *never* was very poetical! O, Basil, dear, I'm afraid we have only come to find out that we were mistaken about everything! Let's leave Rochester alone, at any rate!"

"I'm not troubled! We won't disturb our dream of Rochester; but I don't despair of Buffalo. I'm sure that Buffalo will be all that our fancy ever painted it. I believe in Buffalo."

"Well, well," murmured Isabel, "I hope you're right;" and she put some things together for leaving their car at Buffalo, while they were still two hours away.

When they reached a place where the land mated its level with the level of the lake, they ran into a wilderness of railroad cars, in a world where life seemed to be operated solely by locomotives and their helpless minions. The bellowing and bleating trains were arriving in every direction, not only along the ground floor of the plain, but stately stretches of trestle-work, which curved and extended across the plain, carried them to and fro overhead. The travellers owned that this railroad suburb had its own impressiveness, and they said that the trestle-work was as noble in effect as the lines of aqueduct that stalk across the Roman Campagna. Perhaps this was because they had not seen the Campagna or its aqueducts for a great while; but they were so glad to find themselves in the spirit of their former journey again that they were amiable to everything. When the children first caught sight of the lake's delicious blue, and cried out that it was lovelier than the sea, they felt quite a local pride in their preference. It was what Isabel had said twelve years before, on first beholding the lake.

But they did not really see the lake till they had taken the train for Niagara Falls, after breakfasting in the depot, where the children, used to the severe native or the patronizing Irish ministrations of Boston restaurants and hotels, reveled for the first time in the affectionate devotion of a black waiter. There was already a ridiculous abundance and variety on the table; but this waiter brought them strawberries and again strawberries, and repeated plates of griddle cakes with maple syrup; and he hung over the back of first one chair and then another with an unselfish joy in the appetites of the breakfasters which gave Basil renewed hopes of his race. "Such rapture in serving argues a largeness of nature which will be recognized hereafter," he said, feeling about in his waistcoat pocket for a quarter. It seemed a pity to render the waiter's zeal retroactively interested, but in view of the fact that he possibly expected the quarter, there was nothing else to do; and by a mysterious stroke of gratitude the waiter delivered them into the hands of a friend, who took another quarter from them for carrying their bags and wraps to the train. This second retainer approved their admiration of the aesthetic forms and colors of the depot colonnade; and being asked if that were the depot whose roof had fallen in some years before, proudly replied that it was.

"There were a great many killed, weren't there?" asked Basil, with sympathetic satisfaction in the disaster. The porter seemed humiliated; he confessed the mortifying truth that the loss of life was small, but he recovered a just self-respect in adding, "If the roof had fallen in five minutes sooner, it would have killed about three hundred people."

Basil had promised the children a sight of the Rapids before they reached the Falls, and they held him rigidly accountable from the moment they entered the train, and began to run out of the city between the river and the canal. He attempted a diversion with the canal boats, and tried to bring forward the subject of Rudder Grange in that connection. They said that the canal boats were splendid, but they were looking for the Rapids now; and they declined to be interested in a window in one of the boats, which Basil said was just like the window that the Rudder Granger and the boarder had popped Pomona out of when they took her for a burglar.

"You spoil those children, Basil," said his wife, as they clambered over him, and clamored for the Rapids.

"At present I'm giving them an object-lesson in patience and self-denial; they are experiencing the fact that they can't have the Rapids till they get to them, and probably they'll be disappointed in them when they arrive."

In fact, they valued the Rapids very little more than the Hoosac Tunnel, when they came in sight of them, at last; and Basil had some question in his own mind whether the Rapids had not dwindled since his former visit. He did not breathe this doubt to Isabel, however, and she arrived at the Falls with unabated expectations. They were going to spend only half a day there; and they turned into the station, away from the phalanx of omnibuses, when they dismounted from their train. They seemed, as before, to be the only passengers who had arrived, and they found an abundant choice of carriages waiting in the street, outside the station. The Niagara hackman may once have been a predatory and very rampant animal, but public opinion, long expressed through the public prints, has reduced him to silence and meekness. Apparently, he may not so much as beckon with his whip to the arriving wayfarer; it is certain that he cannot cross the pavement to the station door; and Basil, inviting one of them to negotiation, was himself required by the attendant policeman to step out to the curbstone, and complete his transaction there. It was an impressive illustration of the power of a free press, but upon the whole Basil found the effect melancholy; it had the saddening quality which inheres in every sort of perfection. The hackman, reduced to entire order, appealed to his compassion, and he had not the heart to beat him down from his moderate first demand, as perhaps he ought to have done.

They drove directly to the cataract, and found themselves in the pretty grove beside the American Fall, and in the air whose dampness was as familiar as if they had breathed it all their childhood. It was full now of the fragrance of some sort of wild blossom; and again they had that old, entrancing sense of the mingled awfulness and loveliness of the great spectacle. This sylvan perfume, the gayety of the sunshine, the mildness of the breeze that stirred the leaves overhead, and the bird-singing that made itself heard amid the roar of the Rapids and the solemn incessant plunge of the cataract, moved their hearts, and made them children with the boy and girl, who stood rapt for a moment and then broke into joyful wonder. They could sympathize with the ardor with which Tom longed to tempt fate at the brink of the river, and over the tops of the parapets which have been built along the edge of the precipice, and they equally entered into the terror with which Bella screamed at his suicidal zeal. They joined her in restraining him; they reduced him to a beggarly account of half a dozen stones, flung into the Rapids at not less than ten paces from the brink; and they would not let him toss the smallest pebble over the parapet, though he laughed to scorn the notion that anybody should be hurt by them below.

It seemed to them that the triviality of man in the surroundings of the Falls had increased with the lapse of time. There were more booths and bazars, and more colored feather fans with whole birds spitted in the centres; and there was an offensive array of blue and green and yellow glasses on the shore, through which you were expected to look at the Falls gratis. They missed the simple dignity of the blanching Indian maids, who used to squat about on the grass, with their laps full of moccasins and pin-cushions. But, as of old, the photographer came out of his saloon, and invited them to pose for a family group; representing that the light and the spray were singularly propitious, and that everything in nature invited them to be taken. Basil put him off gently, for the sake of the time when he had refused to be photographed in a bridal group, and took refuge from him in the long low building from which you descend to the foot of the cataract.

The grove beside the American Fall has been inclosed, and named Prospect Park, by a company which exacts half a dollar for admittance, and then makes you free of all its wonders and conveniences, for which you once had to pay severally. This is well enough; but formerly you could refuse to go down the inclined tramway, and now you cannot, without feeling that you have failed to get your money's worth. It was in this illogical spirit of economy that Basil invited his family to the descent; but Isabel shook her head. "No, you go with the children," she said, "and I will stay here, till you get back;" her agonized countenance added, "and pray for you;" and Basil took his children on either side of him, and rumbled down the terrible descent with much of the excitement that attends travel in an open horse-car. When he stepped out of the car he felt that increase of courage which comes to every man after safely passing through danger. He resolved to brave the mists and slippery stones at the foot of the Fall; and he would have plunged at once into this fresh peril, if he had not been prevented by the Prospect Park Company. This ingenious association has built a large tunnel-like shed quite to the water's edge, so that you cannot view the cataract as you once could, at a reasonable remoteness, but must emerge from the building into a storm of spray. The roof of the tunnel is painted with a lively effect in party-colored stripes, and is lettered "The Shadow of the Rock," so that you take it at first to be an appeal to your aesthetic sense; but the real object of the company is not apparent till you put your head out into the tempest, when you agree with the nearest guide—and one is always very near—that you had better have an oil-skin dress, as Basil did. He told the guide that he did not wish to go under the Fall, and the guide confidentially admitted that there was no fun in that, any way; and in the mean time he equipped him and his children for their foray into the mist. When they issued forth, under their friend's leadership, Basil felt that, with his children clinging to each hand, he looked like some sort of animal with its young, and, though not unsocial by nature, he was glad to be among strangers for the time. They climbed hither and thither over the rocks, and lifted their streaming faces for the views which the guide pointed out; and in a rift of the spray they really caught one glorious glimpse of the whole sweep of the Fall. The next instant the spray swirled back, and they were glad to turn for a sight of the rainbow, lying in a circle on the rocks as quietly and naturally as if that had been the habit of rainbows ever since the flood. This was all there was to be done, and they streamed back into the tunnel, where they disrobed in the face of a menacing placard, which announced that the hire of a guide and a dress for going under the Fall was one dollar.

"Will they make you pay a dollar for each of us, papa?" asked Tom, fearfully.

"O, pooh, no!" returned Basil; "we haven't been under the Fall." But he sought out the proprietor with a trembling heart. The proprietor was a man of severely logical mind: he said that the charge would be three dollars, for they had had the use of the dresses and the guide just the same as if they had gone under the Fall; and he refused to recognize anything misleading in the dressing-room placard. In fine, he left Basil without a leg to stand upon. It was not so much the three dollars as the sense of having been swindled that vexed him; and he instantly resolved not to share his annoyance with Isabel. Why, indeed, should he put that burden upon her? If she were none the wiser, she would be none the poorer; and he ought to be willing to deny himself her sympathy for the sake of sparing her needless pain.

He met her at the top of the inclined tramway with a face of exemplary unconsciousness, and he listened with her to the tale their coachman told, as they sat in a pretty arbor looking out on the Rapids, of a Frenchman and his wife. This Frenchman had returned, one morning, from a stroll on Goat Island, and reported with much apparent concern that his wife had fallen into the water, and been carried over the Fall. It was so natural for a man to grieve for the loss of his wife, under the peculiar circumstances, that every one condoled with the widower; but when, a few days later, her body was found, and the distracted husband refused to come back from New York to her funeral, there was a general regret that he had not been arrested. A flash of conviction illumed the whole fact to Basil's guilty consciousness: this unhappy Frenchman had paid a dollar for the use of an oil-skin suit at the foot of the Fall, and had been ashamed to confess the swindle to his wife, till, in a moment of remorse and madness, he shouted the fact into her ear, and then—

Basil looked at the mother of his children, and registered a vow that if he got away from Niagara without being forced to a similar excess he would confess his guilt to Isabel at the very first act of spendthrift profusion she committed. The guide pointed out the rock in the Rapids to which Avery had clung for twenty-four hours before he was carried over the Falls, and to the morbid fancy of the deceitful husband Isabel's bonnet ribbons seemed to flutter from the pointed reef. He could endure the pretty arbor no longer. "Come, children!" he cried, with a wild, unnatural gayety; "let us go to Goat Island, and see the Bridge to the Three Sisters, that your mother was afraid to walk back on after she had crossed it."

"For shame, Basil!" retorted Isabel. "You know it was you who were afraid of that bridge."

The children, who knew the story by heart, laughed with their father at the monstrous pretension; and his simulated hilarity only increased upon paying a toll of two dollars at the Goat Island bridge.

"What extortion!" cried Isabel, with an indignation that secretly unnerved him. He trembled upon the verge of confession; but he had finally the moral force to resist. He suffered her to compute the cost of their stay at Niagara without allowing those three dollars to enter into her calculation; he even began to think what justificative extravagance he could tempt her to. He suggested the purchase of local bricabrac; he asked her if she would not like to dine at the International, for old times' sake. But she answered, with disheartening virtue, that they must not think of such a thing, after what they had spent already. Nothing, perhaps, marked the confirmed husband in Basil more than these hidden fears and reluctances.

In the mean time Isabel ignorantly abandoned herself to the charm of the place, which she found unimpaired, in spite of the reported ravages of improvement about Niagara. Goat Island

was still the sylvan solitude of twelve years ago, haunted by even
fewer nymphs and dryads than of old. The air was full of the perfume that scented it at Prospect Park; the leaves showered them
with shade and sun, as they drove along. "If it were not for the
children here," she said, "I should think that our first drive on
Goat Island had never ended."

She sighed a little, and Basil leaned forward and took her hand
in his. "It never has ended; it's the same drive; only we are
younger now, and enjoy it more." It always touched him when
Isabel was sentimental about the past, for the years had tended
to make her rather more seriously maternal towards him than
towards the other children; and he recognized that these fond
reminiscences were the expression of the girlhood still lurking
deep within her heart.

She shook her head. "No, but I'm willing the children should
be young in our place. It's only fair they should have their turn."

She remained in the carriage, while Basil visited the various
points of view on Luna Island with the boy and girl. A boy is
probably of considerable interest to himself, and a man looks
back at his own boyhood with some pathos. But in his actuality a
boy has very little to commend him to the toleration of other
human beings. Tom was very well, as boys go; but now his con-
tribution to the common enjoyment was to venture as near as
possible to all perilous edges; to throw stones into the water, and
to make as if to throw them over precipices on the people below;
to pepper his father with questions, and to collect cumbrous
mementos of the vegetable and mineral kingdoms. He kept the
carriage waiting a good five minutes, while he could cut his
initials on a hand-rail. "You can come back and see 'em on your
bridal tower," said the driver. Isabel gave a little start, as if she
had almost thought of something she was trying to think of.

They occasionally met ladies driving, and sometimes they encountered a couple making a tour of the island on foot. But none
of these people were young, and Basil reported that the Three
Sisters were inhabited only by persons of like maturity; even a

group of people who were eating lunch to the music of the shouting Rapids, on the outer edge of the last Sister, were no younger, apparently.

Isabel did not get out of the carriage to verify his report; she preferred to refute his story of her former panic on those islands by remaining serenely seated while he visited them. She thus lost a superb novelty which nature has lately added to the wonders of this Fall, in that place at the edge of the great Horse Shoe where the rock has fallen and left a peculiarly shaped chasm: through this the spray leaps up from below, and flashes a hundred feet into the air, in rocket-like jets and points, and then breaks and dissolves away in the pyrotechnic curves of a perpetual Fourth of July. Basil said something like this in celebrating the display, with the purpose of rendering her loss more poignant; but she replied, with tranquil piety, that she would rather keep her Niagara unchanged; and she declared that, as she understood him, there must be something rather cheap and conscious in the new feature. She approved, however, of the change that had removed that foolish little Terrapin Tower from the brink on which it stood, and she confessed that she could have enjoyed a little variety in the stories the driver told them of the Indian burial-ground on the island: they were exactly the stories she and Basil had heard twelve years before, and the ill-starred goats, from which the island took its name, perished once more in his narrative.

Under the influence of his romances our travellers began to find the whole scene hackneyed; and they were glad to part from him a little sooner than they had bargained to do. They strolled about the anomalous village on foot, and once more marveled at the paucity of travel and the enormity of the local preparation. Surely the hotels are nowhere else in the world so large! Could there ever have been visitors enough at Niagara to fill them? They were built so big for some good reason, no doubt; but it is no more apparent than why all these magnificent equipages are waiting about the empty streets for the people who never come to hire them.

"It seems to me that I don't see so many strangers here as I used," Basil had suggested to their driver.

"O, they haven't commenced coming yet," he replied, with hardy cheerfulness, and pretended that they were plenty enough in July and August.

They went to dine at the modest restaurant of a colored man, who advertised a *table d'hôte* dinner on a board at his door; and they put their misgivings to him, which seemed to grieve him, and he contended that Niagara was as prosperous and as much resorted to as ever. In fact, they observed that their regret for the supposed decline of the Falls as a summer resort was nowhere popular in the village, and they desisted in their offers of sympathy, after their rebuff from the restaurateur.

Basil got his family away to the station after dinner, and left them there, while he walked down the village street, for a closer inspection of the hotels. At the door of the largest a pair of children sported in the solitude, as fearlessly as the birds on Selkirk's island; looking into the hotel, he saw a few porters and call-boys seated in statuesque repose against the wall, while the clerk pined in dreamless inactivity behind the register; some deserted ladies flitted through the door of the parlor at the side. He recalled the evening of his former visit, when he and Isabel had met the Ellisons in that parlor, and it seemed, in the retrospect, a scene of the wildest gayety. He turned for consolation into the barber's shop, where he found himself the only customer, and no busy sound of "Next" greeted his ear. But the barber, like all the rest, said that Niagara was not unusually empty; and he came out feeling bewildered and defrauded. Surely the agent of the boats which descend the Rapids of the St. Lawrence must be frank, if Basil went to him and pretended that he was going to buy a ticket. But a glance at the agent's sign showed Basil that the agent, with his brave jollity of manner and his impressive "*Good*-morning," had passed away from the deceits of travel, and that he was now inherited by his widow, who in turn was absent, and temporarily represented by their son. The boy, in supplying Basil with an advertisement of the line, made a specious show of haste, as if there were a long queue of tourists waiting behind him to be served with tickets. Perhaps there was, indeed, a spectral line there, but Basil was the only tourist present in the flesh, and he shivered in his isolation, and fled with the advertisement in his hand. Isabel met him at the door of the station with a frightened face.

"Basil," she cried, "I have found out what the trouble is! *Where are the brides ?*"

He took her outstretched hands in his, and passing one of them through his arm walked with her apart from the children, who were examining at the news-man's booth the moccasins and the birch-bark bricabrac of the Irish aborigines, and the cups and vases of Niagara spar imported from Devonshire.

"My dear," he said, "there are no brides; everybody was married twelve years ago, and the brides are middle-aged mothers of families now, and don't come to Niagara if they are wise."

"Yes," she desolately asserted, "that is so! Something has been hanging over me ever since we came, and suddenly I realized that it was the absence of the brides. But—but— Down at the hotels— Didn't you see anything bridal there? When the omnibuses arrived, was there no burst of minstrelsy? Was there"—

She could not go on, but sank nervelessly into the nearest seat.

"Perhaps," said Basil, dreamily regarding the contest of Tom and Bella for a newly-purchased paper of sour cherries, and helplessly forecasting in his remoter mind the probable consequences, "there were both brides and minstrelsy at the hotel, if I had only had the eyes to see and the ears to hear. In this world, my dear, we are always of our own time, and we live amid contemporary things. I dare say there were middle-aged people at Niagara when we were here before, but we did not meet them, nor they us. I dare say that the place is now swarming with bridal couples, and it is because they are invisible and inaudible to us that it seems such a howling wilderness. But the hotel clerks and the restaurateurs and the hackmen know them, and that is the reason why they receive with surprise and even offense our sympathy for their loneliness. Do you suppose, Isabel, that if you were to lay your head on my shoulder, in a bridal manner, it would do anything to bring us *en rapport* with that lost bridal world again?"

Isabel caught away her hand. "Basil," she cried, "it would be disgusting! I wouldn't do it for the world—not even for *that* world. I saw one middle-aged couple on Goat Island, while you were down at the Cave of the Winds, or somewhere, with the children. They were sitting on some steps, he a step below her, and he seemed to want to put his head on her knee; but I gazed at him sternly, and he didn't dare. We should look like them, if we yielded to any outburst of affection. Don't you think we should look like them?"

"I don't know," said Basil. "You are certainly a little wrinkled, my dear."

"And you are very fat, Basil."

They glanced at each other with a flash of resentment, and then they both laughed. "We couldn't look young if we quarreled a week," he said. "We had better content ourselves with feeling young, as I hope we shall do if we live to be ninety. It will be the loss of others if they don't see our bloom upon us. Shall I get you a paper of cherries, Isabel? The children seem to be enjoying them."

Isabel sprang upon her offspring with a cry of despair. "O, what shall I do? Now we shall not have a wink of sleep with them to-night. Where *is* that nux?" She hunted for the medicine in her bag, and the children submitted; for they had eaten all the cherries, and they took their medicine without a murmur. "I wonder at your letting them eat the sour things, Basil," said their mother, when the children had run off to the news-stand again.

"I wonder that you left me to see what they were doing," promptly retorted their father.

"It was your nonsense about the brides," said Isabel; "and I think this has been a lesson to us. *Don't* let them get anything else to eat, dearest."

"They are safe; they have no more money. They are frugally confining themselves to the admiration of the Japanese bows and arrows yonder. Why have our Indians taken to making Japanese bows and arrows?"

Isabel despised the small pleasantry. "Then you saw nobody at the hotel?" she asked.

"Not even the Ellisons," said Basil.

"Ah, yes," said Isabel; "that was where we met them. How long ago it seems! And poor little Kitty! I wonder what has become of them? But I'm glad they're not here. That's what makes you realize your age: meeting the same people in the same place a great while after, and seeing how old they've grown. I don't think I could bear to see Kitty Ellison again. I'm glad she didn't come to visit us in Boston, though, after what happened, she couldn't, poor thing! I wonder if she's ever regretted her breaking with him in the way she did. It's a very painful thing to think of,—such an inconclusive conclusion; it always seemed as if they ought to meet again, somewhere."

"I don't believe she ever wished it."

"A man can't tell what a woman wishes."

"Well, neither can a woman," returned Basil, lightly.

His wife remained serious. "It was a very fine point,—a very little thing to reject a man for. I felt that when I first read her letter about it."

Basil yawned. "I don't believe I ever knew just what the point was."

"O yes, you did; but you forget everything. You know that they met two Boston ladies just after they were engaged, and she believed that he didn't introduce her because he was ashamed of her countrified appearance before them."

"It *was* a pretty fine point," said Basil, and he laughed provokingly.

"He might not have meant to ignore her," answered Isabel thoughtfully; "he might have chosen not to introduce her because he felt too proud of her to subject her to any possible misappreciation from them. You might have looked at it in that way."

"Why didn't *you* look at it in that way? You advised her against giving him another chance. Why did you?"

"Why?" repeated Isabel, absently. "O, a woman doesn't

judge a man by what he *does*, but by what he *is!* I knew that if she dismissed him it was because she never really had trusted or could trust his love; and I thought she had better not make another trial."

"Well, very possibly you were right. At any rate, you have the consolation of knowing that it's too late to help it now."

"Yes, it's too late," said Isabel; and her thoughts went back to her meeting with the young girl whom she had liked so much, and whose after history had interested her so painfully. It seemed to her a hard world that could come to nothing better than that for the girl whom she had seen in her first glimpse of it that night. Where was she now? What had become of her? If she had married that man, would she have been any happier? Marriage was not the poetic dream of perfect union that a girl imagines it; she herself had found that out. It was a state of trial, of probation; it was an ordeal, not an ecstasy. If she and Basil had broken each other's hearts and parted, would not the fragments of their lives have been on a much finer, much higher plane? Had not the commonplace, every-day experiences of marriage vulgarized them both? To be sure, there were the children; but if they had never had the children, she would never have missed them; and if Basil had, for example, died just before they were married— She started from this wicked reverie, and ran towards her husband, whose broad, honest back, with no visible neck or shirt-collar, was turned towards her, as he stood, with his head thrown up, studying a time-table on the wall; she passed her arm convulsively through his, and pulled him away.

"It's time to be getting our bags out to the train, Basil! Come, Bella! Tom, we're going!"

The children reluctantly turned from the news-man's trumpery; and they all went out to the track, and took seats on the benches under the colonnade. While they waited, the train for Buffalo drew in, and they remained watching it till it started. In the last car that passed them, when it was fairly under way, a face looked full at Isabel from one of the windows. In that moment of astonishment she forgot to observe whether it was sad or glad; she only saw, or believed she saw, the light of recognition dawn into its eyes, and then it was gone.

"Basil!" she cried, "stop the train! That was Kitty Ellison!"

"O no, it wasn't," said Basil, easily. "It looked like her; but it looked at least ten years older."

"Why, of course it was! We're all ten years older," returned his wife in such indignation at his stupidity that she neglected to insist upon his stopping the train, which was rapidly diminishing in the perspective.

He declared it was only a fancied resemblance; she contended that this was in the neighborhood of Eriecreek, and it must be Kitty; and thus one of their most inveterate disagreements began.

Their own train drew into the depot, and they disputed upon the fact in question till they entered on the passage of the Suspension Bridge. Then Basil rose and called the children to his side. On the left hand, far up the river, the great Fall shows, with its mists at its foot and its rainbow on its brow, as silent and still as if it were vastly painted there; and below the bridge, on the right, leap the Rapids in the narrow gorge, like seas on a rocky shore. "Look on both sides, now," he said to the children. "Isabel, you must see this!"

Isabel had been preparing for the passage of this bridge ever since she left Boston. "Never!" she exclaimed. She instantly closed her eyes, and hid her face in her handkerchief. Thanks to this precaution of hers, the train crossed the bridge in perfect safety.

Notes to the Text

15.29ff.   These lines comprise the third stanza of John J. Piatt's "The Morning Street," from *Poems of Two Friends* by Piatt and Howells (Columbus, 1860), p. 2. Knowledge of the authorship gives personal application to Basil March's praise of the poem.

30.34   From Tennyson's "Mariana in the South," l. 39; the line begins, "But day . . . ."

37.22   From Tennyson's "The Lotos-Eaters," l. 153.

82.8–10   A paraphrase of William Cowper's "Verses Supposed to be Written by Alexander Selkirk." The poem begins, "I am monarch of all I survey," and the first half of the second stanza reads:

> I am out of humanity's reach,
> I must finish my journey alone,
> Never hear the sweet music of speech;
> I start at the sound of my own.

86–88   The poem is by Howells. Gibson and Arms (*Bibliography*, p. 25) did not locate any publication prior to its appearance here, and it occurs in the manuscript of the novel in two versions, both extensively revised. Howells reprinted the poem in his *Poems* (Boston, 1873 and 1886), and in both collections, on the line below the title, is "Niagara, 1853," the location and date of the incident.

93.6–7   From Milton's "Lycidas," ll. 168–170:

> So sinks the day-star in the Ocean bed,
> And yet anon repairs his drooping head,
> And tricks his beams. . . .

130.25–26   From Coleridge's "Christabel," Pt. II, ll. 412–413; l. 412 starts, "And to . . . ."

139.1ff.   From Francis Parkman's *Pioneers of France in the New World* (Boston, 1865), pp. 191, 193.

154.25   From *King Henry VIII*, III, ii, 360.

162.22   From Tennyson's "The Lotos-Eaters," l. 9.

178.16   From Marshall Spring Pike's "Home Again," reprinted in *Lincoln Literary Collection*, ed. J. P. McCaskey (New York, 1897), p. 353.

TEXTUAL APPARATUS

Textual Commentary

A considerable number of authoritative documents bearing on the present text require comment. The holograph manuscript, described and discussed more fully on pages 215–218, is incomplete and clearly provisional. Although several revised and corrected versions of text in either holograph, typescript, or proof may reasonably be posited, none is known to have survived; the work was first published in the *Atlantic Monthly* between July and December 1871. The first edition (BAL 9558), under the James R. Osgood and Company imprint, was printed in an initial press-run of 1,440 sets of sheets by H. O. Houghton and Company early in December 1871, first offered for sale on 19 December, and deposited for copyright on 27 December 1871 (though the title page carries the date 1872).[1] This edition featured

---

1. The major source of information about the general publishing history of *Their Wedding Journey* is the business records, now on deposit at the Houghton Library at Harvard University, of Houghton Mifflin and Company and its predecessors—among them James R. Osgood and Company—and of the printing firm of H. O. Houghton and Company. The most pertinent of the many sets of extant records are the Cost Books of Allen and Ticknor and successors (which cover the period 1832–1880) and of H. O. Houghton and Company (1872–1912); the Printing Orders of H. O. Houghton and Company (1894–1901); and the Sheet-Stock Books of the several companies (1880–1924).

The Cost Books offer information about, among other things, the dates and costs of typesetting and plating of books; labor, paper, binding, and advertising costs; royalties; and the number of sets of sheets for which the printer billed the publisher. For the years 1832 to 1858 these records have been edited by Warren S. Tyron and William Charvat, *The Cost Books of Ticknor and Fields* (New York, 1949). The Printing Orders were records kept in the printing shop itself on the progress of the book from date of order to final shipment to the bindery. A typical entry included the number of sets of sheets ordered, a description of the general format of the book (number of pages and signatures), the amount and kind of paper, and the number of sets of sheets actually sent to the bindery. The Printing Orders do not give the date when the book was on the press—nor do any other of the records. The Sheet-Stock Books are exactly what the name suggests: bindery records of the number of sets of sheets received from the printer and a date-by-date ledger of the number taken from this stock for binding.

Of all the sets of records, the Sheet-Stock Books are the most valuable for basic information about the number of re-impressions and their size. None of them is illustrations by Augustus Hoppin. Between December 1871 and September 1887, 32 re-impressions of these plates were made, with the total number of copies reaching approximately 22,000. For the first ten chapters, these three states of the text, as will be made clear below, are the only ones which have primary authority.

Osgood introduced a Pocket Edition in 1875; the first press-run called for 3,000 sets of sheets on 27 April. Thereafter, until 1885, two re-impressions added only approximately 300 to this total. Between 14 February 1888 and 24 August 1900 these plates, with "Niagara Revisited" added (it was originally published in the *Atlantic Monthly* for May 1883),[2] were re-impressed five times for a total of 2,000 copies in this complete form.

Two pirated Canadian editions have been observed. One, under the Belford Brothers (Toronto) imprint, was released in 1876; the other, under the Musson Book Co., Limited (Toronto) imprint, is undated. An authorized British edition, under the David Douglas (Edinburgh) imprint, went through at least seven impressions totaling approximately 28,300 copies between 1882 and 1911;[3] the authorized Tauchnitz Edition (vol. 2186 in the Collection of British Authors) appeared in 1883. There is no evidence that Howells had anything to do with the preparation of these editions; the Belford Edition derives from the 1875 Pocket Edition, the other three from the first-edition plates, and all exclude the "Niagara Revisited" chapter. Of these only the Douglas Edition was fully collated.[4]

---

completely reliable in all aspects. The Cost Books, for example, do include first-impression information, but are inadequate for later printings, particularly during the period when the two sets of Cost Books overlap; and the Printing Orders are random at best, and contain little concerning printings of Howells' books in the various educational series published by the companies. Taken together, however, the records provide uncommonly full information of the kind seldom available to the student of the work of any author.

2. For the interesting story of the separate printing in 1884 of *Niagara Revisited* by the Chicago advertising firm D. Dalziel for the Fitchburg Railroad, see Rudolf and Clara M. Kirk, "*Niagara Revisited*, by W. D. Howells: The Story of Its Publication and Suppression," in *Essays in Literary History Presented to J. Milton French*, ed. Rudolf Kirk and C. F. Main (New Brunswick, N.J., 1960), pp. 177–195.

3. These figures are drawn from the records of T. & A. Constable, London, and are cited with the permission of P. J. W. Kilpatrick.

4. The following printed items, including at least first and last impressions, were collated in the preparation of the present text: copies of the *Atlantic Monthly* in the Indiana University (AP2.A8) and Skidmore College libraries; copies of the 1872 edition, BAL 9558, in the Lilly Library (PS2025.T5, PS2025.T5 1872), in the

The book continued to sell modestly but steadily, and in 1887 Houghton Mifflin and Company, using the plates of the first edition for chapters i-x, brought out what must be called a new edition (BAL 9632) by virtue of the additional chapter ("Niagara Revisited") set here for the first time from the *Atlantic Monthly* text. The twenty-three re-impressions called for between 1888 and 1921 brought the total number of copies for this edition to approximately 7,000.

A new Houghton Mifflin edition with new illustrations by Clifford Carleton appeared in two formats in 1895 (G&A 95-A).⁵ The large paper format in two volumes was "printed at the Riverside Press" in late September or early October 1894 in a press-run of approximately 250 sets of sheets. A trade or "Holiday Edition," bearing the Houghton Mifflin and Company imprint, first printed in early October 1894, is also dated 1895. After these two impressions, the plates were re-impressed five more times between late 1894 and 1916. Altogether, approximately 5,000 copies from these plates were produced. The "Niagara Revisited" chapter in this edition derived from the edition of 1887 (BAL 9632) rather than independently from the serial.

The choice of copy-text from among these phases of the text depends first of all on the nature of the textual variants to be observed. There are hundreds of variants in accidentals between the holograph manuscript and the serial text and some 800 substantive ones (involving as many as 5,000 words). Between the serial and the first edition (BAL 9558) there are over 250 substantive and nearly 300 accidental variants. In addition to normal corruption of accidentals, there are six single-word variants between the *Atlantic* "Niagara Revisited" and chapter xi of the 1887 edition (BAL 9632). Three more substantive variants were introduced when this chapter was set for

Howells Edition Center (HE9558.16), in the Ohio State University Library (PS2029.T5 1872), and in Edwin H. Cady's collection, and of the edition of 1887, BAL 9632, in the Howells Edition Center (HE9632.9), in John Reeves' collection, and in the University of Pennsylvania (813.H835Tᵃ); copies of the Osgood 1875 Pocket Edition in the Howells Edition Center (HE Pocket Ed. 1.1), in William M. Gibson's collection, and in the Ohio State University Library (PS2029.T4 1893); copies of the British edition in the Howells Edition Center (HE British Ed. 2.1) and in William M. Gibson's collection; copies of the edition of 1895, G&A 95-A, in the Lilly Library (PS2025.T5 1895) and in the Howells Edition Center (HE G&A 95-A 5.1). The holograph is the property of John K. Reeves.

5. William M. Gibson and George Arms, *A Bibliography of William Dean Howells* (New York, 1948), pp. 44–45.

the 1895 edition (G&A 95-A). It seems likely that the setting of the 1875 Pocket Edition was the earliest occasion anyone took to look carefully at the text of the first edition, since the misprint in the first edition of "made" for "make" (3.16) was not corrected until then. The pattern of variants suggests, then, that although Howells revised his text line by line at least three times before the first edition, after that he let it alone. There is no evidence that he authorized any change in a later edition. With some notable exceptions (*Venetian Life* and *Italian Journeys*, for example) this represented Howells' typical relationship to his text.

The first edition does incorporate over 250 substantive revisions of the serial text that on the whole reflect Howells' final intention, and almost all of these have been accepted. It could not, however, properly serve as copy-text: it also incorporates nearly 300 accidental variants which reflect the imposition on his text of elements of Osgood house-style and a few compositorial changes and errors, some of which are of substantive character. The choice of copy-text, therefore, had to be made between the provisional holograph manuscript and the *Atlantic* text.[6]

Our decision to use the *Atlantic* resulted from a careful study of both documents and an awareness of Howells' special relationship to them. While this decision would seem to run counter to established editorial practice, which with comparatively few exceptions would make manuscript copy-text because of the prima facie authority of its accidentals, the circumstances which obtain in this case make the choice of serial over manuscript not only defensible but necessary.

In the first place it must be emphasized that the holograph manuscript is radically provisional. Scores of authorial additions of words, sentences, and passages show up in the serial and first edition but are not present in the manuscript. It is heavily revised, and the revisions often call for further changes in both substantives and accidentals which are not made. It offers, moreover, several lengthy passages dropped in the serial—some of them alternative versions of substantially the same material. Finally, it is manifestly inaccurate and inconsistent in its substantive and accidental details. The holograph manuscript constitutes a stage toward a complete first draft. Howells was apparently using it as the basis for a handwritten, typed, or, more

---

6. The *Atlantic* was adopted as copy-text for chapter xi, "Niagara Revisited," since no manuscript is known to have survived.

probably, type-set fair copy. One suspects that it offers at least as many problems to the would-be restorer as would Hawthorne's "wildest scribble of a first draught" of *The House of the Seven Gables.*[7]

The holograph manuscript could not be used as copy-text, moreover, because by and large its accidentals cannot fairly be said to represent Howells' final intention. In scores of instances, substantive changes in the manuscript demanded alteration of accidentals (for correctness or reasonably inferable consistency) which Howells did not make in the manuscript. There are also, in even the unrevised portions, a great many instances of manifest incorrectness and inconsistency which cannot be convincingly attributed to a conscious attempt to achieve some specially contrived effect.[8] Howells was a conventional man in many respects, and he was not much given, on the evidence of other, more finished manuscripts, to radical practices with respect to spelling, punctuation, capitalization, and word-division. He simply took little care with the accidentals in this manuscript, and it makes no sense to preserve the great proportion of these readings, even on the argument that one can at least be sure that they represent Howells' intentions, final or not.

It should also be remembered that as editor of the *Atlantic* Howells had a special relationship to this and many of his other texts over the course of their transmission. He was uncommonly well-prepared for editorial work. He had been trained as a compositor. He set type for and printed himself his first publication at age six or seven and had, before he reached his majority, a wide experience not only of the pressroom but of the several stages of activity between submission of manuscript and its publication.[9] During the years he served the *Atlantic* as assistant editor and editor-in-chief (1866–1881), he not

---

7. Hawthorne–Fields Letter Book, Houghton Library, Harvard University.

8. See, for instance, the following errors and inconsistencies in the manuscript leaf reproduced in this book facing page 219:
   l.11 "moaning" should be followed by a comma;
   l.14 "voice" should be followed by a semicolon;
   l.17 "regularity" should be followed by a comma.

9. Howells' early experiences with the pressroom are recorded in several of his autobiographical writings, especially *A Boy's Town* (New York, 1890), pp. 238–239, "The Country Printer," in *Impressions and Experiences* (1896) and *Years of My Youth* (New York, 1916), pp. 17–18. Before he joined the *Atlantic* staff, Howells on one occasion so effectively communicated his sense of horror over a change in the freshly printed text of his poem "The Pilot's Story" that Fields recalled the sheets of this portion of the *Atlantic* and had them reprinted before the issue was distributed. See

only accepted and rejected, revised and corrected manuscripts, but read, corrected, and was finally responsible for each stage of proof. Indeed, he was hired by Fields precisely because he had the skills and experience which would make him a particularly valuable addition to the *Atlantic* staff. We know, moreover, that Howells did what he was hired to do. His account of his editorial experience in "Recollections of an Atlantic Editorship" records that:

> Except for the brief period of a year or eighteen months, I had no assistance during my editorship. . . . I wrote to contributors who merited more than a printed circular; I revised all the proofs, verifying every quotation and foreign word, and correcting slovenly style and syntax, and then I revised the author's and my own corrections. . . . The proof-reading, which was seldom other than a pleasure, with its tasks of revision and research, I kept for the later afternoons and evenings; though sometimes it well-nigh took the character of original work, in that liberal *Atlantic* tradition of bettering the authors by editorial transposition and paraphrase, either in the form of suggestion or of absolute correction. This proof-reading was a school of verbal exactness and rhetorical simplicity and clearness, and in it I had succeeded others, my superiors, who were without their equals. . . . As I have intimated, I found it [the proof-reading] by no means drudgery; though as for drudgery, I think that this is for the most part in the doer of it, and it is always a very wholesome thing, even when it is real, objective drudgery.[10]

Howells' editorial routine was more precisely described in *Literary Friends and Acquaintance* (pages 138–139):

> In fact, proof-reading of the *Atlantic Monthly* was something almost fearfully scrupulous and perfect. The proofs were first read by the under proof-readers in the printing-office; then the head reader passed them to me perfectly clean as to typography, with his own abundant and most intelligent comments on the literature; and then I read them, making what changes I chose, and verifying every quotation, every date, every geographical and biographical name, every foreign word to the last accent, every technical and scientific term. Where it was possible or at all desirable the proof was next submitted to the author. When it came back to me, I revised it, accepting or rejecting the

"My First Visit to New England" in *Literary Friends and Acquaintance* (New York, 1900), pp. 34–35.
   10. "Recollections of an Atlantic Editorship," *Atlantic Monthly*, C (1907), 597.

author's judgment according as he was entitled by his ability and knowledge or not to have them. The proof now went to the printers for correction; they sent it again to the head reader who carefully revised it and returned it again to me. I read it a second time, and it was again corrected. After this it was revised in the office and sent to the stereotyper, from whom it came to the head reader for a last revision in the plates.

To be sure, there is nothing in these passages that demonstrates Howells was concerned to preserve the forms of his or other authors' words. In fact, the results of that "liberal *Atlantic* tradition of bettering the authors" are precisely what a textual editor is devoted to eliminating. Moreover, that very program of proofing of which Howells was understandably so proud actually created additional opportunities for several editorial and compositorial hands to meddle with the author's intentions.

There are, then, risks involved in taking the serial as copy-text, and if the extant manuscript had been a final draft and if Howells had not controlled the first printing, it would have been necessary to use the manuscript. But such circumstances do not obtain. Howells lavished an extraordinary measure of time and attention on every text printed in the *Atlantic* during his editorship, and one must suppose that his investment in this one was uncommonly high. He understood very well that *Their Wedding Journey* marked for him a new and crucial departure; in it he was taking the first steps along a new path. That he was extremely sensitive to getting his work just right and that he tinkered with large and small substantive elements in the manuscript, Reeves' studies of the nature of the changes between it and serial make clear.[11] That there was ample opportunity for corruption to enter even his own texts is undeniable. But since early and late—and on one occasion, as we have seen, even after the sheets were printed—Howells scrupulously supervised the preparation of his own texts, the conclusion seems inescapable that the *Atlantic* more nearly reflects his final intentions than does the provisional manuscript. Howells did exert a "high degree of control over the printing and proofreading" of his text.[12] Lacking revised proof-

---

11. See his "Introduction" to this volume and "The Limited Realism of Howells' *Their Wedding Journey*," *PMLA*, LXXVII (1962), 617–628.

12. Center for Editions of American Authors, *Statement of Editorial Principles: A Working Manual for Editing Nineteenth Century American Texts*, July 1967, p. 3.

sheets for this novel, it is impossible to claim that Howells stood in the same relation to the text of *Their Wedding Journey* as Whitman stood in relation to *Leaves of Grass*; but by accepting the *Atlantic* serial as copy-text for both chapters i-x (1871) and chapter xi (1883) and by conservatively restoring pre-copy-text forms, one will come as close to reproducing Howells' corrected printer's copy as the available evidence makes it possible to do.

The argument for the serial as copy-text, then, is substantial. It is based solidly on the known circumstances of the publication of the work under Howells' immediate editorial supervision and on the provisional character of the extant manuscript. To say all of this is not to suggest that the accidentals of the *Atlantic* should have been or were taken without question as exclusively authoritative. No such assumption was made. Acknowledging the opportunities there were for other hands carelessly or systematically to alter Howells' manuscript practices, we recorded and scrutinized each variant in accidentals between manuscript and serial in the attempt to recover the texture of Howells' usage wherever this could be done with confidence. The results of this painstaking procedure can best be suggested by discussing the several categories of accidentals.

In this manuscript and others near it in time, Howells consistently spelled words in ways allowably variant from *Atlantic* preferences. Thus, "wrapt," "medieval," "subtle," and other manuscript spellings (listed in the Emendations) are restored in the clear text. The manuscript also records certain variant but allowable spellings involving grammatical usage. Therefore, since Howells usually writes "further" and "furthest" where the *Atlantic* prints "farther" and "farthest," the present text restores pre-copy-text forms.

In general, we have accepted the pointing of the serial as reflecting Howells' final intention. In so doing we surely have chosen to print some corruptions. We are convinced, nevertheless, that the pointing of the present text does in the main represent Howells' final intentions. A careful study of the variations in pointing between manuscript and serial revealed no patterns, no idiom which would make any other decision accountable.

One class of pointing demands a special word—the comma-dash. This pointing was a common indulgence not only of the *Atlantic* but of other publications and publishers as well. If Howells had never or rarely used the comma-dash in his manuscript, the decision could have been straightforward: eliminate the comma-dashes as clearly an aspect of house-style, and restore the punctuation of the manuscript. But such a decision was not possible. Although the comma-dash appears infrequently in this manuscript, Howells unmistakably did use it, and sometimes where the *Atlantic* did not. In some instances the manuscript comma-dash might be attributed to Howells' careless failure to cross out one mark when he made a substantive revision which called for a new and single pointing—either a comma or a dash. But on at least one occasion Howells plainly crossed out a dash only to replace it with a comma-dash. One must conclude, then, that Howells was responsible for at least some of the comma-dashes. But since it is usually impossible to tell which readings Howells intended to point with the comma-dash, we have decided to risk printing some corruptions by following serial copy-text. Exceptions were made only when the manuscript recorded a dash and the *Atlantic* a comma-dash. In these cases, since it would have been a simple matter for a reader or compositor to have introduced the comma before the dash for mere house-style consistency, we have restored the dash of the manuscript. Another exception has been made at 89.13 where a colon in the manuscript is printed instead of the semicolon-dash of the serial.

Where there was no manuscript, the *Atlantic*, of course, became the sole authority for the present text. Throughout we avoided emending on merely editorial authority. With very few exceptions (recorded in Emendations), the authority of one document or the other was the guide. In short, while the serial provided the main copy-text authority, we have restored the texture of Howells' accidentals wherever evidence and common sense permitted.

It was chiefly common sense which suggested the practice respecting capitalization and word-division. Howells paid no observable attention to capitalization in the manuscript. In many instances he failed to capitalize words which required capitalization and vice-versa. He was, moreover, radically inconsistent—sometimes with words that appear twice within the space of a few lines. By contrast, the capitalization of the *Atlantic* is for the most part consistent and sensible; however, such inconsistencies as appeared in the serial (see "rapids" and "Falls" in chapters vi and vii, for example) were not regularized. Much the same can be said about word-division. Howells in manuscript was not concerned to be consistent and was often incorrect (insofar as the rather uncertain contemporary rules for word-division make such a charge meaningful). Sometimes, for example, he hyphenated "New-Yorker," sometimes not. He left un-hyphenated "brandy and water" used as an adjective, but hyphen-ated "night-boat." Every attempt was made to determine the author's distinctive habits in these areas, but the manuscript shows that Howells was perfectly willing to let someone else, perhaps his editorial self, take responsibility for bringing relative order to the initial chaos of his capitalization and word-division. The manuscript in these respects as in so many others records process, not finished product.

With very few exceptions, noted below, all alterations of the copy-text accidentals have been recorded in the Emendations list. For the most part, Howells Edition changes were undertaken to make certain spellings in the 1883 *Atlantic* text accord with Howells' known prefer-ences or to correct obvious mistakes. For example, the spelling changes "traveller" for "traveler" and "O" for "Oh" were made so that the clear text was faithful to Howells' preferences even though no manuscript survives for that chapter. In general, the first edition is cited as the source of these emendations, though in fact it has no authority for accidentals. With respect to correction, the exclusion of a comma after "ways" (134.20) seems justified; the change of "sheeps'" to "sheep's" (132.24) surely is.

No attempt has been made to preserve the merely visual appur-tenances of the copy-text. Thus, the typography of chapter openings, the exact spacing of indentation, and so on, have not been retained. On the other hand, where a visual appurtenance does have a clear substantive value—as in the case of wide spacing between paragraphs to indicate a break—this feature of the copy-text has been retained. Only obviously required pointing has been supplied silently.

R.G.

A Note on the Manuscript

The autograph manuscript of *Their Wedding Journey* is in the possession of the present editor and will eventually be deposited in the Houghton Library at Harvard University. It was purchased from the Mannados Bookshop in New York in 1951, but just how it came to be there is not known.

The manuscript consists of 399 leaves. The text of chapters i, iii, iv, v, vi, and vii is complete; chapter ii lacks the last leaf; chapter ix is incomplete, and chapter viii and all but one leaf of chapter x are missing. Three hundred twenty-seven leaves measure 7¾ in. × 9¾ in., though some are slightly longer or shorter because in revision Howells sometimes cut and then pasted or discarded parts of the original leaves. The 72 leaves of chapters ix and x measure 4⅞ in. × 7⅞ in. and consist of outdated *Atlantic Monthly* rejection slips.

The numbering of the leaves is very complex because of Howells' extensive addition, cancellation, and rearrangement. The original series 1–319 runs through chapter vii and may have continued to the end of the missing chapter viii. However, beginning with chapter iv, Howells in the course of revision marked out the original number (except on wholly canceled leaves) and renumbered the leaves in several sequences. The first new series begins on page 1 of chapter iv and continues almost to the end of chapter v (page 54). The chapter concludes with seven leaves numbered 1–7 and one unnumbered leaf. The leaves of chapters vi and vii are renumbered with a new series beginning in each. Another series begins on the first leaf of the incomplete chapter ix and runs through 122, the last extant leaf of that chapter. The single surviving leaf from chapter x is numbered 135, indicating that the series begun in chapter ix continued through the short final chapter, "Homeward and Home." The numbering is further complicated by several practices of Howells. A few partial leaves, usually insertions, bear no numbers. Longer additions are often numbered by adding A, B, C, etc. or 1, 2, 3, etc. to the leaf they follow. On the other hand, when a whole leaf was discarded or parts of two combined, the surviving leaf was usually given two numbers

(34 and 35, or 24 to 32). The successive series of numbers in these later chapters correspond roughly to the *Atlantic* installments, and one might suppose that these constitute units of composition and revision.

The bewildering variety of paper and ink bears no discernible relation to the pagination and so offers little help in distinguishing stages of composition except as different inks on the same leaf or on one or more sheets of different paper help to distinguish stages of revision in a particular section. However, even such limited deductions are made hazardous by the probability that some of the variations in paper and ink stem from the fact that Howells was moving around and using the materials that came to hand during the summer of 1871 while he was composing the later chapters.

The manuscript begins on white, lined, unwatermarked paper. All but one leaf of the first two chapters are on this paper, and sheets or partial sheets of it continue to appear, though with decreasing frequency, until page 42 in chapter v. For the first three and a half chapters the ink is black and revisions in purple. At this point the inks are reversed, with the original text in purple and revisions in black. Gradually white, unlined, unwatermarked paper replaces the lined. The basic ink remains purple, and revisions are made in both purple and black. In addition, several scattered leaves and occasional revisions are in blue ink. This mixture of papers and inks is further complicated by occasional leaves on the verso of *Atlantic* rejection slips in addition to those in chapters ix and x already mentioned, and eight full-size leaves in chapter v which are made by pasting two rejection slips together lengthwise.

Recently some additional leaves have come to light in the possession of John Noyes Mead Howells, Howells' grandson. These are 39 whole leaves and 19 partial leaves of varying lengths. Some of the leaves are completely or partially canceled, but others bear no mark of cancellation. Some of the material appears in the published text in a revised version, but other parts are not represented in the text at all. Except for one passage each from chapters iii, iv, and vii, all of the material is from chapter vi, which is complete and extensively revised in the main manuscript.

Two generalizations about Howells' methods of revision of this manuscript seem reasonably safe. Revision of words and phrases began during the composition of the first draft. For example, words were crossed out and new ones placed immediately after the cancellation on the same line. The revision ranged all the way from this type of local and immediate change to extensive rewriting of long passages and to probably late changes in diction made above the line in different ink or in pencil. Secondly, the revision of longer passages often shows a pattern of extensive expansion followed at some later stage, sometimes post-manuscript, by cancellation of most or all of the added material. Many of this type involve the life stories of the Marches' fellow passengers on trains and boats. These stories were full of human interest, but Howells seems to have realized eventually that this kind of material was growing out of proportion to the other elements of his narrative.

An unusual feature of the manuscript is the appearance of printed passages from the newspaper articles Howells had written from Niagara and Quebec in 1860. These appear on pages 60 and 66 in chapter vi and page 65 in chapter ix. Another clipping appears on the discarded leaves 254–255 of chapter vi owned by John Noyes Mead Howells. They were not cut from the original papers, for the versos of the clippings are blank. In the late summer of 1869 J. M. Comly of the *Ohio State Journal*, a friend from Howells' days in Columbus, had sent him, at his request, re-settings of the articles for possible use in a collection of his sketches which Howells was then considering.

The large amount of revision in the manuscript as a whole and the substantial variation between its text and the first published version in the *Atlantic Monthly*, not to mention further variation between the serial and the first book versions, indicate that the manuscript represents the early and middle stages of composition.[1] No proof sheets have been found, but the manuscript seems to have served as copy for either a trial galley or a fair copy in longhand or on a typewriter, in which further revisions were made. At first glance penciled names dividing the manuscript into irregular stints and the inky fingerprints on the leaves seem to favor galley, but there are no holes of the compositor's hook. The names are feminine first names and initials: Emma F., Emma N., Addie, Mary, and Carrie, and the fingerprints suggest either the press room or the early typewriters. Either would

1. The two leaves reproduced as plates display together nine single word and short phrase variants. The manuscript as a whole is substantively variant from the serial text in approximately 800 places to a total of as many as 5,000 words. There are approximately thirty-five uncanceled passages of a manuscript page or more in length which were either largely recast or dropped between MS and the serial, and there are ten passages of ten lines or more which appear in the serial for the first time.

be possible, for female compositors were employed by the University Press, which printed the *Atlantic Monthly* at this period.[2] In any case, the names appear as follows:

Chapter i

p. 1	Emma F.
p. 7	Emma F.
p. 8	Emma N.
p. 15	Addie
p. 21	Mary
p. 27	Carrie
p. 31	Carrie
p. 36	Em[ma] N
p. 38	Mary
p. 41	[Note: "stop here."]

Chapter ii

p. 41	Emma F
p. 54	Carrie
p. 69	Addie
p. 78	Mary

Chapter iii

p. 89	Emma N
p. 100	Emma F.
p. 108	Carrie
pp. 111–112	Mary

Chapter iv

p. 1	Emma F
p. 9	Emma N
p. 16	Addie
p. 23	Mary

Chaper v

p. 38	Emma N.
p. 48	Emma F. [penciled in over the erasure "Addie"]

Chapter vi

p. 1	Addie
p. 11	Carrie
p. 22	Emma F
p. 34	Emma N
p. 45	Emma F
p. 55	Mary
p. 65	Addie
p. 72	E[mma] N
p. 78	Emma F

Chapter vii

p. 1	Carrie
p. 17	Mary
p. 28	Addie

Chapter viii [missing]

Chapter ix

p. 1	E[mma] F.
p. 74	E[mma] F.
p. 93	Addie
p. 114	E[mma] N.

Chapter x [missing save one leaf]

The manuscript of chapter xi, "Niagara Revisited, Twelve Years after Their Wedding Journey," which first appeared in the *Atlantic Monthly* for May 1883, has not been found.

J.K.R.

---

2. We are grateful to Mrs. Ellen Ballou, who is writing a history of Houghton Mifflin and Company, for this information. For the employment of women as compositors see the editorials for 1 and 22 December 1849 in *The Protective Union*, a weekly published by the Boston Printers' Union between 1 December 1849 and 9 November 1850. See also George A. Stevens, *New York Typographical Union No. 6; Study of a Modern Trade Union and Its Predecessors* (Albany, 1913), pp. 421–440; and Horace Scudder, *Henry Oscar Houghton* (Cambridge, Mass., 1897), p. 73.

Manuscript leaf, chapter iii, page 111–112

Commentary on Selected Leaves of the Manuscript

These leaves were selected to illustrate a number of the physical characteristics of the manuscript and Howells' methods of revision. Most other leaves do not illustrate as many features as the ones reproduced, though there is hardly one which does not illustrate some aspect of his process of composition.

Chapter iii, page 111–112

This leaf with the double page number is made up of three pieces of paper pasted together. The first and third pieces are lined paper; the ink is black, with revisions in black ink (early) and purple (later), all characteristic of the first three and one half chapters of the manuscript. These two pieces originally formed page 112 before they were cut apart. At some point, probably after Howells had begun to use unlined paper and had changed to purple ink with revisions in black midway in chapter v, he cut page 112 in two and inserted between them a full sheet of unlined paper with purple ink and revisions in both purple and black. Page 111 was discarded, and "111–" was prefixed in purple to the black 112 at the top of the original leaf to keep the numbering continuous. Ten lines from the bottom of the middle section is a lightly penciled "Mary" following a square bracket before the third word of the line. This is one of the five feminine names that divide the manuscript into stints for copying or setting, but it is in an unusual position; most of the names appear at the beginning of a paragraph.

This leaf shows one of Howells' frequent expansions of his original draft, and in this case, as in many of them, the added material was deleted in a later revision. The passage occurs near the end of the scene in which the Marches' night boat runs into a tow-boat. At the end of the first section of this double leaf Howells had originally referred to the stranger at Basil's elbow. Later (in purple ink) at the end of the fifth line he wrote the direction "(Insert A, B, C, D, E)." Still later he canceled this, and these five leaves are among the discarded leaves in the possession of John Noyes Mead Howells.[1] In this passage Basil suddenly recognizes the stranger at his elbow as Lukeson, whose story is one of the passenger histories with which Howells experimented as a means of creating interest in the commonplace. Most were eventually deleted.

Probably at the same time that Howells added the five leaves on Lukeson, he inserted the middle section of page 111–112 between the two parts of original page 112. Using the newly developed Lukeson, Howells introduced a tragi-comic scene when the man who was scalded in the collision was brought on board the night boat. Lukeson saw the "ladies" in widow's black and bridal white watching from the top of the stairs and "giving a truculent cackle of a laugh, kissed his hand" to them and called out, " 'Ladies, ladies! . . . you come too late! The man is past caring for the charms of female society. He's dying, poor fellow. Nevertheless'—." When Basil disgustedly told Lukeson that he was worse than the ladies and wished Lukeson would go away and leave him alone, Basil's "amusing companion" airily agreed saying, " 'Farewell! I will go and speak to our sweet friends, whom I addressed perhaps too abruptly.' " From this parting speech Howells had earlier canceled, " 'Your old frustrations, my dear Basil' " and " 'Never did virtue wear so drear a front as in you.' " The scene as a whole was not canceled until a post-manuscript revision. He must have realized eventually that Lukeson's suggestive innuendoes were not appropriate material for a wedding journey, especially one that started from the vicinity of Beacon Hill. Several similar revisions also suggest that Howells toned down his realism to suit his genteel audience.

The original page 112 (parts 1 and 3 of this double leaf) is essentially what finally appeared in print (page 49).

Chapter v, page 48

Initially this leaf was formed by pasting together lengthwise two outdated *Atlantic Monthly* rejection slips. Except for a plain half-sheet numbered 47, the preceding six leaves and the following three were formed in the same fashion. The ink is purple, with revisions in the same ink and in pencil. Except for the first three lines, which are

---

1. Grateful acknowledgment is made of Mr. Howells' kind permission to examine these leaves and to publish quotations from them.

Manuscript leaf, chapter v, page 48

canceled, the top half of the leaf and the first line of the bottom half are overlaid with a slip of plain paper, with both the first draft and the revisions in black ink. Chapter v begins on page 33 of the new series which started on the first leaf of chapter iv and superseded the first series of numbering. The original page number of page 48 was 164, and the canceled top half is the end of a previously canceled passage which began at the top of page 162. Just below the slip, at the beginning of the last paragraph, "Emma F." was penciled in over the erasure "Addie."

The text on page 48 describes the Marches' entrance into the Bierhaus (page 67). There is considerable variation between the manuscript and the version printed in the *Atlantic Monthly*, which is one of the many indications of revision in one or more post-manuscript stages. The most significant change is the elimination of the passage in which Basil, trying to calm Isabel's fears of going into the Bierhaus among all the Germans, says, " 'They're not our fellow-countrymen, and we needn't be afraid of any misbehaviour or rowdyism.' "

J.K.R.

Textual Notes

3.25　For reasons explained more fully in the Textual Commentary the dash of the manuscript was restored here and at 7.3, 9.25 (twice), 10.36, 13.21, 15.5, 15.6, 16.22, 17.3 (twice), 19.18 (twice), 41.6 (twice), 42.9, 58.24, 60.29, 63.25, 63.26, 65.28, 68.32, 72.9, 72.13, 89.18, 89.22, 99.14, 99.15, 100.1, and 142.16. It is worth noting that manuscript and serial agree for the most part on the use of the comma-dash in the last half of the book. At 15.32 and 15.36 serial copy-text comma-dashes have been emended to dashes to accord with the text of *Poems of Two Friends.*

6.23　Here and at 176.30 the form "wrapt" is restored to accord with the consistent manuscript spelling. At 139.10 the word is part of a quotation from Parkman and was spelled "wrapped" in his text.

6.34　Here and at 6.35, 61.22 and 94.35 the form "moustache" is restored to accord with the consistent manuscript spelling. At 139.2 the word is part of a quotation from Parkman and was spelled "moustache" in his text.

8.33　Howells canceled altogether or replaced many of the "alls" either with a less categorical word such as "many" (11.3) or with an apparently less offensive equivalent such as "every" (11.19).

9.24　Here and at 57.24 and 59.31 the form "behaviour" is restored to accord with the consistent manuscript spelling.

10.6　Here and at 172.36 the form "subtle" is restored to accord with the consistent manuscript spelling.

15.31   Copy-text "Ages" has been emended to "Ages," to ac-
         cord with the text of *Poems of Two Friends*.

19.36   Here and at 30.17, 78.35, 79.12, 79.13, 95.10, 115.14,
         154.36, and 176.3 the forms "further" or "furthest" are
         restored to accord with the consistent manuscript spell-
         ings. Only at 19.33 does the manuscript have "farther,"
         which has been retained.

42.33   The possibilities of compositorial error here and at 43.4
         and 43.8 in setting Howells' rendering of dialect are ob-
         viously great. The carefully revised manuscript, there-
         fore, was the guide in such passages. Observe the
         non-authorial sophistication at 42.32 and 43.1 recorded
         in the Rejected Substantives.

66.35   That Howells meant "he"—in spite of the possibly in-
         tentional ambiguity—is made clear by the manuscript
         in which the "s" of "she" is canceled. A also reads "he."

79.13   Here and at 108.4, 108.8, 113.5, 128.7, and 162.11 the
         form "towards" is restored to accord with the consistent
         manuscript usage.

83.31   Here and (in the "Niagara Revisited" chapter printed
         in 1883) at 186.2, 186.7, 191.8, 195.3, 197.21, 198.23,
         198.36, and 200.4 the form "O" is restored to accord
         with the spelling used consistently in this manuscript and
         in later ones.

89.13   The colon of the manuscript is here restored in preference
         to the eccentric semicolon-dash of the serial.

89.21–22 Here twice and at 115.3, 141.13, and 142.20 the form
         "medieval" is restored to accord with the consistent
         manuscript spelling.

134.20   No manuscript is extant for chapter viii. The comma of
         the serial virtually destroys the rhythm of the sentence.

139.5   Parkman's text reads "south"; the "north" of S 1 makes
          little sense in the context of the quotation.

185.7   Here and at 186.23 and 194.26 the form "traveller" is
          restored to accord with the spelling used consistently in
          this manuscript and later ones.

Emendations

The following list records all substantive and accidental changes introduced into the copy-text, except for required but missing punctuation which has been supplied silently. The reading of the present edition appears to the left of the bracket; the authority for that reading, followed by a semicolon, the copy-text reading, and the copy-text symbol appear to the right of the bracket. The curved dash ~ represents the same word that appears before the bracket and is used in recording punctuation variants. The abbreviation HE indicates emendation made on the authority of the Howells Edition. Occasionally changes in accidentals have been made on Howells Edition authority, with the first or later editions cited as their source, though these editions have no authority for accidentals. An asterisk indicates that the reading is discussed in the Textual Notes. *Om.* means that the reading to the left of the bracket did not appear in the text cited to the right of the bracket.

The following texts are referred to:

MS	Holograph manuscript
S1	*Atlantic Monthly*, XXVIII (July–December 1871)
S2	*Atlantic Monthly*, LI (May 1883)
A	Osgood, 1872: First Edition
B	Osgood, 1875: Pocket Edition
C	Douglas, 1882
D	Houghton Mifflin, 1887
E	Houghton Mifflin, 1888: Pocket Edition
F	Houghton Mifflin, 1895

*3.25	else —] MS; ~, — S1
4.16	together] A; *om.* S1
4.17	this] A; this together S1
4.31–32	June, 1870] A; last June S1
5.13	contrived] A; invented S1

*6.23	wrapt] MS; wrapped S1
*6.34	moustache] MS; mustache S1
8.16	999th] A; 999 S1
8.25	looks] A; looks kindly and S1
*8.33	very] A; all S1
*9.24	behaviour] MS; behavior S1
*10.6	subtle] MS; subtile S1
11.3	many] A; all S1
11.19	every] A; all S1
11.20	chance] A; chances S1
11.20	influence] A; influences S1
11.23	the] A; this S1
12.13	her compassion] A; her shows of compassion S1
12.14	feelings] A; feeling S1
12.36	what] A; how S1
14.3	in] A; in a S1
15.21	or] A; and S1
*15.31	Ages,] HE; ~ S1
16.28	your] F; you're S1
16.35	Thanksgiving] A; Thanksgivings S1
17.29	the feet] A; feet S1
18.17	with the] A; with a S1
19.2–3	Isabel, herself] A; He was, as Isabel—herself S1
19.3–4	conviction, believed her husband the] A; conviction —believed, the S1
19.9	she retorted] A; retorted his wife S1
*19.36	further] MS; farther S1
20.22	sure . . . certain] A; certain . . . sure S1
21.4	eastern sky] A; face of the east S1
21.31	whiling] A; wiling S1
23.3	and first] A; and firs S1
23.7–8	bliss. ¶ "I] A; bliss. If the real Adam and Eve were not able to do likewise in their day, they were not so fortunate as we are apt to think. To be children and to know it,—this is joy's crown of joy, this is the supreme art, the last wisdom of life. ¶ "I S1
24	A MIDSUMMER-DAY'S DREAM] A; A DREAM OF HEAT. S1
24.5	but] A; *om.* S1

25.1	the movement] A; it S1
26.28–29	every impossible phase] A; all its impossible phases S1
28.14	bars, like] A; bars, against which they pressed and struggled like S1
28.15	were] A; were all S1
29.11	year] A; summer S1
29.13	which had wiselier been] A; which had far better and wiselier have been S1
29.28	carrying] A; who carries S1
30.33	again; and evermore] A; again, and found S1
30.35	of] A; of all S1
31.6–7	door had] A; door S1
31.7	it had] A; it S1
31.19	the whole] A; all the S1
32.5	of packages of every shape and size] A; of all shapes and sizes of packages S1
33.6	possessed] A; preyed upon S1
33.7	effect of universal] A; common aspect of S1
33.10	looked on] A; beheld S1
33.10–11	errands] A; errand S1
33.22	issued] A; vanished S1
33.36	the glass he held] A; a tall, slim glass S1
34.9	the apothecary answered, with a laugh] A; laughed the apothecary S1
34.33	little] A; litte S1
36.24	ordinary] A; representative S1
37.3	of] A; of all S1
38.3	than] A; that S1
38.10	much advantage as here] A; good advantage as he does here S1
38.15	now] A; *om.* S1
38.28	regrets] A; sighs S1
38.29	a] A; their S1
39.5	would] A; should S1
39.7	passed] A; passed over S1
39.18	foot] A; feet S1
39.24	keeping up] A; not falling behind S1
39.24	behind] A; back out of sight S1

39.34	being] A; making S1
39.34	were] A; did S1
40.24	loftier] A; grander S1
40.30	satisfaction] A; comfort S1
41.13	them!] A; ~ . S1
41.26	visibly] A; visibly nothing but S1
41.34	bridling,] A; ~ S1
42.20	share] A; see S1
*42.33	a-lookin'] MS; a lookin' S1
*43.4	glothing business] MS; ~-~ S1
*43.8	gind] MS; kind S1
43.15	all have] A; have all S1
43.21	were] A; were all S1
44.30	folded] A; wrapped S1
44.32	but] A; only S1
45.1	as the] A; as that of S1
45.9	every land and time] A; all lands and times S1
45.34	ceased;] A; ~, as S1
47.16	were] A; were all S1
48.1	on. Now] A; ~." "~ S1
49.31	N.Y.,] A; *om.* S1
49.35	yet] A; yet all S1
50.10	Death] A; death S1
50.15	his revery] A; they ran on together in a revery that S1
50.17	it] A; his mood S1
51.16	he] A; *om.* S1
51.20	hot] A; hot, hot S1
54.3	the people] A; them S1
54.7	delicate] A; delicate and vapory S1
55.3–4	concerning] A; concerning all S1
55.27	in the] A; in the very S1
57.20	in] A; in all S1
62.21	what] A; all S1
63.8	am never] A; never am S1
63.24	When] A; When all S1
63.30	or] A; *om.* S1
65.13	They] A; Then they S1
65.33	yet] A; still S1

66.10	*entrepôt*] A; *entrepot* S1
*66.35	he] MS; she S1
69.9	unearthliest love-songs] A; unearthliest love songs S1
70.29	they] A; *om.* S1
71.30	otherwise] A; *om.* S1
71.30	little] A; little other S1
71.35	the other] A; all the S1
72.2	ten-cent note] A; ten cent-note S1
72.18	at] A; at all S1
72.31	meekly. "But] A; meekly, "but S1
75.24	contrasting with] A; related to S1
75.29	next] A; first S1
77.1	profaned] A; haunted S1
77.1	presences] A; phantasms S1
*79.13	towards] MS; toward S1
82.8	suggested] A; gurgled S1
*83.31	O] MS; Oh S1
84.1	seems] A; seems that S1
84.6	at] A; about S1
84.27	on] A; upon S1
84.34	in] A; in all S1
84.34	constantly meets] A; encounters S1
85.32	were] A; were all S1
87.4	that,] A; ~ S1
87.15	foamy] A; foaming S1
87.15	foam-sprent] A; steep, dark S1
87.26	rapids'] A; rapid's S1
*89.13	1812:] MS; ~ ; — S1
*89.21-22	medieval . . . medieval] MS; mediaeval . . . mediaeval S1
91.1	of] A; in S1
91.31	he] A; Basil S1
94.4	tower,] A; tower, on S1
94.4	rocks] A; rocks that S1
94.5	and here Basil] A; he S1
94.8	up on] A; upon S1
94.20	on] A; on the S1
95.14	it upon] A; upon it S1

96.14–15	many treacherous echoes] A; as many echoes as would have followed them in Tara's hall itself, S1
97.1	and it] A; which S1
97.18	mine; yet] A; my own, but S1
98.36	steamer] A; schooner S1
99.11	through] A; about S1
100.13	exchanging] A; changing S1
100.18	*won't*] A; *wont* S1
100.22	nothing] A; nothing even S1
100.25	and] A; *om.* S1
101.5	those] A; those vast S1
101.8–9	surface of that mighty eddy] A; calm, oily eddies S1
101.11	every side] A; all sides S1
101.27	or] A; or then S1
102.7	cliff,] A; cliff, all S1
102.28	rock] A; rocks S1
102.34	forever] A; *om.* S1
104.13	gone] A; ~, S1
104.14	Falls] A; ~, S1
104.17	stand] A; do S1
105.6	tenderness] A; devotion S1
105.31	for a] A; for S1
108.7	Rapids-] A; *om.* S1
108.18	*vis-à-vis*] A; *vis-a-vis* S1
108.23	stretched] A; lay S1
108.28	which] A; which there S1
110.33	and the] A; and all the S1
111.19–20	It is as picturesque as it is historical.] A; *om.* S1
112.12	Either the] A; Either this S1
112.22	her] A; her full S1
113.28	seems] A; is perhaps S1
114.36	way] A; way is S1
115.27	Indians] A; savages S1
115.30	invited] A; called S1
116.4	secret] A; secretest S1
116.10	surprising] A; surprising and puzzling S1
116.15	with] A; with diamonds or S1
116.26	a] A; some S1
118.18	What] A; What cutting S1

118.35	career] A; mad career S1
121.14	French; the] A; French; *om.* S1
121.16	tinkled] A; tinkled the S1
121.17	recalled] A; reminded of S1
121.26	one] A; *om.* S1
122.18	come] A; come to market S1
122.32–33	in the basement] A; *om.* S1
122.34	other] A; all S1
122.35	has] A; had S1
122.36	are] A; were S1
123.1	attend] A; attended S1
123.2	are] A; was S1
123.4	send] A; sent S1
123.5	haggle] A; haggled S1
123.6	gossip] A; gossiped S1
123.22	inattention] A; inattention upon all S1
124.22	always] A; all S1
124.27	the] A; all S1
124.32	whatever] A; for all S1
125.12	painting] A; paintings S1
125.18–19	pictures incredibly bad—but for those in the French cathedral] A; incredibly bad pictures S1
127.33	Church] A; church S1
128.21	from] A; from all S1
131.8	I am] A; I'm S1
131.13–14	insisting so] A; illogicality S1
131.19–20	musingly; and she added after a pause,] A; musingly. S1
132.5	what] A; all S1
132.24	sheep's] C; sheeps' S1
132.28	brown] A; brown and bowed S1
*134.20	ways] A; ~, S1
135.4	in Ireland] A; at home S1
135.15	character] A; life S1
136.14	statute] A; law S1
136.25	lone] A; poor S1
136.31	at] A; *om.* S1
137.30	but] A; but of S1
138.10	even] A; *om.* S1

139.3	moved among] A; mingled with S1
*139.5	south] HE; north S1
139.20	high-born] A; noble S1
140.26	promenade,] A; promenade, eagerly S1
141.8	probably] A; perhaps S1
141.11	the priest] A; him S1
142.3	two hundred] A; a hundred and fifty S1
142.14	Slowly] A; Whoever was worthy to see held his breath at the sight, and slowly S1
142.19	sprang] MS; sprung S1
142.25	shown as] A; shown S1
143.4	dear] A; dear, dirty S1
143.4–5	wanting which Quebec is not to be thought of without] A; without which Quebec is to be thought of with S1
143.10	towering] A; broken S1
144.27–28	bride, never became] A; bride was never S1
145.3	in] A; in all S1
145.14	such] A; all S1
145.14	as are] A; *om.* S1
145.30	make] A; make all S1
146.11–12	Montgomery] A; Mongtomery S1
146.23	the] A; all the S1
147.1	him] A; Basil S1
147.23	pensiveness] A; thoughtfulness S1
148.4	Churchyard,] A; ~ S1
148.21	it] A; this S1
148.23	Another] A; One S1
149.2	was] A; was all S1
149.20	credible] A; credible of all S1
149.35	various] A; all manner of S1
150.29	cleanness] A; cleanliness S1
151.1	only two] F; two only S1
151.30	dinner] A; dinner there S1
152.15	were] A; were all S1
152.18	They] A; They all S1
152.24	Gil Blas-like] A; Gil-Blasian S1
152.27	was] A; were S1
153.20	develops] A; develops all S1

153.23	Montreal, and impartially rejoiced in the] A; Montreal. The S1
153.26	*porte-cochères*] B; *porte-cochéres* S1
154.14	and] A; *om.* S1
154.15	Montcalm.] A; Montcalm;—all these things were inexpressibly dear to their souls. S1
155.2	too] A; *om.* S1
155.10	ponder] A; ponder upon S1
155.19	which] A; that S1
155.19	and] A; and that S1
155.28	joyless] A; bleak S1
155.34	raised] A; placed S1
156.4	rare] A; strange S1
158.31	with the . . . and the] A; with its . . . and its S1
159.16–19	"O, you're not greatly to blame," answered her husband, "and I forgive you the little wrong you've done me. I was quits with the Muse, at any rate, you know, before we were married; and] A; "Yes, you're greatly to blame," answered her husband, "but I forgive you. So many pine away in unrequited affection for the Muse,—even of those who give all their time and money to her,—that S1
160.11	They] A; They all S1
160.13	out of] A; out S1
160.21	But] A; But all S1
160.22	passers-by] A; people S1
160.35	which are] A; which are all S1
161.2	and perhaps] or perhaps only S1
161.18	sorely against] A; sore-against S1
161.25–26	the hapless passengers] A; them, S1
161.30	cataract] A; fall S1
161.32	perilous] A; a *casus belli* S1
161.33	of] A; of all S1
162.8	gate] A; gap S1
162.18	and] A; all S1
163.13	stalked] A; came S1
164.33	Durham] A; the Durham S1
165.18	English] A; ~, S1
165.18	represented] A; represented here S1

166.7	two] A; a S1
166.9–11	a spectacle peculiarly Northern and characteristic of Quebec revealed itself;] A; *om.* S1
166.25	party] A; ladies S1
166.26	of the] A; of their S1
166.31–35	together; as women they could not enjoy these proofs of the jolly *camaraderie* existing among the people of the troupe. They trembled as before the merriment of as many light-hearted, careless, good-natured young men: it was no harm, but it was dismaying;] A; together, S1
167.18	not thinking an instant] A; *om.* S1
167.19	at least two of] A; *om.* S1
167.34	that] A; that all S1
168.1	interval] A; time S1
168.8	solace] A; entertainment S1
168.22	a] A; *om.* S1
168.24–25	They did not stop to ponder this fact, but, with the heedlessness of their sex,] A; With the heedlessness of their sex they did not stop to ponder this fact, but S1
168.35	which] A; which only S1
168.35	alone] A; *om.* S1
169.18–19	left the] A; left her S1
169.28	upbraid] A; bully S1
170.9–14	The momentary . . . friendly word.] A; *om.* S1
170.16–17	The travellers] A; they S1
171.13–14	you," she concluded in a somewhat severe tone,] A; you. Good night, gentlemen," she said with a severity of tone S1
171.14–15	culpable; and vanished as mysteriously as she had appeared.] A; culpable. S1
171.33	drowsy] A; drowsing S1
171.34	wide] A; broad S1
172.14–22	favor. To us . . . and their] A; favor. *om.* Their S1
172.23	comedy] A; ∼, S1
172.23	Basil] A; he S1
172.24–27	He would . . . fiction.] A; *om.* S1
172.33–173.3	better could . . . world.] A; better—" ¶But there he fell asleep. S1

175.11	be] A; be at S1
175.36	till] A; till all S1
176.8	walls;] A; ~, S1
176.20–21	last, having . . . hotel.] A; last. S1
177.5	the] A; these poor S1
177.8	everywhere] A; every where S1
177.13	to] A; to all S1
179.14	having just] A; have just S1
182.6	some] D; *om.* S2
*185.7	traveller] HE; traveler S2
185.28	middle-aged] D; middle-aging S2
185.32	very] D; quite S2
187.19	before,] D; before, he S2
190.7	rumbled] D; rambled S2
192.24	stay] D; stop S2
200.4	easily.] D; ~, S2

Rejected Substantives

The following list records all substantive variants in editions published after the copy-text and rejected as non-authorial in the present text. The reading of the present edition appears to the left of the bracket; the authority for that reading, followed by a semicolon, the variant reading, and the source of that reading appear to the right of the bracket. Any unlisted edition may be presumed to agree with the reading to the left of the bracket.

The following texts are referred to:

MS	Holograph manuscript
S1	*Atlantic Monthly*, XXVIII (July–December 1871)
S2	*Atlantic Monthly*, LI (May 1883)
A	Osgood, 1872: First Edition
B	Osgood, 1875: Pocket Edition
C	Douglas, 1882
D	Houghton Mifflin, 1887
E	Houghton Mifflin, 1888: Pocket Edition
F	Houghton Mifflin, 1895

3.16	make] S1; made A
10.27	had] S1; *om.* A–F
15.29	'gainst] S1; against A–F
30.13	among the] S1; among F
30.27	till] S1; until B
31.30–31	one another] S1; each other B
41.17	eldest] S1; elder B
42.32	believe] S1; pelieve C
43.1	want] S1; wand D
52.20	amusement] S1; amazement A, C–D, F
65.33	his] S1; his eyes B
70.35	cars] S1; car C
91.10	persuaded] S1; dissuaded E

236

102.28	rock] A; rocks B
110.20	undone"; and] S1; ~." And B
116.23	here"; and] S1; ~." And B
123.20	in] S1; at F
124.23	manner] S1; manners F
148.9	the] S1; this F
152.1	a merry] S1; merry F
165.24	dandy; their] S1; dandy; the B
165.26	their profession] S1; the profession B
171.3	dumbly] S1; humbly C
182.32	hollows, of] S2; hollows, or E
187.11	in] S2; in the F
192.25	calculation] S2; calculations F
194.26	influence] S2; influences E
194.33	is] S2; was F
198.36	repeated Isabel] S2; Isabel repeated F

Word-Division

The compounds or possible compounds in List A are hyphenated at the end of the line in the serial copy-texts and were resolved as hyphenated or one word as listed below. If Howells' manuscripts of this period fairly consistently followed one practice respecting the particular compound or possible compound, the resolution was made on that basis. Otherwise Howells' *Atlantic* texts of this period were used as guides. List B records compounds or possible compounds that are hyphenated at the end of the line in the present text; if the compound or possible compound does not appear there it should be transcribed as one word.

LIST A

3.24	honeymoon-shine
5.2	rainfall
6.19	baggage-master
10.34	wild-boar
13.14	night-express
17.1	pigeon-hole
17.7	stairway
17.20	doorsteps
17.26	door-plates
21.18	smoke-stacks
22.18	night-long
27.35	ferry-boat
29.15	ice-creaming
30.32	ice-water
31.2	brown-stone
34.26	sun-stroke
37.2	riverside
37.23	-palace-like
37.33	steamboat
39.31	dreamland
42.16	state-room
53.30	red-cheeked
54.5	hollyhocks
54.23	cook-stove
55.8	headboard
58.32	dining-room
58.36	coal-black
60.21	old-fashioned
61.2	handbook
61.25	Ihlang-ihlang
63.34	re-appeared
65.13	head-waiter
66.15	piano-fortes
68.25	table-rock
71.32	train-boy
73.16	sea-blue
77.20	high-strung
78.25	high-strung
80.33	window-seat
83.7	eavesdroppers

83.35	womankind
85.29	pin-cushion
89.23	guide-books
90.6	undergrowth
90.21	love-making
91.4	suspension-bridges
94.2	rainbow
95.11	nurse-maid
95.22	slaveholder
103.30	whirlpools
104.4	undermining
111.4	careworn
112.16	guide-book
113.21	fellow-passengers
113.26	good-looking
114.4	good-looking
114.13	bridegroom
118.8	double-headed
122.10	fee-taking
122.22	black-haired
122.33	hard-ware
124.22	peasant-like
126.33	sight-seeing
126.36	cold-looking
127.21	self-doomed
131.6	heart-brokenly
132.35	school-house
134.24	dry-goods
137.16	piece-velvets
138.4	warehouses
143.1	high-swung
145.29	river-shores
146.15	drink-money
150.22	self-denying
152.32	dark-faced
153.33	red-coated
153.33	nursery-maids
154.22	rope-dancing
160.16	weekdays

162.11	weather-beaten
164.10	to-night
171.24	landlord's
171.25	tablecloths
171.30	tablecloths
172.22	love-making
174.2	forenoon
176.11	stronghold
176.19	good-natured
177.19	squash-vine
177.21	farm-houses
180.8	gaslight
183.26	superannuated
184.21	woodcutter's
187.10	waistcoat
187.11	retroactively
189.24	pin-cushions
193.13	girlhood
194.22	burial-ground
196.14	middle-aged
197.5	middle-aged

LIST B

7.28	waiting-room
9.14	iron-gray
12.18	wicket-gate
12.21	sleeping-car
18.4	foot-passengers
32.27	foot-passengers
32.34	death-white
36.10	self-respect
36.13	single-columned
36.19	marble-topped
36.25	wedding-journeyers
43.34	twice-told
57.29	well-dressed
59.10	vulture-like

65.13	head-waiter	127.21	self-doomed
65.18	shop-window	127.26	self-sacrifice
67.28	wedding-journeyers	133.19	dark-robed
69.10	matter-of-fact	135.27	half-brother
70.20	wedding-journeyers	136.12	free-trader
71.6	shrill-voiced	138.4	water-side
79.30	verd-antique	139.15	fur-traders'
80.13	mid-air	142.7	traffic-laden
80.31	ice-pitcher	143.15	semi-forbidding
84.8	bead-work	147.14	battle-ground
84.17	bridal-tours	147.26	English-speaking
86.9	heavy-climbing	148.5	to-morrow
88.36	devil-worshippers	150.22	self-denying
90.3	corner-stone	150.36	rose-tree
91.4	suspension-bridges	152.9	sandy-colored
97.35	mill-wheels	152.16	scene-painting
98.22	ticket-agent	153.23	up-and-down
104.17	to-day	153.28	dormer-windows
113.27	self-devotion	153.33	nursery-maids
113.30	white-haired	154.22	rope-dancing
114.11	light-hearted	156.19	nurse-maids
115.29	church-tower	157.5	Sabbath-day
121.14	carriage-drivers	162.3	suspension-bridge
122.10	fee-taking	163.9	greenish-blue
122.21	smooth-cheeked	170.10	good-nature
122.33	hard-ware	172.20	twinkling-footed
123.4	broad-brimmed	180.18	out-goes
126.33	sight-seeing	192.7	twenty-four